I0748571

TABLE OF CONTENTS

CHAPTER 1

STRANGE BEDFELLOWS

Why did I kill her? Why not? Did she deserve to die? Everyone dies, sweetheart, deserves got nothing to do with it. I know that sounds harsh, but life is harsh. Our ancestors crawled out of the primordial ooze, evolved over time, killed plenty of their fellow Homo sapiens, and still survived another day. Hell, Cain killed his brother because God's not a vegetarian. It's rough out there for all of us, but I'm getting ahead of myself. I did have a reason to end her existence—several very good reasons—but I'll leave you to your own judgment. I really don't care either way because I'm a changed man, changed for good.

It was about ten o'clock in the morning. The sun was trying to break through the morning haze. There was a knock at the door to my office—my office being a thirty-seven-foot Holiday Rambler recreational vehicle I lovingly refer to as Coach. At the time, I was camped at Dockweiler State Beach, site 26.

Dockweiler is the only ocean front camp ground in Los Angeles County, and being in Playa Del Rey, its location is convenient for all business dealings in the area. It's also a great base of operations for personal business as well, monkey and otherwise.

I was on my first twenty-day beach vacation at the time. Los Angeles County has some severe rules regarding stays at Dockweiler. The maximum stay is twenty-one days within a sixty-day period, and each owner/operator is limited to sixty days total per calendar year. I like to move around a lot, so living in just under three hundred square feet works. I've lived in more cavernous homes. They just seem to require you to fill them with stuff. And how much stuff does one person really need?

It was mid-July when I heard the knock on my door. "Yes," I said aloud through the partition.

"Mr. Bolt?" replied a clearly female voice from the other side.

"Who's asking?"

"My name is Krista Hartwell. I work for Senator Goldstein, and I got your name from Sam—Sam Truman."

I opened the coach door. As the song says, "she was a black-haired beauty with big dark eyes." Not your stereotypical Aryan princess, but attractive and fit. She wore a bronze chemise, loosely belted around her diminutive waist, black pumps with no hose, but her long legs were tan and lean. She looked at me through dark Maui Jims.

"Sam, you say. How do you know Sam?"

"I met him through a mutual acquaintance."

"Who's the acquaintance? No need to be obfuscatory, Ms. Hartwell. Just the facts."

She told me the senator met Sam at a party in Malibu, but you must know Sam Truman. Sam loved hanging out with celebrity types. I say types because most of his friends were neither celebrated nor likely to be so. Some of them had some measure of celebratory history, but the vast majority of the madding group of celebritards had mostly none. Many were card-carrying members of the Stage Extras Guild, and relying on the one walk-through on a hit television show or blockbuster at the Cineplex was no measure of success in my estimation.

"Danica Thompson. Do you know her, Mr. Bolt?"

"It's Jon. Yes, I do know Danica." It was a lie, of the white variety. I didn't really know her; rather, I knew of her. Sam had some sort of "arrangement" with Ms. Thompson. They spent time together when it was convenient for one or the other of them. They were friends with benefits, and Sam's predilection for C-plus cup sizes didn't hurt. Danica's endowments were a major benefit for Sam.

I invited Ms. Hartwell into my rolling office and bade her sit on the leatherette sofa in the lounge. She sat on the far-left side of the couch, placed her Hermès knock-off bag on the simulated wood floor next to her and crossed her long legs with feigned aplomb. Her choice of seating location spoke volumes. She placed herself at the farthest possible point from where I would most likely sit to interview her. As I looked to the right side of the sofa as a possible landing point, she shifted subtly. I took a seat in the lounge chair directly opposite, giving her the greatest amount of personal separation.

She looked directly at me for a few moments with her eyes still hidden behind her three-hundred-dollar Lilikois. She then averted her glance, looking around the coach's interior. I watched her in silence. After a while, it was clear she was getting anxious. People do that often. Silence has a way of irritating the self-conscious, and the guilty. It's the reason sales gurus and interrogators will make an offer, or offer evidence of wrongdoing, and shut up. He who speaks first loses.

After I allowed her to fidget for several minutes, she said, "The senator is in need of your assistance, Mr. Bolt."

"Jon. Ms. Hartwell, please remove your sunglasses while we speak."

"Why?"

"Well, the senator sent you as her emissary. She is seeking to engage my unique skills, and I don't sell those skills to just anyone. I need to know I can trust you and the senator's judgment."

"You can," she said. I smiled.

"I'm sure. However, will you please indulge me here?"

She removed her glasses hesitantly, folded them gently, and placed them into her purse. She paused before looking up at me, but when she did, I saw her eyes were not coal-colored as I expected. Instead, they were of a dark, violet hue, unique and very beautiful. She appeared to have long eyelashes too, but they were covered in mascara, so the jury remains out on that issue.

"Thank you for indulging me, Ms. Hartwell," I said.

"Please call me Krista."

"So, tell me, Krista, how can I help?"

Nancy Goldstein is the junior senator from the Golden State. She wasn't my pick in the last election, because I rarely if ever vote for an incumbent. I subscribe to the theory that until the government does something, anything of value, I should always give the other guy an opportunity to prove that she or he can do better. It's not that Senator Goldstein did nothing as a legislator, but as a two-term senator, and since the State of California, both fiscally and socially, is in a state of deterioration, I blame the whole lot of them for the mess that we're in. It's like the corporal at Dachau who simply walked the perimeter fence at midnight. Wasn't he as responsible as those who formulated the final solution? No, the problem is with politicians themselves. They're not liars, exactly; they just seem to feel it's okay to deceive the public to win election or reelection. I'm thoroughly convinced every one of them has read "The Prince" multiple times. Senator Goldstein isn't a bad person, but she is a politician.

The senator wanted me to meet her at her home in Malibu. Since I couldn't think of anything I'd rather do than drive through mid-afternoon Los Angeles traffic to visit a powerful politico at her beachside estate, I hopped into my '91 Porsche Carrera and hit Vista del Mar North. I knew the trip well since I'd frequented Malibu in my youth. Dad wouldn't live there because he hated driving to work in traffic, and if you live in Malibu and work in L.A., you have no choice. Mom loved the beach though, so we spent many summers there in rented beach properties or as guests of some of my parents' wealthier friends.

When the senator is in the Golden State, she resides near the end of Zumirez Drive on a bluff overlooking the Pacific. The house sits over eight thousand square feet with a circular driveway, multiple-car garage, a tennis court, pool, and an expansive view all the way to Japan. Not a bad setup if you like that sort of thing. I, however, don't like being beholden to anyone or anything, and most people don't understand that estates like the senator's bring a form of slavery no less insidious than any other.

But the senator's husband has more money than a person could possibly spend in several lifetimes. David Goldstein is a successful venture capitalist. If you look at the most successful high-tech companies from the last twenty or thirty years, David Goldstein had or has a piece of each one. I have no idea how many billions the Goldsteins have accumulated, but I know that David is a legacy member of the Forbes 400. And with that type of wealth comes a sense of entitlement. Never mind the Goldsteins are registered Democrats. Not all Democrats remain altruistic when in office. I prepared myself to reject the senator's offer because I could feel the shackle of obligation beginning to choke me as I drove.

I pulled into the senator's driveway just about an hour after leaving Playa del Rey. Not bad for a twenty-six-mile ride along the coast. Exiting my two-seater, I approached the massive twin mahogany doors. Each was inlaid with mirror-image stained glass representations of Pacific porpoises breaching. I fingered the doorbell button and waited. After a few seconds, a fine domestic named Hobbs opened the left portico and invited me in.

Hobbs encouraged me to follow him, which I did, dutifully. He ended our expedition at a nondescript hardwood door, and opening it, gestured for me to enter. The room I entered was a moderate-sized library with built-in bookcases filled with the classics. Immediately upon entering, I identified at least three dozen rare first editions by the likes of Dickens, Joyce, Hemingway, King, and Koontz.

Hobbs said, "Have a seat, sir. The senator will be with you shortly. Would you care for a beverage?"

I thought about Hobbs' offer. It's funny how the recovering mind goes first to the poison driving one into recovery. "Nothing, thanks."

Hobbs exited with my rejection. I sat down in one of several overstuffed reception chairs placed randomly throughout the library. It was covered in beige calfskin and enveloped me with its luxuriousness. As I sat in the bovine armchair, I looked around, taking in the rest of the room.

Along the east wall hung several portraits printed on canvas-style photographic paper, each one enclosed in an elaborate mahogany frame. The largest one depicted the senator and Mr. Goldstein standing in her senatorial office with Old Glory at their side. Around the portrait, at each corner, hung a smaller one with the same framing. These contained representations of individuals I assumed were the four Goldstein offspring. The west wall of the library held a small fireplace fronted with a tri-fold brass screen.

The door behind me opened, and Senator Goldstein entered. She was wearing a powder blue suit, a string of cultured Japanese pearls, and a Villa Paloma diamond bangle on her right wrist. She extended the Tiffany-enhanced hand to me.

"It's a pleasure to meet you, Mr. Bolt," she said as I shook her hand. "I have heard so much about you."

"Not too much or I wouldn't be here," I said.

"No, Sam Truman was very complimentary. I did have my people vet you, however, so I know about your past, shall we say, indiscretions?"

I didn't like the way she inflected the last word. "Yes, I am a disgrace to my family. What can I help you with, Senator?"

She looked at me disconcertedly. I assume she didn't intend an insult, but the whole episode leading to the end of my legal career, and my subsequent recovery, remains a sore spot for me.

My father, Harrison Walker Bolt, was a partner in one of Los Angeles' two-name law firms. He was a very astute corporate lawyer, and his many satisfied clients led to his accumulation of wealth. When he retired, my parents' net worth was in the mid-eight figures.

Being his only child and son, I was encouraged from a young age to follow in his footsteps. Never mind that I had other aspirations. Law was my chosen vocation, and as a dutiful son, I did as was expected of me, under protest.

I screwed around as an undergraduate, so my grades were not stellar. Luckily, my native intellect got me through the law school admission process, and I attended one of the many training centers for lawyers in Los Angeles.

After graduation and bar passage, I was offered and accepted an associate position with my father's firm. That lasted less than a year. I grew bored with the daily tedium of dealing with petty outrages and the confluence of combatants lacking common concurrence. I considered taking a hiatus when a friend recommended me for a government job.

In the days and years after 9/11, there were those in government who could see the limitations of the CIA and the military in combating terrorist threats. The question was how could a war be fought against an enemy not only willing to die for his, her, or their cause, but wanting to do so? The simple answer was to grant them their wish without incurring any American casualties, but doing so within the confines of the Constitution, international law, and Christian ethos was challenging.

A program was created outside of the confines of government. It was known by the acronym FIDA, which stood for the four tasks required of all operatives: find, interrogate, dissuade, and annihilate. Each task was used to render a perceived enemy invalid. Each subsequent task was presumed to be used only if the predecessor was ineffective.

Annihilation was reserved for the thoroughly recalcitrant or intentionally suicidal suspects.

Selected individuals needed to pass a battery of physical and psychological tests to be considered. Then a comprehensive background check was run to weed out any potential weak links. You see, this program was designed for one thing, and one thing only: murder. But going into foreign countries to kill native sons and daughters required skills far beyond the ability to squeeze a trigger or thrust a blade between two ribs. It required the ability to blend into the local landscape, gather intelligence, determine who could and could not be trusted, and timing the sanction perfectly. Above all, we were trained to make everything look like an accident or a random event of violence.

Now you may be wondering why any program such as this would be interested in a slacker, half-hearted lawyer. Well, the friend who recommended me, Clausen Bonewald, is a lifelong friend. We met as freshmen at Santa Monica High School where we both excelled in athletics. You see, I have a gift—and not what you're thinking. I am blessed with superior visual acuity and extraordinary hand-eye coordination. Claus and I were varsity baseball, basketball, and archery teammates. In four years of high school, I never missed a bullseye, a player's mitt, or the basket on a free throw. I also have a flexible moral compass. It was the latter quality that attracted the government and led to my disgrace as a lawyer.

Senator Goldstein recounted her recent loss of nearly twelve million dollars due to embezzlement by one of her trusted staff members. What I knew of the story was carried for several weeks by the Times, but Nancy Goldstein added several nuances not reported to the masses.

"When did you first suspect Ms. Krieger of embezzlement?" I asked.

"About a year ago," she said.

"What raised your suspicion?"

Senator Goldstein described a convoluted scenario where money collected from donors was deposited into several accounts, then transferred amongst others, and finally ended up in an operating account used by Elsa Krieger. Krieger was responsible for booking media space and time, coordinating fundraising activities, staffing events, and paying vendors. This final step was where the senator lost track of twelve million dollars.

"Obviously, I failed to pay close enough attention to the operation of my campaign," she said. "Do you know how to read financial statements, Senator?" I asked.

She looked at me and flared her nostrils slightly at my impertinence. "Of course I do," she said.

"I mean no insult, Senator. I ask because most people, including highly educated, sophisticated members of society, can't tell the difference between a profit and loss statement, a cash flow statement, and a balance sheet. And someone who wants to hide a misappropriation can do so easily."

"Suffice it to say, Mr. Bolt, a lot of money was taken from me, from my campaign, and I want it back," she said.

I paused before offering my next question and examined the demeanour of the honorable Senator Goldstein. She rose from her chair, moving from behind the large mahogany desk to the floor-to-ceiling picture windows. She stood transfixed, staring at the open ocean. She moved her hand gently down the side of her face and brushed a few stray hairs over her ear. After several moments, she turned to me and said, "I know for someone in my position, being focused on restitution might seem trite and unnecessary, but Ms. Krieger did more than steal from my campaign." She trailed off her speech, turning her head to again watch the vast Pacific Ocean. She asked the blue water, "Can you do it?"

"Frankly, Senator, I don't know," I said. "We just met, I know virtually nothing about her—Ms. Krieger— and you want to extract several million dollars that may be long gone."

I stood and said, “You shouldn’t,” and I walked toward the door to get the hell out of there. “Mr. Bolt, where are you going?” she asked. I turned to address her, bile rising in my throat. I calmed myself because she was, after all, a United States Senator, a member of the legislative branch of our government, of the upper house of the bicameral, law-making branch. “I’m leaving, Senator. You called me because Sam referred you. He did so because I possess unique skills and capabilities to resolve unresolvable problems. There are only two things of which I am certain, and unless you’re dying or evading paying your taxes, I can’t give you any guarantees.”

She stared at me for several moments. Probably she considered my response insolent. Tough. I neither sought her out nor do I need her approval. Finally, she said, “I just want to know you will do your best to retrieve what is mine.” Fine. She understood.

“That I can promise,” I said. “I’ll need what information you have about Elsa Krieger: full name, address, telephone numbers, Social Security, bank accounts, whatever you have. Also, I retain a third of anything I recover.”

“Yes, Sam explained your commission structure. Hobbs will give you everything you need,” she said. “Thank you, Mr. Bolt. You’re my only hope.”

I took that as my cue to leave, so once again I started for the office door. However, I felt that twinge in the back of my neck. It told me something else was coming. That’s when I heard, “Oh, Mr. Bolt, may I ask one other thing of you?” Here we go. I turned.

“Yes?” I said.

“My daughter, my youngest, Tricia. It seems she’s become mixed up in some untoward experimentation with drugs—methamphetamine, I believe,” she said, and then paused, pregnant. I waited for her to continue. I could see the subject was painful for her. She grimaced while trying to continue, and I could see she was holding back some tears.

"I'd like to know who is supplying her with the drugs," she said. "It's probably one of her friends," I said. "Usually is."

"To be clear," she said, "I'd like to know who the source is."

This powerful Washington insider was now treading in some potentially dangerous territory. As I watched her face, staring back at me, I realized she was not easily dissuaded.

"I'll see what I can find out," I said. "Anything else?"

"No, that will do. Thank you again, Mr. Bolt."

I left the senator's office, closing the door behind me. In that moment I couldn't help thinking of what Shakespeare wrote: "misery acquaints a man with strange bedfellows." Ain't that the truth?

Hobbs stood in the large foyer holding a brown pendaflex wallet. It was full of papers and folders, and it was secured by an elastic band. "I assume that's for me?" I said to Hobbs. "Yes, sir. I thought it prudent to be at the ready." Hobbs handed the brown bundle to me. I guess I had a little light reading ahead of me. I thanked Hobbs and exited.

I tossed the package on the front passenger seat of the Carrera. I got in and started the flat-six. Then I noticed the time. It was already 4:30. If I started for Playa del Rey now, it would take me nearly two hours to get there in bumper-to-bumper traffic. I could feel my hypertension increase at the thought.

Plan B. I drove over to the Malibu Country Mart. I figured I'd grab something to eat, maybe a beer, and begin my reading assignment. Hell, I had a couple of hours to kill. I might as well do it in the open air in Malibu, eating a fine turkey burger and fries from Malibu Mutt's.

I ordered my usual: turkey burger with cheddar, grilled onions, pickles, and one slice of tomato. A side of fries is always welcome, but they need to be crisp. There's nothing as unappetizing as limp, greasy fries. I ordered a Corona with a quartered lime to wash it all down.

I sat with my meal in the central commons, enjoying the waning rays of the early fall sun. Several beach moms were allowing their rugrats to recreate with nannies in tow. Discipline was initiated by the matriarch and administered by the governess. I am constantly amazed by the denial of the wealthy and privileged. When their kids turn to alcohol, drugs, or crime, they wonder why. Lack of discipline is the catalyst, in my opinion. And more than likely, lack of discipline led to Elsa Krieger's wayward ways.

Nearly everything I needed was in the dossier. Krieger was born in Van Nuys in the early 1970s. Her father, William Krieger, was a sometime executive producer on several popular television programs in the late '70s and early '80s. He crashed and burned in 1987 due to drugs, alcohol, and adultery.

With her broken family splintered, Elsa was sent to Washington, D.C., to live with her mother's sister, Emily Talbert. Auntie Em worked as a secretary to Senator Bumpers of Arkansas. It was during this time Elsa was first exposed to the connections and contacts that led her to Senator Goldstein.

I had to hand it to Elsa. On the page, she seemed incredibly adept at networking through the halls of power in Washington. Page after page, her dossier revealed a woman hell-bent on becoming a respected and trusted compatriot. What I couldn't figure out at that moment was what caused her to go awry? I needed to gather additional information, and I knew where to get it.

CHAPTER 2

TENDER MERCIES

I called my investigator, Karl Eisner. I met Karl years ago when I started with FIDA. Karl was invaluable to me during the interrogation phase because he was able to provide additional background information that was instrumental to my success. After we both left the committee, Karl settled as a private investigator in West Hollywood.

Karl's cell phone rang three times, and then the call was routed to his voice mail. This was S.O.P. for Karl and most investigators I know. If you answer your phone, anyone with a modicum of technical prowess can discover your location in a matter of seconds. And if someone meant to do you harm, you were going to be harmed. Karl generally keeps his phone off, and he checks his messages at random times during the day from the same location. This meant I would hear back from him within twenty-four hours at the latest. I was hoping for sooner rather than later, but hope and five dollars will get you a coffee at Starbucks.

While I waited for Karl's return call, I jumped into the Porsche to begin my ride back to Dockweiler. I left Malibu and headed south on Pacific Coast Highway. It's a beautiful drive even with the traffic. Just around fifty thousand vehicles a day move through the twenty-five-mile stretch of roadway, and it can be a tedious commute. But the scenery is pretty unbeatable. Ocean breezes, multi-million-dollar homes, beautiful women, and exotic automobiles litter the landscape. If I wasn't so high-strung, I could enjoy the view more.

As I turned right onto Lincoln Boulevard in Santa Monica, Karl's call came in. I touched "earpiece" to answer. "Yello," I said.

"Jon? It's Karl."

"Hey, Karl, what do you know?" A pause. Karl's not amused by innocuous chatter.

"You called?"

"Yes, I did. Sorry for the banter, Karl. You know me. I can't help it."

Nothing but silence on Karl's end. He was waiting for me to get to the point, and it was making him crazy.

"Listen, Karl, I need some information on an Elsa Krieger."

"The Elsa Krieger that's been in the news?"

"The same."

"What are you looking for, and how far back should I check?"

"I'd like the whole ball of wax, Karl: friends, neighbors, habits, sexual proclivities, you know, the usual." I heard Karl scribbling in his spiral wire-bound notebook. Karl is a brilliant investigator, but he's trapped in the twentieth century in some ways.

"And I suppose you want the information yesterday?" Karl said.

"What else? Thanks, buddy. I'll check in tomorrow morning," I said and disconnected the call. We finished the call just as Lincoln Boulevard turns into Pacific Coast Highway in Venice, and as I passed Commonwealth Avenue, I thought I should head up to the Valley to check out Ms. Krieger's apartment building. Maybe I could scrape together the beginnings of an investigation.

I directed the Carrera left onto Rose Avenue and followed the road around the curve as it transformed into Beethoven Street, then a left onto Palms Boulevard, right on Sepulveda, then onto the 405 North on-ramp just south of Venice Boulevard. Traffic on the San Diego Freeway was mercifully light at this time of day, but I knew I would most likely hit some traffic in the Sepulveda Pass. I did.

While sitting at an average speed of twelve miles per hour, I had time to think and plan. I wanted to see where Elsa Krieger lived, what her lifestyle was, because she denied that any of the twelve-some-odd millions she embezzled remained. She claimed she spent it on lavish vacations, gambling, homes, and she even copped to some drug abuse. I understand that triple play of wine, women (or men), and song, but I couldn't calculate how she ran through that amount of money unless she did an incredible amount of high-priced drugs. I guess if she spent the bulk making foolish wagers in Vegas or at any number of Indian casinos in California, it would be possible, but it would also be on video. I made a mental note to have Karl follow up on that.

When I reached the Ventura Boulevard off-ramp, which actually feeds onto Sepulveda Boulevard, I headed north. Elsa's apartment building was in the fifteen-thousand block of Ventura, so I hung a left at the intersection. Passing the Galleria and the freeway overpass, I turned right onto Orion Street.

This area of Sherman Oaks was littered with apartment buildings built in the mid-twentieth century, sturdy wood-frame buildings covered in stucco. It was a solid middle-class neighborhood with residents of various ethnicities living side by side in harmony. People here wouldn't notice the comings and goings of their neighbors. Most were fully engaged in their own day-to-day lives. It was a perfect place for Elsa to "hide out."

I knew the area well. During the '94 Northridge earthquake, many newer buildings suffered severe damage here, but the older ones did not. In fact, the multi-story hotel on the corner suffered serious damage to its parking structure. The hotel was now a Courtyard by Marriott, but back in the nineties, it was a Hilton.

I turned left onto Moorpark Street. Moorpark Street traversed the San Fernando Valley from Toluca Lake to Encino. It ran contiguously from Clybourn Avenue to Van Nuys Boulevard, and then it becomes segmented to Balboa Boulevard. Elsa Krieger lived on a segment cul-de-sac. There was little street parking available due to the time of day and the demographic makeup of the neighborhood. There were eleven large apartment buildings on the street. Each probably had ten to thirty or more units. No more than fifty or so cars could be legally parked on the street, and nearly every space was taken.

I slowly proceeded down the block looking for a place to park the Carrera. Elsa's building was at the end of the cul-de-sac. Several places on the curve were marked in red, but I was fortunate to find an unmarked space. I parked the Porsche and got out. I took a perfunctory look around. There was a parking control sign bolted to the wooden power pole on the passenger side. It was one of many in Los Angeles with multiple days and times listed. It was an understatement to say they were confusing. My analysis was that I was illegally parked. So, I opened the driver's door and set my emergency flashers. I wouldn't be long anyway, and any John Law interference was unlikely.

I got out and walked toward Elsa's complex. It was comprised of four separate buildings, three of which were connected in an "E" shape. Between the buildings were modestly lit courtyards. I checked the mailboxes to confirm Elsa's residence. Krieger was listed as apartment 217. I walked up the first courtyard seeking the door with 217 on it. It was three-quarters of the way down on the upper left. There were no lights on inside. She wasn't at home.

I found the manager's unit on the first floor near the front of the first building on the "E." There were lights on in the living room, and I heard some muffled conversation. Maybe I could gather some additional information from the manager and save this from becoming a wasted trip.

I then proceeded to the manager's apartment and knocked, hard. Through the solid-core door, I heard the faint sound of someone shuffling. I knocked again, harder. "Alright, alright! Keep your shorts dry!" I heard from the other side.

Moments later, I heard the sound of several locks being undone, and the door swung open inward. Before me stood a five-foot-nothing septuagenarian woman, gray hair held tightly in a hairnet, and a cigarette protruding from her bottom lip. The ash was several inches long. "Okay," she said, "can I help you, Mr. Patience?" This was going to be good.

I reached out to her holding one of my many business cards. This one indicated I was a segment producer for a celebrity newsmagazine known for breaking stories about movie star arrests for driving under the influence, divorces, and domestic violence. Very sweet.

"Hello," I said. "I'm Jonas Janus. I'm looking for Elsa Krieger."

The manager stared at me through her finger-smeared glasses, a wisp of smoke undulating from the cigarette. "She's not here."

"I'm sorry," I said. "I didn't get your name." "I didn't give it," she said. I smiled. She was fun. I looked over my shoulder at the bank of mailboxes attached to the building near the atrium entrance. "Easy enough to find out," I said. "Why not play nice?"

I caught a slight smile, which she quickly extinguished. She then removed the cigarette from her lip, allowing the huge ash to drop between us. "Mrs. Bender," she said.

"Mrs. Bender, we are investigating the alleged embezzlement of Senator Goldstein's campaign. Do you have any comments?"

Mrs. Bender took a long, large drag of the cigarette and crushed the filter under her slippered foot. "I didn't vote for her," she said, blowing volumes of smoke into my face.

"Understood," I said. "Any comment about the allegations against Elsa Krieger?"

"I don't know nuthin' 'bout that. Ms. Krieger is a good tenant. She pays on time and is not too noisy. Anything else is nuna my business." I could see I wasn't going to get anywhere with Mrs. Bender, so I decided to end the conversation with a bang.

"So, you're okay with criminals living in your building so long as they pay their rent on time and keep the noise down?"

Her face grew redder than normal, and she almost growled. "Fuck right off!" she said and slammed the door in my face. Some people are so easy to piss off.

I was dictating some notes about my interaction with Mrs. Bender into my iPhone as I walked toward the street. "Hey," I heard from behind. I turned to see the door of the unit below Elsa's ajar. The same unit was catty-corner to Mrs. Bender's. Backlit in the doorway was a short, stout redhead. She looked about forty-five, dressed in her housedress. Nearly transparent with the interior lighting streaming through, her pendulous breasts retreated beneath her armpits. "Hello," I said. "Can I help you?"

"I think I can help you," Red said.

"Really? How's that?"

"I heard you asking about Elsa."

"Go on."

"Elsa lives right up there," Red said, pointing toward the apartment above hers. "She's a party girl, that's for sure."

"What do you mean?" I said.

"Well, she has lots of parties in her place. Usually doesn't end till late. Two or three, usually. And men! All types, all the time. Her cooch must be raw, if ya know what I mean." Red winked at me real sly-like and made a clicking sound with the side of her mouth. I liked Red. She was my kind of source.

"I see," I said. "Did you ever see anyone else coming or going?"
"What do you mean?"

"Aw, come on," I said. "You know. Shady types. Types that your gut tells you are no good. You know what I mean?"

Red got all animated and started jumping up and down a bit. I took a slight step back in case one of her swinging breasts released from its sheer cotton case.

"I know exactly the type. Yup, she has them too. Just the other night, three Russians was in her place. They were pretty near quiet until just before they left. Elsa was screaming at 'em. Calling them 'fuckers' and shit. Yup, they was not good guys, that's for sure."

I gave Red a nice smile, said "thanks," and wished her a good evening. She did invite me in for a knobber, but duty called, so I left.

I walked back into the cul-de-sac. There was a lot of activity now with people returning home from work. Several cars were moving slowly, seeking curb parking, which at this point was becoming painfully scarce. I noticed a black Mercedes CL 63 turn left from the corner. It drove slowly like some of the other cars, but the driver did not seem to have the same hesitation as the parking seekers.

As the sleek Benz moved past me, I tried to get a glimpse of the driver. No such luck. The window tint was not California legal. The driver continued past me down the alley toward the tenant parking in the back of the building. I decided to see who was driving this luxo-boat, so I walked back into the courtyard of Elsa's building.

Earlier I noticed there was only one passageway from the tenant parking into the building, so I positioned myself near the manager's apartment where I could observe everyone who walked through. Several minutes elapsed. I began to think my instinct was wrong. Maybe this Benz captain turned around and left. Then I saw him walk through the passage: tall and lean in jeans, a black button-down shirt, untucked, and black Ferragamo loafers. As soon as the light hit his face, I knew it was Kiril Chesnokov.

Chesnokov came to the United States in the late 1990s flood of Vorovskoy mir. He is a leader in the Dolgoprudnenskaya gang, deeply involved in extortion, prostitution, and narcotics distribution. He was also suspected in several murders. I recall charges were filed on one occasion, but he beat the rap.

My law enforcement contacts indicated that Kiril was a vicious sociopath. He had no compunction about the acts he performed on other human beings. There were tales of rape, of both the female and male variety, torture, intentional maiming, blinding, and hobbling. My private investigator, Karl Eisner, worked a case where it was alleged that Chesnokov sliced off the eyelids of a low-level drug runner because the peon kept wincing in pain when he was being beaten. Kiril insisted that failure to make eye contact would result in the lesson being lost. A real animal.

I watched him enter the atrium. He walked with an air of impenetrability, as if he were untouchable. I thought how easy it would be for me to knock out one of his eyes with a small stone from this distance. The arrogant ass. He walked up a set of stairs and headed directly to Elsa's apartment. He stopped momentarily, and instead of knocking as I supposed he would, he removed a key from his pocket, put it in the lock in the doorknob, and turning it to the right, opened the door. He entered Elsa's apartment and closed the door behind him.

It was becoming clear that Elsa Krieger and Kiril Chesnokov had something more than a casual relationship. If she gave him a key to her apartment, it was probably of the intimate variety. I thought it clever of her to fraternize with a man who would have several conduits available to launder her ill-gotten gains. But there remained too many unanswerable questions. I needed to engage Karl to gather some background intelligence.

I walked out the way I entered the building's courtyard. The cul-de-sac was now completely full of parked cars. Several men and women, arriving home from their daily grinds, were moving from the street into their respective buildings. Their workdays were over, and they all appeared to be ready to unwind.

I noticed two small, black sedans sitting at the curved end of the cul-de-sac. This area's curbs were painted red as a fire zone, so stopping, as well as parking, were prohibited. I noticed each vehicle's engine remained running with light smoke emerging from the tailpipes. The drivers were each sitting behind the wheel looking toward Elsa's building. These had to be a couple of Kiril's men, and if so, it was my chance to see what I could be up against as I moved further along on this case.

I stepped over to the car farthest away from the building. As I approached, the driver sneered at me through the driver's door window. I rapped on the glass with my knuckle. The window slid down into the door.

"You can't park here," I said. "It's a fire zone."

The driver looked like his head was going to explode. "I'm not parked, asshole," he said.

"Well, you can't stop here either." He started to tell me to have sexual relations with my mother when I plucked his windpipe between my thumb and fingers. I applied just enough pressure to make him aware that I resented him assuming I would do that with the woman who bore me.

"No more talking," I said. "Just listen. You need to leave. Now. Just nod if you understand." Because the volume of oxygen flowing to his lungs was minimal, he nodded his comprehension. It was then I noticed his compatriot in the other car exiting the vehicle.

Out of the corner of my eye, I spotted him in the driver's side mirror. He was another gorilla of a man, dressed all in black: slacks, shoes, socks, and shirt. He was bearing down on me rapidly. I watched his progress while I continued to hold my friend's larynx.

When he entered striking distance, I quickly kicked my left foot backward and executed a heel scoop to the groin. The ape fell to the ground holding his nearly ruptured testicles between his hands, hands that were clamped between his knees. It was a funny reaction. When injured, human beings tend to pull inward. It doesn't stop the pain or heal the injury, but it does garner some comfort. Perhaps it's the same reason we enjoy hugging a loved one. There is comfort to be found in tight bodily contact.

With the threat ended, I looked back at my captive. I released my grasp on his throat because I could see his eyelids fluttering. When I did, he began coughing, gasping for air.

"Have a nice day," I said as I walked toward the Porsche. I got in and drove away. As I turned right on Orion, I saw the ape continue to roil on the ground in agony while my former prisoner remained behind the wheel trying to regain some composure. If these two represented the apex of Chesnokov's crew, I felt pretty good about my chances if a confrontation occurred in the future. But I knew that I should not get overconfident. "He who knows when he can fight and when he cannot will be victorious."

Driving down Ventura Boulevard, I called Karl again. Again, I got his voice mail. Not leaving a message this time, I decided to run over to his place. If he was home, great. If not, I would leave a conspicuous note. I needed additional information before I could plan my next move, and Karl was the best source for said information. I knew how efficiently he worked, so I was nearly certain he had uncovered many interesting tidbits by now.

If you've never been to West Hollywood, you should visit sometime. WeHo, as it's known to the locals, has a long, colorful history. The hippies moved there in the 1960s, followed by a large group of Russian Jews after the fall of the Soviet Union. However, most people consider the area a gay enclave, even though the gay population is just about forty percent. I don't really care what your position is on the "gay rights" question, but I'll say this: there are good and bad in all races, creeds, religions, and sexual orientations. I just take them as I see them. West Hollywood is more than the sum of its parts. There are fine restaurants, theaters, and historical points of interest. One of the best medical centers in the world, Cedars-Sinai, calls West Hollywood home. An eclectic blend if ever there was one.

Karl lived in a nice apartment building on North Hayworth Avenue. It was a first-floor one-bedroom deal, sparsely but tastefully decorated. I pulled up in front of the building and saw a light on in Karl's window. Chances were he was home.

I spotted an open space across the street from Karl's building, and I sped the Carrera into it. I walked to Karl's building and rang the buzzer for his unit.

"Yes?" I heard from the speaker.

"Karl, it's Bolt. Let me in." A harsh tone deactivated the front lock, and in I walked. Karl was waiting at his apartment with the door open.

"A little anxious, aren't we?" he said.

"Well, I guess I am. I think our girl's involved with Chesnokov." Karl's face drained of blood. "You're kidding?" he said. "That complicates things. Come on in."

I walked into Karl's apartment. His desk was to the left of the entrance near the large picture window. Karl was a fastidiously organized guy. The desktop was full, but each stack of work-in-progress was neatly arranged. There were several stacks carefully placed near the front of the desk where Karl could have easy access from his chair.

He sat in the chair and began working through some copies of documents he had collected. He examined them cursorily for a few moments when he came upon one that held his attention longer. He sat back in the chair holding the paper in his right hand. He waved the paper slightly in the air and smiled slightly.

"What?" I said. Karl looked at the paper in his hand, then at me, then back to the paper. "I think she's using Chesnokov to launder the money," Karl said.

"Yes," I said. "Why?"

Karl began explaining that he could find nothing linking Elsa to any large expenditures. She hadn't bought any real estate, expensive vehicles, extravagant vacations, precious metals, or other investments. Neither had Karl been able to discover any major substance abuse or gambling addiction. He was perplexed because he hadn't been able to locate any substantial amount of the twelve million dollars Elsa had allegedly stolen, and twelve million is a lot of money to hide. Karl had assumed she had spent it over the years as she stole it, but he could find no assets large enough to represent that amount of spending. When he came up short on that line, he considered various addictions. Again, he was unsuccessful.

"It makes sense," Karl said. "Chesnokov is most likely laundering the money for her. I'll make some inquiries, see if I can confirm that."

"Okay," I said. "Let me know what you find out." I thanked Karl for the information and headed for the door.

"Bolt," Karl said. I turned, looking at Karl.

"Chesnokov is not a nice guy. Be careful." I nodded, acknowledging Karl's concern, then walked out.

I got into my car and headed home. When I pulled into my spot at Dockweiler about an hour later, I noticed several young women sitting on the sand. I decided to cook some dinner on the portable grill outside while I watched the girls. I was feeling anxious anyway, so maybe I could put something together. Time would tell.

I brought several grass-fed steaks out from the coach, fired up the grill, and went back in to collect some beers. Before I did, I noticed the girls had noticed me. The tallest of the three was looking in my direction as one of the other two was talking. I couldn't make out what was being said, but it was clear I could have some company that evening if I so chose.

When I returned with a twelve-pack, Stretch came forward, now standing within the curtilage of my coach. She smiled a bright, orthodontically enhanced smile and told me her name was Julie. I reached out my hand to Julie and told her I was Mick.

"You like steak and beer, Julie?" I asked.

"You bet," she said.

"What about your friends?" I said as we both looked over at the two still standing in the sand. Julie waved them over, mouthing "come on."

They arrived and introduced themselves as Elvie and Katrina. Elvie, the shortest of the trio, had breasts somewhat larger than Dolly Parton's. Her shirt was straining to keep them at bay. And I will state right here that although I don't consider myself a breast man, I was hard-pressed to keep from staring at Elvie as she stood there pivoting from foot to foot. Katrina, on the other hand, was well proportioned for a twenty-something California girl: tall enough, pretty enough, and sexy enough without being overpowering. However, I was really interested in Julie.

Julie stood at nearly my height, so I assumed she was five feet eleven without shoes. She had smaller, perky breasts that, even as she aged, would never fall lower than her breastbone. But her greatest assets were her eyes, Caribbean blue, and her round, uplifted butt. Yes, I am truly an ass man.

I threw the steaks on the glowing grill, and they sizzled into the night. I opened a beer for each of my friends, not knowing if any or all were of legal drinking age.

"I assume you girls are all over twenty-one?" I said, half kidding. To my surprise, they all took out their state driver's licenses to prove it. Not that I gave a fuck, but the fact that they each showed me government identification gave me a solid defense if some overzealous prosecutor wanted to give me shit. The Business and Professions Code in California allows it as a mistake of fact. Good! Time to start drinking.

Elvie and Katrina guzzled down a beer each in a matter of moments. They each grabbed a second one without asking. Their comfort level was total. Julie took her time on her brew. A fine quality.

We made small talk. She asked me about my coach; did I like traveling in one? She seemed concerned when I told her I lived in it.

"Are you homeless?" she asked.

"Does it appear that I am?" I said. Julie smiled.

"I've just never known anyone who lived in one of these," she said. "You're young. Just wait," I said, smiling back into her beautiful blues. I told her my work required that I be mobile, and she asked what I did. I told her I had my own business. This intrigued her.

"What kind of business?" she said.

"I am a freelance dispatcher," I said. I could see Julie's brain working. She wasn't a dummy, but I could see in her eyes she didn't understand how someone could be a freelance dispatcher. "You mean like for the police?" she said. I laughed out loud, which made her face flush.

"Not a police dispatcher. I help people solve their problems quickly and efficiently." Now she didn't know what to think. "Are you hungry?" I said. She smiled again and said she was.

The girls sat down at the dinette while I microwaved some vegetables and a potato for each of us. Elvie and Katrina were feeling no pain. They were telling stories about some of their girlfriends from school. Their words were slurred like there was no tomorrow, and after each slur, Katrina fell into a fit of giggling. A few times I asked if she was alright because it seemed to me that she had completely stopped breathing.

Young women can't hold their alcohol.

Later, the four of us sat in the coach having an intimate supper together. Elvie and Katrina were beginning to come out of their stupor, giggling while sawing through their steaks. Dinner conversation consisted of small talk, inconsequential banter, and descriptions of their various sexual proclivities. I could see where this was going, and as a younger man, I might have been up for a tryst with three sexually voracious vixens. Although I don't need the little blue pill, yet, the thought of having to attend to all of them was giving me a slight headache. I was looking forward to some adult recreation, but I preferred it one-on-one.

After dinner, I decided I needed some fresh air. I left the coach to retire to the makeshift patio just outside. I opened several Tommy Bahama beach chairs in case my guests wanted to join me, and I sat down looking toward the ocean. Moments later, Julie joined me. She looked fine in the filtered moonlight as she sat next to me. Yes, she was my choice. With all the eons of evolution behind us, it struck me that the rules of sexual predation haven't changed much. We identify the one to whom our attraction is stirred, we proceed with our courtship dance, and we move in for the kill.

I kissed Julie. Her mouth tasted mildly of beer and charred beef, but it was an intoxicating blend as far as I was concerned. She responded appropriately with her tongue gently seeking mine as we pulled each other closer and embraced. Moisture grew between us, and I pulled back slightly.

"Let's go inside," I said. She followed my lead as I held her hand. Elvie and Katrina were each in one of the lounge chairs, sleeping off their intoxication. We walked silently to the back of the coach, and I closed and latched the bulkhead door. We would have visual privacy, but my estimation of Julie's sensuality led me to believe there would be no acoustic concealment—only tender mercies. Spiritus promptus.

CHAPTER 3

KILLER ELITE

When I woke up, the sun had been mocking me for several hours. It was castigating me for my insolence, reminding me that I was getting to be an old man, and athletic sexuality is a young man's game. Every muscle in my body ached, and the pain behind my right eye served as a brutal reminder that, although I'd like to think of myself as an experienced imbiber, my physiology and alcohol rarely mix well. I needed ibuprofen, and I needed it now.

That's when I noticed I was alone. There was no sign of Julie anywhere in the bedroom. I assumed she'd left sometime after we'd completed our late-night antics. Too bad—I liked her. She was too young for me, sure, but a nice girl, the product of excellent parenting, I would bet.

I slid the partition back and was immediately assaulted by the sound of deeply resonant snoring. There was Julie, spread out on the sofa bed at the front of the coach, sawing major wood. For such a thin girl, she could make one hell of a racket. I'd been wondering what had caused her to abandon the bedroom after our activities, but now, listening to her cacophony, I was grateful she had.

As peaceful as she looked—relatively speaking—I shook her gently because I needed to get my day started. She awoke immediately, sitting upright and rubbing the sleep from her eyes with the back of her hands.

"What time is it?" she mumbled.

"Time to go," I said. She didn't appear to appreciate my directness, but time was money, and money was wasting.

She pushed back the covers. She was wearing a white bra and matching panties. The term "camel toe" flashed through my mind as she jumped up, grabbed her clothes, and rushed past me to the head. She entered, closed the door hard behind her, and I waited. Several minutes later, she emerged looking considerably less agitated. She glanced around the coach, avoiding eye contact. The silence stretched awkwardly between us, and I decided to break the tension.

"Do you need a ride?" I asked.

"No," she said, "my car is just up the way." Then she made direct eye contact, her eyes clenched slightly in what I recognized as suppressed irritation.

I grabbed my wallet, removed a fifty, and handed it to her. I could see the anger rising in her features like mercury in a thermometer.

"It's not payment for services," I said quickly. "I like you, but I know spending the night had to cause you some inconvenience. I just want to show my appreciation for your company. That's all."

Julie's expression softened. She smiled and took the bill, stuffing it into her bra. I gave her a little kiss on the cheek as I opened the coach door for her. She walked out and headed north toward the parking lot. I watched her just long enough to see if she was going to turn back for one last look. She didn't.

As I was about to go back inside, I noticed a car turning into the RV park. It made a fast left on the aisle nearest the ocean, heading directly toward me. Since I was still standing on the top step with the door open, I reached inside, feeling for my Glock. It was right where it was supposed to be, and I was ready to use it if necessary.

As the car moved closer, I could see Karl Eisner behind the wheel. It was unlike Karl to drive fast unless he had something important and time-dependent to say. Karl muscled his Toyota sedan into a parking space near the coach. He hopped out quickly, carrying a Pendaflex folder under his left arm.

"Are you alone?" he asked as he approached, fully aware of my proclivities.

I answered with a nod. Karl moved past me into the salon, sat on the lounge placing the folder beside him, and simply looked at me. I knew something was wrong, and I said, "What's up?"

"Close the door," he said. I did.

"We have a problem," Karl said.

"What kind of problem?" I asked.

"A big one." Karl began removing sheets of paper from the organizer. As he did, he cursorily looked each one over and placed it down on the table beside the lounge. Several times he rearranged the order of the documents as he spoke.

"Chesnokov," he began, "is an old-time racketeer. He's trying to gain control of all the stereotypical industries: gambling, prostitution, drugs, and extortion. And he's doing very well."

"I'm not following, Karl," I said. "How is this a problem for me?"

"He's also a ruthless killer, Jon. If he discovers you're investigating him, that I'm investigating him, it could be bad." Karl seemed scared, and being scared was unusual for him.

When we were young agents with FIDA, Karl and I were on a case once. We had to locate an al-Qaeda cell in lower Manhattan. After several days sitting in a four-door POS eating bad takeout and drinking gallons of mediocre coffee, we'd identified several members of the cell congregating in an abandoned warehouse. Mahmud Abdulrashid and Salim Saqqaf were wanted for planting several improvised explosive devices around lower Manhattan. If they'd been better bomb-makers, they would have been wanted for mass murder, but they sucked at it. The thing was, if they continued to build bombs, eventually—like everything in life—they would improve and kill Americans. Karl and I were not about to let that happen.

We entered the building surreptitiously. Karl took point, searching for Abdulrashid and Saqqaf while I found a position from where I could provide cover fire if necessary. Karl entered a darkened interior room with his flashlight held high beside the frame of his Sig P226 Scorpion. As he made it to the center of the room, the lights came up, and Karl was surrounded by three men with AKs. Two of the three were Abdulrashid and Saqqaf. The third man was not immediately identified. Most likely he was a new recruit. I presumed this due to his highly agitated demeanor.

They threw Karl to the concrete floor, zip-tied his hands behind him, beat him about the head and neck, then sat him up and began interrogating him. The whole time they were screaming at Karl while the barrels of the machine guns were within inches of his face.

Meanwhile, I was creeping above the fray in the rafters of the warehouse. I positioned myself near a dark, upper corner of the room and held my Glock 19 aimed at the back of Abdulrashid's head. I estimated I would have a second and a half to make the three headshots necessary to eliminate the threat. There would be no second chance. If I missed any of the shots, Karl was dead.

Karl saw me a split second before I squeezed off the shot into the back of Abdulrashid's head. Time expansion made the moment seem endless, and in that brief yet seemingly eternal moment, I saw Karl's slight nod encouraging me to do it. Pop, pop, pop—the shots rang out, and three 9mm Hydra-Shok hollow points turned out the lights on three very bad men. Karl appeared unfazed by his near brush with death. During our debrief, I asked him specifically about this. Karl said he'd accepted the potential possibility that his life could be lost in the pursuit of our goals. He said he was comfortable with this reality.

Yet now I was sensing extreme fear in him. Chesnokov was a ruthless racketeering genius. Yes, he could call out a hit on us. Yes, we could die. So what? Death was inevitable. I remember talking to my dad after I'd accepted the job with FIDA.

"You know you could be killed?" he'd said. "I know," I'd replied.

"Does it bother you at all?" he'd asked. I'd thought about it for a moment, and I realized that I hadn't really done so before then.

"We're all going to die, Pop. Better in the pursuit of bad men than years from now wasting away in some nursing home," I'd said. Dad had smiled at that and slapped me on the shoulder.

The ultimate result of life is death. For some reason, people in America have difficulty getting their heads around that fact. Other cultures don't have the same fear about it. They accept it as a natural progression. So, I was curious why Karl was now fearful about the possibility.

"Karl," I said, "you know we always take precautions. Why is this situation different?"

Karl looked out the side window of the coach toward the ocean. He had that look of someone seeking an elusive response to a benign question. He rubbed his chin with his left hand, then scratched his forehead. He turned to me, ready to respond, and then paused again.

"It doesn't feel good, Jon. I'm not sure why, but I have... reservations. I'm not telling you what to do, but I think I need to bow out."

I could see from Karl's demeanor and the grimace on his face that he was having difficulty sharing his feelings. Over the years, I'd had other team members express reservations about a particular case. Many regarded their potential death for a less-than-admirable goal as unworthy of their sacrifice. Some had simply lost their enthusiasm for the stated goals of FIDA. But in all those years, Karl had not been one of them.

I wasn't sure how to handle Karl's revelation. In our past interactions, Karl had revealed a steadfast commitment to the mission. Lives were always at stake. That was the cost of freedom and security. Karl understood what it meant if actions were not taken, and the alternative to taking action was unacceptable to him. But now, in the present, he seemed overtly nervous, anxious, and riled—quite out of character. I needed to know why my most trusted ally for nearly twenty years had suddenly lost the stomach for the job.

"What's going on, Karl?" I said.

He wouldn't look at me. I assumed the tone of my question had unintentionally relayed my disappointment. I tried again.

"I'm not upset, Karl. I'm just having a hard time understanding your reticence. We've worked together for a long time, and if that relationship is ending... well, it's disappointing."

He looked at me. "Why does our relationship have to end?"

"This is what we do. There's always the possibility of personal danger in this business, and fear won't change a thing."

"Gina's pregnant," Karl said, and I understood.

Although congratulations were in order, I sensed Karl wasn't thinking about the joy of bringing a new child into the world. At that moment, he was more likely thinking about leaving the child an orphan—or worse. Chesnokov and his kind had dysfunctional or vacant superegos. Kidnapping, torturing, and killing were part of his repertoire, and inflicting them on pregnant women and children made no difference to him.

"Okay, Karl. You're out," I said. "But can you use the intel you have and create a complete dossier for me?"

After a short pause, Karl said, "Sure, Jon. It's the least I can do. I saved the initial intel so you keep this hard copy."

Karl laid the Pendaflex down on the settee, looked out at the ocean again, and walked out. When I heard the sound of sand and small stones crunching under his tires, I opened the door and watched him drive away. Karl had always been a good asset and friend, but I couldn't take a chance with his distraction. I figured I'd call him once the job was done so we could talk about the future.

I thought about the conflict Karl must be facing. I don't have any children to my knowledge, and I don't intend to have any. It's not that I dislike the concept of children, but I don't believe everyone capable of procreating should do so. How many times have you been in a public place and observed poor parenting? It seems to me that every day I see people interacting with their offspring—or not interacting—and I'm dumbfounded by the complete lack of skill most parents exhibit.

I see children throwing temper tantrums in restaurants frequently. In nine cases out of ten, the parents do little or nothing to defuse the situation. It's as if ignoring a raging child will make it stop. Perhaps this strategy works, but what about the other patrons? We spend good money to enjoy a meal out, only to have an unruly child inflicted upon us. It's infuriating. Mind you, my anger isn't transferred to the child. No, they're merely acting out to get their needs met. My anger is directed at the parents who fail miserably in training their progeny in proper social etiquette. Don't accept the behavior, and it will become extinct. Just like when my sister, Jenny, was growing up.

Jenny is nearly ten years younger than I am. Although my mother denies it, I'm convinced Jenny's birth was unexpected. Our parents were older when she was born, and Dad died when Jenny was eighteen. The early years were challenging because Jenny was diagnosed with autism spectrum disorder when she was four. My parents grieved at the news, and they proceeded systematically through all five Kübler-Ross stages. The old man basically skipped the bargaining phase because he refused to bargain with an unseen adversary, but Mom prayed daily.

Jenny exhibited many of the stereotypical behaviors: hand-flapping, echolalia, perseveration. I remember being embarrassed when my friends came over to the house. Jenny would sit on the sofa watching Disney videos, flapping her hands and yelling. Mom was great at redirecting her to appropriate behaviors, but it was a long process. Once, a friend of mine—I believe it was Davy Ducomin—referred to Jenny as a "retard." I saw red and beat Davy to a pulp. It was then, at fifteen, that I realized I was to be Jenny's protector and advocate.

Through intensive therapy and time, Jenny developed communication skills. Her greatest leaps, however, came in mathematics. She has the innate ability to recognize and interpret patterns in complex number systems. Over the years, she's learned how to live a semi-independent life, holds a job in an accounting office, and she seems happy. I speak with her most days and visit every week when I'm in town. I made a mental note to visit Jenny at the end of the day. In the meantime, I needed to regroup and replace Karl.

I needed a drink, so I poured myself three fingers of single malt, neat, and tossed it back. I wiped my mouth with the back of my hand and sat down at the dinette. On my phone, I began looking through names of potential replacements. It didn't take me long to come upon the name Maggie Dunlevy. I nodded to myself. Yeah, Maggie would do nicely.

I knew Maggie through Master Parker's dojo; I was one of her instructors there. She was a spitfire. Standing five feet six in her stocking feet, most people—bad people—would think she was a less-than-able adversary. Her red hair, blue eyes, and slightly crooked smile added nothing to make a villain quake. But if you touched her, you would instantly know you were wrong. Maggie is also an expert in Kenpo Karate, the same style I practiced, a killer elite. She's one of only a handful of women I've met in my life whose musculature is similar to a man's. I once slapped her on the back and was surprised to find her muscles hard. I remember Maggie smiling at my recoil. "What's the problem, Jon?" she'd said. "Never had a hard woman?" I was instrumental in getting Maggie recruited by FIDA.

After I left FIDA, I kept in touch with only a handful of my co-agents. Maggie was one. Her career with the agency was short-lived, however. I never could get her to tell me all the details, but she was dismissed and prosecuted for battery. Evidently, Maggie had crushed the testicle of a senior operative, one Al Ashton. Al was actually Maggie's supervisor for about three days when the assault took place.

My recollection is that Al claimed Maggie didn't accept criticism well. He testified during the trial that he'd called Maggie into his office to discuss his expectations after reviewing Maggie's work record. She'd entered his office, and he'd closed the door behind her. He told her that he had a low tolerance for shenanigans, and she needed to change her methods. Then he claimed Maggie had hit him with a knee strike to the groin.

Maggie's story was slightly different. She actually took the stand in her defense, and yes, Al had asked her to report to his office. Yes, he'd opened the door and allowed her to enter. Yes, he'd closed the door behind her, but then the stories diverged. Maggie claimed she'd heard the sound of a zipper. She'd turned around to see what was going on, and Al was standing before her with his fly open, his erect penis pointing at her.

Al had smiled and begun slowly stroking his member, increasing its turgidity. Maggie had started laughing, softly at first, but with increasing intensity until it was uncontrollable. With tears streaming down Maggie's cheeks, Al had said, "What's so fucking funny?"

Maggie had stopped laughing. "You," she'd said. "You're funny."
"Yeah, how so?"

"You're pathetic, that's how."

Al had removed his hand from his dick and said, "You won't find me pathetic when I bend you over my desk and fuck you in the ass. Far from it. You'll think I'm a god!"

Maggie had shaken her head in pity and turned to leave. She'd felt his hands grab her neck from behind, fingers wrapping around her throat, pressure increasing.

Maggie was a little hazy on the details of what transpired next—a not uncommon experience for active martial artists. Muscle memory is great for self-defense, but relatively poor for testimony. She remembered feeling the constriction around her neck. She remembered stepping back with her left foot, striking Al in the groin with her right fist, and then following up with her right elbow to his throat. She remembered Al falling backward into his desk, his now-deflated prick still poking out like a baby turtle.

She remembered Al's anger and how he'd charged her, but then she was blank until she saw Al lying on the burgundy carpet, unconscious. Maggie was arrested for assault and battery and mayhem. After the detectives interviewed Al and Maggie, the district attorney filed charges against Maggie for battery. During discovery, a private detective named Myer ascertained that Al had tried his bullshit before. A young lady named Maya Golding came forward and decided to press charges against Al for sexual assault. The charges against Maggie were dropped after the defense proffered their opening statement.

I pressed Maggie's name on my phone. After three rings, I heard a crisp, energetic female answer. "Yeah?" she said.

"Maggie?"

"Who is this?"

"It's Jon, Jon Bolt."

A few seconds elapsed. I wasn't sure if she'd failed to recognize my name at first, but then her voice exploded.

"Holy shit! Jon fucking Bolt! How the hell are you, Jon?"

We talked for a few minutes, catching up on years of minutia. Finally, I said, "Do you miss it, Mags?" Silence again. I waited, patiently, which is torture but necessary. I heard Maggie exhale deeply after a few moments. Poor girl had been holding her breath at my question.

"Sometimes," she said. "But I'm also glad I don't work for the agency anymore. Too much political bullshit." I so wanted to ask her if she kept tabs on Al, but that would be a topic for another time. Instead, I continued: "Would you be interested in working together again?"

More silence. It was unnerving because my recollection of Maggie was that she was rarely, if ever, at a loss for words. A blurter was the technical term, but now each question was met with utter, lonely silence. As I waited for a response, I wondered if Maggie had simply learned to analyze what was being said before speaking.

Maybe she'd learned that silence is power. Maybe she'd decided her quick wit and trash mouth had caused her innumerable grief in the past, so now she was always going to wait before speaking—think first and shoot second. Or perhaps she was simply stunned by my questions.

My patience at an end, I asked her to meet me for a cup of coffee. No promises, no commitments. I just wanted to get her perspective. I waited several seconds in total silence. Then I said, "Come or don't, Mags. I'll be there at ten. I'll wait fifteen minutes, and then I'm gone."

I pulled the phone away from my ear, preparing to end the call, when I heard Maggie's voice. I returned the phone to my ear and listened.

"Where?" was all I heard.

"The usual place. Our Starbucks in El Segundo," I said.

After the charges against Maggie were dropped, we met several times at Starbucks. I wanted to support Maggie because I, like her, felt justice had not been served since after the defense proffer, no charges were filed against Al the Perv for his assault on Mags. The district attorney was a coward and opined that a conviction would be difficult to get because Maggie wouldn't make a great witness.

I get that L.A. juries are notoriously sucky, but to let a predator like Al walk away virtually ensured there would be other victims of his abuse. I believe Maggie appreciated the moral support and the outlet for her rage every time we met for coffee talk.

Then I heard Maggie end the call from her end. I wasn't certain this was a good idea, but I cleaned up a bit, got into the Porsche, and headed south on Vista Del Mar.

CHAPTER 4

RED SCARE

I pulled into the lot on the corner of Grand and Eucalyptus in El Segundo, a thoroughly modern strip center with a pizza shop, hair salon, and various other small businesses. I left the 911 parked in front of a dentist's office two hundred feet away from the coffee shop. I got out and walked toward the Starbucks. As I got closer, I could see Maggie was already there. She was looking west, but her huge mass of red hair was hard to miss.

As I approached, I cleared my throat. It had the effect I was hoping for as Maggie turned and smiled. Her teeth caught my attention first. Brilliantly white, they seemed to reflect the sunlight directly into my eyes. I couldn't recall that particular characteristic, and I immediately thought it had been longer than I'd realized since we'd seen each other. Maggie hugged me tight, and I returned the gesture. She was good people— deadly, but good.

We went inside, ordered some Pike Place, Grandes both, and found a table in the back. The preliminary chitchat wasn't as tedious as with others. Maggie's sharp wit and sense of humor were effortless.

"So, old man," she said, "you still fucking that whore?"

"That was a long time ago, Mags," I said. "Anyone special in your life?"

She took a long, deep sip of her obviously steaming beverage and said, "A few, but who really has time for that?"

We continued catching up for a while. I found out Maggie had had one long-term relationship that had ended about eighteen months prior. She said it was the first time she'd actually felt a loss when it was over. I couldn't tell from watching her because there was no indication of sadness in either her tone or her countenance. Maggie was always disconnected in a way, and I attributed that to her upbringing.

Maggie grew up in Van Nuys. Her parents were divorced, father absent, mother addicted to painkillers and alcohol—the standard story for maladjusted teenagers. She'd started to hang around the "wrong" types in high school, so in a moment of clarity, her mother had enrolled her in Tatum Parker's karate school. At the time, I was one of the instructors there.

I remembered Maggie's tenacity and unbridled energy. For a young girl with a challenging home life, she'd stuck with the rigorous routine required in martial arts. Her ability to absorb and repeat forms and techniques was impressive. We'd quickly become friends, and I'd mentored her through her time at the studio. When I left to join FIDA, I brought Maggie with me.

Maggie was a tremendous agent. There were no assignments too tedious or dangerous for her tastes. I remember one time we'd had a local group of young, white Muslims causing all manner of disorder. The group was headed by an expelled UCLA student by the name of Todd Wanamaker. Todd had been expelled for plying a girlfriend with Rohypnol and committing sexual misconduct with her. Todd was prosecuted for rape, but a hung jury had set him free. The victim hadn't wished to prolong the awful event through a new trial, so charges were dropped. Todd later changed his name to Rashad Karim.

Rashad and his cohorts came to the attention of FIDA when an IED was found, unexploded, near the federal building in Westwood. Someone in the organization had claimed responsibility for the bomb before it detonated. Clearly, Todd/Rashad's management skills left much to be desired. The fact was, the construction of the IED wasn't even close to being effective. I'm no explosives expert, but I was told there was no way the device would have detonated unless it was surrounded with some C4.

"So, Mags, what have you been doing to keep yourself busy?" I asked.

"Oh, you know," she said. "A little of this, and a little of that. Mostly PI work with some security work thrown in for good measure."

Maggie showed little enthusiasm for her current trade. I knew that she made great money. Celebritards pay well and are among the most paranoid group of people you'll ever find. But what I knew about Maggie was that money was far down on the list of things important to her. She and I were the same there. No, Maggie sought fulfillment through challenge and testing. Like steel quenched with fire and water, Maggie grew tough and resilient through trial and tribulation.

"Would you like to work with me again?" I asked. Maggie's countenance changed. She looked at me the same way she had the first day she'd discovered Kenpo's dynamic system working out in Master Parker's dojo. "Fuck yes!" she said a little too loudly for Starbucks. Several of the patrons and staff turned to look at the crazy redhead screaming profanity in the family-friendly drug emporium.

"What's the deal?" she said next. I explained the Senator Goldstein case. Maggie knew some of the details as reported in the news, but she was naturally unaware of some of the most pertinent.

"Isn't the senator's husband one of the richest men in California?" she asked. "Yes," I said.

"Kinda petty for her to go after Krieger with such a vengeance, don't you think? Why not let the law handle it and let the chips fall where they may?"

"Mags, you and I don't make money a priority, but for most people, twelve million dollars is far from petty. I also think the senator was hurt by Elsa's betrayal. I believe she considered her a surrogate daughter." Maggie nodded at this. "So where does Chesnokov fit in?" she asked. "That's what I need you to find out, but, Mags, he's not a very nice person." Maggie stared at me for a moment and then burst out laughing. "Are you shitting me, boss? I didn't think you wanted me to hold hands with him."

I explained what had happened with Karl. I wanted Maggie to understand what Chesnokov was capable of. I wanted her eyes completely open. I sugar-coated nothing.

"Jon," she said, "I appreciate your concern and your directness. I understand the risks. Hell, it's what gets me off. I'm in."

I told Maggie to follow Elsa for a few days, reconnoiter her movements. I told her I would gather intelligence on Chesnokov. I said we should meet in a few days to compile the information, but we should also keep in touch periodically if anything important arose. Maggie disagreed.

"Jon," she said, "I think I should go after Chesnokov. You should follow Krieger." "Mags, Chesnokov is a killer. He's a dangerous guy. Hell, Karl backed out."

Maggie shot me that famous smile of hers, slightly crooked but filled with subtext. "That's sweet, Jon," she said. "But I can handle him. Trust me."

Trust me. There's a saying that the three biggest lies in the world are "trust me," "I love you," and "I always pull out in time." What was I going to do? I knew Maggie could handle herself, but I also knew Chesnokov could be unpredictable. The most dangerous people in the world are those unafraid of prison or death. By all accounts, Chesnokov didn't give a shit about either. The guy had survived years in the most vicious prison system in Mother Russia. And death was an inevitability to most Russians. Life was cheap to them. If I had to guess, I'd say Chesnokov considered each day above ground a bonus. He probably loved the game of staying alive but still accepted the fact that someday death would ride in on his horse and reap.

Maggie and I argued a bit about her plan versus mine. Ultimately, I came around to her thinking. She would be less conspicuous around Chesnokov's men. I told her to be cautious. She laughed and said, "Always am." I told her I was serious. "Be doubly cautious, Mags. I mean it."

We hugged it out as she left Starbucks. I watched her get into her car and drive away. I couldn't shake the feeling that I'd just placed Maggie in a very precarious position. I needed to work out the anxiety, so I decided to drive to Pasadena.

I arrived at Master Parker's dojo in about an hour. The dojo in Pasadena was situated on a tree-lined street, one-way, which carried four lanes of traffic. Pasadena is such a grand old dame, having been founded in the late nineteenth century. Many of her streets are lined with hundred-year-old oak, maple, and sycamore trees. The canopy always yields a grand filtered lighting that transports me back to an earlier time in the city's history. It has an old-world feel to it.

And every time I drive up to the school, the memories flood back into my brain. I first met Tatum Parker when I was eight years old. Back then, Dad could see that I had an undisciplined streak in me. I was incorrigible, and "no" was my favorite answer. Dad knew Tatum because they'd been in the war together. Dad said they'd each saved the other's life, so they'd become responsible for each other.

On my first day at the school, Master Parker walked around me as I stood on the mat in my gi. I recall standing askew in an "I don't give two shits" stance. Master Parker told me to stand at attention. I ignored his request for the last time. The next thing I knew, I was on the floor, and my stomach, knee, and chest hurt.

I've always had a stubborn side, and as a kid, it was very pronounced. However, once I was under Master Parker's influence, I mellowed greatly. My mom and dad noticed it immediately. I started saying "thank you" and "please" spontaneously. The man had that much effect on me. Even to this day, I respect him more than most people I know. That's why my dad put him in charge of my trust.

Dad was a great lawyer. I know, I know—most lawyers are scumbags. They would fuck you out of your last dime and then send you a bill for their out-of-pocket expenses. I'm being facetious, of course. There are many reputable attorneys in the world. It's just difficult to find many ordinary people who think so. Doctors have a much better lobby.

Dad was different. He didn't look at litigation as war. Instead, he considered it chess. He knew he would win some and lose some, but he also knew that by practicing diligently, he would win more often than he would lose. He was pretty successful professionally and financially, so when it came time to plan for his estate, he set up irrevocable, spendthrift trusts for both Jenny and me. We were children when he did this, but Dad knew enough to know what he could not know: where either of us would end up in life. For Jenny, it was clear she would be limited. Her trust had special needs provisions so any government benefits would not be forfeited. Mine protected me from lawsuits. And Tatum Parker is the trustee for both trusts.

I was practicing Defying the Storm and Long Form Six when Master Parker called to me from his office. I saluted out to my partner, a young first-degree brown belt named Kevin, and strode over to see my sensei, sweat and all.

Tatum Parker is not a man anyone would fear on first impression. He's not overly tall or muscular. He doesn't have a deeply resonant voice. And he doesn't normally have an intimidating visage. However, underestimating this man would be a mistake.

Master Parker started Kenpo karate lessons when he was nine years old. A skinny kid with red hair, he was mercilessly beaten nearly every day after his family moved to Pasadena from Chicago. His mother, Marjorie Parker, had heard about a self-defense studio nearby that offered classes for children as young as four. She enrolled Tatum the next day.

At first, Tatum was little interested in self-defense. He didn't care that he was being beaten up several times a week. He only wanted to go back home, to Chicago where his friends were. And he assumed that if he was beaten frequently enough, his mother would agree to move back to the Midwest.

On the fourth day of class, young Tatum Parker skipped out and spent the two hours in the library. When the two hours had elapsed, he got up to leave. However, standing behind him was the founder and head instructor of the school, Sam Mitose. Sensei Mitose frowned at him, and young Tatum Parker withered. He didn't know why this man, whom he'd known for less than a week, had such an effect on him. But he did. It was a power not even his mother held over him. And it distressed him.

They walked out of the library in silence, but when they exited, Sensei Mitose said, "I am disappointed in you, Deshi. Why have you disrespected me?" Tatum didn't know what to say. He stammered out something about missing his friends and wanting to go back home. "Have you heard of Lao Tzu and the Tao Te Ching?" Young Tatum Parker had not. "Lao Tzu said, 'Life is a series of natural and spontaneous changes. Don't resist them—that only creates sorrow. Let reality be reality. Let things flow naturally forward in whatever way they like.'" Sensei Mitose then became severe and curt. "You are meant to be here in this time. You are my pupil, and I will teach. Will you learn?" The rest, as they say, is history. Tatum Parker became Sam Mitose's protégé and one of the preeminent martial artists in the world. And as the strange karmic wheel we call life turns, I have the unique privilege to call Master Parker my sensei.

I entered Master Parker's office as I had many, many times before. His office was intentionally small, leaving the majority of the space in the dojo for training. Each wall was fully adorned with awards, trophies, photographs, and copies of magazine articles about the man. Tatum Parker was once the west coast teen full-contact karate champion three years in a row, and he had the medals to prove it. His desk was cluttered, but there was a zen-type organization to the clutter. Out of chaos comes order.

Master Parker was sitting at his desk. He was wearing a pair of reading glasses and perusing several pieces of paper. I took a seat in front of the desk to the left. I waited. Minutes passed. Most people get edgy in silence, especially when a requested meeting is taking place. But I'd learned long ago that Master Parker was on no schedule, and he was most likely testing me. So, I sat. I waited, in silence. I could hear the traffic noises from the street and the sounds of students practicing in the dojo. Then I focused on my breathing. In, out, in, out. Rhythmic. Several minutes later, Master looked up at me and said, "How have you been?" "Me?" I said. "Sterling." Master sighed. "Can we have a real conversation?" he said. I smiled to myself. "Sure, what do you want to know?"

Master Parker first asked if I'd spoken to my mother recently. I had, but I wasn't sure what Master was getting at, so I played dumb.

"Not really. Why?" I said. He shook his head almost imperceptibly from side to side. "A man is not a man if he does not honor his family," he said.

"Lao Tzu?" I asked.

"Don Corleone," he said.

"I spoke to her Sunday. Call her every week. Is that okay?"

"I think you should spend some time with her. She's worried about you." "She's always been worried about me," I said.

It was true. My mother spent an enormous amount of time worrying about me. You would think Jenny would be a better focus of her attention, but Abigail Bolt's concern always ran to me, the prodigal son. It was part of the reason I limited my interactions with her to once-weekly telephone calls, short and sweet. I couldn't abide the constant state of anxiety I would cause if Mother knew what was really happening in my life. I'm afraid it might kill the old girl. Better to keep a safe distance than to cause your mother's death. I always end every call with "I love you, Mom," and she replies, "I love you too, Nathan."

I looked at Master, trying to discern his concern. He looked back at me sternly. He didn't appreciate levity when he wanted a serious discussion. I sat up in the chair and apologized for not being serious.

"I don't want you to be serious. I just want you to listen." Master Parker paused, inhaled deeply, and continued, "I think your mother is not well."

This wasn't what I was expecting. Mom had sounded fine when we'd spoken a few days ago. "How do you know?" I asked.

"I don't. It's just a sense I got when I saw her earlier. Be a good son and check on her. It's what your dad would want."

Although I wasn't in shock, I wasn't prepared for Master's declaration about my mother's state of health. I fully accept that she will die someday, but since Dad died several years ago, I'd somehow thought she would live well into her nineties. Would I need to revise my expectations? What about Jenny? I would need to think about these things later. Right then, I had another pressing issue to attend to.

I refocused my thoughts. "Is my trust bulletproof?" I said. "Bulletproof?" Tatum Parker asked.

"Yes. What I mean is, is there any way someone can sue me, win, take a judgment, and collect against the trust?"

Master Parker smiled. "Why are you asking this? You know the answer." "Humor me," I said.

"No, no one can get to the trust without my consent," he replied. "Jon, what have you gotten yourself into?" I looked out the window toward the street. An old pickup truck drove by and backfired. "Nothing yet," I said to the window. "But you never know." I looked back at Master Parker and offered my hand. He accepted it and responded with a firm shake, once up and down, then disengaged.

"Let me know if you need anything," he said, and with a stern look repeated, "anything."

I walked to the locker room and changed back into my street clothes. Swinging my duffel over my shoulder, I exited the locker room back into the dojo. As I did, I performed an unconscious bow of respect. Martial artists always bow before entering or leaving the dojo, and after years of performing this ritual, it had become part of muscle memory like all the Kenpo techniques, forms, kata, and exercises. I don't even recall doing it anymore. I'm not sure that's a good thing.

I tossed the duffle into the front passenger seat and jumped into the Porsche. The flat six growled to life, and I sped away from the curb. I headed East on Imperial Highway toward its conversion into the 105 freeway. Minutes later I was racing south on the Arroyo Seco Parkway, Highway 110. Traffic moved well until I hit downtown Los Angeles. It always amazes me how people don't understand traffic flow. Most jams are caused by drivers failing to anticipate their exit and stopping dead to cross multiple lanes. Come on, Google! Let's get those self-driving cars on the road!

Back at the coach, I poured myself another scotch and sat down with Karl's intelligence file. Chesnokov's dossier made for interesting reading. Born in Vladivostok in 1975, he'd spent his early years in the dying Soviet system before emerging as a player in the post-Cold War chaos. His father had been a mid-level party official who'd managed to position himself well during the transition. Young Kiril had learned early that survival meant adapting quickly to changing circumstances.

His criminal record in Russia was extensive but incomplete—typical of the corruption that plagued law enforcement there. What was clear was that Chesnokov had worked his way up through the ranks of organized crime with a combination of intelligence, ruthlessness, and an uncanny ability to avoid lengthy prison sentences. The few times he'd been incarcerated, he'd emerged stronger and with more connections.

His arrival in the United States in 2010 was part of the emigration of many former Soviet mobsters to the United States, the so-called Red Scare. Chesnokov's arrival had been facilitated by what appeared to be legitimate business investments. He'd purchased several properties in Los Angeles and had established himself as an importer of Russian goods. On the surface, everything looked legal. According to FIDA intelligence, he was building a network that would eventually challenge the established organized crime families for control of traditional rackets.

What made Chesnokov particularly dangerous was his understanding of modern technology and finance. Unlike the old-school mobsters who relied primarily on muscle and intimidation, Chesnokov employed sophisticated money laundering schemes, cyber-crime operations, and international trafficking networks. He was a criminal for the digital age.

The file also contained surveillance photos. Chesnokov was a big man, probably six-foot-three and two hundred forty pounds. He kept himself in excellent physical condition and was known to practice Sambo, the Russian martial art developed for the military. His face was unremarkable except for a thin scar that ran from his left ear to the corner of his mouth—a souvenir from his prison days, according to the intelligence report.

More troubling were the psychological profiles included in the file. Multiple sources described Chesnokov as having sociopathic tendencies combined with above-average intelligence. He was capable of extreme violence but only when it served a strategic purpose. He didn't kill for pleasure; he killed to send messages or eliminate obstacles. This calculated approach to violence made him more dangerous than the typical street thug who might act impulsively.

The connection to Senator Goldstein's case was still unclear from the file. There were notations about Chesnokov's interest in high-end art and antiquities, which could provide a link to Elsa Krieger's world. There were also references to his involvement in various money laundering operations that might have attracted Krieger's attention as a financial advisor.

I closed the file and walked out onto the small deck of the coach. The ocean was black now except for the white foam of the waves catching the moonlight. A few other RVs had lights on, their occupants probably settling in for the evening with a book or television. It was a peaceful scene that belied the dangerous game I was about to enter.

My phone buzzed with a text message. It was from Maggie: "Initial recon complete. This guy's got serious security. Three bodyguards minimum, armored Mercedes, changes routes frequently. Professional operation. Meeting tomorrow at 2 PM?"

I texted back: "Copy that. Same place. Be careful."

I knew Maggie could handle herself, but Chesnokov wasn't some Hollywood celebrity with more money than sense. He was a predator who'd survived in one of the world's most dangerous environments. If he suspected Maggie was surveilling him, she could disappear without a trace.

I made myself a sandwich and opened a beer, trying to push down the nagging feeling that I was making a mistake. Karl's warnings echoed in my mind, but I'd committed to Senator Goldstein, and more importantly, I'd brought Maggie into this. There was no backing out now. As I prepared for bed, I thought about my conversation with Master Parker about my mother. I made a mental note to drive up to see her in the next few days. Whatever was going on with the Chesnokov investigation, family came first. Dad had taught me that, and Master Parker had reinforced it.

I checked the locks on the coach door and ensured my Glock was within easy reach. In this business, paranoia isn't a mental illness—it's a survival skill. As I drifted off to sleep, I couldn't shake the feeling that I was about to step into something much bigger and more dangerous than a simple investigation into embezzled funds.

The last thing I remembered before sleep took me was the sound of the waves against the shore and the distant hum of traffic on Vista Del Mar. Tomorrow, the real work would begin.

CHAPTER 5

CROSS HAIRS

I was sitting at the dinette finishing off my second cup of coffee when I heard horns blaring and tires screeching. I stepped outside of the coach to see what all the hubbub was about. I could see a car blasting into the parking lot at Dockweiler, horn blasting and the driver threw a bird toward the other vehicles on Vista Del Mar. Moving closer, I saw it was a late-model Mercedes coupe. Through the darkly tinted passenger window, I could barely make out a figure in the driver's seat—a female form with which I was intimately familiar. The Benz pulled into a spot just East of the coach.

As the driver exited and turned, I saw a twenty-something woman. She stood five-seven with brunette hair, sunglasses, and a smile. "Can I help you?" I asked, knowing full well I couldn't and wouldn't. She removed her sunglasses, and I could tell she posed no immediate threat. At least not then. She had no visible weapons, and both hands were in plain sight. She continued smiling and began walking toward me. Her unsteady gait told me she was either high or nervous. I remained in condition orange.

"Hi, Mr. Bolt. I'm Tricia," she said, extending her hand as she wobbled closer. "Ms. Goldstein," I said. "What brings you to the Playa?"

"I wanted to talk to you about my mother." "What about her?"

As Tricia Goldstein reached me, she tripped over her own feet, nearly falling flat on her face. Nearly—had I not been standing directly in front of her, my body breaking her fall. She was very high on something, most likely meth. Quickly returning her to an upright position, I could see her pupils were dilated and her eyes were rolling. She was high, alright, and I knew she needed to come down soon. It was inconceivable that she'd been able to drive from Malibu, or wherever she'd come from, to here.

"You were asking about your mother," I said.

"Yes. I know she hired you for something." There was a long pause before I said, "Yes." Tricia looked toward the ocean.

"Why did she hire you?"

"I'm not at liberty to say. Why do you think she did?"

"She doesn't like my boyfriend very much, and I think she wants you to follow him. I can't have that. I won't stand for that!"

Tricia Goldstein was ranting with slurred speech, spittle spraying as her indignation grew. It was time for her to get sober.

I directed her to get into the Coach, shower, and relax for a while. At first, she objected and resisted. "Fuck you, motherfucker," she cursed. I wasn't upset about the language, but the way she slandered my dear mother—a woman with whom she was unacquainted—hit me kind of hard.

"Tricia," I said, "I'll caution you to refrain from defaming my mother like that."

She said something else about dear mom. I don't remember it exactly, but suffice it to say she described my mother performing a rather explicit sexual act with a female bovine.

"That's some mouth on you," I said. "You better watch it."

Tricia, still high, telegraphed a punch to my head. I parried the blow and placed her in a Sankyo wrist lock. She cried out in pain immediately, struggling to free herself. I applied additional torque to her hand with each attempt to escape.

"Stop it, fucker!" she yelled.

"Keep it up," I said. "Let me know when you hear your wrist snap." That calmed her down. Once she relaxed, I asked her if she was going to be a good girl. She nodded affirmatively. I told her I needed to hear her say it.

"Yes!" she yelled.

"Yes, what?"

"I'll be a good girl!"

I released the lock, and she stood up, rubbing the soreness away. I told her to get into the shower, clean up, and come back out when she was ready. She walked to the back of the coach, and as she entered the head, she stared at me and stuck out her tongue.

Tricia, like most youngsters, takes long showers. Maybe it was the methamphetamine. Maybe she enjoys the hot water running down her nubile body. Or maybe it's neither, and she just likes showers. I don't know, but she stayed in there for at least a half hour.

When the water stopped, I could hear her toweling dry. After an additional ten minutes, she emerged. "How do you feel now?" I asked.

"Better," she said. "Do you have any beer?"

I grabbed her a Stella Artois from the cooler when it dawned on me that she might not be twenty-one. "You're old enough to drink, right?"

Her smile told me she wasn't, but she was on her way to becoming a full-blown meth-head. One beer wasn't going to kill her.

Tricia sat down on the lounge, and I sat across from her in one of the two recliners. Although the shower and time had brought her back from her high, she was still not one hundred percent. She appeared agitated, nervously playing with her beer bottle. She took several sips, looked at me, then turned to look out the side window. The silence was killing her. Good. I needed to find out what she wanted, and in any good interrogation, silence works wonders.

After a while, when she could take no more, Tricia looked at me and said, “I need to know what my mom hired you for.”

“I’m sorry, but I can’t discuss that.”

“Why’s that?”

“Attorney-client privilege,” I said. I know it’s a stretch, but I was an attorney once, so I use it when necessary.

“Bullshit!” she spat back. “You’re not a lawyer. You lost your license because you stole from your clients!”

I grabbed the spoiled rich bitch by the scruff of her neck, opened the door to the coach, and tossed her down onto the asphalt parking lot. I slammed the door closed behind me.

Maybe I overreacted, but the whole situation leading up to the loss of my law license remains a raw wound. I hate talking about it because I always feel like I’m seeking forgiveness, which I’m not. There’s a big difference between malfeasance and misfeasance in my book, and I don’t give a shit what anyone else thinks. But since it’s out now, maybe sharing it will help with the healing process. At least my therapist thinks so.

After leaving the agency, I screwed around for a few months. I lived at my parents’ home in Malibu then, and Dad did not abide someone of my age wasting time surfing, sunning, drinking, and screwing. He told me to get my shit together, so I did. I rented a small office space, put up a shingle, and started a small law practice.

It was great at first. I took any case if I felt I had or could obtain the necessary level of competence to effectively represent the client. About a year in, I found the majority of my cases were real estate related: unlawful detainer, fraud, breach of contract, and broker malpractice. All this happened when the bottom fell out of the real estate market. I had clients coming in daily wanting to sue someone—anyone— because the home they’d recently bought at the top of the market was falling rapidly in value. Many of them were hit with the double whammy of unemployment as well. Unfortunately, many of these prospective clients I could not help. There's very little the law can do to help someone stupid enough to buy real estate at the top of a bubble market.

However, after the crash, I found that negotiating loan concessions with lenders was a forte of mine. I had an innate ability to convince certain unscrupulous lenders to either reduce the principal amount of the loan or otherwise modify the terms of the note to allow my clients to remain in their now vastly overpriced California real estate. I ran a simple ad in the Times, and I was inundated with struggling homeowners looking for a way to save their homes. The problems started when I hired Tim Jenkins.

Tim responded to an internship offer I'd filed with the UCLA law school. I needed someone to vet the homeowners because at the time, most banks were reluctant either to reduce the principal balance due on the loan or to modify the mortgage terms. This was before several attorneys general filed suit against the large national mortgage banks. Tim understood we couldn't take on clients we couldn't help—or so I thought. Turns out, Tim was taking on everyone who walked through the door, collecting a $3,500 fee up front, and only advising me of the cases where we could do some good. Later, during my bar association investigation, I discovered Tim had misappropriated over a million dollars in fees. Since it was my duty to supervise my employees, the responsibility for the theft fell on me the same as if I had stolen from my clients myself.

During my bar prosecution, I could see the real possibility of disbarment, so instead of trusting someone else with my fate, I resigned and forfeited my law license permanently. Many of my peers thought I was crazy for doing so. In fact, one of the mediators commented that the average lifetime revenue attributable to having a law license in California is over two million dollars, and I should take that into account before making a "rash" decision. It was the mediator's opinion that I should find a way to settle with the bar association rather than resign.

I disagreed. My only "crime" was negligence—failing to act reasonably under the circumstances. Yet I was facing a possibility, small though it might be, of having my license taken from me. I'll tell you what: I'd rather choose my own destiny than rely on the questionable sense of justice held by lawyers who decided a good career path was prosecuting other lawyers. If I never have the opportunity to practice law again, so be it. I never really liked it that much anyway. Que sera, sera.

I could hear Tricia Goldstein's sobs. I opened the door slowly and saw she was lying supine on the blacktop. Her cheeks were moist with remnants of tears shed in distress. I was mildly empathetic because I had overreacted to her attack. Let's face it—I'd screwed up my life before with my attitude and resistant nature. Tricia was lashing out because she wanted something I was unwilling to give, and she's a spoiled Malibu heiress. I'm not excusing the behavior, but I understand it.

"Nice weather we're having," I said.

Tricia rolled her head in my direction. "You're an asshole!"

Yes, I am, but I wanted to be less of one, so I apologized. "Forgive me, Tricia. What can I say? You hit a still-raw nerve."

She looked at me, I suppose to ascertain my level of sincerity. Then she sat up and lifted herself from the ground, wiping the grime from her hands as she arose.

"No, I'm sorry," she said. "I shouldn't have picked on you."

"You're right. Apology accepted," I said. "Want to come back in?" She responded by pushing past me, re-entering the coach.

Tricia retook her seat on the lounge, and I grabbed her a beer from the fridge. It was a lite beer, but beer just the same. She cranked the cap off and took a long swig. Then she masked a small burp with her lips and hand.

"'Scuse me," she said.

I smiled, sat back in my chair, and looked across the space in silence. It's funny how powerful carefully placed silence can be. The adage is true: He who speaks first, loses. I did not intend to lose.

In law school, I read a study about the power of silence. The researchers found many valuable insights, including the common misperception of time. Most people become uncomfortable after only a few moments of silence, especially after a question has been asked. When asked to estimate the amount of time that had elapsed, most respondents answered with a number of minutes when the true time was more likely a matter of seconds.

The study also concluded that silence gives the user a window into the emotions of the other person. If given enough silence, most people will fill the void with information about themselves. If you use silence and active listening, you can gather much information about anyone with whom you come in contact.

After forty-five seconds of silence, Tricia was fidgeting uncontrollably. I continued to stare at her without affect. Finally, she blurted, "What the fuck! What do you want from me? I came here for help, and you're interrogating me. Just leave me alone!"

I stepped across the floor and sat on the lounge beside her. She wouldn't look up at first, but slowly she turned to look at me. I smiled and said, "I will help if I can. What do you need?"

Tricia began a diatribe familiar to many a methamphetamine addict. She went on and on about tweaking, crashing, and the hangover. I asked why she'd fallen into addiction. Of course, she said it "feels good," but when she realized I wasn't buying that crap, she told me she started using heavily when she discovered her boyfriend, Jared Fitzpatrick, was cheating on her. She started whimpering as insecure, narcissistic, spoiled children do. It amazes me how rich kids tend toward severe daddy or mommy issues. I'm not amazed that it happens, but one would think that wealthy parents would have more time, not less, to spend with their children. The freedom of money would dictate that. However, the reality tends toward the opposite. It's the less well-to-do, the impoverished, who seem to find time for their offspring. I've seen mothers and fathers who worked multiple jobs find a few precious minutes each day dedicated to their kids. It boggles the mind.

"How do you know Jared is cheating?" I asked.

"I just know," Tricia said.

"You know nothing. You suspect he cheated, so why don't you just confront him about it?"

Tricia wilted at my suggestion. "I can't do that. I love him. I couldn't take it if he got angry and left me."

There are many things in this damaged world that simply turn my stomach, and insecurity and hopelessness are right there at the top. At that moment, I wanted to toss her the hell out of Coach and tell her where the dog died. But, to show you I'm not a complete prick, I could see Tricia was in a fragile state. I didn't want to add to her issues. So I said, "Then why don't you just forget about it and go on loving him?"

She started to cry and buried her face in my shoulder.

When her sobbing subsided, she looked up at me with those bloodshot brown eyes and asked if I would find out if Jared was cheating or not. I asked her how she would pay for those services. She started unbuttoning her blouse. All I could do was shake my head in disbelief. I lifted her from the settee, told her I would think about it, and showed her the door. I walked Tricia to her Benz, opened the driver's side door, and made certain she was lucid enough to drive.

"Tricia?" I said.

"Yes?"

I moved my face to within an inch of hers. The poor kid thought I was moving in for a kiss. She was all puckered up when I said, "Get off the drugs." She frowned and pushed me away from her car. She pulled the door closed, revved the engine, and peeled out as she drove away. All I could do was wave and laugh.

As Tricia made a left onto Vista Del Mar, I realized I'd neglected to ask her who her drug connection was. More than likely she gets her stuff from her boyfriend, but I wouldn't hang anyone out to dry without at least a scintilla of evidence. I made a mental note to ask her about it next time our paths crossed. But the fun and games were over. I needed to work. I hopped into the Carrera and headed to the valley. I needed to gather more intel on Ms. Krieger.

I made it to Sherman Oaks in just under thirty minutes. I found a place to park across the street, diagonally from Elsa Krieger's apartment building. I walked across the cul-de-sac and then through the building's courtyard, feigning interest in the unit for rent in case someone got nosy. Krieger's second floor apartment in building one was viewable from the "for rent" bulletin board. I couldn't make out if she was home or not, so I decided to check the parking area for her car.

Her car, a late-model Buick SUV, silver, was parked in her assigned space 217 to match her apartment number. I snapped a photo of the license plate with my phone and made sure there was no one around. Then I bent down at the rear hatch to attach a real-time GPS tracker under the bumper. Just as I completed the job, I saw someone walk around the side of the building. The guy saw me too and obviously thought I was up to no good. He approached me rather quickly.

"What are you up to, pal?" he said.

I flipped open my wallet, displaying my authentic FBI badge and ID card. The card identified me as Special Agent Ben Walters. The guy backed down but was displaying guilt-related behavior: scratching his head and nose, looking around anxiously. It was time to have some fun.

"I'm Special Agent Walters. What's your name, pal?"

"Jerry," he said.

"Jerry? Jerry what?"

"Jerry Durbin."

I moved off the X in case Jerry Durbin decided to run or escalate and continued: "Say, Jerry, you live around here?"

Jerry pointed to the building adjacent to Elsa Krieger's. I found it humorous that this non-descript douchebag thought he was clever. Why would he be questioning me if he wasn't a resident of the building? Jerry cleared his throat with a fake cough and said, "That's Elsa's car. What do you want with it?"

I moved closer to dear Jerry. The poor schlub had it bad for Ms. Krieger. "What's your relationship to Elsa Krieger, Jerry?" I said.

Jerry started fidgeting. I watched in silence to get a read on him. Jerry's not a ladies' man. Standing, I would say, five-six in his bare feet, several dark moles on his face with sporadic mustache growth on his upper lip, he was not the epitome of male beauty. But it was his attire that truly said it all about dear Jerry. His button-down shirt was partially tucked into his thirty-eight-inch waistband, and I could tell he'd eaten something with tomato sauce either earlier in the day or the day before. Let's face it—Jerry was a hot mess.

"So tell me, Jerry," I said, "what business do you have with Elsa Krieger?"

"She's my neighbor," he said.

"Anything else?" I said.

Jerry swallowed harshly and said, "We're friendly, I guess." I moved in closer. "She's pretty, Elsa is, right, Jerry?"

His crooked smile answered.

"Looking to get you some of that?" I asked.

Jerry's smile faded, and I could see I was agitating him. I moved further away in a circular pattern, making sure I was off the X. Just in case. Jerry was not only enamored with Ms. Krieger but also very protective of her virtue. And guessing Jerry had some type of cognitive deficit, I didn't want a confrontation. I held out one of my faux FBI business cards and told him to give it to Elsa when he saw her next.

Jerry slid the card into his pocket and said, "You bet I will." Then he walked away.

With Jerry gone, I checked to make certain the GPS was securely fastened to Elsa's vehicle. It was, so I walked back into the atrium. As I reached the bank of mailboxes, I heard Elsa's door open. I quickly spun around the wall near the mailboxes to limit my exposure. Elsa exited her second-floor apartment, closing and locking the door behind her. She was as stunning in person as she was in her photos: nearly five-nine, shoulder-length blonde hair pulled back into a tasteful ponytail, ice-blue eyes, and a rack straining against its spandex prison. Nice!

As Elsa walked through the portico to the parking area, I waited a few moments, listening. I heard the Buick's engine come to life and move out toward the street. I walked around the front of the building to ensure Elsa left the area. She did.

I spent the next twenty minutes collecting as much intel as I could. I took note of the names on the mailboxes in the atrium, watched the comings and goings of several residents, and wrote down the license numbers of several vehicles exiting and entering the parking area of Elas's building. Some of these residents might be able to add "color" to my investigation.

I noticed that several of the names had changed on the mailboxes since my last visit. There seemed to be some transient residents using Elsa's building. I thought about asking Mrs. Bender about the transients, but on second thought I wasn't up for another encounter with her just then.

I walked out to the front of the building taking some photos with my phone. I wanted to make note of the other building, existing exits, and other geographical and architectural features of the neighborhood. Just in case I needed to enter or exit Elsa's place in the future.

I walked the neighborhood up to the entry of Moorpark at Orion and watched traffic patterns for a few minutes. From there I continued to Ventura Boulevard. Although there was plenty of traffic on Ventura, there didn't seem to be a large volume of vehicles entering or exiting onto Orion at this time of day. Good to know for entries and exits.

Walking back down Orion, I turned left into the Moorpark cul-de-sac and back to where I'd parked the Carrera. I hopped in and activated the tracker I placed on Elsa's Buick. The signal strength from the car was four bars, and when the map triangulated her location, she was on Melrose Avenue near Fairfax in West Hollywood.

I hopped on the 101 southbound at Van Nuys. Driving along, I couldn't help thinking I was traveling eastward more so than southbound. All major roads in the country have odd numbers running north and south and evens running east and west, but in this section of the San Fernando Valley, the highway runs more east. Not that direction carries much importance today with every cell phone containing GPS. Hell, even a few decades ago, people would be given directions like, "Just hop on the 101 south and exit at Union." No one considered north, south, east, or west to any greater extent. I think maybe directionals are a holdover from the pioneer days.

I exited on Highland and quickly sprinted to Melrose. Hanging a quick right, I headed toward the locator signal from Elsa's Buick. Her car was parked in a small alley off the street. I found an empty spot across the street and parked the Carrera. The drive over from Sherman Oaks took thirty-five minutes total.

There are many storefronts on this section of Melrose. It's in a hot area of town, so many entrepreneurs open up to exploit the opportunity. Most fail, but some remain. As I stepped onto the sidewalk, I could see the barbershop, a tennis shoe store, and a nail salon. Directly next to the nail salon was a cigar shop called "Smokes." Originality is in short supply in LA. I scanned the front windows of all four establishments, trying to catch a glimpse of Elsa.

Bingo! I saw her blonde tresses cutting through the smoke-filled atmosphere in the tobacconist shop. She was standing at the front counter, discussing something with a fat man behind it. Fats sucked long and hard on his stogie and blew a huge cloud directly into Elsa's face. She didn't flinch. Me, I would have shoved el stogito up the fat man's shit pipe so fast he wouldn't have had time to adjust his girdle. I despise that crap.

After a while, a black Benz pulled up in front of Smokes. It was a long, lean machine: CL63 with dark tint on the windows. The back passenger door opened. I almost couldn't believe who got out. Chesnokov! Son of a bitch! The murdering bastard was right here! I thought about storming the place just to shake Kiril's cage, but I remembered I was working a job. Anger is a stern taskmaster. You have to finesse her some, or things can get butt ugly.

Then I had a dark thought: Where's Maggie? I hate that my head veers toward darkness frequently. I always considered it part of my training. We were taught to consider every conceivable outcome, and in that business, most outcomes were not pretty. So now I drift that direction frequently. Not good.

Kiril entered the cigar shop, hugged Elsa, and they began to talk. Elsa was very animated using isometric language, flailing hands in time with her mouth flapping. She was clearly upset about something, but from my vantage point I could not make heads or tails of it.

Suddenly, while Elsa was in mid-isometric rant, Kiril slapped her hard across the face. Ms. Anger was ready to rock, but I reined her in. I hate when piece of shit men think smacking around a woman makes them more of a man. I took note of this incident and would make Chesnokov pay later.

After Elsa rubbed the side of her face for a few minutes while Kiril was intensely speaking to her, he smiled and hugged her again. The look of Elsa's reciprocal smile indicated they'd made up. Whatever. Pure Stockholm Syndrome, I guess.

Finally, the two walked toward the back of the store. I watched a few moments to see if they were going to return, but they didn't. I decided to check out the alley just in case they decided to rabbit.

I walked around the corner to the alley entrance on the east side. I watched down the way first, just to see if they'd exited. There were no cars parked close to the smoke shop. Either they'd left like lightning, or they were still inside the store. I walked slowly down the alley, acting as nonchalant as I could. There were no signs of anything awry—that is, until I reached Smokes.

Outside the rear entrance to the shop were two very large Russians. Each one was six-four or taller, about two-fifty, two-sixty pounds, not kilos. Each one had ink running the entire length of his arm from wrist to shoulder. I recognized several of the tattoos as Russian prison emblems. They were having a heated conversation in Ukrainian, so they hadn't noticed me. It was just the break I needed to back up a bit to observe a little more clandestinely.

"What the fuck do you want here?" one of the Slavs said.

I had to play it down, or this was not going to be good. "Tell me, do you know if there's any commercial space for lease on this block?" I asked.

Both behemoths turned now to face me directly in a clear aggressor stance. I played it down. "I'm thinking about opening a wine tasting room."

"Go fuck yourself!"

Okay, they weren't in the mood, so I turned to walk away. "Sorry to bother you," I said as I began walking back the way I came.

"Yes, run away, little pussy-man!"

Okay, I have a pretty good sense of humor, but Ms. Anger hates being called a pussy. Naturally, I turned around and gave them the bird. They didn't like my gesture. They both bolted in my direction and were on me in half a second. My training kicked in. Poor fuckers.

If you've never seen Kenpo Karate in action, it's a sight to behold. I remember first seeing Master Parker demonstrate several techniques before I decided to begin taking lessons. This was when I was ten years old, and many of my friends were taking Taekwondo. Taekwondo is impressive too. The high kicks attract many people. But when I watched Tatum Parker landing blow after blow with blinding speed during that demonstration years ago, I was hooked. I couldn't wait to begin training.

The two Ukrainian mountains rushed me from the front, but they were in my cross hairs. Instinctively, I parried their frontal assault with a blocking blow, and as they tried to regain their footing, I landed multiple heel-palm, knife hand, and snap kick blows to each of them in rapid succession. It was clear from their reactions they weren't expecting any of this from someone like me. It's always a mistake to underestimate your opponent.

They were pissed. They exchanged a few words in Ukrainian, and then one approached me from the front as the other began a move toward my rear. It's funny how muscle memory takes over in combat situations. You don't even understand how you're reacting; no thought is involved whatsoever. So, when I subconsciously analyzed the attack, I immediately went into a gathering of the snakes technique.

The first opponent came at me, swinging his left hand toward my face. I stopped the blow with a left outward block and continued with a back knuckle strike to the ribs. Checking his arm, I delivered a right overhead shot to the back of his neck and immediately collapsed his left knee with a sidekick. Then I pushed him toward the second man.

The second opponent was easier to handle. While he was occupied with his companion, I delivered a left roundhouse kick to his head, a horizontal back knuckle strike to his head, and finally a spinning back kick to his solar plexus. I watched the second man drop to the ground like a rock. But it was a mistake to observe because I missed the first man rising again. He got a good punch to the left side of my rib cage, and I thought I heard a crack. I quickly finished him off with a series of strikes, chops, and kicks, and he fell to the ground also.

I decided to get out of there while the getting was good, so I quickly left the alley toward the street. As I walked, I was more convinced than ever that my rib or ribs were fractured. Son of a bitch! I hate it when I make a mistake. I should have kept my attention on both men. Stupid.

When I got to the Carrera, I eased myself into the driver's seat. I'd definitely sustained an injury, but I wasn't sure of the extent. No bleeding, so I had time to get to my doctor. That would be my next stop, but before I drove away, I saw Elsa and Chesnokov through the cigar store window. Chesnokov handed Elsa a gym bag, and her body language indicated it was a heavy bag. They exchanged a few words when I saw the two men from the alley stagger back into the shop. Time to exit, so I started the flat six and sped away westbound on Melrose.

CHAPTER 6

STOLEN INNOCENCE

I knew my injuries were severe enough that I had to see my doctor, Steven Roth, MD. Since his office was in Malibu, I continued driving west toward the Pacific. I've known Steve for a long time. I met him when I was a new agent at FIDA. Steve was the main MD handling any trauma and injuries incurred by the agents. He was really good at his job, but his most important quality was his discretion. Unfortunately, Steve developed a taste for cocaine hydrochloride and underage women. With the help of Dad's connections in the legal community, Dr. Roth avoided the penitentiary. However, his medical license was suspended after he flunked out of diversion. Several of my friends and I have kept Dr. Roth in business since then. He's a good man and an excellent physician. He succumbed to his darker self, but who among us is fully clean? If you are, the first stone is yours.

Steven Roth's "office" operated out of his home in Malibu. Since he inherited the home from his parents, and they'd had the foresight to hold their sizable estate in a spendthrift trust, Steve didn't lose it during his long legal battle. Good for him because I'm not sure where he'd be without it. Even though I provide an annual "retainer," it's not enough to support the lifestyle to which he was accustomed. I mean, growing up in Malibu leaves one with a vastly different view of society, one completely askew with reality.

I continued driving surface streets all the way from WeHo to Malibu because after 3:00 p.m. on a weekday, the freeway traffic is unpredictable. One careless driver can cause an hours-long pile-up. As it was, I reached Dr. Roth's place in about an hour. I pulled into his drive and parked the 911 next to his black Lexus. Steve's vanity plates read NOTADOC.

I walked up to the door and realized I'd injured myself pretty good. With each step along the concrete path on the curtilage was a reminder of my stupidity. I'd let my guard down. I was cocky. Jackass! My hitched breathing was a tell to anyone watching that I was injured. It had been a while since I'd been this injured. Ever since I left the agency, I'd been extremely cautious, so I hadn't had more than a bruise or two in several years.

I knocked on the solid teak door with as much force as I could muster in my current state. I couldn't hear much through the door, but I waited about a minute before knocking a second time.

"Doc," I yelled. "I need help!"

A moment later, Doctor Steve Roth opened the door. He was dressed in his bathrobe and pajamas. He was also wearing sunglasses and holding a cocktail in his left hand.

"Jon!" he said. "How are things?"

"Not great, Steve. Can I come in?"

His response was to simply step out of the way.

I moved past him, and he noticed I was guarding my left side. "What happened?" he asked.

"A little scuffle," I said.

"I'd say it was more than a scuffle."

"You should see the other guys."

"There was more than one? Jon, buddy, what were you thinking?"

"I wasn't. Obviously. I think my ribs are busted."

Doctor Steve held my left arm and guided me to the back of his house.

He kept his office in the back. We entered, and I sat down on the examining table. Steve slid open several drawers across from where I was sitting and retrieved a stethoscope and an infrared ear thermometer. He placed the thermometer in my right ear. Several seconds later it beeped.

"Ninety-nine," he said. Then he asked if I could remove my shirt. I did, but it was painful.

Dr. Roth then inserted one ear tip into each of his ears and held the diaphragm gently to the center of my chest. He moved the diaphragm to the left upper quadrant and said, "Deep breaths."

I inhaled as deeply as I could several times as he listened to my lungs from the front and back. "I don't hear any congestion or edema. That's good. Let's get an X-ray," he said.

Steve's home office had an older model X-ray machine. It still functioned well enough, so he stood me against the Bucky diaphragm and took a posterior/anterior shot of my chest, removed the X-ray film cartridge, and inserted a fresh cartridge for the lateral view. I returned to his waiting area while Dr. Roth developed the films.

While I waited, I went over in my head the whole Elsa/Chesnokov meeting. That duffle bag had to contain either drugs or cash, and lots of either. The bag was heavy, judging by the way Chesnokov handed it to Elsa and the way her whole body lurched when Chesnokov let go of it. This whole case was starting to piss me off. I think that's why I brain-farted during my run-in with the two Ukrainians. I really need to work on that.

A few minutes later, Steve returned, holding several developed X-rays. "Well," he said, "no fractures that I can see. Come here a second," he said, gesturing for me to follow him into his office.

Steve shoved the X-rays onto the read box attached to the back wall. He then turned the backlight on. He used a pen to point out the areas where he would expect a fracture if one was present, but then he said, "I don't see any evidence of a new fracture. Plenty of old healed ones, though."

Too true. I've had my share of broken ribs, starting when I was ten years old. Skateboarding is a California rite of passage, and my friends and I partook whenever we could. My first break happened while attempting an ollie-grind on a metal handrail at school.

"So what's causing the pain?" I said.

"Most likely you have several contusions in the area where you were hit. They should resolve in a few days," Steve said. He picked up his script pad from the desk and began scribbling. "Apply ice for the next three days." Dr. Steve completed the prescription, tore it from the pad, and handed it to me. "Take some Advil for the pain, but if it becomes severe, here's a prescription for Vicodin. Use it only as needed."

Another thing you need to understand about me is I hate pain medication. Maybe hate is a strong word, but let's just say I loathe it. I think too many people succumb to the pity party when they're in a small amount of pain. I know everyone has different pain tolerances, but I've seen too many friends and family end up addicted to painkillers. Personally, I believe they hastened my dad's demise.

"Thanks, but no thanks, Doc. I'm not a fan," I said.

Steve Roth, MD, has known me a very long time, and he knew a debate would be unwinnable, so he backed off. "Fine. Just use Advil. Also, Jon, you need to rest and let the ribs heal."

I smiled at Dr. Roth. Fat chance. "I'll give it my best shot, Doc. Thanks for all your help." I shook his hand and headed for the door.

"Jon," he said. "Next time, protect yourself better." No shit, Doc!

I left the doc's house and headed toward the Pacific Coast Highway. As the Porsche merged into late afternoon traffic, I could see everything stopped about half a mile ahead. You never can tell about PCH. Sometimes traffic surprises you. Not today. It was the usual parking lot. I decided I could put the rush hour to good use and dialed Maggie's number.

The phone rang nearly ten times before Maggie answered, per usual. Maggie is a great operative. She's smart, cunning, strong, fearless, and loyal. She has one main flaw. She loves to bake.

"Boss man!" I heard her say through the hands-free. "Wassup!" She was so high.

"Maggie, you okay?" I said.

"Sincerely, yes. Very well indeed."

"Okay, I guess you're in for the night, yes?"

"No way, José. You'll never believe what I found at Chesnokov's place," she said. "Try me," I said.

"Well, come over so we can talk in private."

"Mags," I said, "I'm not really in the mood. I just want to hit the rack and get some sleep. I was in a tussle with some of Chesnokov's men. I'm in some pain."

Maggie let out a guffaw, or what can correctly be described as a "stoner's laugh." "Come on, ya big pussy! You can lie down on the sofa. I'll even give you some ice for your boo-boo."

I was getting a little pissed, but baked Maggie was always combative. Giving in only made it worse. "Fine," I said. "I'll be there in a bit. Ciao."

I ended the call before she could say anything else.

Traffic still sucked. I was passing Duke's on the coast highway, so I figured I would be to Maggie's in about forty-five minutes or so. I decided a few mellow tunes would help take my mind off Maggie and the pain. Satellite radio isn't good for many things. Howard Stern and commercial-free music are about it, but it does help when driving long distances. If you ever drove across country in the days before Sirius XM, you know what I mean.

I tuned to 80's on 8 because it always calms me down. Listening to the songs from my youth does something to my psyche. The British New Wave, the End of Disco, Michael Jackson, Billy Joel, Prince, and Van Halen when they were really Van Halen instead of Van Hagar. I enjoy

80's music so much that I've said before if I'm ever diagnosed with a terminal illness, I want to listen to it on my way out.

It was also the beginning of the hip-hop era, but I have to say, for a kid who grew up in Malibu, hip-hop wasn't my preference back then. I like it more today, but I guess everything in life is personal preference.

Three-quarters of an hour later, I arrived at Maggie's apartment. Maggie lived a bohemian lifestyle, and her choice to reside in Venice was an exhibitionist example of it. Venice is a vast refuge for counter-culture, the avant-garde, and new-age thinking. It's nice in small doses, but some of the rants I've heard while walking along the strand make me lament the lack of mental health care.

Maggie's apartment was decorated in what she calls "shabby chic." I call it post-modern pothead. The sofa and love seat are different colors and fabrics. The former is covered in well-worn red leather and the latter with chartreuse muslin. Every internal doorway is adorned with a beaded curtain. The atmosphere was composed mostly of exhaled marijuana smoke. The environment in her place can be off-putting to some, but overall, Maggie keeps the place clean if not tidy. I've heard it said, "Cluttered home, cluttered mind." If so with Mags, you wouldn't know it when she's working. Hell, maybe she's a savant.

I knocked once, and Maggie swung the door wide. "Hey, Jon! Come on in!"

Maggie stumbled a little bit when she turned toward the living area. I closed the door behind me and followed. As expected, I walked through a thick mist of Cannabis indica vapor. I knew indica from sativa only from previous conversations with Mags when she told me indica was her preferred variety because it helped her sleep.

"Geez, Mags, a guy could get eyeball cancer just walking through this place! How about better ventilation?"

Maggie laughed her ass off at the quip, but getting a stoner to laugh requires no special talent. Just say anything.

"Dope doesn't give you cancer, Jon. And if it did, you wouldn't give a crap."

"I don't know, Mags," I said. "I think you're addicted."

"No way, José. It's also non-addictive," Maggie said.

"I don't know about that. I read somewhere that twenty-five percent of users are addicted."

"Addiction means continued use leads to compulsive behaviors that are difficult to manage. I don't know anyone who smokes frequently who will steal, miss work, or lie because they use. It's just not that kind of drug."

I should know better than to debate with a stoner, but this was part of the fun. "Really?" I said. "Can you quit?" Maggie stared at me, and her jovial look changed. She looked like a kid being told for the first time there was no Santa Claus. "Well?"

"I can stop anytime I want," Maggie said. "I just don't wanna!" Touché, Mags.

"So, fill me in on Chesnokov," I said.

Maggie appeared sober as she described the goings-on at Chesnokov's headquarters. She'd reconnoitered the place for nearly twelve hours and observed multiple drops. The couriers entered the building with two large suitcases, remained inside for several minutes, and exited empty-handed. Maggie took a great risk and surreptitiously witnessed stacks of cash being offloaded inside.

"Did you see any drugs, specifically methamphetamine?" I asked.

"No," Maggie said. "But what else throws off that amount of cash?"

True. Other than petroleum and Apple products, I couldn't think of a thing.

Methamphetamine is a major problem in the United States. Somewhere around ninety million tons of the stuff is seized every year. And that's just what gets intercepted. Mexican drug cartels upped the ante in recent years by providing high-quality meth at drastically lower prices.

And the youth of this country seem powerless to reject the quick, powerful, and long-lasting high it produces.

All drug abuse is a form of self-medication, but just what do millions of American teenagers have to be concerned about that they're willing to risk a lifetime of addiction and likely early death? It boggles the mind.

Even though lots of methamphetamine is floating on the streets every day, it would be a big coincidence if Tricia's boyfriend wasn't involved with Chesnokov in some way. I'm a firm believer that true coincidences are rarer than dodo eggs, so I made a note to check into a connection.

I thanked Mags for the intel and told her I was going to get some rest. "Here," she said, offering her dragon-shaped bong.

"Thanks, Mags," I said. "I only participate in activities in which I can rank number one or number two. And you fill both positions effortlessly!"

"Fine," Maggie said. "Don't let the door hit you on the ass."

I left Maggie's place quickly, heading to Highway 1 south. The sun was touching down into the Pacific as I hung a right onto Culver Boulevard, heading toward the deep blue sea. The light coming off the ocean amazes at times. The orange, red, and yellow hues can be blinding, but this evening there were several low clouds hugging the horizon. They dispersed the light, lending a dramatic flair to the ride home.

Just before the turn for Vista del Mar, I stopped at "The Shack" for a quick burger. Southern California has its share of great burger joints. The best known is "In-N-Out," but I'll tell you what, the Shack Burger just hits the spot sometimes. A national chain tried to imitate the success of the Shack Burger by offering a double patty topped with a split hot dog. Personally, I think they missed the mark by a long shot by using a hot dog instead of the Shack's split Louisiana sausage. Maybe their addition of potato chips had something to do with the failure too, but next time you're in Los Angeles, check out the Shack Burger.

The burger was great as usual, and as I sat watching the diminishing rays of the day sublimate into the sea, I thought about Elsa, Chesnokov, and Maggie. What are you doing, Bolt? You swore you were getting out of the "complicated" stuff. You're a glutton for punishment. But this was going to be the last one. I needed to simplify. There's plenty else to do without lives being at risk at every turn. This was it.

I hopped into the Carrera and sped along Vista del Mar, heading toward Dockweiler. The headlights were needed now, but there was still a sliver of glow arising from the horizon, almost as if the sun refused to let go of the day. What did it know that I didn't?

I parked beside the coach, got out, and headed in for the night. As I entered, I began to feel the ache again from my bruised ribcage. Maybe the secondhand smoke in Maggie's apartment provided an analgesic effect because until that moment I was unaware of the pain. I walked into the head and got myself a couple of Advil gelcaps. I swallowed both without water. I stripped down to my skivvies, gingerly. Then I crawled into the bunk, leaving my left leg hanging out of the covers. Sleep came fast.

CHAPTER 7

FRIENDLY FIRE

One of the benefits of living on the beach is the natural background music of the ocean waves. It helps achieve sleep if insomnia roosts. I've never had a problem falling asleep—I can usually shut off my mind when I need to recharge—but awakening to the surf is the best early morning experience. Preferable to being roused by the sound of small arms fire.

The windows on Coach were all wide open, and the sweet salt air of the morning was flooding in, strained through the screens. I rolled onto my back, kicking the covers off so I was lying supine in my boxer briefs. I reached down, unsticking my balls from my thigh, making sure the boys were receiving their fair share of the ocean air. It's nice waking up to no schedule to keep. Maggie and I had to continue our surveillance of Chesnokov, but there was no urgency. I would text her later in the day to get something on the schedule.

I got up, took a piss, and went into the galley to make a cup of coffee. When the coffee was done, I took a steaming cup and sat on the settee, watching the dawn's early light illuminate the day while I lost myself in thought.

I thought about the prior few days: my meeting with the senator, Tricia's impromptu visit, and the actual gathering of intelligence on Elsa and Chesnokov. "You've gotten yourself into a hot mess, haven't you?" I said to myself. I had to laugh. The more I try to remove myself from the complicated cases, the more I seem to attract them. Maybe it's Murphy. Maybe it's karma. Hell, I don't know. I do know it's taxing me, and I need to figure out how to deal with it or get out altogether.

Then I thought about my sister. Christ! I threw on a pair of board shorts and a wife-beater, brushed my teeth, put a little gel in my hair, and combed it back. I exited the RV, jumped into the 911, and headed toward LAX.

Jenny lived in Westchester, so at this time in the morning the traffic would be light. I can't friggin' believe I forgot to see her. Patterns are important to Jenny, as they are to most people on the spectrum. I hoped my faux pas didn't set her off, so I called her while I drove.

Her cell rang three times before she picked up. "Jon?" I heard over the hands-free.

"Morning, buttercup," I said.

"Where have you been, Jon? I've been waiting for you."

"I'm sorry, Jen," I said. "I'm coming over now. Can we have breakfast together?"

There was a long silence. "Jen?" I said. "Are you there?"

"I already ate a Pop-Tart. Strawberry."

Jenny loves strawberry Pop-Tarts. I remember when she was about five years old and was just starting to talk. You see, Jenny was nonverbal for the first four years of her life. That's how my parents knew something was wrong. Our pediatrician, Dr. Myron Spelling, was on vacation one summer when Jenny was about to turn four years old, and she had one of those terrible summer colds—terrible for Malibu, California anyway. Mom took Jen and me to Dr. Spelling's office and met his associate, Dr. Janice Ghassemi. She examined Jenny, prescribed some antibiotics, Tylenol, and lots of fluids. Before we left the examination room, Dr.

Ghassemi said, "I'm concerned about Jennifer's lack of language. You might want to get her tested to see if she has autism."

It was the first time I'd ever seen the blood rush out of my mother's face. She didn't know how to respond, but she was clearly upset. We left the office in a hurry.

Later that night, Mom and Dad were discussing what happened. Mom was ranting: "How dare she imply there's something wrong with Jenny. She's just speech-delayed, that's all. I never want to see her again."

Dad was calmer. Maybe because that was his nature, or maybe because he wasn't present in the office when Dr. Ghassemi insinuated that a Bolt progeny was less than perfect.

"Dear heart," he said, "perhaps we should have her tested, if only to rule out anything other than a speech delay."

Mom looked at the old man with a wicked glare, but Dad just looked back with his soft, handsome smile. His chiseled chin jutted forward ever so slightly, as if to indicate Harrison Walker Bolt was correct and there was no argument left. Mom melted when Dad presented things this way. It was his strength and commitment, I believe, that she respected most.

Ultimately, Jenny was diagnosed at UCLA. A large team of experts tested Jenny's hearing, her IQ, and her social quotient. She went through comprehensive behavioral and physical evaluations. The outcome of the battery of tests indicated she was on the autism spectrum, but she also had a high IQ. This one fact could preclude lifelong institutionalization, provided interventions were started immediately.

And so, my parents' lives and mine changed. The house was filled with consultants, teachers, and aides, all of whom were tasked with teaching my little sister how to operate in a world that was no doubt confusing to her. They had to teach her how to speak, how to dress and maintain herself, how to relate to other people, and how to cope with the huge influx of stimuli bombarding her on a daily basis.

I have to say I was impressed by the magnitude of the program set up by several nonpublic agencies. Comprehensive it was, but more than that, the people involved with Jenny seemed to actually care about her. They attended birthday parties every year, brought her small gifts, and many of them shed actual tears as she made grand leaps in her progress. The whole ordeal almost made me reevaluate my opinion of humankind. Almost.

"Okay, Jen," I said. "Can I stop by for a cup of coffee then?"

"Okay, Jon, see you in a few minutes."

Jenny disconnected, and I continued driving to her apartment.

Ten minutes later I arrived. I parked the Carrera in front of Jenny's quadplex and bounced up the walk to the door. Before I could knock, she opened it. Jenny stood staring at me. I could tell she was disappointed, and the disappointment may have set off a cascade of neurological events within her. I stepped forward and hugged her closely. Physical contact used to cause Jenny stress, but over the years she's become accustomed to it. The Bolt family, for all our flaws, is loving. She hugged me back, and I whispered in her ear, "Forgive me?"

She pushed me away, gave me a pseudo-slap on the shoulder, smiled, and said, "Yes."

I followed her as she walked back into the home.

Jenny lived in a four-unit building in Westchester, fairly close to LAX. Not so close that the air traffic noise was a problem, but close enough to check in on her when our parents were traveling. The folks bought the multi-family property with the intention of creating a group home for Jenny. She now lived in one unit, and two other units housed other disabled adults. A caregiver, Melissa, lived in the final unit. She acted as a sorority mother of sorts and checked on the other residents daily, making sure they were clean, fed, and not in need of anything. The system actually worked pretty well for Jenny.

Jenny went directly to the kitchen. She started washing some dishes that were set beside the sink. I looked around to see if coffee was made, but I saw none.

"Hey, sis, do you have any coffee in this place?"

Jenny neither said anything nor turned to look at me. She simply pointed to the pantry with her left hand.

I grabbed the open bag of Starbucks House Roast, a paper filter, and placed them on the small cart next to the refrigerator that held the coffee maker. I filled the pot with water from her bottled water dispenser and filled the reservoir with enough water for ten cups. Maybe overkill, but I thought I needed additional caffeinating.

I sat down at Jen's round pub table and sipped my coffee. Jen finished washing the dishes, dried them with a hand towel, and put everything away. Jen's autism resembled obsessive-compulsive disorder sometimes. Each plate, cup, and bowl was placed in the cabinets in a specific orientation. Those who know ASD know this isn't an OCD trait, but rather some on the spectrum are fastidious about patterns and "sameness." Jen just liked all her things in the same place all the time. It was most likely comforting to her to have everything just so.

Jen sat down across from me. "Don't you want a cup of coffee?" I asked.

"I already ate my Pop-Tart. I don't want coffee now."

"Jen, I'm sorry. I messed up. I've been busy, but I'm here now."

Jen looked at me, and she was tearing up. "I miss you when I don't see you, Jon. I need to see you."

"I miss you too, Jenny. I do." I reached across the tabletop and put my hand over hers. "I promise. If I get caught up in work again and I can't make it over, I will call you. Okay?"

Jen wiped her eyes with the back of her hand. "Okay, but try to get here."

"Dealio!" I said.

Jen and I had a little small talk. I asked her about her job. She works at a small accounting office as a bookkeeper. Jen always had an aptitude for math, so her job fits right in with her strengths. Jen's major challenges with verbal communication and socialization don't hinder her performance. She can focus on balancing the books, reconciling statements, and keeping all the numbers working.

"Work is good," she said.

I remembered Jen had a friend at work, Lisa, so I also asked her how Lisa was.

"She's fine," Jen said.

Jen's curt responses may or may not have been due to her disappointing brother. Her autism sometimes made her answer questions in a staccato manner. Then again, she might have just been pissed at me. A different tack seemed in order.

"Jen," I said, "how can you know if someone is laundering money?"

Jen's eyes lit up. "Look for multiple bank deposits of just under ten thousand dollars."

"Why is that?" I asked.

Jen was on a roll. She explained how the government Financial Crimes Reporting Network requires banks to file a form 112 for cash transactions greater than ten thousand dollars. Banks also must consider separate transactions as a single transaction if they have reason to believe the multiple transactions benefit the same person.

"So should I look for multiple accounts as well?"

"Maybe," Jen said. "It depends on how often and how close to ten thousand dollars the deposits are."

Hmm, I needed to get Maggie on this.

I finished my coffee and gave Jen a hug goodbye. Hugging Jen was an exercise in futility. She rarely responded in kind. Instead, it was like wrapping your arms around a loosely packed bag of incompressible jelly—no reaction. This lack of reaction is a far cry from how Jen was as a young child. I remember an incident when Jen was about five years old. She'd been completely nonverbal up until that time. One day, Jen spontaneously said, clear as a bell, "I want pizza."

Mom was overjoyed. She was standing at the sink, rinsing a glass, when Jen first spoke. Mom put the glass down and briskly walked to Jen.

She sat next to her on the sofa, stroked her hair, and said, "I am so proud of you, Jennifer." Then Mom hugged Jen.

The meltdown was stupefying. Jen screamed at the top of her lungs, the staccato cacophony continuing for several minutes. Mom's reaction was equally perverse. She began rapidly pacing back and forth with her arms folded, hands rubbing the opposite arm. She wasn't prepared for Jen's reaction; she didn't have a clear coping strategy for her autism.

By the time Jen calmed down, Mom was talking to herself. "What have I done? What have I done?" she kept repeating. I told her it was all right, that Jen was better now, but she was inconsolable. I also remember when the old man returned from work, Mom immediately ran to him and broke down crying. Dad comforted her until she regained her composure. She then told him what happened.

"Meltdowns are common with autism, Abby. The doctors told us," Dad said.

"But she spoke, and I just wanted to tell her I loved her for it," Mom replied.

"I understand," Dad said. "But perhaps next time you can tell her without touching her. Some people with autism don't like to be touched."

"I stroked her hair, Harry," Mom said. "It's not the touching. She just doesn't like me."

That was it. Mom felt unloved by Jen. It wasn't true. Even as a kid, I could see that Jenny loved our parents. She may not have shown it the way a typical child did, but she showed it in other ways. The fact that Jen allowed Mom to stroke her hair before the breakdown was indicative of Jen's affection for her. It was several years before Jen could tolerate a hug, but even to this day she rarely hugs back.

I hopped into the Carrera and headed back to Dockweiler. As I pulled into the lot, I saw Tricia's Benz parked beside my coach. She was sitting on the driver's side fender, Maui Jims on, head tilted to the sky. When she turned her head in my direction, I could see she smiled. Then the smile turned to a severe look. I just knew her visit was going to cause me agita.

I parked beside the Benz and hopped out. “What brings you back to this beach, Trish?” I said.

She said nothing. I waited about half a minute in total silence to give her a chance to converse. No such luck. She just looked in my direction, her eyes hidden behind a polarized blind.

“Why don’t you come on in?” I said as I entered the coach.

She followed me moments later and closed the door behind her.

I parked my keister on the settee. Tricia continued standing with her shades on. I was getting a little pissed at this point because I still didn’t know what she wanted. And she was refusing to show me her eyes. Passive-aggressive bullshit!

Finally, I said, “What do you want?”

My tone of voice indicated my aggravation.

“I need your help,” she said.

I was losing my patience with her lack of candor. “That’s obvious. Take off your shades.”

She removed them and slipped them into her purse. “Sorry,” she said.

“So, what’s the problem?” I said.

“I’m afraid my boyfriend is going to kill me,” Tricia said.

I’ve handled paranoia before, many times. It’s difficult to know when someone’s concern is valid and verifiable or if they’re simply unbalanced. Tricia’s behavior in the past indicated an unbalanced nature, so I needed to do a little more probing.

“What makes you think Jared wants you dead?”

Tricia looked down at her wringing hands before speaking. “I fucked up,” she said.

Tricia Goldstein was a methamphetamine addict. She detailed her foray into that world where she smoked, snorted, and shelved meth.

Jared introduced her to the stuff. He said it would heighten their sexual relationship. Yeah, Jared is a real piece of shit.

"You know you need to quit that shit, right?"

"I'm trying," she said. "It's really hard."

Hard? Understatement of the year, but Tricia grew up with a sense of entitlement. I'm sure many things were easy for her: making friends, traveling, retail therapy. But in the world of major drug use, quitting is never as easy as it seems. We've all heard stories about addicts saying, "I can quit anytime I want... I just don't want to." Horse shit!

Methamphetamine makes users feel good because it releases large amounts of dopamine in the brain. Dopamine is the chemical that makes everyone feel good. These meth addicts use so often that the stores of dopamine in their brains become depleted, and so they can't feel good any longer without using. It's a vicious circle.

"Check yourself into rehab. Your folks have money."

"I can't tell them," Tricia said. "It would kill them."

"Trish, you live in Malibu. Do you think your family is the only one dealing with drug abuse?"

She stood staring at me for a moment. I maintained eye contact to see if I saw hesitation or acknowledgment. Then I heard a faint sound outside the coach—a car squealing its tires in the distance.

Tricia said, "I guess, but it's so embarrassing."

I heard a vehicle pull up closer to the coach outside. I stood to get a look. A late-model convertible Mustang pulled up behind Tricia's Benz. There were two surly men inside, both wearing sunglasses and knit caps. This was not good.

I was just about to warn Tricia when the two douchebags outside pulled semi-automatics from their waistbands and aimed for the side of the coach.

"Get down!" I yelled as I grabbed Tricia, pulling her to the floor with me.

Bullets penetrated the aluminum sidewalls of the coach like spikes piercing tissue paper. My mind was racing so fast that Tricia's screams seemed distant. I crawled over to the galley and reached up. Opening the lower silverware drawer, I removed my loaded Glock 19. This gun was loaded with sixteen rounds of 9mm +P+ of 115 grains. This load throws lead at 1,400 feet per second. Pretty good for most situations.

I heard one of the shooters say something in Spanish. Through the door it sounded like "vamos a salir de aquí," then I heard a car door close. I jumped up off the floor and moved to the door with my Glock ahead of me. I kicked the door open. The two bastards were hauling ass in the Mustang. I was about to fire but held off because even with my natural skills there was too much chance I could miss or hit an innocent with a ricochet. I didn't even get the license plate. Fuck!

I tucked the Glock into my waistband, pulling my shirt over for concealment, and stepped outside to survey the damage. There were several nice holes in Coach's sidewalls. It didn't appear any utility lines were severed, but I would need to do a full diagnostic check to be certain. This fiasco was going to cost me time and money.

The next question was: who were these fucks who trashed my home and threatened Tricia's life and mine? I ran through the list of my potential enemies. I didn't think Chesnokov knew anything about me yet. I would check with Maggie to see if she was made. Not a likely scenario, knowing Maggie as I did, but when someone tries to shoot the life out of you, prudence is the word of the day.

What about Tricia? Could I have underestimated Jared's boldness? Not likely. From what I gathered, Jared was a punk drug dealer/pusher. A bully, plain and simple. His threats achieved their intention: to scare Tricia enough so she would toe the line. Like most bullies, my guess was he would never back up his threats with action. I made a mental note to interrogate him just in case.

So that left a big, empty suck-hole of nothing, and that was unacceptable. Unless the attack was a gang initiation row, not many people attempt homicide without motive. Forget everything you've heard. Unless you're a certified sociopath or psychopath, killing another human being is never easy. Even people who kill in self-defense often claim they wish they'd been killed instead. There's substantial survivor guilt for some people.

It's infuriating not knowing who the culprit was. Maybe it's my innate sense of justice or my vengeful streak, but I was pissed! I started thinking Tricia brought these pieces of shit here, to my home. I was not a happy puppy. I looked at Tricia, sitting there on the floor, staring at her hands, and cold rage overcame me.

"Get the fuck out!" I yelled as I picked her off the floor and pushed her out the door.

She fell to the blacktop pretty hard. No injuries as far as I could tell, but tough tits. I still wasn't sure who the shooters were or what they wanted with me, but it was becoming more and more likely Tricia Goldstein was involved. Throwing her out was protective—it would stop me from strangling her.

She was hysterical. "Jon, please don't do this," she said. "I'm sorry!"

"Better if you go now. You won't like who I am at this moment. Call me tomorrow."

Hyperventilating, she got up, wiping her eyes dry with the back of her hand. She headed for the Benz but stopped short and turned.

"You know," she said, "maybe those guys weren't trying to get me. You do have a knack for pissing people off."

With that gem hanging in the air, she got into her Benz. She was right. I couldn't be sure who the target was. I had to find out.

"Trish," I said.

She rolled down the window of the coupe.

"Where can I find Jared?"

CHAPTER 8

NO REGRETS

Tricia told me Jared worked at the Viper Room in West Hollywood. I decided to get over there to have a talk with him. I figured it would be the best first step to determine if Tricia was targeted. Jared would be the most likely person to want retribution considering the meth connection. However, Tricia Goldstein could have other enemies. Her mother, the senator, has made some of her own. Those people could use their children to pressure the senator to do something. Then again, maybe Tricia was right, and I was the target.

I changed my shirt, grabbed my keys, took the Carrera, and hit the road. The Viper Room was on the Sunset Strip between San Vicente and Larrabee. It was less than a twenty-mile trip, but the drive could take anywhere from forty minutes to an hour and fifteen. You gotta love LA traffic!

I took Vista Del Mar north to Imperial Highway, which merged into the 105 Freeway east. I exited the 105 onto the 405 north to La Cienega, which took me all the way to Sunset. Traffic was light, as was the steering on the 911, so I was there in forty minutes. As luck would have it, there was a parking space just in front of the joint. And what a joint it was.

The place opened in the early ‘90s, and some famous actor owned it. The year it opened, a good friend of this actor—another famous actor—died of an overdose on the sidewalk in front of the place. Some people think the place is cursed because it was the former home of a jazz club frequented by various Los Angeles-based mobsters. Me, I don't put too much stock in curses. People. It's always about the people. And bad decisions.

Since it was midday, mid-week, the place wasn't crowded inside. I stopped briefly as I entered to allow my eyes to adjust to the change in light. Once I could see again, I noticed no one behind the bar. There were two guys sitting there talking and nursing what appeared to be scotch rocks in old-fashioned glasses. I sauntered closer to the bar. I overheard some of the conversation of the bar boys.

"She's a fucking bitch, bro. You need to take control."

"Man, fuck you, ese. I am in control. Smacked her real good. She won't play that shit again."

Great, I thought—two real misogynist assholes who believe abusing women is an acceptable pastime. I made a mental note to give each one a good ass-whipping if I got the chance.

As I got closer to the bar, a tall blonde woman came out from the back room. She stood about five-eleven with her bleached blonde do cut in a long mohawk. The strip of hair began on the top of her head and reached the top of her butt crack. The sides of her head were shaved clean. She also had two small bolts piercing each earlobe and a nice wire half-loop piercing her columella. Both arms were covered in full-sleeve ink to her wrists. The left depicted a full version of the "Lord of the Rings" mythology. The right was a fusillade of dark, goth-inspired images: the Grim Reaper, a heart being sliced in half with a flaming sword, a satyr holding a bloody unicorn horn standing above the dying creature. What in the world!

I stepped up to the bar and asked Sleeves, "Is Jared working today?"

Continuing to dry a scotch rocks glass with a suspiciously dirty bar towel, she said, "Who's asking?"

"I'm a friend of a friend. And you are?"

"Call me Bitch," she said.

"Stage or birth?" I said.

"It's just a name. You got one or not, funny man?"

"I'm Jon. Jared?"

Sleeves looked at me square in the eyes and yelled, "JARED! GET YOUR SORRY ASS OUT HERE!"

Jared, or who I assumed was Jared, sauntered out. He had the appearance of a typical dirtbag druggie: long, greasy black hair pulled back into a tight ponytail. His facial hair was trimmed in a goatee—I use the term "trimmed" lightly. Jared had neither the fine motor skills nor the inclination to keep his beard neat and tidy. And it was clear he rarely laundered his work clothes. His blue jeans held various stains on and around his knees, ass, and crotch. I couldn't tell if the stains were of food origin or if some bodily functions of either Jared or one of his drug buddies had gone haywire, leaving remnants on Jared's pants. I couldn't for the life of me understand what Tricia Goldstein saw in this sorry sack of shit. Most likely he was the lowest form of humanity she could find to torque her senator mother's tits.

"I'm here, Bitch. What?"

Sleeves looked at him, then gestured at me with her head. Jared followed her lead and looked.

"I know you?" he said.

"Be glad you don't," I said. "We know people in common."

"For instance?"

"Tricia Goldstein. You've been seeing her?" I said.

"Fucking her is more like it."

Yup, I was right. Jared is a real piece of shit.

"You're a charmer, aren't you?" I said.

"Guess that's why the ladies love me so, right, Bitch?" Jared said.

Sleeves double-flipped him off and mouthed the words "Go fuck yourself."

I had to laugh. "Not all of them."

"Who, her?" he said. "She's no lady, Mac. She's pure dyke."

The witty repartee was beginning to annoy me. I could taste the bile rising in my throat. I closed the gap between us with only the bar separating Jared from me. I leaned in, saying, "You're done. No more Tricia. Understood?"

"Who the fuck do you think you are, man?"

"I'm the guy who can make life uncomfortable for you. Just do what I say, and you'll never see me again."

I could see it in his eyes. Jared was going to need a little more "persuading." I reached out provocatively toward Jared's throat, and he reacted as expected by swinging a wide right to my head. I grabbed his right hand and performed a thumb lock, bending it back against the ulnar nerve.

"Lemme go, you fucking asshole!" Jared screamed.

I increased the pressure on his thumb until his fat head slammed against the bar top.

"Stop fighting me, or I'll break it off," I said. "Try jerking off without a thumb."

He wasn't a complete moron because he stopped resisting.

"Are you gonna listen to me, or do I need to break something?"

"I'll listen. Just let me go."

I released the lock, and he swung his head back, nearly falling against the liquor wall.

"Are you going to stop seeing Tricia?" I asked.

Jared wiped the sweat from his face using both hands and said, "I don't like being threatened, man. You feel me? I don't give a shit about her, but don't fucking threaten me."

I don't get people sometimes. This guy couldn't give half a turd about Tricia, but he still wanted to provoke a confrontation. Ego. It will get a body killed.

Jared called over two bouncers standing near the entrance. He told them to escort me out. Not in those exact words, but you get the drift. I threw my hands up and said, "No problem. I'm leaving. Remember what I said, Jared. I won't say it again."

I walked toward the exit, and just before I could push the door open, the bouncer on my left threw a punch at my head. I blocked the punch and executed a five-swords technique on him. He dropped to the floor, gasping for air. His partner just stood there staring with his "O" face on. I watched the other bouncer for a moment just to be certain he wasn't planning anything. He wasn't. I backed out of the bar and let the door close in front of me.

I got into the Porsche and got the hell out of Dodge. I find fighting distasteful. There are times when it's completely justified—like when a life is at stake, especially my own—but hurting someone who, although meaning to do me harm, is just following orders causes me some consternation. Don't get me wrong, the government trained me well. I have the ability to hurt, maim, or kill anyone with several well-placed strikes to vital locations on the human body. In fact, I could do it with one strategically executed strike. It doesn't change the fact that every now and then I feel remorse after beating someone's ass. Maybe I'm getting soft.

I ran the Carrera west on Sunset, heading toward the ocean, then onto Santa Monica to the 405. Parking lot! LA traffic is a punchline. You only have to say the words, and most people know what you mean. There's a visceral reaction to hearing them. And the west-side strip between Wilshire and LAX is perennially bumper-to-bumper. I once saw a vanity license plate that read HATE 405, or something to that effect. I understand the sentiment.

It took forty-five minutes to travel twelve miles. When I pulled into Dockweiler, the sun was just beginning to touch the cool Pacific. It was some panorama—the yellow-orange ball of fire slowly submerging itself into the largest body of water that we know. I stood watching the light show until the disk of ol' Sol disappeared beneath the waves, leaving a yellow-orange horizon that slowly faded to orange to red and to black. It was a nice way to end a taxing day. I was going to have a couple of beers and then hit the sack. I went inside to start my solo party.

CHAPTER 9

CARPE DIEM

I called Karl. Karl is one of those people who carries his phone with him everywhere, and he usually answers before the second ring. Obsessive-compulsives are successful in Karl's line of work.

"You got me," I heard just before the second ring. "Tell me your story," Karl finished.

"Karl, I'm gonna get you one of these days."

"Not likely, Jon, but I appreciate your tenacity. What's up? This is not about Chesnokov, is it?"

"No, Karl. I respect you too much. It's about Trisha Goldstein."

I caught him up on everything that had happened at the Viper Room. The confrontation with Jared, the drug dealing, the whole clusterfuck of a situation I'd stumbled into. I could hear Karl's breathing change as I described the scene—the way Jared had squared up to me, the casual arrogance of a dealer who thought he was untouchable, the underlying threat that had permeated the entire encounter.

"Jesus, Jon," Karl said when I finished explaining the situation. "So this pretty boy is dealing meth to a senator's daughter? That's a special kind of stupid."

"That's what it looks like. And he's not just dealing to her—he's got her hooked. She's completely under his control."

"Fuck." Karl muttered. "This changes the whole surveillance profile. We're not just watching some dirtbag anymore. We're potentially dealing with someone who's got serious distribution connections. Meth dealers don't operate in isolation."

"I know. That's why I need someone with your skills on this. Someone who understands how these operations work."

Karl was quiet for a long moment. I could practically hear the gears turning in his head, calculating risks, weighing options. "Why don't you believe in backup, Jon?" he finally asked.

I thought about that for a millisecond. It's not that I don't believe in it. It's just that most of the training I've had focused on stealth and deception. It's hard to be stealthy and deceptive when you have a posse comitatus around. I know this attitude will bite me in the ass someday, but it's the way I roll.

"Training," I said. "I'm too old to be retrained."

"Bullshit," Karl shot back. "You're stubborn. There's a difference. But I get it. Old habits die hard, especially when they've kept you alive this long."

"Look, Karl, I'm not asking you to hold my hand. I just need professional surveillance on Jared. Even though Karl was wary of anything connected to Chesnokov, I figured Jared was relatively safe compared to direct involvement with the Russian mob. Feel free to refuse. I respect your position, but I need additional eyes to catch him in the act so I can get Goldstein's daughter free."

"Define 'in the act,'" Karl said. "Are we talking about catching him dealing drugs, or are we talking about the abuse? Because if this kid's really got a serious distribution network, his definition of 'problem solving' might involve more than just slapping his girlfriend around."

"I need to show Trisha who this guy really is. The abuse, the drug dealing, the way he's controlling her through addiction. Whatever it takes to break the spell he's got over her."

Karl sighed heavily. "Okay, I'm listening. But this isn't going to be a standard surveillance job. If Jared's got a serious drug operation, he's going to have security protocols. Street dealers learn to watch for tails, especially when they're dealing to high-profile clients like a senator's daughter."

"That's why I need you, Karl. You've worked narcotics surveillance before."

"Yeah, and I know how paranoid these guys get. What kind of documentation do you need?"

"I want photos, audio, and video."

The silence that followed was longer this time. When Karl finally spoke, his voice had taken on that flat, professional tone he used when he was mentally calculating operational complexity.

"Christ, Jon. You want me to document a drug dealer who's smart enough to hook a senator's daughter? Why don't you just ask me to surveil a DEA operation while I'm at it?" I could sense Karl was getting frustrated. Gathering any of the three was difficult enough, but collecting photos, video, and audio complicated any reconnaissance exponentially.

"Why do you need all this stuff? If photos won't convince her, nothing will."

"Karl, this is a young woman who has lived a very privileged and protected life. She needs to see what a piece of shit this guy is, so I'd rather throw the whole shebang at her. Make it undeniable."

The silence on the other end told me Karl was processing this. He understood my reasoning, even if he didn't like the complexity it added to his work.

"Look," I continued, "Trisha Goldstein isn't some street-smart kid who's seen the dark side of human nature. She's been insulated from reality her entire life. When someone like that finally gets hit with the truth, it needs to be overwhelming enough to break through years of conditioning. She trusted the wrong people."

"And you think a multimedia presentation is going to snap her out of it?"

"I think it's our best shot. Karl, I've seen what happens when sheltered people get a glimpse of real evil. They either shut down completely, or they wake up fast. I'm betting on the latter with Trisha."

Karl made a noise that might have been a laugh, but it came out more like a growl. "You know what this reminds me of? That case in Miami, back in '02. Remember the pharmaceutical heiress?"

I remembered. The congressman's daughter who'd gotten hooked on oxycontin by her dealer boyfriend. It had taken two weeks of surveillance and a mountain of evidence to convince her that her supplier was slowly killing her. "That worked out, didn't it?"

"Yeah, after she overdosed and nearly died. You sure you want to go down this road?"

"I don't see another option. Trisha's in danger, Karl. And not just from Jared's fists. If she's this deep into meth addiction, she could die from an overdose, or worse."

Karl sighed. "Alright, I get it. But this is going to take time, and it's going to cost extra. We're talking about surveillance equipment that won't be detected by standard counter-surveillance. We're talking about establishing multiple observation points, probably using different operatives for different types of contact. And if this goes sideways, we're talking about dealing with people who solve problems with violence."

"Bill the senator. She can afford it."

"Fair enough. But I want hazard pay included in that bill. And I want a clean exit strategy if things get too hot."

"Done. What else do you need?"

"Give me a few days to set up the operational framework. Other than the Viper Room, send over any addresses you have for the guy. I'll run a trace on him as well. Maybe we'll luck out and the douche has some warrants outstanding."

"What about his daily routine? Can you establish a pattern?"

"That's surveillance 101, Jon. I'll map his movements, identify his regular haunts, figure out his security protocols. If he's really dealing to high-profile clients, he'll have some kind of protection, even if it's just a couple of guys who watch his back during transactions."

"And if he spots the surveillance?"

"Then we abort and hope he doesn't connect it back to you. Drug dealers are paranoid by nature, but I'm good at my job, Jon. I don't get made easily."

I could hear Karl's fingers tapping against his phone, probably already making mental notes. "I'll need to bring in some additional assets for this. People who understand the drug trade, who know how these dealers operate. It's going to be expensive."

"How expensive?"

"Let's just say the senator's going to feel it in her campaign fund. But if you want this done right, if you want to get the evidence you need without ending up in a shallow grave, it's going to cost what it costs."

"I trust your judgment, Karl. Just get me what I need."

"I'll also need backup extraction protocols. If this goes bad, I need to know you can pull my people out safely."

"You'll have whatever you need. Just tell me what that is."

Karl was quiet for another moment, and I could practically feel him weighing the risks against the potential rewards. Finally, he spoke. "Alright, Jon. I'll do it. But we do this my way, with my timeline, and with my safety protocols. And if I say we abort, we abort. No heroics, no cowboy shit. Understood?"

"Understood. Thanks, Karl. I owe you one."

"You owe me several, but who's counting? And Jon? Be careful. If Jared really is connected to Chesnokov, this thing could spiral out of control faster than you can imagine. These people don't just eliminate threats—they eliminate everyone connected to threats."

"I'll watch my back."

"Watch everyone's back. Including the girl. If she's dating someone in Chesnokov's organization, she's already in more danger than she realizes."

The line went dead, and I sat there for a moment, staring at my phone. Karl was right to be worried. The Russian mob didn't operate like other criminal organizations. They were ruthless, efficient, and completely without conscience. If Jared was really connected to them, then Trisha wasn't just in an abusive relationship—she was in mortal danger.

Karl was the epitome of efficiency. If there was anything on Jared—any dirt, any secrets, any leverage—he would find it. The man had contacts in places I didn't even know existed, and a talent for uncovering information that people thought they'd buried deep. More importantly, he understood the stakes we were playing for. This wasn't just about exposing a bad boyfriend anymore. This was about survival.

Since I had a few hours to kill before my next move, I decided to take a well-deserved respite on the beach. I grabbed a few requirements: beach chair, towel, and most importantly, a cooler containing a six-pack of brews. I found a nice spot on the sand, set everything up, and sat down to enjoy the sunset. I popped open a can of suds, took a nice big swig, and sat back.

The Pacific stretched out endlessly before me, its surface catching the dying light like scattered diamonds. A few surfers were still out there, silhouettes against the amber sky, waiting for that perfect last wave of the day. There's something about the ocean that puts things in perspective. All our problems, all our schemes and machinations, they're just ripples on the surface of something vast and indifferent.

But even the ocean's majesty couldn't completely quiet the tactical side of my brain. I found myself analyzing the situation from every angle, looking for weaknesses, potential complications, and exit strategies. The conversation with Karl had clarified some things, but it had also raised new questions. If Jared was really connected to Chesnokov's organization, what did that mean for Trisha? Was she an unwitting pawn, or was she somehow complicit in whatever game was being played?

I thought about Trish, Jared, Senator Goldstein, and this frigging mess I'd gotten myself into. The Russian Mob. What the fuck! This could be a slippery slope for sure. Chesnokov and his men don't fuck around. They'd sooner shoot you in the face than look at you. And if you give them a reason, it could be worse than that.

I'd dealt with the Russians before, back in my agency days. They operated by a different set of rules—if you could call them rules. Honor meant nothing to them. Fear was their currency, and violence was their language. The fact that Jared had gotten himself tangled up with them meant this situation was more dangerous than I'd initially thought.

The memories came flooding back unbidden. Moscow, 1995. A blown operation that had cost three good operatives their lives. I'd been lucky to escape with just a scar and a healthy respect for Russian ruthlessness. Chesnokov hadn't been a major player then, but even as a mid-level enforcer, he'd had a reputation for creative brutality. Twenty years later, he'd built an empire on that foundation of fear.

What worried me most was the randomness of Russian mob justice. They didn't just eliminate threats—they eliminated anyone who might potentially become a threat. Families, friends, casual acquaintances. The concept of innocent bystanders didn't exist in their world. If they decided Trisha was a liability, her privileged background wouldn't protect her. If anything, it would make her a more attractive target.

And I never understood how some women tolerate abusive men in their lives. Especially women from so-called "good" families. Trisha's mother is a United States senator, and her father is a billionaire businessman. Her upbringing was the envy of the other ninety-nine percent of the world. I know because, although I wasn't brought up in a billion-dollar lifestyle, my sister and I still had many more opportunities than the vast majority of people on this planet. Sure, we had—and have—our challenges, but why Trish would suffer a fool like Jared is beyond me.

But then again, privilege doesn't protect you from psychological manipulation. In some ways, it makes you more vulnerable. When you've been shielded from the harsh realities of life, when you've never had to develop street smarts or survival instincts, you're easier prey for predators like Jared. They know exactly which buttons to push, exactly how to exploit the insecurities that privilege can create.

I understand enough about psychology to know that she might be acting out to get her parents' attention. You know—date the biggest dick cheese she can lay her hands on to get a reaction, any reaction, from her self-absorbed, narcissistic parental units. Just from my brief interactions with the senator confirmed for me that Trish is mostly an afterthought for her mother, at least. That is, until something happens that might impact her career aspirations.

The pattern was depressingly familiar. Rich kids acting out, seeking attention through increasingly dangerous behavior. The difference was that most rebellious rich kids didn't end up dating enforcers for the Russian mob. Most of them settled for drug dealers or petty criminals. Trisha had managed to find someone who could get her killed in truly spectacular fashion.

Am I being overly critical of the senator and her relationship with her only child? Perhaps. But where there's smoke, one will usually find fire as well. Senator Goldstein struck me as the type of woman who saw her daughter as an extension of her political brand rather than as an individual human being with her own needs and desires.

The irony wasn't lost on me. A woman who'd built her career on family values and protecting children couldn't protect her own daughter from an abusive relationship. But then again, that was often how it worked. The people who talked the loudest about family values were often the ones who'd failed most spectacularly at actually practicing them.

I took another swig of beer and tried to push down the cynicism. It wasn't productive, and it wasn't fair to Trisha. She was a victim, regardless of her parents' failings. The question was whether she'd remain a victim or whether we could wake her up before it was too late.

Jared is another matter entirely. He coaxed me into violence. I do it when I have to, but I don't like it. Anyone who has a hand in extracting that behavior from me can become a problem—a problem I don't need. Yes, I have anger issues. So, I try to avoid physical confrontations if at all possible.

The confrontation at the Viper Room had been a test, I realized now. Jared had been probing, trying to figure out what kind of threat I represented. Siccing the bouncers on me hadn't been an accident—it had been a warning. He'd been telling me that he had backup, that any move against him would have serious consequences.

But he'd also revealed something else: he was insecure enough to need that backup. A truly confident predator doesn't need others for protection. They will use intimidation, violence, and sometimes humor to get out of difficult situations. The fact that Jared had felt compelled get those two to engage me suggested that he knew he was vulnerable, that he needed the threat of other muscle to maintain his hold over Trisha.

That gave me hope. If Jared was vulnerable, if he was dependent on external protection, then he could be separated from that protection. And without other backing, he was just another abusive boyfriend—dangerous, but manageable.

The agency trained me well in many facets of interdiction. Ultra-violence was one area where I excelled, unfortunately. And when I last let myself partake in it freely, they nearly locked me away for the majority of my life. I don't want to go there again if I can help it. The darkness that lives inside me, the part that enjoyed the work a little too much—that's a door I prefer to keep locked.

The memories of that darkness were never far from the surface. The satisfaction I'd felt when targets begged for mercy. The clinical efficiency with which I'd eliminated threats. The way my pulse had remained steady even as I'd ended lives. The agency psychologists had called it "compartmentalization," but I knew better. It was something deeper and more dangerous—a part of me that had enjoyed the power of life and death.

That part of me had been useful once. It had kept me alive in situations where hesitation would have meant death. But it had also nearly destroyed me. The line between necessary violence and sadistic pleasure had blurred until I couldn't tell the difference anymore. It had taken years of therapy and careful self-monitoring to lock that part of myself away.

But Chesnokov could force me to open it. Everything I know about the Russian Mob, and Chesnokov in particular, leads me to believe this. He has no ability to feel empathy for other human beings. Like all sociopaths, he gets pleasure from the pain of others. This is the kind of person ultra-violence was made for. This could get messy.

The thought sent another chill down my spine that had nothing to do with the ocean breeze. I took another long pull from my beer and tried to push those memories back where they belonged—in the past. But I couldn't shake the feeling that the past was about to become the present again. If Karl's surveillance revealed that Jared was more than just a local drug dealer, if he was connected to Chesnokov—if he was actually working for him—then this case would evolve from a simple domestic dispute into something far more dangerous.

And if that happened, I'd need to decide how far I was willing to go to protect Trisha. Would I be able to stop at just enough violence to neutralize the threat? Or would I let that dark part of myself take control again? The honest answer scared me more than Chesnokov's entire organization.

And then there's Elsa. I'm stuck in this mess because of greed, plain and simple. Stealing twelve million dollars is bad enough, but when you steal from people in powerful places, it's easy enough for all hell to break loose. Dumb, but it was her choice to be stupid.

But as I sat there watching the waves roll in, I began to wonder if there was more to Elsa's story than simple greed. Twelve million dollars was a lot of money, but it was also a very specific amount. It wasn't the kind of round number that suggested opportunistic theft. It was the kind of precise figure that suggested planning, calculation, purpose.

What if Elsa hadn't just stolen the money? What if she'd been forced to steal it? What if she'd been caught between the same kind of impossible choices that Trisha was facing now? The more I thought about it, the more the pieces seemed to fit together. Elsa works for Senator Goldstein. Trisha is dating someone connected to the Russian mob. Twelve million dollars goes missing.

Still, I couldn't help but feel a grudging respect for her audacity. It takes balls to embezzle that kind of money from a U.S. senator, especially one with Goldstein's connections. Either Elsa was incredibly naive about the consequences, or she was more desperate than I'd given her credit for. Either way, she'd painted a target on her back that was visible from space.

The question was whether that target was painted by the senator's people or by someone else entirely. If the Russians were involved in the theft, then Elsa wasn't just a thief—she was a loose end. And Russian criminals were notoriously efficient at tying up loose ends.

The sun was setting now, painting the sky in brilliant shades of orange and red. A couple walked by hand-in-hand, their laughter carried on the evening breeze. For a moment, I envied them their simplicity, their apparent freedom from the kind of complications that defined my existence.

But even as I envied them, I couldn't help but analyze their body language, their positioning, their situational awareness. Old habits die hard, and paranoia was one habit I'd never been able to shake. In my line of work, the moment you stopped being paranoid was the moment you died.

As the final slice of the sun settled into the deep Pacific for the night, I picked up my empties and gathered my beach accoutrements. Tomorrow was going to be a busy day of surveilling Elsa Krieger. It's all shits and giggles until someone gets hurt. I just needed to make sure that someone wasn't me.

Walking back to the RV, I couldn't shake the feeling that I was walking into something bigger than a simple embezzlement case. The Russians, the senator, the boyfriend with violent tendencies—all the pieces were there for a perfect storm. And I was standing right in the middle of it, trying to keep everyone from drowning.

The problem with perfect storms is that they're unpredictable. You can see them coming, you can prepare for them, but you can never be sure exactly how they'll unfold. Variables cascade into other variables, creating chaos that even the most experienced professional can't anticipate.

In this case, the variables were human ones, which made them even more dangerous. Trisha's psychological state, Jared's connection to Chesnokov, the senator's political ambitions, Elsa's motivations—any one of these could shift unexpectedly, changing the entire dynamic of the situation.

The moon was rising as I reached my RV, its silver light creating a path across the waves. Tomorrow would bring new challenges, new dangers, and probably new complications I hadn't even considered yet. But tonight, I had cold beer, a comfortable bed, and the sound of the ocean to lull me to sleep. Seize the day, right? Sometimes, that's enough.

But as I settled in for the night, I couldn't shake the feeling that the day had already seized me. The pieces were in motion, the players were taking their positions, and the game was about to begin in earnest. Karl would start his surveillance, I'd track down Elsa, and somewhere in the background, Chesnokov's people would be watching all of us, waiting for the right moment to make their move.

The only question was whether I'd be ready when that moment came. Whether I'd be able to keep the darkness locked away long enough to save the people who needed saving. Whether I'd be able to navigate the perfect storm without losing myself in the process.

Outside my window, the ocean continued its eternal rhythm, indifferent to human concerns. But for the first time in a long while, I found its indifference comforting rather than unsettling. Tomorrow would bring what it brought, and I'd deal with it the way I always did—one crisis at a time, one decision at a time, one day at a time.

Seize the day. Sometimes, that's all you can do.

CHAPTER 10

TEMPUS FUGIT

I hopped out of my bunk at quarter after five, put on my running gear, and headed out on the oceanside bike path for a quick five-mile run. Southern California is a great place in which to be fit. You'll always see someone in better—and worse—physical shape than you are. It's the kind of clarity that stops a thinking person from believing their own press.

The morning air was crisp and clean, carrying the salt scent of the Pacific and the promise of another perfect California day. My feet found their rhythm on the concrete path, and soon I was in that meditative state that long-distance runners know well—where the body moves automatically and the mind is free to wander.

As I ran along the concrete paseo through the clean ocean air, jogging mothers, businesspeople, and others riding bikes passed coming and going. The variety of people attracted to the Southern California lifestyle is mind-boggling. Of course, you have stereotypical hard bodies. These folks spend the majority of their day in the gym, exercising and sculpting in an attempt to find perfection. These are men and women too shallow to consider the frivolity of their regimen. Staying fit is healthy and wise. Reducing your body fat percentage below three percent is worthless. We are worm food, after all.

I've never understood the obsession with physical perfection that drives so many people out here. Don't get me wrong—I believe in taking care of myself, maintaining the body as the tool it is. But when it becomes your entire identity, when you spend four hours a day in the gym and can't hold a conversation about anything except protein intake and workout routines, you've lost something essential about what it means to be human.

I looped around Playa del Rey, past The Shack, and headed back toward Dockweiler. The morning joggers were out in force now—an eclectic mix of dedicated athletes, weekend warriors, and people just trying to stay ahead of middle-age spread. I nodded to the regulars I recognized, the same faces I'd been seeing for months on this same stretch of path. There's a camaraderie among early morning exercisers, an unspoken acknowledgment that we're all fighting the same fight against entropy and time.

When I got back to the coach, I heard the muffled sound of my cell phone ringing. I don't jog with my phone. Why? Because I'm just old enough to remember a time when the telephone was not portable. It was fixed to a wall or sitting on a table but still tethered to the wall with a cord. If you left the house to do anything, you either missed a call completely, or if you had an answering machine, you returned any calls after reviewing your recorded messages. Nothing was so urgent that it couldn't wait minutes or hours.

Today, however, it seems everyone is thoroughly connected 24/7/365. Christ, I see morons texting while driving. The need for constant connectivity has created a generation of people who can't be alone with their thoughts for five minutes without reaching for their devices. Me? I prefer a less anxious existence, at least where phone calls are concerned.

I caught the last ring on the cell. "It's Bolt," I said.

"Good morning, Mr. Bolt. Senator Goldstein here," was the reply. "I need to see you today."

There was a pregnant pause between "you" and "today." Not good. The tone in her voice had shifted from the polite but distant professionalism of our previous conversations to something harder, more urgent. Whatever happened since our last meeting, it wasn't good news.

I wasn't really in the mood to trade pleasantries with the good senator, but a client is a client. The customer is always right, right? Not really, but bills don't pay themselves.

"What time is good for you, Senator?"

"Meet me at my office downtown. Let's say 3:30. You know the address?"

"333 North Hope Street," I said, testing her.

"No, it's South Hope. 333 South Hope. Be on time, Mr. Bolt," she said, and the call disconnected.

I did know the address, but my anti-authority voice always interjects when engaging with those in power. It's a character flaw I've never been able to shake completely. I need to work on that. After all, many—if not most—of my current clients could be included in that group, and if not, they're encumbered with many entitlement issues. It just rubs me the wrong way.

Maybe it's because I was born into a family of privilege. My pop could be the ultimate entitled jagoff at times even though I had and have great respect for the man. His pontifications on money, prestige, etiquette, and duty made my stomach turn. Living in Malibu as a kid wasn't easy either. Nearly everyone was just like my dad. My peers were too. It's challenging living each day dealing with a bunch of entitled pricks trying to tell you how to live your life.

I thank God I met Master Tatum when I did. He helped put me on the straight and narrow, taught me that true strength comes from discipline and self-control, not from the accident of being born into wealth. The old Korean War veteran had seen enough of the world to know what really mattered, and he wasn't impressed by money or status. He was impressed by character, and he demanded it from his students.

I got a pot of coffee going, jumped into the shower, dressed, grabbed a travel mug full of joe, and headed to the Valley. The traffic was unusually light going over the Sepulveda Pass. I thought for a moment it was a holiday, but I couldn't think of one landing on a Tuesday in May. I'll take it. Hello, gift horse—no need to look you in the mouth.

The drive gave me time to think about what Senator Goldstein might want to discuss. The urgency in her voice suggested something had changed, some new development in the case that required immediate attention. In my experience, when politicians summon you with that tone of voice, it usually means one of two things: either they're about to fire you, or they're about to ask you to do something that will probably get you killed.

I exited the 405 at Ventura Boulevard, then headed west toward Elsa's apartment. I parked at the end of the street and walked toward her building at the end of the block. People were leaving for work, school, etc., so I was inconspicuous. The suburban morning routine provided perfect cover—just another guy in casual clothes walking through the neighborhood.

I walked down the alley between Elsa's building and the neighboring one. The Buick SUV was parked in her assigned carport. Good. Now I just need to wait.

I walked back to the Carrera, got in, and watched. This was the part of "the job" I hated most. Surveillance sucks. There's no other way to put it. You sit on your ass and wait. Sometimes you wait for days trying to catch a break. Sometimes you do catch that break, but other times you get bupkis. There's no glamour in it, but it's a necessary evil.

The psychology of surveillance is fascinating in its own way. You have to find the balance between alertness and patience, between focus and relaxation. Stay too tense, and you'll burn out before anything happens. Get too comfortable, and you'll miss the crucial moment when it finally does. It's a skill that can't be taught in books—you must develop the instinct through hours of mind-numbing practice.

I knew Elsa had to leave sometime. She did work for a living, after all. It was already past 9:00 in the morning, but perhaps she started her shift later than most. Then again, maybe she's just the type who's never on time for anything. I couldn't imagine the senator would have accepted that type of person for a sensitive position, but you never know. There must have been something that gave Senator Goldstein confidence in her. I aimed to find out what that was.

Elsa's Buick pulled out of the alley about ten minutes later. As she turned right on Orion, I followed, keeping several cars between us. She drove west on Ventura toward Encino. I stayed several cars behind her, trying to remain as inconspicuous as possible. Since traffic was typical mid-week heavy, the Carrera and I disappeared in plain sight.

She signaled a move into the left lane as we passed Hayvenhurst Street, and as we neared Balboa, she signaled again to turn left into the parking structure of an office building. I drove past the building and swung a U-turn mid-block—an illegal move, but necessary for expediency's sake.

I snaked into a small parking space near the curb and double-timed it to the parking structure. As luck would have it, I reached the elevator just before Elsa did. Perfect timing is one of those things that separates successful surveillance from amateur hour.

"After you," I said when the door opened.

She walked in, I followed, and she pressed 10. "Floor?" she asked politely.

"Ten, please," I said, feigning ignorance.

The elevator ride was awkwardly silent, filled with that peculiar tension that exists between strangers in a confined space. Elsa checked her phone, and I studied the floor indicator, both of us avoiding eye contact. She was prettier than her photos suggested—not stunning, but attractive in that California way that comes from good genes, regular exercise, and expensive skincare.

When the door opened, I gestured for Elsa to exit first. Chivalry is not dead, it's just in a coma most days. She exited to the left, and I went to the right. I watched her enter an office about halfway down the hall. After the door closed behind her, I turned and followed.

The suite was 1011, and the sign indicated it was a financial planning office. "Robert Barnes, Financial Consultant," the sign read. I jotted a note in my phone, including date and time, and turned back toward the elevator. I had no sense whether this was her place of employment or what. This stake-out could be a long one. Fuck!

I took the elevator down to the parking garage. There were attendants at the exit about forty feet away from the elevator. I looked around to see if Elsa's car was close. It didn't appear there was valet service in this garage, so I started searching for her car. I found it parked on the second level, nestled between a BMW and a Mercedes in what was clearly the "nice car" section of the garage.

I looked around to see if there were any cameras in the garage. Security was lighter than I'd expected for a building this size—either they were overconfident in their safety, or they were cutting corners on operational costs. I opened the GPS tracking app to confirm the tracker on Elsa's car was still active. It was. Most times these small, usually reliable, devices have sufficient battery life, but I've experienced failures so confirmation is a good idea.

I waited in the garage for about twenty minutes before deciding to head back upstairs. Elsa emerged from the elevator carrying a manila envelope, looking pleased with herself. Whatever business she'd conducted with Mr. Barnes had gone well. She walked briskly to her car, and I followed at a discreet distance, but as we got close to it, I exited the parking structure and proceeded back to my ride. I saw Elsa exit the structure several minutes later, and I pulled away from the curb to follow.

She moved into the far right lane as we approached Hayvenhurst Street. I followed her lead as she signaled a right turn ahead. Elsa turned north onto Hayvenhurst and immediately drove into the strip center on the corner of Ventura and Hayvenhurst. She parked in a space just in front of the Starbucks. I drove past her and found a spot further down the long row of parking spaces. It was a great vantagepoint from which to observe. I backed the Porsche into a spot between two SUVs. Concealment is beneficial to surveillance.

Elsa got out of her car and went into the coffee shop. I find Starbucks to be a fascinating success story. I enjoy my coffee the same as anyone else, but I never would have thought you could open several thousand coffee shops and be successful selling what amounts to burned beans at premium prices. I guess that's the story of all founders of successful businesses—they can see an opportunity where others can't. McDonald's is another example.

She left the place holding a venti something in her left hand. She was looking at her iPhone as she walked, completely absorbed in whatever was on the screen. The modern condition—unable to walk fifty feet without digital stimulation. She headed toward Whole Foods, and I had a hunch that was her planned destination, so I walked across the sea of Valley vehicles to follow her in.

If you've never been to a Whole Foods store before, it's kind of a sight to behold. Unlike all the supermarkets that I frequented as a child with my parents, Whole Foods is set up to present its wide range of organic and natural foods first. My recollection of walking through Safeway when I was eleven is that the produce department was usually in the back of the store. The front of the store was filled with shelving units comprised of standard grocery items from multiple different food producers.

Whole Foods is arranged differently. Most of the stores that I've been in—and I don't frequent Whole Foods often because they're twice as expensive as most of the other supermarkets I shop at—have the produce department right up front as you walk in the doors. Their vast range of unique and exotic organic fruits and vegetables are there staring you in the face. And only for twenty-five dollars per pound. They generally have food service departments also at the front for those who are not only looking to shop for groceries but to grab a quick, healthy bite on the way out.

The store was busy this afternoon. I kept a safe distance behind Elsa as she traversed the aisles. I was holding my iPhone in my hand as I watched her shop, wanting to make some notes. You never know what facts will be important down the road.

In the produce section, Elsa purchased the usual items: tomatoes, lettuce, celery, carrots, and something else I thought was a little strange—rhubarb. She then moved to gather some fruit. Among the various apples, she picked out two pairs each of mixed green and red varieties, a handful of plums, and a bag of red seedless grapes. Nothing too unusual so far.

Elsa then walked up and down the aisles, stopped briefly in the meat department, and bought two organic chicken breasts, boneless and skinless. She picked up a box of cereal—one I believe is a generic brand of Cheerios, but gluten-free—a dozen eggs, gluten-free multigrain bread, a small triangle of Camembert cheese, and some crackers.

Her shopping habits revealed someone who was health-conscious but not obsessive about it. The combination of organic produce and processed gluten-free alternatives suggested someone trying to eat well within the constraints of a busy lifestyle. The rhubarb was interesting—not many people buy rhubarb on impulse. Either she was planning something specific, or it was part of a regular routine.

She stepped in line at a register that had three customers ahead of her. The older gentleman at the front of the line seemed to be conducting some high-minded international finance. He had two items on the conveyor belt: a cheap bottle of Pinot Grigio and a bag of string cheese. He was paying for it with that vestige of the twentieth century—a handwritten check.

Elsa was clearly not amused, standing there waiting. When the line two registers down started moving quicker, she quickly moved her cart that way and got back in line. I made a note to myself about her lack of patience. That trait could be beneficial to know about.

After bagging her groceries, Elsa pushed her shopping cart out through the exit sliders, returned the cart to the collection area, retrieved her bagged items, and walked toward her Buick. I followed at a fair distance, but maintaining a tail in the busy parking lot of a strip mall is easy. I could have walked side-by-side with Elsa, and she wouldn't have been the least bit suspicious.

Her cell phone rang in her purse. I heard one of the default iPhone ringtones. She stopped walking and retrieved the phone from her purse.

"Hey," I heard her say.

She was holding the bag of groceries with the crook of her right elbow while holding the iPhone in her right hand. From Elsa's facial expression, the caller was someone with whom she had a close relationship. She smiled, brushed her blonde hair back with her left hand, and then placed her hand on her left hip in a gesture that was both casual and unconsciously flirtatious.

Suddenly, I heard the distinct sound of an automobile engine revving hard. I looked to Elsa's left and saw a large Chrysler 300 sedan bearing down on her fast. The car was accelerating directly toward where she stood, and from the angle and speed, there was no question about the driver's intent.

Time slowed to that hyper-focused state I remembered from combat situations. Every detail became crystal clear: the determined expression on the driver's face, the way Elsa remained completely oblivious to the approaching danger, the exact distance I needed to cover to reach her.

I sprinted toward Elsa, who was clearly too involved in her phone conversation to notice the approaching threat. I reached her a split second before the 300 would have made contact, wrapping my arms around her and diving to the side. We hit the asphalt hard, rolling between two parked cars as the Chrysler roared past, close enough that I could feel the heat from its engine.

The 300 sped out of the parking lot, burning rubber as it turned north on Hayvenhurst, leaving behind the acrid smell of scorched tires and the echo of its racing engine.

Elsa looked up at me from the ground, her eyes wide with shock and confusion. "Fuck!" I thought. I'd blown my cover completely. Then an earth-shattering scream came, followed by tears. Elsa was hysterical.

I gently helped her sit up, scanning the parking lot for any sign that the Chrysler might return. "It's okay. You're safe," I said, trying to keep my voice calm and reassuring.

She looked at me again, and with breath hitching she managed, "S-s-safe? W-w-who w-w-was th-th-that?"

"Don't know," I said, sounding like a moron even to myself. "Obviously someone in a hurry."

She didn't find my attempt at levity funny, which I couldn't blame her for. Someone had just tried to run her down in broad daylight, and my stupid joke wasn't helping the situation.

Elsa removed a tissue from her purse and wiped her eyes and face. She was beginning to regain her composure, though I could see her hands were still shaking. She smiled at me tentatively and said, "Thank you."

"No worries," I said. "Are you alright?"

"I think so. Other than being freaked out a little bit." She paused, studying my face carefully. "You think that asshole was just some random asshole?"

Elsa was paranoid now, which was good. She should be after embezzling millions from a U.S. senator. But I played along, not wanting to reveal how much I knew about her situation.

"Why? Do you think someone's after you?" I asked, watching her reaction carefully.

She looked at me, and I could see the fear in her eyes, but then I smiled broadly, and she started laughing—that slightly hysterical laughter that comes after a close brush with death.

"Me? Of course not. Who would want to hurt little old me?"

Three black-and-white LAPD units pulled into the parking lot, their lights flashing and sirens wailing. Someone had called in the incident, which meant there would be reports, statements, and official documentation. That was my cue to leave. I needed to get to Senator Goldstein's office downtown, and I couldn't afford to get tangled up in a police investigation.

"The cops are here now," I said, getting to my feet and brushing off my clothes. "They'll want your statement."

I started walking away, but Elsa called after me. "Wait! What's your name?"

"Jon," I said, turning back. "Jon Steele."

"Can I have your number?" she asked, her voice still shaky but determined. "I'd like to thank you for saving my life."

I told her it wasn't necessary, but she insisted. So, I gave her the number to Brooklyn Pizza in Hermosa Beach. At least she could get a great slice to ease her disappointment when she discovered the deception.

As I walked back to my car, I couldn't shake the feeling that the attempted hit-and-run hadn't been random at all. Someone wanted Elsa Krieger dead, and they were willing to do it in broad daylight in a crowded parking lot. The question was: who? And more importantly, was I walking into the middle of a war I didn't fully understand?

The tracking device would let me keep tabs on her movements without having to maintain close surveillance, which was good because after this incident, she'd be more alert to potential threats. But she'd also be more desperate, and desperate people make unpredictable choices.

I had a meeting with Senator Goldstein in a few hours, and I had the distinct feeling that the conversation was going to be far more complicated than I'd anticipated. The case was evolving rapidly, with new players and new dangers emerging every day. And somehow, I was right in the middle of it all, trying to keep everyone alive long enough to figure out what the hell was really going on all while time was flying into the abyss.

CHAPTER 11

TAKE FIVE

I flipped a hard right out of the Whole Foods parking lot onto Havenhurst, heading north, then jumped on the 101 South toward downtown L.A. The time read 2:55 on my dashboard. Traffic was moving nicely, so I figured making it to the Senator's office on time was possible—until I hit the Hollywood area.

As I approached Sunset, I slammed into a dead stop. A three-car accident stretched across the lanes ahead, fresh enough that the wreckers hadn't arrived yet. Fuck! 3:10 already. No way I'd make it to the Honorable Senator at this rate.

I maneuvered the Carrera toward the Sunset exit, weaving through the infamous Ventura Parking Lot. You ever notice how some people accommodate you when you're clearly trying to move through traffic, while others act like complete assholes? Several cars moved aside or let me cut in as I worked from lane to lane. That is, until I reached some bald jackoff in a Rolls-Royce Phantom.

This chrome-domed bastard ignored my friendly attempts to get his attention. I waved, smiled, pointed toward the off-ramp. I even called out "Excuse me, sir" through his open window. He kept staring straight ahead like I didn't exist.

When my blood pressure hit about 220, I threw the shifter into neutral, set the e-brake, and got out. Baldy and I were going to have ourselves a little tête-à-tête.

I walked over to the Rolls, reached through the window, and grabbed cue ball's windpipe. "Listen, friend," I said as Mr. Clean writhed in my grip. "This is a nice, expensive vehicle. You obviously live a comfortable life. Want to keep it that way?"

Homer Simpson tried to respond, but without the ability to inhale or exhale, coherent speech proved challenging.

"I'll take that as a yes. Now, next time someone tries to exit this packed freeway, you'll let them pass, right? Just nod."

Skullet nodded vigorously. I released my grip and he started coughing like he'd swallowed a hairball.

"Have a nice day," I said, returning to the 911.

I shifted into first and started moving toward the off-ramp again. Curly backed the Phantom up a few feet to give me room. I smiled and waved as I sped away.

I headed south on Van Ness toward Beverly, making nearly every light thanks to my sixty-two-mile-per-hour average speed. But when I turned left on Beverly, it was already 3:20. This was going to be close.

I did five miles in four minutes and forty seconds. Not bad time through downtown Los Angeles. Don't judge me—you know you've driven like that at least once in your lifetime. It's the name of the game.

I left the Carrera with the building valet, hopped on the elevator, and arrived at the senator's office at 3:32. Walking into the outer office, I greeted the dowdy receptionist.

"Jon Bolt to see Senator Goldstein."

The receptionist looked up at me. She reminded me of Mrs. Hughes from Downton Abbey, but with cat-eye glasses. She touched a button on her phone, waited a moment, then said, "A Jon Bolt is here to see you." Another pause before she said, "Very well," and disconnected.

"Please have a seat, Mr. Bolt. The senator is running a little late, but she'll be with you shortly."

I wasn't amused, but I sat down anyway. I should have known better than to take a case from an overly entitled, overly wealthy politician who also happened to have a mile-wide passive-aggressive streak. Sometimes I can be such a jackass.

The Honorable Senator was pissed that I was two minutes late, so now she was going to make me cool my heels in her front office. What a load of fucking bullshit! I had half a mind to get the hell out of there, commission be damned.

Mrs. Hughes could tell I was upset—my mumbling to myself might have been a hint. She asked if I'd like some water or something.

"You got any scotch?"

She smiled the first genuine smile I'd seen from her. "Nothing that strong, but we do have flavored sparkling water."

I smiled back. "Plain water is fine."

She brought me a cold bottle of Fiji. I twisted off the blue cap and took a long sip. The cold liquid cooled my throat and my temper. I started to calm down.

About fifteen minutes later, there was a buzz on Mrs. Hughes' console. I heard her say into her earpiece, "Yes, ma'am." Then she looked up. "You can go in, Mr. Bolt."

I got up, replaced the cap on the Fiji bottle, and walked toward the senator's office door. As I passed Mrs. Hughes' desk, I said, "It's Jon."

She smiled as I entered the senator's inner office.

Senator Nancy Goldstein was staring out one of the floor-to-ceiling windows in her corner office on the twenty-seventh floor. The view of downtown was stunning, but I could tell the senator wasn't enjoying it. It hit me that I'd been standing in her office for nearly thirty seconds and Nancy Goldstein hadn't said a word about my tardiness.

"Is everything all right, Senator?"

She turned toward me. Her eyes were bloodshot, lids red and puffy. She was clearly distraught, shooting glances all over the office, her breathing hitched. She sat down in her big, overstuffed burgundy leather chair, slid open the bottom right desk drawer, and poured herself a double shot of Glenfiddich. She inhaled deeply and tossed back the scotch, then set the empty rocks glass on the desk and placed both hands over her face.

I decided this was going to take longer than expected, so I sat down in one of the chairs facing her desk and waited.

After several minutes, I heard her say from behind her hands, "Tricia is in the hospital."

"What happened?"

"The doctors say she suffered a psychotic break, a nervous breakdown of sorts. They're keeping her medicated and calm. She's sleeping now."

"When did this happen?"

"Earlier today. Before noon, so morning is more accurate."

"I guess the shooting got to her."

Nancy Goldstein sobered up quickly and screamed, "What shooting?"

I brought her up to speed on Tricia's visit to the coach, our conversation, and the exchange of gunfire. I left out Tricia's state of intoxication, not wanting to add fuel to the fire.

"Why didn't you tell me about this incident? And why have you been seeing my daughter behind my back?"

"Calm down, Senator. That's not how it is. Tricia came to see me a couple of times."

"A couple of times! For Christ's sake! Who are you working for, Mr. Bolt?"

I was starting to regret meeting the Right Honorable Senator from California.

"Senator, we can change our arrangement anytime you like, but if you'll listen to me, you'll see there's nothing untoward here."

The tension dropped from her shoulders. She clasped her hands together, rested them on the desk, and said, "I'm listening."

"The first time Tricia visited, she wanted to know why you and I met at your home. I told her in no uncertain terms it was none of her business. That if she wanted to know more, she should ask you. I also told her to get off the drugs."

I left out the part where Tricia tried seducing me. I figured no mother wants to hear that about her "little girl." I also didn't want to feel like a creepy old guy.

"The second time she was very scared."

"Scared? Why?"

This wasn't going to be an easy conversation. "Jared. It was about Jared."

I gave her the quickest synopsis I could: Jared is a drug dealer; Tricia is his client and sex partner. That tidbit caused a visceral reaction in the senator, like she'd thrown up a little in her mouth. I continued by informing her that I'd visited Jared at his workplace and let him know to stop dealing to and screwing Tricia.

"What did he say to that?"

"I had to fight my way out of the club, but I've handled turds like Jared before. He'll come to understand the wisdom of following my directives, trust me."

Nancy Goldstein—a United States Senator who'd been elected and re-elected to that office multiple times and had served her country for many years—lost her shit.

"What the FUCK, Bolt! Are you fucking kidding me? You had my daughter's dealer within your grasp and you let him go? Jesus Christ!"

She marched over to her desk and picked up the telephone.

"What are you doing, Senator?"

"I'm calling the police, that's what I'm doing. Since you don't seem to think dealing methamphetamine is a problem, I'll get the authorities involved."

I stepped beside her, took the phone from her hand, and hung up. I could see she was about to explode again, but I simply placed a finger to my lips and said quietly, "Shh."

I wasn't certain this tactic would work, but it did. She relaxed her shoulders and let her arms drop to her sides.

"Senator, take five. Do you really need a scandal now with the election coming up in less than a year? Drugs and sex are the top two things that garner negative media attention, don't you think?"

I could see that she understood. Before she could retort, I continued, "You need to trust me. I will take care of the Jared problem."

She looked me straight in the eye. "Will you? Will you, Mr. Bolt, 'take care' of Jared?"

Damn! This conversation was taking a nasty turn.

"Senator, I'm not in that line of business."

"You're a fixer of sorts, no?"

"Senator...Nancy, let me be blunt and cut to the chase. Yes, I am a 'fixer' of sorts, but I don't sanction people. That's not in my wheelhouse. Also, many of the rich and famous have been taken down by exactly the kind of shenanigans you're suggesting. I assure you, you would not enjoy a moment in prison."

She stared at me, ruminating on my words. I took the lull in conversation as my cue to leave, so I walked to the office door. At the threshold, I turned and said, "But never fear—I have the Jared situation under control."

Then I left.

As I walked through the outer office, Mrs. Hughes was engaged in a phone conversation, so I smiled and winked as I passed her desk. When I got to the elevators, three businesspeople were waiting: two women—a redhead and a brunette—and a younger man. They were having a heated conversation about "objection deflecting" or something. Obviously, a sales team leaving a less-than-successful meeting.

Red said, "Darcy, I told you before we went in not to bring up the technological challenges with the new release. Why did you do that?"

Darcy replied, "I didn't want to lie to him, and he asked us specifically about it."

Red shook her head and looked at the young man, who I assumed was some sort of trainee. "You see, Tim, as you go out on calls, you need to listen to your trainer and follow instructions. That is, if you want to close deals!"

"So, we're supposed to lie to get deals?" Darcy asked.

Red got right in Darcy's face. "You are 'supposed' to do whatever it takes to close a deal."

I couldn't resist. "Yes, Darcy, you should probably take a pistol on all your sales calls from now on. Nothing screams 'buy or else' like a Glock!"

All three stared at me, dumbfounded, just as the elevator doors opened and I stepped inside.

Salespeople. Unbelievable.

CHAPTER 12

IGH ANXIETY

It was 4:35 when I drove out of the parking structure on South Hope. I decided to drive to the dojo in Pasadena for a workout. Traffic was about average, but I'd driven this route so many times over the years that I knew a few shortcuts. I bobbed and weaved until the 101 became the Arroyo Seco Parkway.

Arroyo Seco was the first freeway built in Los Angeles—hell, in the entire U.S., if I recall correctly. Built in the 1940s, it was considered a marvel of futurism at the time. Traffic would no longer be impeded by lights and stop signs. Commuters could move rapidly from Pasadena into downtown Los Angeles in one continuous flow.

Not the case anymore. The designers of Arroyo Seco probably never imagined how the population and traffic would explode over the years. The greater Los Angeles area was fairly sleepy in the 1940s. After World War II, everything exploded. Real estate developers bought cheap land, subdivided it, and built many of the suburbs we know today, especially in the San Fernando Valley. Freeways followed the urban sprawl.

By modern standards, the Arroyo Seco Parkway is a narrow, outdated roadway, but in its day, it was the shit.

I made it to Master Parker's dojo in just over thirty-five minutes. Not bad for afternoon rush. As I entered, I saw the empty office up front. Master Parker must be teaching a class, and indeed he was on the west-side training floor. I made my way back to the locker room, bowing in respect as I stepped onto the training mat and again when I stepped off.

I donned my black gi top and pants, then wrapped my well-worn black belt around my waist. I'd earned my black belt many years ago and never upgraded to a new one. In fact, in Kenpo, as you move through the upper ranks of black belts, you're entitled to add red tips to your belt. I don't adhere to such nonsense.

I remember when I was promoted to second-degree black. Master Parker handed me a new black belt with two red tips attached.

"No thanks," I said.

Master Parker gave me an incredulous look.

"I once heard that an old sensei, when asked by a new student, 'Master, how long will it take me to earn my black belt?' replied, 'I don't know. Work hard and your white belt will turn black by itself.' I'm happy to be a black belt. I don't need to know or show how 'black' I am."

I remember Master Parker laughing uproariously at this. "Always the rebel, Jon," he said, but I knew he meant it as a compliment.

After I warmed up on the mat, I began practicing Long Form 8—the knife form. I also worked on several black belt techniques dealing with handgun attacks. Why? As Sun Tzu said, "If your enemy is secure, be prepared for him." I wasn't sure what was coming down the pike, but better to keep my skills sharp.

When I was finishing my workout, Master Parker came over to the east side of the dojo where I was training. I immediately bowed as he approached.

"Jon, how are you?"

"Fine, Sensei."

"Fine? Fucked-up, insecure, neurotic, and emotional?"

I smiled. "Well, sir. Well."

He asked me to walk with him to his office. I demurred because I was stinking and sweating. He placed his left hand on the back of my neck as we walked. I don't know what it is about the man, but there's an energy that radiates from his strong, rough hands. When I used to work out with him in my lower blackbelt classes, I could feel the energy hit me before his hand connected. The chi is strong with him.

Master Parker sat in his big office chair behind his desk. I stood at the doorway.

"Sit," he said.

"I stink, Master."

"Jon, take a big whiff."

He was right. The whole dojo had the faint aroma of body odor and sweat. With that, I wiped my head and face with my hand towel and sat down.

He just looked at me for several moments. I knew he was testing to see if I could handle the silence. It's a great interrogation technique. Silence is a knife—it cuts to the bone on most people, especially the guilty. I started playing with my fingernails and noticed I had a tiny hangnail on the edge of my right pinkie. I tried to bite it off.

"How's your mom?" he said.

Point, Parker!

"I guess she's all right. I haven't spoken to her in a few days."

I knew what was coming. "I know that. She called me today."

"How did she know I'd be coming to the dojo? I didn't even know I was coming today."

"Mother-sense. They all have it. Give her a call."

Master Parker has been a great friend to my family for many years. I know my mother truly appreciated how his training and guidance helped me become a better man, a better human. My old man, on the other hand—I'm not sure those things were important to him. He did trust Tatum Parker, however. Otherwise, he never would have named him trustee. That was something, I guess.

Master Parker was also there for my family during challenging times. When the old man died, Tatum and his wife June brought food and comfort to my mom, Jenny, and me. Mom and Jenny really needed it. I actually found more comfort working out at the dojo in the early days after his death.

Dad and I had a confrontational relationship from the beginning, and it went downhill from there. He loved and respected the law so much that I believe he could never understand how his son could not. I understood the concept of the law—the concept is superior. However, after practicing for several years, I came to understand that there are vast differences between concept and reality. Like most things in life, reality bites.

I left the dojo around 7:40. About ten minutes into my drive, I got a call from Karl. He said he'd have his preliminary report on Chesnokov completed that evening.

"Great work, Karl. When can I see a copy?"

"Why don't we grab some dinner tonight? I can give it to you then."

I hate eating dinner after seven o'clock. It always makes my GERD worse. Also, Karl's the kind of guy who'll invite you to dinner and conveniently forget his wallet.

"Can't I just swing by and get a copy?"

Silence. Well, I guess I owe him dinner... NOT!

"Okay, Karl. Where and when?"

"Meet me at Izzy's. Where are you now?"

I was coming up on the 10 interchange from the 110 South and told Karl so.

"I'll see you there between 8:30 and 8:45," and with that, Karl hung up.

Izzy's is a great place—one of my favorites. Locals in Santa Monica are frequent patrons, and I have fond memories of matzo ball soup and corned beef sandwiches with my mother and sister. It opened in 1973 and serves great deli food twenty-four hours a day. It's also been used as a location in many Hollywood movies and television episodes.

I arrived at Izzy's at 8:35 and parked the Carrera in the lot around the back. Walking into the restaurant, I passed the long counter housing cakes, pies, cookies, hamantaschen, various salads, and cold cuts. I moved to the left of the counter to see if Karl was already there. He wasn't.

The fifty-something waitress, who I guessed had worked there since the beginning, asked, "How many?"

I held up two fingers. She took two menus from the hostess stand and said with a snort, "Follow me."

Ms. Friendly seated me in a two-top booth by the window and dropped the menus on my side of the table. I sat down and opened one of the menus—not that I needed to look it over. I just like to peruse. I always have my usual at Izzy's: hot corned beef on rye, a bowl of matzo ball soup, and a big silver dish of pickles and pickled green tomatoes. Boring? Maybe, but delicious.

Just as I reached the last page of the menu, Karl walked in. He looked disheveled: sports coat askew, one black sock, one navy sock, and his saddle brown messenger bag—which he hated when I called a "murse"—was slung over his left shoulder at an odd angle.

He saw me from the hostess station, gave me a nod, and walked over to the booth. He removed his murse, tossed it into the booth opposite me, and slid in after it.

"Not even a smile hello?" I said.

Karl grunted his mirth. He reached into his bag, removed a two-inch-thick dossier on Chesnokov, and plopped it in front of me. Karl then picked up and perused his menu.

I opened the dossier. Chesnokov was running one of the top ten methamphetamine syndicates in the country. By all accounts, he had operations in at least seven states, mostly in the Southwest and South.

That made sense due to the proximity to Mexico—easy to transfer raw materials and finished product across the border with little interference. Genius.

His money laundering operation was even more sophisticated. Kiril had acquired multiple cash-based businesses over the past ten years: convenience stores, laundromats, bakeries, restaurants, and carwashes. Every one would allow the cash proceeds from the meth operation to disappear. All he needed to do was co-mingle the drug cash with legitimate receipts from each business, and it would be virtually undetectable.

Furthermore, he also used old and new money laundering vectors. Chesnokov was heavily invested in Bitcoin, using it in every business, legitimate and illegitimate. Karl's research couldn't ascertain exactly how much Bitcoin Chesnokov had amassed—secrecy and anonymity are part of its allure—but conservative estimates were in the low ten figures. That's between one and nine billion, with a B, dollars in Bitcoin alone.

He also made use of very ancient informal value transfer systems, or IVTS. These systems have been used for thousands of years in China, India, and the Middle East as a way for villages to keep track of money owed and remit payment. Because these systems are based in foreign countries, they're more difficult for the Feds to monitor accurately.

I had to hand it to the guy—Kiril Chesnokov was smart. Don't get me wrong, he's a dirty bastard criminal piece of shit, but he runs his business like a businessman, not like your average criminal moron. He'd set it up to minimize risk, and there's a ton of risk in the drug trade, both financial and mortal. He also had the mortal risks in check.

Chesnokov's army, as Karl called it in the report, consisted of multiple sub-bosses, captains, and enforcers from some of Russia's most infamous criminal enterprises: Dolgopruadnanskaya, Orekhovskaya, Solntsevskaya Bratva, and Izmaylovskaya. This group of miscreants not only had street credibility—most had lived through multiple sentences in some of Mother Russia's most infamous penitentiaries—but they also had access to post-Cold War Soviet military hardware: flamethrowers, rocket-propelled grenade launchers, as well as thousands if not tens of thousands of Kalashnikovs.

This was not going to be easy.

I heard the waitress say, "Are you guys ready to order?"

Karl ordered Judith's Mish Mash Soup and a half tongue sandwich on rye. Animal! The Mish Mash soup is good—chicken soup with egg noodles, rice, matzo ball, and kreplach, which is Jewish ravioli. But I don't abide tongue as sandwich meat. I'm not sure why. Maybe because I was raised a WASP, or maybe because the thought of eating something the animal used to eat with makes me want to puke.

I closed the dossier. Karl said, "Well, what do you think?"

"I think I'm fucked, that's what I think."

Karl ran his left hand over his nose, mouth, and chin. This was one of his "tells," and it meant what was coming next would include some deception.

"You just need to be careful. These Russian mob types are pure sociopaths. They have no empathy. They'd just as soon shoot you in the face as shake your hand."

"Thanks, Karl. You really should work on your cheerleading skills."

I told Karl about the incident at Whole Foods, how someone tried to run down Elsa, how I saved her life—Karl put both hands over his face for that tidbit—and how I'd blown my cover with my target. After he absorbed the gravity of my stupidity, he reminded me how becoming involved with a surveilled target can be extremely dangerous.

As much as we all hate to admit it, once we become intertwined in someone else's life, we form an emotional bond. It can be slight or serious. We generally don't appreciate the significance while we're connected. It's after some sort of disaster when we come to understand the error of our ways. And my stupid reflexes had dropped me right into this great big pile of shit.

"What do you suggest now that I've screwed up the surveillance?"

"As I see it, you have two options. Have Maggie continue the surveillance of Ms. Krieger or come clean with Elsa and deal with her reaction." Neither option appealed to me, and I told Karl so. Passing responsibility for Elsa's surveillance to Maggie meant I'd need to take over surveillance of Chesnokov, which would greatly increase the likelihood of a confrontation.

I know—I need better control of my emotional outbursts. My therapist calls it Intermittent Explosive Disorder. I call it just desserts. When I see a wretched piece of crap like Chesnokov getting away with the shenanigans he does, it makes my blood boil. This quirk of mine could cause significant complications if I was watching Kiril on a daily basis.

Coming clean with Elsa was equally unappealing. First, because I had no idea what her reaction would be. Second, no matter what reaction she had, my ability to clandestinely observe her movements would be hampered. Finally, it would hamper my recovery efforts. This last one was the biggie for me.

Our food arrived. If you've never been to Izzy's, or any Jewish-American deli for that matter, the sandwiches are huge. Karl immediately split the heaping pile of boiled beef tongue into two piles on his plate, squirted brown mustard on each pile, and added additional rye bread from the basket placed on our table earlier by Ms. Friendly. He picked up one of the divided sandwiches—now normal sandwich size, meaning Karl wouldn't have to dislocate his jaw to eat it—and took a big bite of the tongue, smiling.

"Why can't you order corned beef like a normal person, Karl?"

He just lifted both eyebrows and continued enjoying his food.

Karl and I finished our meal, I paid the check—Karl is great at mooching—said our goodbyes and left. I got back to the Coach at 10:15, took a quick shower, got ready for bed, and called Maggie. I got her voicemail, as usual.

"Mags, it's Bolt. Can you meet for breakfast in the morning? Call or text either way. Ciao."

I knew I wouldn't hear back from Maggie until morning, so I hit my rack and was fast asleep in five minutes.

At 3 a.m., I was awakened by a loud bang outside the coach. Training kicks in at times like this. I grabbed my Glock off the nightstand, sprinted to the front of the coach, and looked out the window to see what was happening.

There was a small group of young guys milling around one of the vacant RV parking spots about six spaces away from me. I couldn't hear everything being said, but I did pick up, "Man, fuck you, dude! I think you broke my hand." Then laughter, a right hook, and both guys fell to the ground to grapple.

Since I didn't see any firearms or other deadly weapons, I went back to my bunk. They'd burn off the alcohol or drugs in a few hours anyway, and I couldn't afford to risk any injuries trying to corral these idiots.

Before I went back to sleep, I checked my phone. Maggie replied by text. Her response was simple: Where? Brevity is the soul of... bitch. I loved Mags for that. I didn't text her back in case she was asleep. I made a mental note to text her after five.

At 5:15, I heard seagulls in the background, most likely scrounging for discarded food from the trash cans on the beach. Sanitation was supposed to empty beach trash cans nightly, but I'd say they make it to Dockweiler about every other or every third evening, unless the main office receives a complaint.

I texted Maggie to meet me at Du-Par's in the Farmers Market at nine and started the coffee pot. I don't know about you, but I'm funny about coffee. I love the taste of a good cup, but sometimes I feel like the morning joe is just habit. Do I need it, or do I think I need it? Who really cares? Not me. All I know is I want it.

When the coffee finished brewing, I poured myself a big sixteen-ouncer and added two sugars and cream. One of my FIDA buddies,

Chino Velasquez, grew up in the Bronx. Chino calls coffee with two sugars and cream "coffee, regular." It's a New York thing, but I'm sticking with it.

I took my cup and iPad outside the coach, sat in a Tommy Bahama beach chair I kept set up under the awning, and watched the sun come up as I perused the news. Sunrises on the West Coast are different from those on the East. I still enjoy watching the light traverse the Pacific horizon even though the sun is behind me. It gives me hope for a new day. Sappy? Sure, but a little sap never hurts anyone.

I finished up at about six and was feeling restless. I was spending too much time thinking about Chesnokov, Maggie, and me. I decided to head out toward the Farmers Market early. There's an L.A. Fitness gym near Fairfax on Wilshire. I'd get in a workout, shower, then meet Maggie for breakfast.

I put on my workout clothes: shorts, t-shirt, and sneakers. I'm not a metro, so when I work out at the gym, it's just the basics. I couldn't give two shits how I look working out. Not a very L.A. attitude, but tough.

I grabbed a change of clothes, towel, and deodorant and threw them into my gym bag. I also grabbed my Smart Carry holster and my Glock 19 and tossed them in.

The Smart Carry wraps around my waist with Velcro adjustments on the straps. The holster hangs in front, covering my genitals. In my experience, it takes a very secure-in-his-masculinity dude to frisk another man over his junk. Between the legs all the way up to the balls, yes, but actually patting down a guy's Johnson? Not happening.

I tossed the gym bag in the passenger seat of the Carrera and headed out. Traffic at that time of morning is usually pretty good and today was no exception. I exited the 405 north at La Cienega out of habit and still made it to Fairfax and Wilshire in thirty minutes.

I made a right on Ogden, then a left on Genesee. As luck would have it, there was a meter available just across from the parking garage for the gym. Saved me from having to play the "lost ticket" game when I was done working out.

You see, I'm not a member of L.A. Fitness or any other fitness club. I just get a day pass for free. Every club will do that—they hope to entice you with their facilities so you'll agree to pay a monthly fee for the rest of your life. Not me, baby. Free is a whole lot better.

I finished my workout, showered, holstered my Glock, dressed, and headed over to Du-Par's. First off, I love Du-Par's. The Farmers Market restaurant opened in 1938 and has been in operation since then, as far as I know. Second, if you like pancakes, you'll have a hell of a time finding better ones anywhere. At Du-Par's, pancakes are hotcakes, but six of one, half dozen of another. Fluffy, light, and chewy, they serve them with butter and your choice of boysenberry or hot maple syrup.

I know carbs are out, but the way I look at it is this: if a city bus is bearing down on me and my mortality is certain, my last thought will not be, "Boy, I'm glad I skipped that full stack of Du-Par's hotcakes!"

The only downside of going to Du-Par's is the parking during peak hours. The lot surrounding the restaurant is limited and cramped, but meeting at nine in the morning should be all right. The place is open twenty-four hours, so I guess Maggie and I could have scheduled our meeting for anytime, but I also know Maggie is not an "early riser." During FIDA training, she was ordered to complete extra calisthenics for being tardy. It happened so often that I sort of believe she just loves working out. Fit as hell, she is.

I pulled up to the parking kiosk at ten minutes before nine, got my parking ticket from the attendant, and found a spot right near the restaurant entrance. Lo and behold, Maggie was already there waiting at the entrance. She was dressed in black Lululemon pants, a matching black tee-shirt, and her red leather jacket. Her red hair was pulled back in a ponytail, and she was wearing dark Wayfarers and MAC Ruby Woo lipstick. I was in trouble.

"I guess you weren't in the mood for a hazing, Mags," I said.

"Shut up, old man. You're lucky I'm here at all. Nine fucking o'clock in the morning? What do you think I am?"

"Human?" I said.

She triple-flipped me off for that one but gave me a big hug and a smile at the door. I smelled the slight aroma of hours-old whiskey oozing from her pores.

"Rough night?" I said.

She punched me in the stomach and walked into Du-Par's.

I held up two fingers when the hostess asked, "How many?" and pointed to a booth by the window. The hostess, whose name tag read "Rita," looked to be about forty-five with plenty of miles ridden over that time. Her bleached blonde hair was pulled up into a bun on top of her head, and she had gray-green eyes nearly hidden behind oversized, blue-framed spectacles.

Rita stopped us at the booth, threw down two menus and an additional "breakfast specials" card. "Coffee?" she said. I held up the same two fingers I'd shown her moments before, and she left.

Maggie was slumping slightly across from me, still wearing her sunglasses. By the way she was positioned in the seat, I could tell Maggie was hurting. Not physically injured, but I surmised she'd partaken in some serious partying in the past twenty-four hours. I held up my hand to flag down a member of the wait staff so I could get her a big glass of water.

While waiting for our coffee and Maggie's ice water, I sat across from her wondering who would speak first. This was quite out of character for Maggie. She has a genuinely bubbly personality and is not at a loss for words. She's not a motormouth by any stretch, but she can hold her own in conversation.

The waiter brought two cups of steaming hot coffee, a small pewter pitcher of cream, and a large glass of ice water. He placed the coffee cups in front of each of us, then paused a moment before setting the ice water and a wrapped straw on the table in front of Maggie. Even a total stranger understood she needed hydration.

Maggie looked up at the waiter through her dark Wayfarers as if to say, "I didn't order this, asshole!"

"You need water," I said. "You're welcome."

She wrinkled her nose and canted her head slightly to the right, unwrapped the straw, slid it into the water glass, and drank some.

"Do you need any Advil or something?"

Maggie reached into her right jacket pocket and retrieved two blue-green gel caps. She popped them both in her mouth and sucked up enough water to swallow them.

She was still sitting across from me with her sunglasses on, so I reached over and removed them.

"What the fuck, Jon?"

"We need to talk, and I hate talking to a pair of cheap sunglasses."

"They're not cheap, you moron. Set me back over a hundred. Now give them back."

I handed them to her, but when she attempted to put them back on, I held up my right index and middle fingers joined together. She folded them and slipped them into her right jacket pocket.

"I'm going to need to switch surveillance targets with you," I said.

"Why's that?"

There was no other way to say it. "I fucked up."

Maggie smiled for the first time since she'd flipped me off at the Du-Par's entrance. "Do tell," she said.

I gave her the complete rundown. I told her about surveilling Elsa's apartment, the conversation with the manager, Elsa's downstairs neighbor, and how Chesnokov had visited her.

"You didn't engage with him then, did you?" Maggie said.

"Nope, but I had some interactions with members of his crew."

Maggie shook her head from side to side. "Living on the edge," she said.

I continued updating Maggie about my surveillance all the way up to the point when I saved Elsa Krieger's life. That tidbit drew an incredulous look from Maggie.

"Nice job, Jon. So, you screw the pooch, and I have to pay the ticket?"

"That's it in a nutshell, Mags. It sucks."

"It sucks donkey, Jon. I despise Krieger. Is there any other way?"

"Karl's done with fieldwork, and there's no one else I trust enough to take over. And there's no time to train anyone. When we're done with this, I'll recruit someone else as backup, but right now it's you, princess."

"I don't want to watch the bitch."

"I'm sorry I screwed up, Mags, but we have no choice here. My cover is blown with her."

"Yeah, but it's blown with Kiril's men too. What about that?"

It was a good point. "I believe it's less risky than me continuing to follow Elsa. I can handle the two chumps I interfaced with. Just do what I ask, okay?"

Maggie was clearly unhappy and anxious about the turn of events, but what was she going to do? That's one of the reasons I always have her on the team—she's a true team player.

Our waitress came over and took our order. Of course, I ordered the hotcakes. Over breakfast, Maggie caught me up on her reconnaissance of Chesnokov. Her information confirmed most of what Karl had uncovered. Chesnokov's group is highly involved in drug trafficking, fraud, identity theft, money laundering, illegal gambling, kidnapping, racketeering, robbery, extortion, and murder. Maggie presented the last beauty thusly: "Oh, and murder. Kiril has zero compunctions about taking a life." I placed my hand between my legs and patted my Austrian friend at that.

We finished eating, drinking coffee, and engaged in a little small talk. Maggie really isn't good at small talk.

"Dating anyone special?" I said.

"Screwing, yes, but I wouldn't say dating."

"Well, as long as you're happy, Mags."

"Who said I'm happy? I'm just passing the time between cases."

"All right. Maybe you should settle down, raise a family?"

"Maybe you should blow me."

I gave her a big hug as we walked out of Du-Par's. She did return the hug, so I knew she wasn't pissed. "Talk soon, Mags." She flipped me off one last time, but she also smiled as she spun around to leave. I got into the Carrera and figured since I was so close to Melrose, I'd drop by Chesnokov's place just to observe the day-to-day operations.

CHAPTER 13

KING CASH

The drive to Melrose took twenty minutes in morning traffic. Chesnokov's headquarters occupied the ground floor of a two-story building sandwiched between a vintage clothing store and a yoga studio. The juxtaposition was almost comical—enlightenment and criminality separated by thin walls and good intentions.

I parked my Porsche 911 across the street, positioned so I could see the front entrance while remaining inconspicuous among the other cars lining the busy street. The morning crowd provided perfect cover: joggers, dog walkers, people heading to work with their eyes glued to their phones.

At ten-fifteen, a black Mercedes S-Class pulled up in front of the building. Two men got out first—thick-necked, wearing suits that barely contained their bulk. They looked like they'd been ordered from the same catalog: Eastern European Intimidation, size extra-large. They scanned the street with professional paranoia before one of them opened the rear door.

Kiril Chesnokov emerged like a shark surfacing from dark water. Even from across the street, I could see the predatory grace in his movements. Even though I had seen him at Elsa's place a few days before, in the full light of day he looked younger than I'd expected, maybe fifty, with silver at his temples and the kind of expensive haircut that costs more than most people's rent. His suit was tailored, his shoes Italian leather, his watch probably worth more than my car. He disappeared into the building, followed by his bodyguards. I settled back to wait.

Surveillance is ninety percent boredom and ten percent terror. The boredom part involves sitting in uncomfortable positions for hours, drinking lukewarm coffee, and trying not to think about how badly you need to use the bathroom. The terror part comes when something happens.

For the next two hours, I watched a steady stream of people enter and exit the building. Most were young men, late twenties to early thirties, with the lean, hungry look of soldiers awaiting orders. They came and went in groups of two or three, never staying long enough to suggest actual business meetings. More like check-ins. Status reports. The kind of brief encounters that keep a criminal organization running smoothly.

At twelve-thirty, Chesnokov emerged with four of his men. They stood on the sidewalk in a tight circle, voices low, gestures sharp. I couldn't hear what they were saying, but body language is a universal tongue. Someone was getting instructions. Someone else was asking questions. Chesnokov was clearly in charge, his presence commanding even from a distance.

The conversation ended abruptly. Three of the men headed back inside while Chesnokov and one bodyguard walked to the Mercedes. The engine started with a purr that spoke of German engineering and illegal profits.

I waited until they'd pulled into traffic before starting my own engine. Following someone in Los Angeles requires patience and luck in equal measure. The traffic provides cover, but it also means you can lose your target at any red light. The key is staying close enough to maintain visual contact while remaining far enough back to avoid detection.

The Mercedes headed east on Melrose, then north on Highland. We were moving toward the valley, away from the glittering surface of West Hollywood and into the grittier industrial neighborhoods where real business gets done.

Twenty minutes later, we were in North Hollywood, winding through streets lined with warehouses and manufacturing plants. The Mercedes turned into an industrial complex, a collection of beige buildings surrounded by chain-link fence topped with razor wire. A sign by the entrance read "NoHo Industrial Center" in faded letters.

I drove past the entrance, watching as the Mercedes disappeared around a corner inside the complex. A block away, I found a parking spot with a clear view of the gate. This was going to be more complicated. I couldn't follow them inside without being spotted, and surveillance from the street would be limited.

I sat in my car for ten minutes, weighing my options. The smart play was to wait for them to come out, then continue the tail. But smart plays don't always yield results, and I was running out of time. Every day that passed was another day for trails to go cold, for evidence to disappear, for people to die. The decision made itself. I got out of the car.

The chain-link fence was eight feet high, but there was a section near the back of the complex where the razor wire had been damaged, probably by weather or vandalism. It wouldn't be comfortable, but it was passable. I've been in worse situations.

Getting over the fence took longer than I'd hoped. My jacket snagged on the wire, and I landed harder than I'd intended, my knee protesting the impact. But I was inside, crouched behind a dumpster, listening for any sign that I'd been detected.

The complex was quiet except for the distant hum of machinery and the occasional rumble of traffic from the street. I moved carefully, keeping to the shadows between buildings, until I found the Mercedes parked outside a warehouse in the center of the complex.

Before approaching the building, I took a moment to plant a GPS tracker on Chesnokov's car. The device was no bigger than a matchbox, magnetic backing strong enough to hold it securely to the undercarriage. If I lost visual contact, at least I'd be able to track his movements electronically.

The warehouse was a standard industrial building, flat roof, concrete walls, minimal windows. I worked my way around the perimeter until I found what I was looking for: a window about halfway along the south wall, positioned high enough to provide a view inside but low enough for me to reach.

From my jacket pocket, I retrieved a device that looked like a small telescope but was actually something much more useful: a slide-rule periscope. It allowed me to look around corners and through windows without exposing myself to detection. In my line of work, staying invisible often means staying alive.

I extended the periscope to its full length and carefully positioned it at the bottom corner of the window. The view inside made my blood run cold.

The warehouse had been converted into a money-counting operation. Long tables filled the center of the space, covered with stacks of cash in various denominations. Men in suits moved between the tables with the mechanical efficiency of bank tellers, counting, sorting, and bundling bills. The amount of money was staggering—millions of dollars in small bills, the kind that comes from street-level drug sales and other cash businesses.

I counted at least eight men working at the tables, with several others standing guard near the entrances. This wasn't some small-time money laundering operation. This was industrial-scale financial crime, the kind that required connections to legitimate banks and businesses to clean this much dirty money.

As I watched, a door at the far end of the warehouse opened, and Chesnokov entered with another man. Even through the periscope, I could see the tension in their postures. They were arguing, their voices carrying across the warehouse space.

They were speaking Russian, and while my command of the language was limited to basic phrases learned during a brief stint in Eastern Europe years ago, I could pick up fragments of their conversation. They were discussing quantities, schedules, and what sounded like concerns about security. Then I heard a name that made my heart race: "Krieger."

The name was unmistakable, even with a Russian accent. They were talking about Elsa. But in what context? Was she a customer? A threat? A business partner?

I adjusted the periscope, trying to get a better view of the second man's face. He was shorter than Chesnokov, maybe sixty years old, with thinning hair and the soft features of someone who'd spent more time behind a desk than on the street. His suit was expensive but ill-fitting, the uniform of new money trying to buy respectability.

Their argument was escalating. Chesnokov's gestures became more animated, his voice rising above the general noise of the counting operation. The other man seemed to be pleading, his hands spread in a gesture of supplication.

Suddenly, Chesnokov grabbed the man by the lapels and said something that made every worker in the warehouse freeze. Even without understanding the words, the threat was clear. The man nodded frantically, his face pale with fear.

The confrontation ended as quickly as it had begun. Chesnokov released the man and walked back toward the entrance, his bodyguard falling into step behind him. The counting operation resumed its mechanical rhythm, but the tension in the air remained palpable.

I had to move. If Chesnokov was leaving, I needed to be back at my car before his Mercedes reached the gate. I collapsed the periscope and began working my way back through the shadows, my mind racing with the implications of what I'd seen.

The money laundering operation explained a lot about Chesnokov's resources and influence. If he was cleaning this much cash, he had connections to legitimate financial institutions and the kind of money that could buy protection, silence, and death in equal measure.

But what was Elsa's connection to all this? The mention of her name in that context suggested she was more than just a peripheral figure in whatever game was being played. She was central to it, important enough to argue about in the middle of a major financial crime.

Getting back over the fence was easier than getting in, gravity being a reliable assistant in such matters. I reached my car just as the Mercedes was pulling out of the industrial complex. I started the engine and settled in for the next phase of what was becoming a very long day.

The Mercedes headed east on the 101, back toward the city, but instead of returning to Melrose, it continued to the 110 south. I followed four cars back as we moved through the afternoon traffic. When he exited the 110 onto the 105 west, I assumed we were heading to the beach.

We ended up in Redondo Beach, specifically at the Red Bull Lounge, a high-end bar and restaurant that catered to the kind of people who considered hundred-dollar meals a casual expense. I'd been there once before, tracking a cheating husband who'd been meeting his mistress. The place was all dark wood and ambient lighting, designed to create an atmosphere of discrete luxury. It was the perfect spot for conversations that couldn't happen in public.

I parked in the lot across the street and watched as Chesnokov and his bodyguard entered the restaurant. Through the large windows, I could see them being seated at a corner table, positioned to provide a clear view of the room while maintaining privacy.

That's when I saw her.

Tricia Goldstein was sitting at the bar, nursing what looked like a martini. She was dressed casually—jeans, silk blouse, expensive handbag—but her posture suggested she was anything but relaxed. She kept checking her watch and glancing toward the entrance.

The pieces of the puzzle were starting to come together, but the picture they formed was more complex than I'd imagined. Tricia was connected to Chesnokov, which meant she was connected to the money laundering operation. But how did that fit with her role in the Krieger case?

A black Range Rover pulled into the parking lot in front of the Red Bull and pulled parallel to the curb in front of the building. A tall brunette woman wearing sunglasses and a very haute couture outfit got out and walked into the building. I saw through the window that Trisha clearly knew this woman because a big smile grew on her face as the two hugged hello. The woman kissed both of Trisha's cheeks as well. They spoke animatedly for a few minutes and then the woman left. She got back into the Range Rover and quickly exited the lot. As she drove past me on Pacific Coast, I was able to take down the license number: 1ZARINA.

My phone buzzed. A text from Maggie: "Elsa shopping in Manhattan Beach. Nordstrom. Thought you should know."

Manhattan Beach was only fifteen minutes away. If I left now, I could intercept Elsa before she finished her shopping trip. It would mean abandoning surveillance on Chesnokov, but the opportunity to confront Elsa directly was too valuable to pass up. I could follow up on Chesnokov, Trish, and Zarina soon enough.

I made the decision quickly, the way you must in this business. Sometimes you have to choose between following a lead and creating one. I started the car and headed for Manhattan Beach.

Nordstrom in Manhattan Beach was busy with the kind of afternoon shoppers who had both time and money to spend. I found a parking spot near the entrance and went inside, scanning the crowd for Elsa's distinctive blonde hair.

I found her in the women's clothing section, examining a rack of designer dresses. She was alone, which surprised me. Someone with her apparent resources and paranoia should have had security or at least been more careful about her public appearance. Unless she wanted to be found.

I approached casually, picking up a men's shirt from a nearby rack pretending to examine it. She was only twenty feet away, close enough for me to see the concentration on her face as she selected items to try on. She was beautiful in the way that expensive maintenance can make anyone beautiful—perfect skin, perfect hair, perfect teeth. But there was something else, a hardness around her eyes that spoke of experiences that couldn't be bought or sold.

I moved closer, timing my approach to seem coincidental. When she turned toward the fitting rooms, I was there, just another shopper navigating the crowded store.

"Excuse me," I said, as if I'd just noticed her. "Aren't you Elsa Krieger?"

She froze, her eyes met mine. For a moment, confusion flickered across her features, then recognition dawned. Her expression shifted through several emotions—surprise, relief, and then something that looked like hope.

"Jon?" she said, using the name I'd given her after the parking lot incident. "Jon Steele?"

I had to think fast. The adrenaline from that day had kept me from thinking straight, but now I needed to be honest if I wanted her trust.

"My real name is Bolt," I said. "Jon Bolt. I think we need to talk."

Her eyes narrowed, studying my face as if trying to read my intentions. "So, Jon Steele was a lie? Just like the phone number that went to a pizza place in Hermosa Beach?"

I couldn't help but wince. I'd forgotten about that detail. "I can explain."

"Can you? Because I called that number, wanting to thank the man who saved my life. Instead, I got Brooklyn Pizza asking if I wanted to order a large pepperoni." She glanced around the store, probably looking for escape routes or potential threats. "I don't think we have anything to discuss."

"I did save your life," I said. "I'm only kind of a heel. Can we agree on that at least?"

The question hung between us like a challenge. Other shoppers moved around us, oblivious to the drama playing out in their midst. To them, we were just two people having a conversation. They couldn't see the undercurrents of danger and deception, or the complicated history between a woman and the man who'd saved her life while betraying her trust.

"What do you want?" she asked finally.

"The truth. About Chesnokov, about the twelve million dollars you stole from Senator Goldstein."

Her face went pale. "How do you—"

"I know more than you think. I know you've been using Chesnokov to launder the money, and I know he's decided you're more trouble than you're worth."

She was quiet for a long moment, studying my face as if trying to decide whether to trust me. When she spoke, her voice was barely above a whisper.

"You have no idea what you've gotten yourself into," she said.

"Then enlighten me."

"Not here. Too many people." She glanced around again, then made her decision. "There's a coffee shop on Manhattan Beach Boulevard. Café Luna. Meet me there in an hour."

"How do I know you'll show up?"

A sad smile crossed her face. "Because Mr. Bolt, I'm tired of running. And after what happened in that parking lot, I think you're the only person who might be able to help me."

She turned and walked away, leaving me standing among the racks of designer clothing with more questions than answers. But for the first time since this case began, I felt like I was getting closer to the truth.

I watched her leave the store, then followed at a distance. She got into her Buick and drove away, but I didn't try to follow. If she was going to meet me at the café, I needed to use the next hour to prepare.

I found a quiet corner of the store and called Maggie.

"How did it go?" she asked without preamble.

"She's going to meet me. But Maggie, this is bigger than we thought. Chesnokov is running a major money laundering operation, and Elsa is one of his clients."

"How much money are we talking about?"

"Much more than the twelve million she stole from Senator Goldstein. Chesnokov is cleaning all of it."

"Jesus. You just can't trust anyone anymore?"

"I need you to do something for me. Run a deeper background check on Tricia Goldstein. I saw her meeting with Chesnokov at the Red Bull Lounge."

"Tricia? The senator's daughter?"

"The same. I'm starting to think she's not the innocent victim she pretended to be."

"I'll get on it. But Bolt, be careful. If Elsa is connected to Chesnokov's operation, meeting her could be walking into a trap."

"I know. But it's a risk I have to take."

"Want me to provide backup?"

"No. If she sees anyone else, she'll run. I need to do this alone."

"I don't like it."

"Neither do I. But sometimes you have to play with the hand you're dealt."

I hung up and left the store, my mind racing with possibilities. The next hour would either provide the breakthrough I needed or get me killed. In my experience, those were often the same thing.

Café Luna was a small, intimate place with outdoor seating and the kind of relaxed atmosphere that encouraged conversation. I arrived early and chose a table with a clear view of the street and multiple exit routes. Old habits die hard, especially when they're the reason you're still alive.

Elsa arrived exactly on time, which told me something about her character. She was someone who kept her word, even when it might not be in her best interest. She'd changed clothes—now wearing a simple black dress and sunglasses despite the late afternoon overcast—and moved with the careful grace of someone who was used to being watched. She sat across from me without saying a word, her hands folded in her lap, waiting for me to begin.

"Thank you for coming," I said.

"I almost didn't." She removed her sunglasses, revealing eyes that were intelligent and infinitely sad. "But I realized I'm tired of being afraid."

"Afraid of what?"

"Of him. Of them. Of the consequences of what I did."

"Tell me about the money. Why did you steal it from Senator Goldstein?"

She was quiet for a moment, collecting her thoughts. When she spoke, her voice was steady but soft.

"I worked for the senator's campaign. I was her finance director, in charge of managing donations and expenditures. I discovered she was skimming money from campaign contributions—taking cash donations and funneling them into her personal accounts."

"So, you decided to steal it?"

"I confronted her about it. She said if I reported her, she'd destroy my career. She had the power to do it, too. So, I started taking the money she was stealing, thinking I was just... evening the score."

"Twelve million dollars is a lot of evening."

"It built up over time. Small amounts at first, then larger ones. I told myself I was just borrowing it, that I'd pay it back somehow. But then..."

"Then you realized you couldn't put it back without getting caught."

She nodded. "I needed to clean it, make it legitimate. That's when I found Chesnokov."

"How did you find him?"

"Through Tricia. She introduced us."

The pieces were falling into place. "Tricia is working with Chesnokov?"

"More than that. She's his inside connection to legitimate financial institutions. Her trust fund, her social connections—they provide cover for his money laundering operations."

I thought about how convoluted this whole mess was getting. Did you ever hear of a Mongolian Cluster Fuck? I was beginning to believe I was in the center square of one. "Why are you telling me all this now?" I said.

"Because I think he's planning to kill me. The money laundering operation is getting too much attention. The FBI is sniffing around Senator Goldstein's finances, and Chesnokov thinks I'm a liability."

"The attempt on your life in the parking lot?"

"A warning. Next time, he won't miss."

I studied her face, looking for any sign of deception. She seemed genuine, but in my experience, the best liars always did. Still, what she was telling me made sense of everything I'd observed.

"I saw the laundering operation. Do you know where Chesnokov keeps the cash after it has been cleaned?"

"I have an idea. Why?"

"Don't you want to give the money back to the senator, to make amends?" I needed this information. I couldn't break into the North Hollywood industrial yard and walk out with twelve million in cash.

She reached into her purse and pulled out a piece of paper. On it was written: 34.037939, -118.232233, 1247,SSH.

"This was written down by Yuri, one of Kiril's men. I copied it when he went to the bathroom. I think it's a code, coordinates to where the money is."

I studied the numbers. The first two were definitely GPS coordinates for somewhere in Los Angeles. The others could mean anything—a time, a date, an address.

"We need to check out those coordinates," I said.

"Together?"

"If you're willing to trust me."

She was quiet for a moment, then nodded. "I don't have much choice. And after what you did in that parking lot... I think I trust you."

"Why?"

"Because you're the first person who's bothered to look for the truth instead of just accepting what you were told."

I paid for our coffee, and we left the café together. As we walked to our cars, I couldn't shake the feeling that we were being watched. Every shadow seemed to hide a potential threat, every passerby a possible enemy.

"I'll follow you," I said. "If anything happens, if you see anything suspicious, call me immediately."

She handed me a piece of paper with her real phone number. "And Mr. Bolt? Thank you. For saving my life, and for believing me."

"Don't thank me yet. We still have to find the money."

"Do you think we can?"

"I think we're going to try. And sometimes that's enough."

We got into our respective cars and pulled out onto Manhattan Beach Boulevard. The coordinates on the paper would lead us somewhere in the city. Whether it would provide the answers we needed or lead us deeper into danger remained to be seen.

As I followed Elsa's Buick through the late afternoon traffic, I thought about the chain of events that had brought me to this point. A simple recovery case had evolved into something much more complex and dangerous. But that's the nature of truth—it's rarely simple, and it's never safe.

The GPS coordinates led us toward downtown Los Angeles, into the heart of the city where old buildings housed new secrets and the past refused to stay buried. I still wasn't sure what we were about to find out. I just hoped we'd live long enough to find it.

The setting sun painted the sky in shades of orange and red as we drove toward our destination. Behind us, I noticed a black SUV that had been following us since we left Manhattan Beach. Either we were already being hunted, or we were about to walk into the trap that would end this case one way or another.

In the rearview mirror, I could see the SUV maintaining a careful distance, professional in its surveillance. They were good, but not good enough to avoid detection by someone who'd spent years learning to spot a tail.

I reached for my phone to warn Elsa, then decided against it. If she was legitimate, she was probably already scared enough. If she was part of a trap, showing my hand wouldn't help.

The coordinates were taking us to an area of downtown, which I knew well—the Arts District, where old warehouses had been converted into lofts and galleries. It was the kind of neighborhood where someone could hide something and have it remain hidden indefinitely.

The warehouse sat at the end of a dead-end street, its brick facade weathered by decades of Los Angeles sun and smog. Graffiti covered the lower walls, but it was old graffiti, faded and layered like archaeological strata. The building looked abandoned, which in this neighborhood meant it was either genuinely empty or housing something that preferred to stay invisible.

Elsa parked first, and I pulled up beside her. The black SUV had disappeared three blocks back, but that didn't mean we weren't being watched. In fact, it probably meant we were being watched more carefully.

"This is it," Elsa said, checking the coordinates on her phone against the address painted in fading numbers above a steel door. The door hung slightly ajar, as if someone had left in a hurry and forgotten to secure their exit.

I drew my Glock and motioned for Elsa to stay behind me. The door opened with a rusty creak that echoed through the cavernous space beyond. Afternoon light filtered through grimy skylights, casting everything in a sepia tone that made the emptiness feel deliberate.

The warehouse was vast and hollow, our footsteps echoing off concrete floors and bare brick walls. But it wasn't the emptiness that caught my attention—it was what the emptiness revealed. Long tables had been arranged in precise rows, now cleared but leaving behind the geometric impressions in the dust where equipment had sat. Power cables snaked across the floor to outlets that had been recently installed, their copper still bright against the industrial gray.

"Money counting machines," I said, following one of the cable runs to where it terminated near a wall outlet. "Industrial grade, from the look of these power requirements."

Elsa knelt beside one of the dust outlines. "They were big machines. Professional operation." She pointed to smaller rectangular impressions nearby. "And these would be for currency strapping machines, bill sorters."

There were a few scattered receipts and other papers, spreadsheets mostly, scattered about. I picked up a few of them. Each one was either a bill of lading, a drop ship receipt, or some other evidence of business being conducted, however, most were difficult to read. It appeared someone attempted to conceal the information contained on each record.

The air still carried a faint chemical smell—the kind that comes from processing large quantities of cash, mixing the metallic scent of coins with the organic compounds in paper money and the ozone from electronic counting equipment. In one corner, I found a small pile of rubber bands, the kind banks use to bundle bills, and a few scattered plastic ties.

But it was the sophisticated ventilation system that really told the story. New ductwork had been installed, powerful enough to handle the heat and humidity generated by industrial money processing. This wasn't some small-time operation—this was the kind of setup that could handle millions of dollars in a single session.

"They cleared out recently," I observed, running my finger along a windowsill. The dust was thin, maybe a week's worth. "But they were here for months, maybe longer." I gestured toward the floor where heavy equipment had worn permanent impressions into the concrete.

Elsa stood near what had clearly been a staging area, where pallets had left their mark and a small forklift had carved tire tracks in a perpetual figure-eight pattern. "This was their distribution center. They'd process the cash here, then move it out in organized shipments."

The sophistication of the operation was impressive and disturbing. This wasn't amateur hour—whoever had run this warehouse understood both the technical and logistical challenges of large-scale money laundering. They'd had time to establish routines, refine their processes, and then vanish without leaving anything behind that could directly implicate them.

Except they had left something behind. They'd left the story written in dust and wear patterns, in electrical installations and chemical residue. And they'd left questions that were rapidly becoming more dangerous than answers.

"We need to leave," I said, holstering my weapon. The warehouse felt too exposed, too much like a stage set waiting for actors to return. "This place served its purpose, and now it's a liability. To them, and to us."

As we walked back toward our cars, I realized the black SUV's disappearance made more sense now. They didn't need to follow us anymore—they knew where we were going. The coordinates hadn't been a clue we'd discovered; they'd been an invitation we'd accepted.

"Bolt," Elsa said as we reached our vehicles, "I think we're in deeper than either of us realized."

I nodded, but my mind was already moving to the next steps. The warehouse had told us what we were dealing with—a professional organization with resources and planning capabilities that went far beyond what I'd initially assumed. That changed everything about how I needed to approach this case.

"I need to regroup and think this through," I told her. "Why don't you head home and stay low for a few days? I'll be in touch."

Elsa looked like she wanted to argue, but something in my expression must have convinced her this wasn't negotiable. She got into her Buick with a nod that managed to convey both understanding and frustration.

As she drove away, I pulled out my phone and dialed Maggie's number. She answered on the second ring.

"I need to see you," I said without preamble. "The Kettle in Manhattan Beach. Can you meet me in an hour?"

"That serious?" she asked.

"Serious enough that I need someone I trust to help me sort through what I just learned."

"I'll be there," she said, and I knew she would be.

I stood beside my car for a moment, looking back at the warehouse. Somewhere in this city, people were moving millions of dollars through a network sophisticated enough to require industrial-grade money processing equipment. They were professional enough to abandon expensive infrastructure rather than risk exposure and connected enough to know when private investigators were getting too close to their operations. We all know that cash is king, and Chesnokov's operation appeared to be flush with cash. The risk level had risen ten-fold; a simple recovery case had just put me directly in their path.

CHAPTER 14

WAR DOGS

The afternoon sun was already beating down on Manhattan Beach when I pulled into the parking lot of The Kettle, a retro diner that had been serving overpriced comfort food to tourists and locals since the 1980s. The chrome and neon exterior gleamed in the California light, a monument to artificial nostalgia that somehow managed to feel authentic in a city built on illusions.

Maggie was waiting for me in a corner booth, a cup of black coffee growing cold in front of her. She looked tired—the kind of bone-deep exhaustion that came from too much partying and too little sleep. I'd seen that look in the mirror plenty of times during my own rebel years.

"You look like hell," I said, sliding into the seat across from her.

"Fuck off." She managed a weak smile. "Some friends from college are back in town. It's been a non-stop jamboree for three days straight."

I signaled the waitress for coffee. "Glad to know you still have friends."

"You're such a dick." Maggie straightened up, her expression shifting from casual to business. "So, what's this about? Your message said it was urgent."

The waitress appeared with my coffee, and I waited until she was out of earshot before speaking. "I found an abandoned warehouse in the Arts District. It looked like a money laundering enterprise was being conducted there."

"A money laundering operation?" Maggie's voice dropped to barely above a whisper, her eyes scanning the diner to make sure we weren't being overheard.

"There were some empty pallets and the telltale signs of forklifts. It had to be a big operation. That's just the tip of the iceberg." I pulled out a small notebook and flipped to the pages where I'd documented everything I'd discovered. "I found evidence of a massive operation—shipping manifests, import documents, financial records scattered everywhere like someone left in a hurry."

Maggie leaned forward, her party girl fatigue replaced by the sharp focus I'd seen her use in dozens of dangerous situations. Despite her love of nightlife, she was one of the toughest investigators I knew. Her Kenpo black belt wasn't just for show, and neither was her instinct for recognizing when something was seriously wrong.

"What kind of evidence?" She reached for her own notebook, pen poised. "Give me specifics, Jon. I need to understand the scope here."

"Bank routing numbers, offshore account information, shell company registrations. But here's the thing—it was completely cleaned out. Professional job. Nothing left but dust and the smell of bleach."

"Someone tipped them off?"

"Had to be. The timing was too perfect. I'm talking about warehouses that were full of activity just days before, according to my surveillance notes. Then suddenly they're empty, like they never existed."

I showed her the photographs I'd taken with my phone—images of scattered paperwork, shipping containers with suspicious manifests, and finally, the sterile emptiness.

"Jesus, Jon. This is bigger than we thought." She studied each photo carefully, her expression growing more serious with each swipe. "Look at these container numbers. These are international shipping codes. This isn't just local distribution. They're moving product globally."

"That's what Elsa said."

"Elsa? Jon, what the fuck? Elsa was with you?"

I could see this detail had riled Maggie. I was getting a little upset as well because I knew I had screwed up. "Yes. Elsa was with me, and someone followed us."

"Dude, you're thinking with the little head. She's the rat. She's got to be trying to get you off track because isn't she the main one who benefits from the laundering?"

Mags was right. I needed to pull my head out of my ass. My chivalric side got the best of me again. Damn it! I needed to get back on track and remember Elsa is not the victim. She's the perp and she's in deep with Chesnokov.

"You're right, Mags. I am a dick. I'll do better."

"You better. This is not playtime. People can get killed, and I'm not looking for it to be either of us." She leaned back, studying my face. "Tell me everything that happened with Elsa. From the beginning. Don't leave anything out."

I took a long sip of my coffee, gathering my thoughts. "She contacted me, said she had information about the warehouse. Claimed she was scared, that Chesnokov was threatening her. The whole damsel in distress routine."

"And you bought it?"

"Hook, line, and sinker. She seemed genuinely frightened, Mags. The tears, the shaking hands—if she was acting, she deserves an Oscar."

"Or maybe she's just good at her job," Maggie said dryly. "What exactly did she tell you?"

"She said Chesnokov was using the warehouse for more than just drug distribution. That there were financial records, shipping manifests, evidence of money laundering. She offered to show me where it was."

"And you went with her? Alone?"

"I thought I could handle it. I thought—" I stopped, realizing how stupid it sounded even to me.

"You thought with your dick instead of your brain," Maggie finished. "What happened when you got there?"

"The place was cleaned out, but there was just enough evidence to corroborate Elsa's story. In hindsight, it was too perfect."

"Because she'd been there before. Because she helped set it up."

The realization hit me like a physical blow. "She was testing me. Seeing how much I knew, how close I was to the truth."

"And when you found the evidence?"

"She seemed surprised. Genuinely shocked that it was all cleaned out. But now that I think about it ..." I replayed the scene in my mind, looking for tells I'd missed. "She kept checking her phone. Said she was worried about Chesnokov finding out where she was."

"She was probably texting him updates."

I shook my head, took another sip of my coffee, and said, "It gets worse. There was some paperwork that I photographed. It showed connections to import-export operations from Eastern Europe. Specialty items, they called them. Art, antiques, luxury goods. All legitimate on the surface."

"Money laundering through high-end merchandise?"

"That's what it looked like. You buy expensive art with dirty money, sell it at auction for clean cash. Classic technique but scaled up to industrial levels. We're talking about hundreds of millions of dollars moving through these operations."

Maggie absorbed this information, her expression growing more serious. "Walk me through the financial records. What exactly did you see?"

I flipped through my notebook, finding the pages where I'd documented the key findings. "Multiple offshore accounts in the Cayman Islands, Cyprus, and Switzerland. Shell companies registered in Delaware, Nevada, and the British Virgin Islands. The paper trail showed money coming in from drug sales, then being converted into purchases of high-end art and antiques."

"How much money are we talking about?"

"Conservatively? Based on what I saw, they're laundering at least fifty million a year through just this one operation. And Maggie, there were references to other warehouses, other operations. This could be a billion-dollar enterprise."

"Jesus." Maggie leaned back in her seat. "And you think Elsa is managing this?"

"I think she's a key player. The paperwork showed payments to something called 'E.K. Consulting Services.' Want to bet what the 'EK' stands for?"

"How much was she getting paid?"

"According to the records I photographed, she pulled down two million. Not bad for a scared victim."

Maggie whistled low. "No wonder she was so eager to help you find the warehouse. She needed to know how much you'd figured out."

"And now she knows everything I know."

"Which means Chesnokov knows everything you know."

The weight of my mistake settled on me like a physical burden. I'd been played, manipulated by someone who was probably laughing about it right now. "I fucked up, Mags. Big time."

"Yeah, you did. But we can work with this. What else did you find?"

"There's something else," I continued. "I found evidence that they've been using the operation to fund more than just drug trafficking. Arms dealing, human trafficking, moving money for international criminal organizations. This isn't just a local operation—it's part of something global."

"How global?"

"Connections to organized crime families in Russia, cartel operations in Mexico, terrorist cells in the Middle East. Chesnokov isn't just a local drug dealer—he's running a hub for international criminal activity."

Maggie leaned forward, her voice dropping even lower. "What kind of connections? Be specific."

"I found shipping manifests showing arms shipments to Somalia, financial transfers to accounts linked to the Sinaloa cartel, and payment records for what looked like human trafficking operations in Eastern Europe."

"Holy shit, Jon. You're talking about a criminal network that spans continents."

"That's exactly what I'm talking about. And I walked right into their trap."

"What about the other people involved? Who else is on the payroll?"

I consulted my notes again. "There were payroll records for at least thirty people. Some I recognized—dock workers, customs officials, shipping inspectors. Others were just names and numbers. But the payments were significant. We're talking about systematic corruption at multiple levels of law enforcement and customs."

"Any federal agents?"

"That's what scares me. There were payments to someone with the initials 'J.M.' at what looked like a federal pay grade. If they have someone inside the FBI or DEA ..."

"Then taking this to the feds could be suicide."

"Exactly. Which is why I need to decide what to do next. Do I take what I have to the FBI and risk it disappearing into bureaucratic hell? Or do I keep digging and risk getting myself killed?"

"What about your client? Senator Goldstein? Are you thinking she's involved?"

"Tangentially, because it appears her daughter has some connection, but maybe only to the drug enterprise."

Maggie studied me carefully. "You don't sound convinced."

"I'm not. The more I dig into this, the more I realize that everyone has connections to everyone else. Goldstein's daughter is dating Jared Fitzpatrick, who may be connected to Chesnokov's drug operation. Elsa is connected to Chesnokov's money laundering. What are the odds that a U.S. Senator's daughter just happens to be dating someone connected to a billion-dollar criminal enterprise?"

"You think Goldstein knows?"

"I think she knows more than she's telling me. The question is whether she's a victim or a participant."

"What makes you think she might be involved?"

I took another long sip of coffee, organizing my thoughts. "The money I'm supposed to recover—twelve million in campaign funds. That's a lot of money to just disappear. And the way she hired me, it felt rushed. Like she needed someone to investigate quickly, before someone else could."

"Before someone else could what?"

"Find out where the money really went. What if the twelve million wasn't stolen? What if it was invested in Chesnokov's operation?"

"Are you talking about a sitting U.S. Senator investing in money laundering?"

"I don't think so, but what if Elsa was 'allowed' to take the twelve million in order to connect to the money laundering? It could look really good for the senator at election time. Helping to take down a huge crime syndicate. But maybe I'm just full of crap and the only connection is Trisha."

Maggie was quiet for a long moment, processing this information. "Then why would she be so eager to get the money back quickly and quietly?"

"Subterfuge?"

"And why doesn't she want law enforcement involved?"

"Probably so she gets the credit and not some L.A.P.D. stiff. Which means I'm not just hunting criminals. I'm hunting someone who is being hunted by my client. This caper is getting better and better."

The weight of the decision pressed down on me like a physical force. I'd started this investigation looking for twelve million dollars of stolen campaign funds. Now I was staring at evidence of a criminal empire that spanned continents and possibly involved my own client.

"You know what you have to do," Maggie said quietly.

"Yeah. I just don't know if I'm ready for the consequences."

"Since when has that stopped you?"

She was right. In twenty-three years with FIDA and three years as a private investigator, I'd never backed down from a case because it was dangerous. I wasn't about to start now.

"I'm going to need backup," I said. "This isn't something I can handle alone, and Karl is more out than in."

"You've got it. What do you need?"

"Additional surveillance on Chesnokov's known associates, financial analysis of the accounts I photographed, and someone watching my back in case they decide to eliminate the problem."

"I can handle the surveillance," Maggie said. "I've got contacts in the private security world who owe me favors. They can put eyes on Chesnokov's people without raising suspicions."

"What about the financial analysis?"

"I know a forensic accountant who specializes in money laundering cases. Former FBI, now private practice. He'll keep it quiet if I ask him to."

"And watching my back?"

"That's what partners are for." Her smile was sharp and predatory. "Besides, it's been too quiet lately. I could use some excitement."

"This isn't excitement, Maggie. This is war."

"Even better."

We spent the next hour going over the details of what I'd found, making plans for how to proceed, and discussing the risks we'd be taking. Maggie took detailed notes, asking probing questions about every aspect of the operation I'd uncovered.

"What about Elsa?" she asked as we prepared to wrap up. "How do you want to handle her?"

"I need to keep her thinking she's still got me fooled. If she believes I trust her, she might lead me to other parts of the operation."

"That's dangerous, Jon. If she figures out you're onto her ..."

"Then I'll deal with that when it happens. But right now, she's my best source of information about the operation."

"And if she tries to set you up again?"

"Then I'll be ready for it. This time, I won't go in blind."

By the time we finished, the afternoon sun was starting to sink toward the horizon, casting long shadows across the parking lot.

"One more thing," I said as we prepared to leave. "If something happens to me, make sure Senator Goldstein is updated. She wants her money back, but I don't want to put that on you."

"Nothing's going to happen to you. You're too stubborn to die."

"Famous last words."

"Not yours. Trust me."

I drove back toward the Playa with more questions than answers, but also with something I hadn't had before—a true partner I could trust and a plan for moving forward. The warehouse investigation had revealed the scope of Chesnokov's operation, even if it had also cost me the element of surprise.

The real work was just beginning. Elsa couldn't be trusted. Her life might be in danger, but if it became a question of her or me, she was toast. I just wanted to recover the money. The commission was too important. My phone rang as I merged onto the freeway. The caller ID showed Nancy Goldstein's number.

"Mr. Bolt? I would like an update on the Jared," her voice trailed off. "Situation."

"Hello, Senator, I hope you are having a fine day," I said.

"Please, Mr. Bolt, can we agree there is no need for pleasantries between us?" I made a mental note to never again work for a politician. Too narcissistic for my taste.

"Fine. I have it under control. I will have a further update by the end of the week."

"See that you do," she said and ended the call.

"G'Bye, Cunt." I said to the air.

After she hung up, I drove the rest of the way in silence, planning what I would say and how I would say it. Nancy Goldstein was rightfully concerned for her daughter and the connection to Jared Fitzpatrick, but what would she do when she discovered her "sweet" little girl was involved with an international criminal enterprise? She deserved to know that truth, but I wasn't certain how she would take it.

But first, I had to make sure I lived long enough to collect her money. The warehouse investigation had given me the evidence I needed, and I now understood Chesnokov's operation. Now I had to figure out how to use that evidence without getting myself killed in the process. Could I take down Chesnokov and his empire without sacrificing Elsa, Tricia, Maggie, or Karl? The adventure was about to enter a new phase. And this time, I wasn't going in alone.

I pulled into Dockweiler as the last light faded from the sky, carrying with me the weight of what I'd discovered and the responsibility for what came next. Somewhere in the city, Kiril Chesnokov was probably planning his next move, trying to figure out how much I knew and what I planned to do about it. He'd find out soon enough. But not before I was ready for him.

The case that had started with stolen campaign funds was about to become something much larger—a battle between justice and corruption, between truth and the kind of power that thought it could make money and people disappear without consequences. The war against Kiril Chesnokov's empire was about to begin. And I intended to win it.

CHAPTER 15

CRASH CART

The insurance adjuster arrived at nine sharp, clipboard in hand and suspicion etched into every line of his weathered face. I'd been up since six, arranging the coach's exterior to look as convincing as possible. The bullet holes needed to look like hail damage, which meant I'd spent the better part of an hour with a ball-peen hammer, trying to create the right pattern of dents around the genuine articles.

His name was Peterson, according to the business card he'd handed me with a limp handshake. Mid-fifties, thinning brown hair, and the kind of pale complexion that suggested he spent most of his time behind a desk, pushing papers and denying claims. He walked around the Holiday Rambler like a detective at a crime scene, making notes on his clipboard and occasionally stopping to examine the damage more closely.

"Quite a storm," he said, running his finger along one of the larger dents. "When did you say this happened?"

"Three nights ago." I grabbed a Sam Adams from the cooler to keep my hands busy. "Came out of nowhere. Hail the size of golf balls, maybe bigger. Never seen anything like it."

Peterson nodded but didn't look convinced. He crouched down near the driver's side door, where I'd been particularly creative with my hammer work. The actual bullet holes were scattered among the fabricated ones, and I'd done my best to make them all look uniform. Still, there was something different about the way metal tears when it's punched through by hot lead versus cold ice.

"Funny thing about hail damage," Peterson said, standing up and making another note. "Usually creates a more random pattern. This looks almost..." He paused, searching for the word. "Organized."

I took a long swig from my beer and shrugged. "Nature's weird that way sometimes. You want some coffee? I've got a fresh pot going. Or would you prefer a beer?"

"That's kind of you, but I'm trying to cut back. On caffeine. And I don't drink on the job." He walked to the back of the coach, where the damage was heaviest. This was where Chesnokov's boys had really opened up, and despite my best efforts with the hammer, it was obvious something high-velocity had punched through the aluminum siding.

"How did this happen?" Peterson asked, pointing to a cluster of holes near the rear window.

"Hail," I said without hesitation.

"Right." He made a long note on his clipboard, and I could practically hear him thinking. "Mr. Bolt, I have to tell you, I'm not entirely sure there's coverage for this kind of damage."

My stomach tightened, but I kept my expression neutral. "What do you mean? It's comprehensive coverage. Acts of God, right?"

"Well, yes, but..." He gestured at the holes. "This doesn't look like hail damage to me. It looks like gunfire."

The word hung in the air between us like smoke. I put my beer bottle on top of the cooler, buying myself a few seconds to think. Peterson was sharper than I'd given him credit for, but he was also just an insurance adjuster, not a cop. He suspected something, but he couldn't prove it.

"Gunfire?" I laughed, but it came out forced. "Come on, Peterson. You think I'm running around getting shot at? I'm a traveling salesman, for Christ's sake. I sell kitchen knives to housewives."

"What kind of knives?"

The question caught me off guard. I'd been using that cover story for so long, I'd forgotten that people might actually ask for details. "Japanese steel," I said quickly. "High-carbon content. Stays sharp longer than German blades."

Peterson nodded and made another note. "And you were where when this supposed hailstorm hit?"

"Parked at a truck stop outside Bakersfield. Plenty of witnesses, if you need them." I had read about a hailstorm that hit the grapevine a few weeks ago. I had some friends in the area who could provide affidavits if needed.

"I'll need a list of those witnesses," Peterson said. "Names and contact information, if you have them."

"Sure thing. Let me grab my notebook."

I climbed into the coach, partly to get my notebook and partly to give myself a moment to breathe. The conversation wasn't going well. Peterson clearly suspected something, and the more questions he asked, the deeper the hole I was digging for myself. But I wanted the insurance money. The coach was my home, my office, and my transportation all rolled into one. Without it, I was just another cog in the wheel. I liked the freedom the coach provided.

I found my notebook and flipped to a blank page, then started writing down names and phone numbers. Most of them were real—truckers I'd met over the years, people who might remember seeing me if Peterson bothered to call. I also added Pedro Perez. Pedro was the maintenance supervisor at the TA Travel Center on Wheeler Ridge Road in Arvin, a little truck stop on the grapevine. Pedro was good people, and he owed me a favor or two. I added a few names that were pure fiction, but I made sure to include enough legitimate contacts to make the list look credible.

When I climbed back down, Peterson was taking photographs of the damage with a small digital camera. He snapped shots from multiple angles, paying particular attention to the holes that looked most like bullet wounds.

"Here's that list," I said, handing him the notebook page.

He glanced at it and folded it into his clipboard. "Mr. Bolt, I'm going to be honest with you. This claim is going to require further investigation. The damage pattern is highly unusual for hail, and there are several inconsistencies in the physical evidence."

"Such as?"

"The entry angles are too uniform. Hail bounces when it hits the ground, creating secondary impacts at different trajectories. This damage all comes from roughly the same direction and elevation." He pointed to the cluster of holes. "That's consistent with gunfire from a moving vehicle, not falling ice."

I felt sweat beading on my forehead despite the cool morning air. "Look, Peterson, I don't know what to tell you. A storm came through, my coach got damaged, and now I'm filing a claim. Isn't that what insurance is for?"

"Insurance is for legitimate claims, Mr. Bolt. Not for covering up whatever you've gotten yourself involved in."

The accusation stung because it was true, but I couldn't afford to show it. "I think we're done here," I said. "You've got your photos, you've got your witness list. File your report and let me know what the company decides."

Peterson nodded and tucked his camera away. "You'll hear from us within seven to ten business days. In the meantime, I'd suggest you avoid any more hailstorms."

He walked to his car—a sensible gray sedan that probably got excellent gas mileage—and drove away without looking back. I stood on the blacktop and retrieved my beer wondering how much trouble I was in. The legitimate repair estimate was running close to eight thousand dollars, money I didn't have and couldn't get without the insurance payout or finding the senator's money and collecting my commission. The trust had plenty, but having to ask Master Parker for the funds to fix my coach because of gunfire would open up all sorts of interrogation I just didn't have the time to deal with now.

The rest of the morning crawled by like a wounded animal. I called Jenny to confirm our dinner plans, then spent an hour on the phone with a guy in Tucson who claimed to have information about Chesnokov's operation. It turned out to be a dead end—just another wannabe informant looking to make a quick buck with secondhand gossip and wild theories.

By the time evening arrived, I was ready for some genuine human contact. Jenny had suggested a family restaurant called Giuseppe's, a red-checkered-tablecloth kind of place that served generous portions and didn't ask too many questions about why a guy in a worn leather jacket might be dining with a young woman who talked to herself between courses.

I arrived early and got us a corner booth where we could talk without being overheard. Jenny showed up right on time, wearing a bright yellow dress that made her look younger than her twenty-eight years.

She'd been living in the group home for almost three years now, ever since our father died and left us both adrift in different ways.

"Jonny!" she said, sliding into the booth across from me. She always called me Jonny, a holdover from when we were kids and she couldn't pronounce Jonathan properly. "You look tired."

"I'm fine, Jen. Just work stuff. How are things at the house?"

Her face lit up the way it always did when she talked about her living situation. The group home housed six adults with varying degrees of autism, and Jenny had found her place among them like a puzzle piece clicking into position. She had her own room, her own routine, and enough supervision to keep her safe without making her feel trapped.

"Marcus got a job at the grocery store," she said, unfolding her napkin with careful precision. "He's stocking shelves in the produce section. He knows everything about vegetables now. Did you know that there are seventeen different types of lettuce?"

"I did not know that."

"It's true. He told me. And Sarah started taking art classes. She's really good at drawing birds. She showed me a picture of a cardinal that looked exactly like the one that sits outside my window."

The waitress came by and we ordered—spaghetti and meatballs for Jenny, chicken parmesan for me. Jenny insisted on garlic bread, which she would eat methodically, one piece at a time, always starting from the left side of the plate.

"Tell me about your work," she said once the waitress was gone. "Are you still selling knives?"

I nodded, maintaining the fiction even with her. "Business is good. People always need sharp knives."

"But you travel so much. Don't you get lonely?"

"Sometimes. But it's the job, you know? Can't sell knives sitting in an office."

She studied my face with the kind of directness that most people found uncomfortable. Jenny had never learned to mask her curiosity or soften her observations with social niceties. When she looked at you, she really looked.

"You have new scars," she said. "On your hands."

I glanced down at my knuckles, where scratches from the broken glass of the coach's windows were still healing. "Accident at work. Cut myself on a display case."

"Jonny, why aren't you married?"

The question came out of nowhere, delivered with the same matter-of-fact tone she'd use to ask about the weather. I nearly choked on my water.

"What brought that on?"

"Everyone at the house talks about their families. Marcus has a sister who visits every Sunday. Sarah's parents send her letters. I have you, but you're not married, and you don't have children. What about Victoria? I like her."

I'd known Victoria, Vicky, for many years. I met her in Washington, D.C. on my first FIDA assignment. We dated on and off for years, but we are both "success oriented," whatever that means, so opportunity and timing have not coalesced . . . yet. "Victoria is terrific, but we both have very busy careers."

"You should be with her," Jenny said. "I worry about you being alone."

The concern in her voice was genuine, and it cut deeper than Peterson's accusations had that morning. Jenny saw through the stories I told myself about being better off solo, about how relationships were just complications I couldn't afford.

"My job takes me away for long periods," I said. "It wouldn't be fair to someone, being gone so much."

"You could find different work."

"It's not that simple, Jen."

"Why not?"

Because I'm not qualified for anything else. Because I spent years at FIDA and three as a fixer, and now I'm involved with an international crime syndicate that might just get people killed, people I care about and some I could give zero fucks about.

"It just isn't," I said instead.

The food arrived, and we ate in comfortable silence for a while. Jenny attacked her spaghetti with surgical precision, twirling each bite exactly three times before lifting it to her mouth. She'd been eating pasta the same way since she was six years old, and I found the consistency oddly comforting.

"I worry about you," she said suddenly.

"Why?"

"You seem sad. Sadder than before."

Before our father died, she meant. Before I was forced out of my law practice. Before everything went wrong and I started living in a motorhome, taking contracts from people like Nancy Goldstein and running down people like Kiril Chesnokov.

"I'm not sad," I lied. "Just busy."

"Busy people can still be sad."

She was right, of course. Jenny had a way of cutting through bull-shit that would have made her a hell of a detective if she'd been wired differently. But she wasn't, and that meant she lived in a group home, held a bookkeeping job, and worried about her brother the traveling knife salesman who came to visit every few months with new scars and hollow eyes.

"I'm working on some things," I said. "Trying to make some changes."

"Good changes?"

"I hope so."

We finished dinner and I walked her back to the group home, a converted Victorian house in a quiet neighborhood where the biggest threat was jaywalking tourists. She hugged me goodbye at the front door, holding on longer than usual.

"Be careful, Jonny," she whispered. "Whatever you're really doing, be careful."

I wanted to ask her what she meant, but the door was already closing, and she was already gone, leaving me standing on the porch with the weight of her words settling in my chest like a stone.

The drive back to the coach took me through the commercial district, past strip malls and fast-food joints and the kind of businesses that stayed open late to serve the night shift workers and insomniacs. I was stopped at a red light, thinking about Jenny's questions and Peterson's suspicions, when I heard the screech of brakes and the sick crunch of metal meeting metal.

The accident happened right in front of me. A small Toyota Corolla had rear-ended a black Mercedes G-Wagon that was waiting to make a left turn. It wasn't a hard impact—maybe fifteen miles per hour, at most—but the sound of it snapped me back to the present moment.

The driver of the Corolla got out first, a young Latino man in work clothes who was already reaching for his wallet. He approached the G-Wagon with his hands visible, the universal gesture of someone who knew he was at fault and wanted to handle things peacefully.

The driver of the Mercedes took longer to emerge, and when he did, my blood went cold. I recognized him immediately: Viktor Petrov, one of Chesnokov's senior lieutenants. He was thickly built and ugly, with prison tattoos covering his forearms and the kind of dead eyes that came from years of inflicting pain for money.

The young man from the Corolla was already apologizing, his words tumbling over each other in accented English. "I'm so sorry, sir. My insurance will cover everything. Here's my card. I wasn't paying attention. This is all my fault."

Petrov looked at the offered insurance card like it was a piece of garbage. Then he looked at the minor scuff on his rear bumper. Then he looked back at the young man, and I saw something shift in his expression.

"You stupid fucking spic," Petrov said, his Russian accent thick with rage. "You have any idea what this car costs?"

The young man's face went pale. "Sir, please, I said I'm sorry. My insurance—"

Petrov's fist caught him in the solar plexus, doubling him over. The insurance card fluttered to the asphalt as he gasped for air. Other drivers were starting to notice the commotion, but no one was getting out of their cars. This was the kind of neighborhood where people minded their own business.

"Your insurance?" Petrov grabbed the young man by the hair and lifted his head up. "You think your fucking insurance can pay for my time? For disrespect?"

The second punch caught him in the face, splitting his lip and sending him stumbling backward into his car. Petrov followed, methodically now, working the body with professional efficiency. Ribs, kidneys, solar plexus again. The young man tried to protect himself, but Petrov was bigger, stronger, and experienced in the art of inflicting maximum pain without killing.

I sat in my car, engine running, watching a man get beaten half to death for a fender-bender. The smart thing would be to drive away. Petrov hadn't seen me, and getting involved would only complicate an already complicated situation. I was supposed to be laying low, avoiding attention, staying off Chesnokov's radar until I could figure out my next move.

But the young man was on the ground now, curled in a fetal position while Petrov kicked him in the ribs. And I could hear Jenny's voice in my head: "Be careful, Jonny. Whatever you're really doing, be careful."

What I was really doing was sitting in a car, watching an innocent man get beaten by a psychopath, and doing nothing about it.

The light turned green. Cars behind me started honking. Petrov delivered one final kick to the young man's head, then climbed back into his G-Wagon and drove away like nothing had happened. I followed the traffic flow, keeping my eyes straight ahead, telling myself I'd made the right choice.

By the time the police arrived, I was three blocks away. But I could still hear the sirens, and I knew that somewhere behind me, paramedics were loading an unconscious man into an ambulance while witnesses pretended they hadn't seen anything.

I stopped at a 24-hour diner and ordered coffee I didn't want, trying to wash the taste of cowardice out of my mouth. The waitress was friendly and chatty, but I barely heard her. All I could think about was the sound of Petrov's boot connecting with the young man's skull, and the way his body had gone limp afterward.

I paid for the coffee and walked back to my car. The night was cool and clear, full of stars that were invisible from the city but bright enough here to cast shadows. I sat behind the wheel for a long time, thinking about Jenny's questions and Petrov's violence and the young man who was probably in surgery right now because he'd had the misfortune to rear-end the wrong Mercedes.

A police cruiser drove past, moving fast with its lights on but no siren. Probably heading to the hospital to take a statement from the victim, if he was conscious enough to give one. The cops would ask if he'd seen who attacked him, and he'd probably say no because he was smart enough to know that identifying Viktor Petrov would be a death sentence.

Just like I was smart enough to know that getting involved would have been suicide.

But sitting in that diner, staring at my reflection in the black coffee, I couldn't shake the feeling that smart and right weren't always the same thing.

I sat there for another minute, watching the police cruiser's taillights disappear into the distance, then started the Carrera and drove back to Dockweiler. As I pulled into the RV court, there were several travelers sitting on beach chairs under their outstretched awnings taking in the night air and enjoying some adult beverages. There was one loudmouth standing and spewing his life philosophy in halting slurred speech. This audience appeared unimpressed, but perhaps they were just too intoxicated to care one way or another.

I pulled up and parked next to Coach, exited the 911, unlocked the door, and stepped inside. The coach was a small space in which to live life, but she was mine and smelled like home. I poured three fingers of Makers Mark from the bottle I kept in the galley, then sat on the settee and stared out the window toward the vast Pacific.

Jenny was right to worry about me. I was sadder than before, lonelier than I'd ever been, and getting deeper into a situation that was going to get me killed if I wasn't careful. The insurance adjuster suspected I was lying. Chesnokov's men were on to me. And somewhere in the city was Elsa. I punched myself in the head for letting my guard down with her. Never again. She was a perp plain and simple, and I needed her for one thing only: to lead me to the money she took from Senator Goldstein. I felt I had already earned my commission, and I wasn't about to give it up without a fight.

I finished the bourbon, walked back to the bedroom, and lay down fully clothed, staring at the ceiling until exhaustion finally pulled me under. My last conscious thought was of Petrov's dead eyes, and the sound of sirens in the distance, and the question Jenny had asked that I still couldn't answer: Why aren't you married, Jonny?

Because this is what I am, I thought as sleep took me. Because this is what I do. Because men like me don't get to have normal lives.

Outside, the city hummed with late-night energy—cars on Vista del Mar, planes heading out of LAX, emergency vehicles racing toward other people's disasters. But inside the Holiday Rambler parked in space 26, Dockweiler RV Park, there was only silence and the smell of bourbon and the dreams of a man who'd forgotten how to be anything other than what he'd become.

CHAPTER 16

PEER PRESSURE

I spent most of the morning sipping coffee and listening to the ocean. During this caper, I hadn't had many chances to just chill, so it was nice to relax or at least try. Type A personalities have difficulties with relaxation.

After looking over newsfeeds on X, I came across a thread about a guy who was scammed out of tens of thousands of dollars by some blond chick he'd met in a bar. Most of the replies were virtually beating this poor schmuck about the head and neck, but there were a few sympathetic responses as well. I felt like a compatriot after my recent faux pas with Elsa. I decided to get my ass in gear and follow her around for a while to see what else I could discover or shake loose. I grabbed the Glock and my Smart Carry holster and jumped into the Porsche. The flat six roared to life and I headed toward the San Fernando Valley.

As I exited the 105 to the 405 north, I checked the GPS app on my phone. I wanted to make sure Elsa was at home. Well surprise, surprise she was not at home. The GPS tracker I'd planted on Elsa's Buick showed a steady blue dot on Robertson Boulevard, parked outside a building I recognized but had never entered: the Kabbalah Center. I looked at the screen of my phone wondering what the hell she was doing at a spiritual center in West Hollywood. I exited the 405 at La Cienega and headed toward Elsa's location.

It was three in the afternoon when I arrived at 1062 South Robertson and found a parking spot on Whitworth Drive. I'd been watching the dot for twenty minutes. Elsa arrived at 2:45 and hadn't moved since. The tracker was military grade—a favor from an old contact at Camp Pendleton—and accurate to within three feet. Elsa was inside, probably sitting in some meditation circle talking about chakras and energy healing.

I minimized the GPS app and called Maggie. The phone rang twice before she picked up.

"Bolt," she said, her voice carrying that slight rasp that indicated she was still in party mode. "What's up?"

"I need an extra pair of eyes on something. You available?"

"Depends. Who and what?"

"I'll send over the coordinates of an abandoned warehouse in the Arts District. Can you check the ownership records for me?"

There was a pause, and I could hear her taking a deep drag on something that definitely wasn't tobacco. "Don't you have a street address?"

"Are you high right now, Maggie?"

"So?"

The word came out flat and unapologetic, exactly the way Maggie delivered most of her responses to questions she considered irrelevant. Most people could barely function when they were baked, but Maggie was different. Marijuana seemed to sharpen her focus rather than dull it, made her more observant and methodical. I'd seen her work a crime scene while stoned out of her mind, cataloging evidence with the precision of a Swiss watchmaker.

"Never mind," I said. "You want to join me on a stakeout at the Kabbalah Center."

"The spiritual tourist trap? What's there?"

"Elsa showed up a few minutes ago. I need someone who can get inside, blend in with the crowd."

"And you can't because she'll recognize you? Nice way to stay incognito."

"Yes, I screwed the pooch. Are you available or not?"

Maggie laughed, a sound like gravel in a cement mixer. "Sure, Boss Man. I can be there in 30 minutes. I'll bring some toys with me."

"Toys?"

"Surveillance equipment. Microphones, recording devices, that sort of thing. If you want me to get close to your Elsa, I might as well grab some audio while I'm at it."

The line went dead. I expanded the GPS app and got out of the 911. Since the blue dot remained stationary on my screen, I knew Elsa's car hadn't moved. I put on my shades and grabbed my Dodgers cap from the back seat. Not a great way to hide myself, but in this part of L.A. I would blend in.

The Kabbalah Center was housed in an old mission style house of worship; all stucco with red roof tiles like the many Spanish missions that ran through California from San Diego to Sonoma, with Hebrew letters etched into the facade. Cars came and went from the parking lot—mostly expensive German sedans and Japanese hybrids driven by the kind of people who could afford to pay three hundred dollars for a meditation workshop.

Elsa's Buick was parked near the back of the lot, tucked between a white Tesla and a silver Bentley. I had to hand it to her. She had stolen millions of dollars and continued to drive a Buick SUV. In West Hollywood! Either she's extremely disciplined or she doesn't give a rip about status. Point, Elsa.

And then I saw it. The Zarina's black Range Rover. It was parked on the end of the same row as Elsa's Buick. I made my way between the cars in the lot, to confirm it was the same, and indeed there was the proof: 1ZARINA. I sprinted back to the Porsche because I couldn't afford to lose the opportunity to tag Zarina's car. I grabbed a GPS unit from the glove box, checked the battery, and turned it on. I proceed back to the Kabbalah lot and to the Range Rover. I stood at the rear of the vehicle and looked around to make sure I wasn't being watched, and when I was sure I looked down at my shoes and then bent as if needing to tie them. I quickly placed the GPS under the rear bumper and stood back up. Ten seconds and it was done. Now I would be able to get additional information on Zarina because it was killing me that I still didn't know who she was.

My phone buzzed with a text from Maggie: "I'm about 20 minutes out. See you stone." I assumed Mags was using voice to text or she was really, really high. This should be good.

Twenty minutes later, Maggie's Honda Civic pulled into the parking lot. The car was fifteen years old and looked like it had been through a demolition derby, but the engine was pristine and the interior was loaded with more electronic equipment than a Best Buy. Maggie climbed out wearing jeans, a black t-shirt, and a canvas messenger bag slung across her shoulder.

She walked over to the sidewalk where I was standing facing Robertson so as to maintain as low a profile as possible in case Elsa exited the center. Maggie smelled of marijuana and patchouli oil. "So," she said, opening her messenger bag and pulling out what looked like a smart phone but was actually a sophisticated recording device.

"In your previous interactions with Elsa, was there anything that might tip you off that she would be into the kind of services provided by this place?"

"She's an attractive, insecure young woman. How's that? In public, Elsa presents as confident and competent. Why else would Senator Goldstein have given her the kind of access she had to the campaign finances?"

"So, she's an actress and is pretty good in the role. Nice. You go, sister." Maggie made a few notes in a spiral notebook.

"She's also involved in Chesnokov's organization, and you want me to spy on a Russian mobster's princess."

"I want you to observe and record. Big difference."

"Not to the people who'll kill me if they I.D. me. Surveilling Chesnokov and his crew is relatively safe since I'm pretty good at blending in from fifty or one hundred yards away. Being close enough to count the pores on Elsa's face is another story." She pulled out a second device, this one about the size of a credit card. "What's your interest in her connection to the Kabbalah Center?"

"Professional curiosity."

"Bullshit. You don't do professional curiosity. You do professional violence."

She was right, of course. Maggie had known me long enough to see through most of my evasions. But the truth—that I was supposed collect the campaign funds and make sure Elsa never did anything like it again—wasn't something I could share with anyone, even someone I trusted.

"Let's just say I need to understand her better. I got played, Mags. I don't aim to have that happen again."

Maggie studied my face for a moment, then shrugged. "Understood. What's she doing in there?"

"That's what I want you to find out."

She nodded and tucked the devices into various pockets. "Give me her description again."

"Five-foot-seven, blonde hair, blue eyes, expensive taste in clothes. Late twenties, probably grew up with money and lost it."

"Got it. How long do you want me to stay inside?"

"As long as it takes to get a sense of what she's doing. If she's in some kind of regular session or class, I want to know about it. If she's meeting with someone specific, I want to know who."

Maggie adjusted her messenger bag. "If this goes sideways and I end up floating in the harbor, I'm haunting your ass."

"Noted."

She walked across the parking lot toward the center's main entrance, moving with the casual confidence of someone who belonged there. Maggie had a gift for blending in anywhere—cop bars, high-end restaurants, meditation centers, crack houses. It was something about her body language, the way she carried herself like she had every right to be wherever she was.

I returned to the Porsche to wait, keeping one eye on the GPS tracker and the other on the building's exits. The afternoon sun was warm through the windshield, and I found myself thinking about Jenny's questions from the night before. Why wasn't I married? Why did I seem so sad? The simple answer was that people like me didn't get to have normal lives, but the complicated answer was that I'd chosen this path one decision at a time, and now I was too deep in to find my way back.

Forty-five minutes passed. The blue dot hadn't moved, and neither had Elsa's Buick. I was starting to wonder if something had gone wrong when my phone buzzed with a text from Maggie: "Found her. In group session. Getting good audio. Stay put."

I typed back: "Copy that."

Another thirty minutes crawled by. I watched people come and go from the center—mostly women in yoga pants and designer handbags, a few men in expensive casual wear that screamed entertainment industry. The afternoon crowd was winding down, and I was starting to worry that Elsa would leave before Maggie could extract herself when I saw movement near the Buick.

Elsa emerged from the building alone, walking with the loose, relaxed gait of someone who'd just spent an hour meditating. She was wearing dark jeans and a cream-colored cashmere sweater that probably cost more than most people made in a month. Her blonde hair was pulled back in a simple ponytail, and she had the kind of natural beauty that didn't require much enhancement.

She climbed into the Buick and started the engine. The blue dot on my tracker began moving toward the parking lot exit. I started my car but didn't follow—no point in risking exposure when I could track her electronically. Instead, I waited for Maggie to emerge.

Ten minutes later, she walked out of the building and crossed the parking lot toward Whitworth and my car. She slid into the passenger seat with a satisfied expression on her face.

"Well?" I asked.

"That chick? She has some interesting spiritual needs," she said, pulling the recording device out of her pocket. "I managed to get within about ten feet of her during the group session. The audio quality is pretty good."

"What kind of session?"

"Something called 'Kabbalah and Consciousness.' Basically, a guided meditation with some Hebrew mysticism thrown in. About twelve people sitting in a circle, talking about their spiritual journeys and personal struggles."

"And what did Elsa talk about?"

Maggie grinned. "That's the interesting part. She spent twenty minutes discussing stress, meditation techniques, and her relationship issues."

"Her relationship issues?"

"Apparently she's having some problems in that department. Trouble connecting with men, issues with intimacy, that sort of thing. The group leader—they call him a 'guide'—spent a lot of time talking to her about opening her chakras and releasing emotional blockages."

I felt a twist of something in my stomach that might have been sympathy. I wasn't sure why because Elsa was out for herself. That has been made clear. And she sought out Chesnokov so being surrounded by violence and paranoia was her choice. Her struggling to form normal relationships? It wasn't hard to imagine why she might have intimacy issues.

"Did she mention anyone specific? Boyfriend, family members?"

"No one in particular. I was getting the sense she has lots of free-floating anxiety, which makes sense. There was another woman there, a brunette with a Russian accent."

I think Mags found Zarina. "Did you get a name?"

"Don't recall, but it'll be on the recording. They run this place like a 12 step program. 'my name is Elsa K, and I'm fucked up!'"

"You didn't record the Russian's introduction?"

"No, douche, I didn't. She must have roll-called before I arrived."

"Ok, Mags, just the facts. Did the Russian say anything?"

"She talked about her father, but not by name. Called him 'a powerful man with many enemies' who didn't understand her spiritual needs. Said she feels trapped between his world and the life she wants to live."

"She said 'didn't'?"

"I believe so. It's on the recording. Why?"

I thought Zarina's dad might be dead and she has unresolved "daddy issues." "No reason," I said. "Anything else?"

Maggie scrolled through the recording device's menu. "Elsa's planning to attend a weekend retreat next month. Something called 'Sacred Sexuality and the Divine Feminine.' Three days in Malibu, very expensive, very exclusive."

"A sex retreat?"

"More like spiritual enlightenment through sexual awareness. It's a thing in certain circles. Lot of wealthy women trying to find meaning through tantric meditation and goddess worship."

I processed this information, trying to figure out how it might be useful. A weekend retreat would get Elsa away from Chesnokov's goons, isolated in a location with other like-minded women. But it also meant she'd be surrounded by other people, witnesses who might complicate any operation.

"I want a copy of that recording," I said.

Maggie pulled a micro SD card from the device and handed it to me. "Already made you one. But Bolt, whatever you're thinking, be careful. That girl is trouble with a capital "T". And I think there's something else going on between her and the Russian."

"What do you mean?"

"During the session, the Russian mentioned some things that didn't add up. Said she's been studying martial arts since she was twelve, that her father insisted on it for protection. But the way she talked about it, it sounded like more than just self-defense classes."

"Such as?"

"Combat training. Real stuff, not the McDojo bullshit they teach at strip mall karate schools. She mentioned weapons training, tactical awareness, and threat assessment. This girl has been groomed for something more than just being daddy's little princess. And I recall Elsa saying something like, 'you need to teach me.'"

I thought about the way Elsa had carried herself when I'd observed her earlier; she was nearly run down in a supermarket parking lot. Her situational awareness sucks. She could use self-defense training.

"Anything else?"

"Yeah. She's scared."

"Of what?"

"Everything. Men, women, probably Chesnokov, his minions, her own future. She talked about feeling like she's living on borrowed time, like something bad is coming and she can't stop it." Maggie tucked the recording device back into her bag. "Whatever game you're playing with her, remember that she's not just a pawn. She's a victim too."

I thought 'give me a little break.' This woman stole millions and was now laundering it with one of the most dangerous criminals in the city. Victim, my ass.

Maggie climbed out of the car and walked back to her Honda without saying another word. I sat parked in the street for another ten minutes, staring at the SD card and thinking about what I'd learned. Elsa

Krieger wasn't just a thief and novice money launderer—she was like a rat in a trap, and a trapped rat can be dangerous. But she was also a young woman struggling with loneliness and intimacy issues, seeking spiritual guidance from strangers because she couldn't trust anyone in her real life.

I needed to find out who Zarina was so I texted Dan Brennan.

Dan was my go-to guy for anything involving technology, surveillance, or information that wasn't supposed to be publicly available. He'd worked for the NSA before going private, and he maintained a network of contacts in government agencies, telecommunications companies, and data brokers that would have impressed a Fortune 500 corporation.

I texted, 'Hey, Dan. It's Jon Bolt. Can you run down a license plate for me? Plate is 1ZARINA. California plate. Need name and address. THX!'

I started the car and pulled out onto Robertson, following the GPS tracker's signal toward Beverly Hills. Elsa was heading home, probably to spend the evening alone in her apartment, meditating on chakras and sexual energy.

My phone rang as I was headed west on Pico. Karl's number appeared on the display.

"Jon," he said.

"Howdy, Karl. What's the haps?"

There was a long pause. I could hear Karl breathing. I've seen this before. Karl has trouble expressing regret. After a few moments he said, "I've been thinking about how we left things." Another long pause. I turned right on Cotner and then onto the on ramp for the 405 north. Then to shake things loose, I said, "How's Gina doing?"

"She's great. Thanks for asking. Actually, Gina is why I'm calling." Another pause. I couldn't take it anymore. Something you need to know about me: I hate wasting time. "Karl, please get to the point. I'm gonna have a stroke."

"Gina said I was being a pussy not continuing to work with you. She said I needed to have faith that everything would be fine, and whatever happened it was the Lord's plan anyway." Gina was very religious, a devout Catholic.

"You got a good woman there, Karl. Are you sure you want back in?"

For a second I thought I was going to get another pause, and I was preparing to drive off the embankment.

"Yes. This is what I do."

"Excellent. I'm on my way to Elsa's place again for some additional surveillance. When I get back home, I will send you a recording Maggie collected earlier today. I'd like you to parse it. Oh, and I've been having Dan Brennan do some of the work so you guys should connect so we don't duplicate effort." I knew this would be ok with Karl. Dan and he worked together at NSA and they were friendly.

"Cool. I will call Dan now. Thanks, boss. Talk to you soon."

The line went dead. I pocketed the phone and continued driving north, thinking about Karl's reluctance to continue on the case in light of Gina's pregnancy, and Gina shreking Karl for his pussification, made me smile. Maybe I should recruit Gina after she delivers; let Karl be Mr. Mom. That would be something to see. Karl, six feet three, face like a bald boulder, and the hairiest arms I'd even seen outside of the gorilla case at the L.A. Zoo changing diapers and cleaning up infant puke all day, every day. I'd have to record that and upload it to Tik Tok.

The GPS tracker showed Elsa's car pulling into the parking garage of her apartment building. When I arrived in the valley, I drove onto Moorpark and circled the cul-de-sac without slowing. The only parking spot was all the way back at Orion. I parked and walked back to Elsa's building. I entered the atrium near the mailboxes and looked up at Elsa's apartment. I could see her shadow on the blinds as she walked around the living room. After a few minutes, I started to feel like a peeping Tom so I thought better of the plan. It appeared Elsa was in for the night, and if not the GPS would let me know if she left again. Besides, it had been a long day and I was getting tired.

I walked back up the street, got into the 911, and drove back to Dockweiler. When I got in the coach, I grabbed a beer and sat at the dinette. I opened my laptop and transferred the audio file from the SD card. The recording was clearer than I'd expected, with Maggie's equipment picking up most of the conversation despite the ambient noise from the group session.

Elsa's voice came through the speakers with crystal clarity: "I have trouble connecting with men. There's always this wall between me and them, like I can't let anyone get close enough to really know me."

The guide's response was delivered in the kind of soothing, professional tone that probably cost three hundred dollars an hour: "This wall you describe—where do you think it comes from?"

"Probably from my father. He was loving but cold. Does that make sense? I never felt good enough for him."

Then another voice came from the recording, one with a Russian accent.

"I understand what she's saying. Fear of not being good enough? I live with that and other fears as well."

The guide followed up with Zarina, "What causes those fears for you, Elena?"

Bingo! Zarina is Elena. Noted.

"Fear, I think. My father... a powerful man with a bad temper. I grew up knowing that anyone who got close to me could be used against him, or against me. It's hard to trust people when you know how easily they can be turned into weapons."

"And how does this fear manifest in your intimate relationships?"

There was a long pause before Elena answered. "I can't let go. Even when I want to, even when I care about someone, there's always this part of me that's watching, analyzing, looking for threats. It's like I'm two different people—the woman who wants to love and be loved, and the soldier who knows that love is just another weakness to be exploited."

The soldier. Maggie had been right about Elena's training. This wasn't just a girl who'd taken a few self-defense classes. This was someone who'd been raised in a world where trust was a luxury and intimacy was a liability.

I listened to the rest of the recording, taking notes on names, locations, and personal details that might be useful later. Elsa mentioned the retreat in Malibu, her meditation practice, her struggles with intimacy. Elena talked more about her father's expectations. She talked about wanting to travel, to see the world beyond Los Angeles, to find some kind of meaning beyond the violence and paranoia that defined her family's existence.

By the time the recording ended, I had a much clearer picture of who Elsa Krieger really was, but I was also seeing the new woman, Elena. She wasn't just the daughter of a vicious man—she was a young woman trapped between two worlds, trained for violence but yearning for peace, surrounded by wealth but starved for genuine human connection. And I still wasn't sure who she was and how she was connected to Elsa, Trisha, Elena, and Chesnokov. So much for a simple "collection" case. This deal was getting very sticky.

I sent an email to Karl with a copy of the recording. I told Karl to break down the background noise and parse the other conversations. I closed the laptop and poured myself three fingers of bourbon. Outside, the ocean waves were lightly crashing on the sand. There was a lull of a few vehicles traveling on Vista del Mar, but mostly the sound of the ocean was intoxicating. Maybe it was the booze.

My phone buzzed with a text from Karl: "Got it. Working on it now. I'll have it back to you within 48 hours."

I finished the bourbon and lay down on the bed, staring at the ceiling, listening to the ocean, and thinking about choices and consequences. Somewhere across the city, Elsa Krieger was probably sitting in her apartment, meditating on chakras and sexual energy while in a state of free-floating anxiety. Tomorrow, she'd wake up and continue living the complicated life she's created for herself, not realizing that a burned-out ex-operative was analyzing her spiritual struggles for weaknesses he could exploit.

The SD card sat next to my laptop, containing an hour of intimate confessions from a young woman who wanted to connect with someone, anyone, without having to worry about betrayal or manipulation. But in my hands, those confessions had become intelligence, weapons that could be used to destroy everything she cared about.

Then my phone rang. The number was in my contacts list: Victoria Stetson.

"Well, well, well, Vicky Stetson. How the hell are you?"

"I'm good Jon. Long time... no hear. Are you alright?" I sensed that Jenny was connected to this call by the way Vicky asked. "Did Jenny put you up to this?"

"She called. She's worried about you." I was hoping beyond hope Jenny didn't mention Vicky and I getting hitched. "I know she is, but I'm doing well."

"Liar," Vicky exclaimed. "I've known you too long, Jon." She was right. She knew me well. That was one of her most attractive traits. We talked for ten or fifteen minutes just catching up with each other when I said, "Vic, how about we get together soon?"

"Why?" She was teasing. I loved it.

"So, we can catch up some more. I'm kind of beat now."

"Didn't we just do that?" Oh, she was something else.

"Yes, but I think everything you told me is bullshit, so I want to look in your eyes when I hear it all again." Vicky laughed.

"Sounds good. When?"

"Tomorrow night? Where?"

"Perfect. I'll text you a time and place." There was a substantial pause before she said, "See you then, Jonny," and ended the call.

I closed my eyes and tried to sleep with the thoughts of Victoria Stetson swimming around my brain. I didn't deserve a woman of her caliber. This I know, but we definitely had a connection unlike any other I've experienced with a woman. I was actually looking forward to something which had been a rare experience for me lately.

Then I thought about the case and Elsa. Her voice kept echoing in my head: "It's like I'm two different people—the woman who wants to love and be loved, and the soldier who knows that love is just another weakness to be exploited." She wasn't the only one living with that split. The difference was that she was trying to heal it, while I was using it to justify what I was about to do.

The digital clock beside the bed showed 11:47 PM in red numbers. In a few hours I would be back at it trying to recover the money Elsa took from Senator Goldstein. Focus Bolt. That was the objective. And somewhere adjacent to that objective, Elsa's spiritual struggles and intimacy issues would play a role, transformed from genuine human pain into tactical advantages.

I pulled the pillow over my head and tried to drown out the sound of my own conscience, but some noises are too loud to ignore, no matter how hard you try.

CHAPTER 17

OPENING DAY

The Los Angeles Police Department headquarters on Spring Street looked exactly the same as it had when I'd walked out of it for the last time three years ago—a concrete monument to bureaucratic efficiency and broken dreams. I parked across the street and sat in my car for a moment, watching cops and civilians flow in and out of the building like ants around a disturbed hill. Some things never changed in this city, and the LAPD's ability to generate paperwork and frustration was apparently one of them.

I needed information about Chesnokov's operation—the kind of intelligence that only came from active investigations and surveillance reports. The Russian mob task force would have files on every major player, organizational charts, financial records, maybe even intercepted communications. Getting access to that information as a private citizen would be impossible, but I still had a few contacts in the department who might be willing to bend the rules for an old colleague.

The lobby smelled of industrial disinfectant and coffee, with an undertone of human desperation that seemed to permeate every police station I'd ever been in. The duty officer behind the bulletproof glass was a kid who looked like he'd graduated from the academy about fifteen minutes ago. His nameplate read "Officer Martinez," and he had the eager, slightly overwhelmed expression of someone who was still figuring out that real police work was nothing like what they'd shown him in training.

"Help you?" he asked, looking up from a stack of forms that seemed to stretch from here to Riverside.

"I need to speak with whoever's running the Russian organized crime task force."

Martinez consulted a directory on his computer screen, pecking at the keyboard with two fingers like he was afraid it might bite him. "That would be Detective Valenzuela. Luis Valenzuela."

The name didn't ring any bells, which probably meant he'd transferred in after I left FIDA. "Is he available?"

"Not today, sir. It's Dodgers' Opening Day."

I stared at him for a moment. "What does that have to do with anything?"

Martinez looked at me like I'd asked him to explain quantum physics. "Detective Valenzuela has season tickets. He's had them for twelve years. Never misses an opening day."

"And is this considered acceptable by the department?"

"Well, sir, it's his day off. And it is Opening Day."

The kid said it like it was a religious holiday, which in Los Angeles it practically was. The Dodgers had been playing in Chavez Ravine since 1962, and for a certain generation of Angelenos, baseball wasn't just a sport—it was a sacred ritual that connected them to something larger than themselves.

"Can you give me his contact information?"

Martinez reached into a desk drawer and pulled out a business card. "This has his cell number. But like I said, it's Opening Day. He probably won't answer."

I took the card and studied it. Detective Luis Valenzuela, Russian Organized Crime Task Force. The address was Parker Center, the old LAPD headquarters that had been demolished years ago, which meant the cards were either old or Detective Valenzuela wasn't big on updating his contact information.

"Thanks," I said, pocketing the card.

"You want to leave a message? I can have him call you tomorrow."

"That's all right. I'll try the cell number."

I walked back to my car, thinking about the peculiar relationship between Los Angeles and its baseball team. The Dodgers had been transplanted from Brooklyn in 1958, a move that had broken the hearts of East Coast fans but given the sprawling western city something it had never had before—a shared identity, a reason for strangers to high-five each other on the street.

The drive to Chavez Ravine took me through some of the oldest neighborhoods in Los Angeles, past buildings that had witnessed the city's transformation from a sleepy pueblo to a metropolitan sprawl of four million people. I'd grown up hearing stories about what this area had been like before the Dodgers arrived, back when it was home to three thriving Mexican American communities: Chavez Ravine, La Loma, and Bishop.

The history was uglier than most people wanted to remember. In the early 1950s, the city had used eminent domain to seize hundreds of homes, promising residents that their neighborhoods would be replaced with public housing. Families who had lived there for generations were forced to sell their property for far less than it was worth, their tight-knit communities scattered to the four winds. But the public housing project never materialized. Instead, the city sold the land to Walter O'Malley, owner of the Brooklyn Dodgers, who was looking for a new home for his team.

By 1959, bulldozers had erased three neighborhoods to make room for a baseball stadium. The last holdout, an elderly woman named

Abrana Arechiga, had to be physically carried from her home by sheriff's deputies while news cameras rolled. Her house was demolished the same day, along with the last remnant of a community that had existed for nearly a century.

It was a perfect metaphor for Los Angeles—a city built on the bones of what came before, where progress and profit mattered more than people or history. The Dodgers brought championships and civic pride to their new home, but they'd also brought the knowledge that in America, no community was safe if someone with enough money wanted the land beneath it.

I took the Stadium Way exit and followed the winding road up into the hills. Dodger Stadium sat on top of Chavez Ravine like a concrete crown, its clean lines and modernist architecture a stark contrast to the urban chaos below. It was a beautiful ballpark, I had to admit, with panoramic views of downtown Los Angeles and the San Gabriel Mountains. But I couldn't look at it without thinking about the families who'd been displaced to build it.

The parking lots were already filling up with cars, RVs, and tailgating fans. Opening Day was always a celebration in Los Angeles, a ritual that marked the beginning of spring and the renewal of hope that maybe this would be the year the Dodgers won it all. I found a parking spot in Lot K and walked toward the stadium, pulling out my phone to call Detective Valenzuela.

The call went straight to voicemail, as expected. Valenzuela's recorded message was brief and professional: "This is Detective Luis Valenzuela, LAPD Russian Organized Crime Task Force. Leave a message and I'll get back to you as soon as possible."

"Detective Valenzuela, this is Jon Bolt. I'm a former federal agent, currently working private investigation. I need to speak with you about Kiril Chesnokov and his organization. It's urgent. Please call me back at this number."

I hung up and immediately dialed Dan's number again. He answered on the second ring.

"Bolt. What do you need now?"

"I need another favor. Two favors, actually."

"I'm listening."

"Can you track a cell phone location from a call I make?"

"Whose phone?"

"LAPD detective named Luis Valenzuela. I just called his number and left a message."

"Jesus, Bolt. You want me to track a cop?"

"I need to find him, and he's not answering his phone. It's important."

There was a pause while Dan considered the request. "I can probably triangulate his position based on cell towers, but it's not going to be precise. Maybe within a few hundred yards."

"That's good enough. What about vehicle information? Can you find out what he drives?"

"DMV records? That's easy. Give me his full name and badge number if you have it."

"Detective Luis Valenzuela, Russian Organized Crime Task Force. I don't have a badge number."

"I'll work with what you gave me. This is going to take some time, maybe an hour or two."

"How much time do you need for phone tracking?"

"That I can do right now. Hold on."

I could hear Dan typing on his computer, probably accessing databases that ordinary citizens weren't supposed to know existed. The man had skills that bordered on the supernatural, and he'd saved my life more than once by providing information that law enforcement agencies would have killed to possess.

"Okay, I've got a general location on that phone number. It pinged towers in the Chavez Ravine area about twenty minutes ago."

"Chavez Ravine? Okay, so Dodger Stadium area or are there other towers in the ravine?"

"There are several towers that could ping, but the last ping was closest to the stadium. The signal is stationary, which means he's probably sitting in one place. Makes sense if he's at a baseball game."

"Can you narrow it down any further?"

"Not without more sophisticated equipment. But if he's at the stadium, there are only so many places he could be."

I looked up at the concrete structure rising in front of me, thinking about 56,000 seats spread across multiple levels and sections. Finding one detective in that crowd would be like looking for a needle in a haystack, but at least I knew he was here.

"Send me whatever you find on his vehicle registration," I said. "And Dan? This stays between us."

"Always does."

The line went dead. I pocketed the phone and walked toward the stadium entrance, joining the stream of fans flowing through the gates. The crowd was a cross-section of Los Angeles—families with young children, elderly couples who'd been coming to games since the stadium opened, young professionals in Dodger blue jerseys, construction workers still wearing their hard hats from the morning shift.

The atmosphere was electric in the way that only Opening Day could create. Vendors hawked peanuts and Dodger Dogs, kids ran around wearing oversized caps and dragging foam fingers behind them, and somewhere in the distance a mariachi band was playing "Take Me Out to the Ballgame" in Spanish. It was pure Los Angeles—a melting pot of cultures united by their love for a team that had been transplanted from three thousand miles away.

I was about to join the line at Gate A when my phone rang. The caller ID showed a number I did not recognize but it was local, 424. I let it go to voice mail.

Lines were beginning to form at the stadium entrances. It was a beautiful day, and when Dodger Opening Day fell on a beautiful day you could bet the crowds would be massive. My phone vibrated in my pocket announcing a voice mail from whomever called. I pulled out my phone to listen to the message.

Son of a bitch! The caller was the driver of the Range Rover, Zarina/Elena, but she introduced herself as Elena Pavlov... daughter of Kiril Chesnokov! The connections in this case were getting out of hand. Elena asked me to return her call as soon as possible. I have to admit my curiosity was getting the best of me so I clicked the number on her voice mail and her phone began ringing.

She answered on the fourth ring.

"Hello, Mr. Bolt? This is Elena Pavlov. I think we need to talk."

Her voice was different than it had been on the voice mail. She sounded more direct, more confident. She sounded like someone used to getting what she wanted.

"It's a pleasure to meet you, Ms. Chesnokov. You did say in your message that he is your father."

"I use my mother's maiden name. I'm sure you understand why." She was correct. Using Chesnokov could cause a whole range of complications in both Elena's life and in Kiril's. She then said, "Where are you right now?"

The question caught me off guard. "Why do you ask?"

"Because I know you've been following me. The GPS tracker on my car, the surveillance at the Kabbalah Center, the background checks you've been running on my family. Did you really think I wouldn't notice?"

My blood went cold. If Elena knew about the tracking device, then she probably knew a lot more about my activities than I was comfortable with. "I'm not sure what you're talking about."

"Mr. Bolt, I've been trained to spot surveillance since I was twelve years old. You're good, but you're not invisible. Now, where are you?"

I looked around at the crowd of baseball fans, wondering how many of them might be working for the Chesnokov organization. "Dodger Stadium. Opening Day."

"Perfect. I am also attending the opening day. I'm close. I will be parking in Lot K, near the shuttle stop. Meet me there in ten minutes."

"I don't think that's a good idea."

"Mr. Bolt, you have two choices. You can meet me in the parking lot for a civilized conversation, or I can have this discussion with the district attorney. Stalking is a crime. Which would you prefer?"

The threat was delivered in the same calm, professional tone she'd used at the spiritual center, but there was steel underneath it. This wasn't the vulnerable young woman struggling with intimacy issues. This was a woman trained in combat and tactical awareness, and she was making it clear that she held all the cards. Or at least she thought she did.

"Ten minutes," I said.

"Thank you. And Mr. Bolt, come alone."

The line went dead. I stood in the middle of the crowd, surrounded by families heading to ball game, and tried to figure out how badly I'd screwed up. Elena Pavlov née Chesnokov knew about my surveillance, which meant she probably knew about Maggie's infiltration of the Kabbalah Center. She might even know about the recording. Or she might be bluffing. The only way to find out was to meet her face to face.

I walked back through the parking lot, weaving between cars and tailgating fans. The smell of grilled meat and beer filled the air, and somewhere nearby someone was playing "I Love L.A." on a radio. It was such a normal, American scene that it felt surreal to be walking through it toward what might be my execution.

Lot K was on the far side of the stadium complex, a section reserved for season ticket holders and VIPs. The cars here were newer and more expensive—BMWs, Mercedes, the occasional Ferrari or Lamborghini. I found the shuttle stop and looked around for Elena, wondering if she'd come alone or brought backup.

She was standing next to the black Range Rover, wearing jeans and an official Dodgers jersey, and an unzipped Dodgers jacket. Her brunette hair was pulled back in a ponytail, and she was wearing sunglasses despite the overcast sky. She looked like any other wealthy Los Angeles woman heading to a baseball game, except for the way she positioned herself with clear sight lines in all directions and her back to the vehicle.

"Mr. Bolt," she said as I approached. "Thank you for coming."

"Ms. Pavlov. You said we needed to talk."

"We do." She gestured to the Range Rover. "Get in. We're going for a drive."

"I'd rather stay here."

"I'm sure you would. But this conversation requires privacy, and there are too many ears in a place like this." She opened the passenger door. "Please."

It wasn't really a request. I could see at least two men in the vicinity who were trying a little too hard to look like baseball fans, and the bulge under the left arm of Elena's jacket suggested she was carrying more than just car keys and lip gloss.

I climbed into the Range Rover. The interior was leather and luxury, with more electronic equipment than the space shuttle. Elena got behind the wheel and started the engine, pulling out of the parking lot with the smooth confidence of someone who'd been driving expensive cars since she was sixteen.

"Where are we going?" I asked.

"Nowhere in particular. I just want to have a conversation without worrying about who might be listening."

She drove us out of the stadium complex and onto the surface streets, heading east toward downtown. The radio was tuned to the pre-game show, with announcers discussing the starting lineup and the prospects for the season. It was such a normal soundtrack for such an abnormal situation that I almost laughed.

"So," Elena said, stopping at a red light. "Tell me about Vincent Russo."

The question hit me like a punch to the solar plexus. Vinny Russo is well-known by the criminal elements in Los Angeles. He's private muscle, a ronin of sorts, open to working for anyone and doing anything for a price. But what she thought Vinny had to do with me left me clueless. "I don't know what you mean."

"Mr. Bolt, I appreciate your discretion, but we're past the point of playing games. Vincent Russo hired you to kill my father. The contract is for two million dollars, with half paid in advance. You've been conducting surveillance on me for the past two weeks, trying to find weaknesses you can exploit."

She recited the facts with the casual precision of someone reading a grocery list. The light turned green and she accelerated smoothly, heading toward the concrete canyon of downtown Los Angeles.

It was a rich theory Elena had concocted. Here was a likely spoiled princess, mob princess, who was proving to also be a talented manipulator who was trying to extract information from me. Information I didn't have, and what's more her hypothesis was wacky as all hell. However, this might be fun, so I decided to play along to see where this lead.

"How do you know all this?"

"Because I make it my business to know when someone is planning to murder my family." She glanced at me in the shotgun seat. "The real question is why you haven't tried yet."

"Maybe I'm still planning."

"Maybe. Or maybe you're having second thoughts."

We drove in silence for several blocks, passing through neighborhoods that had seen better days. Boarded-up storefronts, chain-link fences topped with razor wire, groups of men standing on corners with nothing to do and nowhere to go. This was the Los Angeles that tourists never saw, the part of the city that existed in the shadows between the beaches and the Hollywood sign.

"You want to know something interesting about my father?" Elena said, turning onto Spring Street. "He's dying."

"What?"

"Pancreatic cancer. Stage four. The doctors give him maybe six months, probably less."

I stared at her profile, trying to process what she'd just told me. "You're lying."

"Why would I lie about something like that? He was diagnosed three months ago. We've kept it quiet because knowledge of his illness would create instability in the organization. But the truth is, Vincent Russo is paying you to kill a man who's already dying."

She pulled into a parking garage beneath one of the downtown high-rises. The attendant waved her through without checking her ticket, which suggested this wasn't her first time here.

"Assuming that's true," I said, "why are you telling me?"

"Because I have a proposition for you."

She parked the Range Rover on the third level and turned off the engine. The garage was empty except for a few scattered cars, and the sound of our voices echoed off the concrete walls.

"I'm listening."

"My father's death is going to create a power vacuum in the organization. There are already people positioning themselves to take over, and most of them are considerably more violent and unpredictable than he is. Vincent Russo thinks removing my father will solve his problems, but actually it's going to make them much worse."

"And you want to prevent that?"

"I want to control it. When my father dies, I want to be the one who determines what happens to his organization."

I studied her face, looking for signs of deception or manipulation. But Elena Chesnokov was harder to read than most people. She'd been trained to conceal her thoughts and emotions, to present whatever facade was most advantageous in any given situation.

"What does this have to do with me?"

"Vincent Russo hired you because he believes you're the best at what you do. I want to hire you for the same reason."

"To do what?"

"To help me eliminate the people who pose a threat to my succession. There are three men in my father's organization who have the resources and connections to challenge me when he dies. I want them removed before that happens."

"You want me to kill three people instead of one."

"I want you to complete three contracts instead of one. The payment would be considerably more than what Vincent is offering."

She reached into her purse and pulled out a manila envelope, placing it on the console between us. "There's a million dollars in bearer bonds in that envelope. Consider it a down payment. Successfully complete the contracts, and I'll pay you another four million."

Five million dollars total. More money than I'd made in the past five years combined. Enough to disappear completely, to buy a house somewhere far from Los Angeles and start over with a clean slate. Enough to take care of Jenny for the rest of her life, to make sure she never had to worry about money or security.

"Why should I believe anything you've told me?"

"Because it's the truth. And because you're smart enough to recognize a better deal when you see one."

She was right about that. If Kiril Chesnokov was really dying, then Vincent's contract was essentially meaningless. The mob boss would be dead within six months regardless of whether I pulled the trigger. But eliminating his potential successors would require real skill, careful planning, and significant risk.

"I need time to think about it."

"Of course. But don't take too long. My father's condition is deteriorating rapidly, and the window for action is closing."

She started the engine and backed out of the parking space. "I'll drive you back to the stadium. Your car is still there, I assume?"

"Yeah."

We drove through downtown in silence, the radio still playing pre-game coverage of the Dodgers' season opener. The announcers were discussing the team's prospects, the new players they'd acquired during the off-season, the hope that this might finally be the year they won another World Series.

Hope. It was such a fragile thing in a city like Los Angeles, where dreams came to die and people reinvented themselves on a daily basis. The fans heading to Dodger Stadium were hoping for a championship, the players were hoping for career years, and I was hoping to survive long enough to figure out who was telling the truth and who was trying to get me killed.

"One more thing," Elena said as we pulled back into the stadium parking lot. "That GPS tracker you planted on my car? I've known about it since the second day. I left it there because I wanted you to think you were being clever."

She stopped next to my car and waited for me to get out. "Think about my offer, Mr. Bolt. But remember—in this business, standing still is the same as moving backward. And people who move backward tend to end up dead."

I climbed out of the Range Rover. Elena tossed the manila envelope to me through the open window. She smiled as I watched her drive away. I looked at the envelope. A million dollars in bearer bonds, untraceable and immediately negotiable. More money than I'd ever held at one time, offered by a woman who might be trying to save her father's criminal empire or destroy it completely. I opened the drivers door on the 911 and tossed the envelope on the passenger seat.

My phone buzzed with a text from Dan: "Found your detective's vehicle. 2018 Honda Accord, blue, license plate 7G4J829. Registered address in Alhambra."

I looked around the parking lot, scanning for a blue Honda Accord among the thousands of cars scattered across the asphalt. Finding Detective Valenzuela was still important—I needed information about Chesnokov's organization, about the power structure and potential successors that Elena had mentioned. But now I also needed to verify her story about her father's illness, about the looming succession crisis, about everything she'd told me.

The manila envelope sat on my front passenger seat like a loaded weapon, tempting and dangerous in equal measure. Inside were bonds worth a million dollars, the first payment for a contract that could set me up for life or get me killed in the process.

I started my car and drove deeper into the parking lot, looking for a blue Honda Accord and a detective who might have answers to questions I was just beginning to understand. Somewhere above me, 56,000 fans were settling into their seats for the ritual of Opening Day, hoping that this season would be different, that this year would bring something better than disappointment and broken dreams.

In Los Angeles, hope was the most dangerous emotion of all. But sometimes it was the only thing that kept you moving forward, even when you weren't sure where you were going or who you could trust when you got there.

The game was about to begin, and I still didn't know which team I was supposed to be playing for.

CHAPTER 18

NOT NECESSARILY

The phone buzzed against my ear as I sat in the Carrera, watching the afternoon shadows lengthen across the landscape near the corner of Gregory Way and Wooster Street in Beverly Hills. Three hours I'd been sitting here, nursing a cold coffee and pretending to read the same page of a paperback thriller that was proving to be far less thrilling than my actual life had become. Elena's apartment building, the Beverly-Wooster, was visible from my vantage point parked on Wooster near the parking entrance for the building. I'd watched her come and go twice today already. Each time, I'd felt that familiar knot in my stomach—the one that reminded me I was crossing lines I'd sworn I'd never cross again.

"Bolt." I answered the phone without looking at the caller ID, though I already knew who it was. Elsa's voice had become as familiar to me as my own breathing over the past few weeks.

"Hi there, stranger." Her voice carried that particular quality that made me think of honey poured over broken glass—sweet, but with sharp edges underneath. "I was wondering... are you following me?"

The question hit me hard. Elena and Elsa must be in sync. My grip tightened on the phone as I scanned the area, looking for any sign that she might be watching me. The question could mean anything—could be innocent curiosity, could be a trap, could be that she'd figured out about my extracurricular surveillance activities or Elena was sharing intel with her. But as the seconds ticked by, I realized there was something almost playful in her tone, like she was fishing for something specific.

"Of course," I said, keeping my voice light and easy. "Why wouldn't I?"

The pause that followed was pregnant with possibility. I could hear her breathing on the other end of the line, could almost picture her processing my response, trying to figure out if I was being serious or sarcastic. The silence stretched between us like a tightrope, and I found myself holding my breath, waiting to see which way she'd fall.

Finally, I couldn't stand it anymore. "Because I have nothing better to do than follow you around daily."

Her laughter bubbled up through the phone, genuine and relieved, and I felt some of the tension drain from my shoulders. "Oh God, I'm sorry," she said, still chuckling. "That came out wrong. I didn't mean to sound paranoid or accusatory. I just... I don't know. Sometimes I get this feeling like someone's watching me, you know? Probably just my imagination running wild."

If only she knew how right she was. But not about me—at least, not directly. I was watching Elena, not her, at least not today, though the distinction was becoming increasingly blurred in my mind. Every time I saw Elena leave her apartment, I wondered where she was going, whether she was meeting Elsa, whether they were discussing me. The whole situation had become a twisted web of surveillance and paranoia, and I was right in the center of it, pulling the strings.

"Where are you now?" Elsa asked, her tone shifting to something warmer, more intimate.

I glanced around the neighborhood, taking in the familiar landmarks—the Vendome liquor store with its flickering neon sign, and the other shops and offices on South Robertson; the dry cleaner with the handwritten "Back in 15 Minutes" sign that had been hanging in the window for the past hour, the small cafe where I'd bought my now-cold coffee. "I'm about to head into the San Fernando Valley," I said, which was technically true. I'd been planning to drive back through the Valley on my way home, though I hadn't been planning to leave for another hour or so.

"Would you like to get a drink together?"

The question caught me off guard, though it shouldn't have. Our reconnoiter of the Arts District warehouse was both anxiety ridden and intimate. I generally react to stress with the fight-or-flight impulse, and nine times out of ten I default to fight. Women, Elsa, generally default to tend-and-befriend behavior. The difference is which hormones are acting on which participant. For men, they are adrenaline and cortisol; for women, it's oxytocin. It made sense that after the warehouse visit Elsa was feeling close to me even though for me, I felt like a moron for letting my guard down. I should probably refuse this invitation outright, but something internal was compelling me.

I found myself running through the possible outcomes in my head like a detective working a case. Scenario one: we meet for drinks, keep things professional, and I learn something useful about her connection to Elena and whatever scheme they might be running together. Scenario two: we meet for drinks, things get personal, and I compromise my objectivity, again, in the investigation. Scenario three: we meet for drinks, she figures out that I've been investigating her, and I blow the whole case wide open. Scenario four: we meet for drinks, and I finally get some answers to the questions that have been eating at me for weeks.

But there was another scenario I didn't want to admit to myself—the one where we meet for drinks and I discover that I care more about Elsa than I do about the case, more about her smile than about whatever truth I'm supposed to be uncovering. That was the scenario that scared me the most, because it was the one that felt most likely.

"Yes," I said finally, surprised by how easily the word came out.

"Great! Where would you like to meet?"

I expected her to suggest some upscale bar in Beverly Hills or West Hollywood, the kind of place where drinks cost twenty dollars and everyone was either an actor, a producer, or someone pretending to be one of the two. Instead, she surprised me.

"How about my apartment? I've got a full bar, and it's much more private than anywhere in public."

The suggestion sent a jolt through me that was part excitement, part caution. Her apartment meant privacy, intimacy, the kind of setting where conversations could take unexpected turns and professional boundaries could disappear entirely. It also meant I'd be on her turf, in her space, where she'd have all the advantages and I'd be operating blind.

"I think I'll have to politely decline," I said, trying to keep my tone light and conversational.

"Oh, come on," she said, and I could hear the teasing in her voice. "Are you afraid to be alone with me?"

The question hung in the air between us, loaded with implication. She was flirting with me, that much was clear, but there was something else underneath it—a challenge, maybe, or a test. I thought about the hours I'd spent sitting in my car, watching her apartment, wondering what secrets she and Elena and perhaps even Trisha might be sharing. I thought about the case files spread across my kitchen table, the photos, the notes, the growing sense that I was missing something important.

"Not necessarily," I said finally. "I'm thinking about your safety."

"My safety?" She laughed again, but this time there was something different in it—surprise, maybe, or curiosity. "What do you mean?"

"I haven't been alone in an intimate environment with a beautiful woman in a while," I said, letting the words hang in the air for a moment before continuing. "I'm not sure I trust myself to be a perfect gentleman."

It was a dangerous thing to say, walking the line between honesty and flirtation, between professionalism and something much more personal. But it felt true, and truth had become a rare commodity in my life lately. I'd been alone for months, throwing myself into work to avoid thinking about the emptiness that had settled into my life like dust on furniture that nobody ever used. The idea of being alone with Elsa in her abode, of talking to her without the barrier of a phone line between us, or without other people around, was both disturbing and appealing. The warehouse was different because we were both in a heightened state of alertness, it was a "public" place, and we were being watched.

"I think I can take care of myself," she said, and there was steel underneath the silk of her voice. "But I appreciate your honesty."

Playing dumb seemed like the safer option, so I shifted gears. "Where do you live, anyway? I realize I don't even know what part of town you're in."

"Sherman Oaks," she said. "I've got a little place off Ventura Boulevard, on Moorpark Street. Nothing fancy, but it's home."

"Tell you what," I said, thinking fast. "How about we meet somewhere in between? There's a place called El Mariachi on Ventura Boulevard. Good margaritas, decent food, and public enough to keep us both honest."

I'd driven past El Mariachi dozens of times during my surveillance runs, had even eaten there once or twice when I needed a break from sitting in the car. It was the kind of neighborhood Mexican restaurant that served strong drinks and minded its own business—exactly the sort of place where two people could have a conversation without attracting attention.

"El Mariachi," she repeated, and I could hear her thinking it over. "I know the place. Sure, that sounds perfect."

"How does five-thirty sound to you?"

"It's a date," she said, and then the line went dead.

I sat in the car for a moment, staring at the phone in my hand and trying to process what had just happened. A date. She'd called it a date, which meant this was crossing definitively into personal territory, leaving professional concerns in the rearview mirror. I should have said no. I should have made up an excuse, postponed, suggested we meet during business hours in a more formal setting. I should have done a lot of things differently.

But before I could head to the restaurant, I had another matter to attend to. Elena had mentioned Vinny Russo during our conversation on opening day—a freelance hitman who supposedly had a contract on her father, Kiril Chesnokov. She'd been vague about the details, but something in her tone had convinced me it wasn't just paranoia. If Vinny was real, and if he was planning to move against Chesnokov, that changed the entire dynamic of the situation I'd found myself in. Since it was three-fifteen, I had plenty of time to talk to Russo.

I'd spent the morning tracking down information about Russo through my contacts in the underworld—the kind of people who knew things but didn't ask questions about why you wanted to know them. What I'd learned wasn't encouraging. Vinny Russo was a professional, someone who took contracts seriously and completed them regardless of obstacles. He was also someone who could be reasoned with, if you approached him the right way and had something valuable to offer.

According to my sources, Russo frequented a dive bar called The Scene on Saticoy Street, usually showing up around four in the afternoon for a beer and a shot before heading home to his apartment in North Hollywood. It was a routine that had been consistent for months, which meant I had a narrow window of opportunity to approach him before my meeting with Elsa.

I started the engine and pulled away from the curb, driving toward a confrontation that could either solve one of my problems or create several new ones. The traffic was light for a weekday afternoon, and I made good time through the hills that separated Beverly Hills from the Valley.

The Scene was exactly the kind of place you'd expect to find a contract killer—dimly lit, sparsely populated, with bartenders who minded their own business and customers who paid in cash.

I parked across the street and watched the bar for ten minutes, looking for any sign of surveillance or unusual activity. The place seemed dead, which was either a good sign or a very bad one. In my experience, the most dangerous situations often appeared the most peaceful on the surface.

Vincent Russo was sitting at the far end of the bar when I walked in, a half-empty beer bottle in front of him and a shot glass that had been recently emptied. He was smaller than I'd expected, maybe five-eight with a slight build, but there was something about the way he held himself that suggested coiled violence. His dark hair was slicked back with pomade, and he wore a cheap suit that had seen better days.

He looked up as I approached, his eyes taking in my appearance with the professional assessment of someone who was used to evaluating potential threats. "You're not a regular," he said, his voice carrying a slight Brooklyn accent that hadn't been softened by decades in Los Angeles.

"No, I'm not." I took the stool two seats away from him, close enough to talk but far enough to give him space. "I'm looking for Vinny Russo."

"Depends on who's asking." He signaled the bartender for another shot. "And why they want to know."

"The name's Bolt. I'm a private investigator, and I understand you might have a business arrangement that involves Kiril Chesnokov."

The change in his demeanor was immediate and subtle. His shoulders tensed slightly, and his right hand moved closer to his jacket pocket. "I don't know what you're talking about."

"I think you do." I ordered a beer I didn't want, using the time to choose my words carefully. "I also think you're smart enough to know that Chesnokov is dying. Cancer. Maybe six months left, if he's lucky."

Russo's shot arrived, and he downed it in one smooth motion. "Even if that were true, which I'm not saying it is, what's that got to do with me?"

"It means any contract on him is worthless. You'd be taking a risk for payment on a job that'll complete itself in a few months." I took a sip of my beer, watching his face for any reaction. "That's not good business."

"You seem to know a lot about business arrangements I may or may not have." He turned to face me fully, and I could see the calculation in his eyes. "Makes me wonder why you care."

"Because I'm not going to let you complete that contract," I said simply. "But I'd rather make it worth your while to back down than have to stop you the hard way."

The silence that followed was heavy with implication. Russo studied my face, looking for signs of bluff or weakness. What he saw there seemed to satisfy him, because when he spoke again, his voice had lost some of its hostility.

"You're serious."

"Dead serious."

"Seven figures," he said quietly. "That's what we're talking about. You got seven figures to make this worth my while?"

"Not in cash. But I've got something better." I leaned closer, keeping my voice low. "I've got access to Elena Chesnokov."

His eyebrows rose slightly. "The daughter?"

"The heir. When the old man dies, she takes over everything. The legitimate businesses, the not-so-legitimate ones, all of it." I paused, letting him process that information. "Someone with that kind of power could throw a lot of work your way. The kind of work that pays better than one-time contracts."

"Assuming she survives to inherit."

"She will. I'll make sure of it."

Russo ordered another shot and sat in silence for a moment, thinking. When he spoke again, his voice was purely business. “What kind of work are we talking about?”

“Competitors who need discouraging. Business partners who become problems. The kind of situations that arise when you’re running a criminal enterprise in a competitive market.” I finished half my beer, trying to project confidence I didn’t entirely feel. “Elena’s going to need someone reliable, someone professional. Someone who can handle problems without creating new ones.”

“And you speak for her?”

“I speak for her interests. And right now, her interests include keeping her father alive long enough to die naturally.”

Russo laughed, a dry sound that held no humor. “You’re asking me to walk away from guaranteed money for the promise of maybe getting work from someone who might not even survive the transition.”

“I’m asking you to think long-term. Seven figures sounds like a lot, but it’s one payday. What I’m offering is a relationship that could be worth ten times that over the next few years.”

“Assuming the old man doesn’t have other enemies. Assuming his daughter can hold onto power. Assuming she honors agreements made on her behalf by private investigators she barely knows.” He drained his beer and stood up. “That’s a lot of assumptions.”

“Then let me make it simpler.” I stood as well, making sure he could see that I was unarmed and ready for trouble, but also confirming my six-inch height advantage. “The contract is off. You can take what I’m offering, or you can walk away and find other work. But you’re not touching Kiril Chesnokov.”

For a moment, I thought he might reach for whatever weapon he was carrying. His hand moved toward his jacket, then stopped as he reconsidered. “You’re either very brave or very stupid.”

“Maybe both. But I’m also right about this. The smart play is to walk away.”

"I need to think about it."

"Don't think too long. The offer expires when Chesnokov does."

He nodded once, a gesture that might have been agreement or acknowledgment. "I'll be in touch."

"Don't take too long to decide. And Russo?" I waited until he was looking at me directly. "If you decide to ignore my advice, remember that I know where to find you. And I won't hesitate to make sure you can't complete your contract."

He walked out without another word, leaving me alone at the bar with my thoughts and half a beer I didn't want. The confrontation had gone better than I'd expected, but I knew it was far from over. Men like Russo didn't make decisions quickly, and they didn't abandon lucrative contracts without careful consideration. I'd bought myself some time, but I hadn't eliminated the threat.

I checked my watch and realized I needed to leave for my meeting with Elsa. The drive to El Mariachi would take me back through the Valley, giving me time to shift mental gears from the violence of Russo's world to the more subtle dangers of whatever game Elsa was playing.

Instead, I started the engine and pulled away from the curb, driving toward a meeting that I knew was going to change everything, one way or another.

The drive to El Mariachi from Saticoy took me onto Coldwater Canyon and then onto the Ventura Freeway. The traffic was horrendous as expected. I breathed deeply in an attempt to cool my jets. The eight-mile drive took thirty-two minutes.

My phone rang. I recognized the number as Detective Valenzuela. I answered hands-free. "Bolt here," I said.

"Mr. Bolt, it's Detective Luis Valenzuela from L.A.P.D. How can I help you?"

"Thanks for returning my call, Detective. I'm a private investigator working a missing person case, and it appears there may be some Russian mob connection. I understand you're running the task force?"

"Who's the missing person?"

"Rollo Tomassi," I took a chance that Detective Valenzuela was too young to know the movie L.A. Confidential from the '90s.

"How is Rollo connected to the Russian mob?" Bingo! He didn't get it.

"I'm not sure, but I have reason to believe he is involved with Kiril Chesnokov." I could hear Valenzuela inhale hard.

"Mr. Bolt, Kiril Chesnokov is a killer, pure and simple. I suggest you give all your information to the missing person's unit." This joker thought I was an amateur.

"I appreciate your concern, Detective, but I was twenty-three years with the FBI." It was a white lie he wasn't likely to confirm. "I know how to handle dirtbags like Chesnokov. Do you have any information that might be helpful?"

"Sorry, Mr. Bolt, I didn't realize you had federal law enforcement experience. We have information that Chesnokov has a warehouse in Desert Center. Do you know where that is?"

"Middle of the desert, I suspect. What's the intel on the warehouse and operation?"

"We have a team going out there next week. Call me back a week from Friday, and I can give you an update." Yeah, I'll wait a week to find out Chesnokov closed down the operation two days before they arrived. He probably had a mole in the department and knows exactly when the cops are coming.

"Thank you very much, Detective. I will do that. Have a nice day."

The call ended just as I was approaching El Mariachi. I parked three blocks away from the restaurant and walked the rest of the way, using the time to clear my head and try to figure out what I was walking into. The evening air was warm and dry, carrying the scent of jasmine from the landscaping around the apartment complexes and the faint smell of car exhaust from Ventura Boulevard. The sun was setting behind the hills, painting the sky in shades of orange and pink that would have been beautiful if I'd been in the mood to appreciate them.

My encounter with Russo had left me unsettled in ways I hadn't expected. There was something about the casual way he'd discussed seven-figure murder contracts that reminded me of the world I'd left behind—a world where violence was a tool and human life was a commodity to be bought and sold. I'd thought I was done with that world, but here I was, making deals with killers and threatening violence of my own.

El Mariachi was tucked between a nail salon and a used bookstore in a strip mall that had seen better days. The neon sign flickered intermittently, and the parking lot needed repaving, but the place had character in the way that only authentic neighborhood joints could. I'd always liked it here—the food was good, the drinks were strong, and nobody bothered you if you wanted to sit in a corner booth and think.

I pushed through the heavy glass door and was hit by the familiar combination of cumin, cilantro, and the subtle tang of lime that permeated every surface. The interior was dimly lit, with red vinyl booths and walls covered in faded photographs of Mexico and hand-painted murals of desert landscapes. A mariachi trio played softly in the corner, their music mixing with the low hum of conversation and the occasional laugh from the bar.

I'd arrived a few minutes early, which gave me time to scope out the place and choose a strategic seat. I picked a booth near the back that had a clear view of the entrance but was far enough from other customers to allow for private conversation. The waitress, a middle-aged woman with kind eyes and hands that suggested she'd been working in restaurants for decades, brought me a beer without being asked.

"You want to wait for your friend before you order?" she asked in accented English.

"Yeah, thanks. She should be here soon."

I nursed the beer and tried to organize my thoughts. What did I know about Elsa, really? She was beautiful, intelligent, articulate. She claimed to be a journalist, though I'd never seen any of her bylines. She had some spiritual and emotional issues she hoped could be helped by attending classes at the Kabbalah Center, but she was composed enough during our reconnoiter of the abandoned warehouse downtown. She called me at odd hours, asked probing questions about my work, and seemed genuinely interested in my thoughts and opinions.

Any one of those things could be innocent. Taken together, they painted a picture of someone who was either exactly what she appeared to be—a smart, attractive woman who was interested in getting to know me better—or someone who was playing a much deeper game than I'd given her credit for.

The door chimed, and I looked up to see Elsa scanning the restaurant. She was wearing a simple black dress that probably cost more than a monthly car payment, and her dark hair was pulled back in a way that emphasized the elegant line of her neck. She moved with the kind of confidence that came from knowing she was beautiful and being comfortable with that fact.

When she spotted me, her face lit up with a smile that made my chest tighten. She walked toward the booth with a fluid grace that drew glances from every man in the place, but her attention was focused entirely on me.

"Jon Bolt," she said as she slid into the booth across from me. "You clean up nice."

"Just Bolt is fine," I said. "And you look..." I paused, searching for a word that wouldn't make me sound like a teenager on his first date. "You look incredible."

"Thank you." She flagged down the waitress and ordered a margarita, then turned her attention back to me. "So, this is nice. I was starting to think you were avoiding me."

"Why would I avoid you?"

"I don't know. You tell me." She leaned forward slightly, resting her elbows on the table. "Every time I suggest meeting in person, you find a reason to postpone or change the subject. I was beginning to think you didn't want to be seen with me."

The directness of her approach caught me off guard. I'd expected small talk, the usual dance of getting to know each other that preceded more serious conversations. Instead, she was cutting straight to the heart of things, forcing me to either lie or reveal more about myself than I was comfortable sharing.

"It's not that," I said carefully. "My work keeps me busy, and I've learned to be cautious about mixing business with pleasure."

"Yes, I know. Your business is... interesting."

Her margarita arrived, and she took a sip while waiting for me to respond. The statement hung between us like a challenge, and I realized that how I responded would set the tone for everything that followed.

"That's one way to describe what I do," I said honestly. "I'd like it to be pleasure, but I've got some professional concerns that are hard to ignore."

"Such as?"

"Such as the fact that I don't really know who you are or what you want from me."

She leaned back in the booth, studying my face with an intensity that made me uncomfortable. "Fair enough," she said finally. "What would you like to know?"

"Start with the basics. What do you do for a living?" I said. Because of her attempted murder in the Whole Foods parking lot, I hadn't really had a chance to discover how Elsa covered her lifestyle.

"I'm a journalist."

"What kind of journalism do you do? Who do you write for?"

"Freelance mostly. I do investigative pieces for various magazines and online publications. Nothing too glamorous—corporate corruption, political scandals, that sort of thing." She took another sip of her margarita. "I specialize in stories that other people don't want to touch, the kind of things that make powerful people nervous."

"Such as?"

"My last piece was about a real estate development company that was using dummy corporations to buy up property in low-income neighborhoods, then flipping them for massive profits while displacing longtime residents. The piece ran in LA Weekly three months ago."

It sounded plausible, the kind of story that investigative journalists actually wrote. But I made a mental note to check whether such an article had actually appeared in LA Weekly. Trust but verify had become my motto where Elsa was concerned.

"And how did you meet Elena?" I asked, trying to keep the question casual.

"Elena?" She seemed genuinely surprised by the question. "Why do you ask?"

This was going to be good. "Elena is the daughter of Kiril Chesnokov. You are connected to him as well. I'm not sure how other than some money laundering, maybe, but connected you are. So, one thing leads to another, and I am curious about the connection."

"Oh, that." She waved a hand dismissively. "We know each other through a group we both belong to, the connection is not because of her father."

I assumed Elsa was referring to the Kabbalah Center, but I wanted to see if she added any color to her story.

"What group?"

"Are you familiar with the Kabbalah Center on Robertson?"

"I think so. Isn't that a Jewish spiritual organization? I didn't know you were Jewish."

"I'm not. I'm Christian or was Christian. Currently, I'm a seeker. I'm not sure what I believe."

Holy crap! She is one messed up puppy. She continued.

"Turns out we had some mutual interests, including apparently knowing you."

I didn't recall any conversation about me on the recording Maggie gathered. And since I hadn't had my "conversation" with Elena until after the Kabbalah surveillance, I was becoming more concerned that I was being surveilled by either Elena or by her father. Not good.

However, the explanation was smooth, plausible, and completely unsatisfying. It answered my question without really answering it, giving me information while revealing nothing of substance. Either Elsa was naturally evasive, or she was deliberately avoiding giving me details that might allow me to verify her story.

"What kind of mutual interests?" I pressed.

"Justice, truth, the usual things that idealistic people care about." She smiled, but there was something sharp in her eyes. "Why all the questions about Elena? Are you two...?"

"No," I said quickly. "Nothing like that. I just like to understand the connections between people in my life."

"People in your life?" She raised an eyebrow. "Is that what I am?"

The question caught me off guard again. She had a talent for turning conversations back on me just when I thought I was getting somewhere, for making me reveal more about myself than I intended while keeping her own cards close to her chest.

"I hope so," I said, and realized I meant it.

The admission seemed to please her. She reached across the table and touched my hand, her fingers warm against my skin. "Good," she said. "Because I like you, Bolt. I like talking to you, I like the way your mind works, and I think we could be good together."

"Together how?"

"However we want to be." Her thumb traced a small circle on the back of my hand. "I'm not looking for anything complicated or demanding. I'm just looking for someone interesting to spend time with, someone who understands that life is short and should be enjoyed."

It was a tempting offer, made more tempting by the touch of her hand and the way she was looking at me. But something in her phrasing nagged at me, something about the careful way she'd constructed her sentences to sound intimate while committing to nothing specific.

"What about your story?" I asked. "The one you're working on?"

"What about it?"

"Are you still planning to write about police corruption?"

She pulled her hand back and picked up her margarita, buying herself time to think. "That depends," she said finally.

"On what?"

"On whether I find a story worth telling."

We stared at each other across the table, and I had the distinct feeling that we were negotiating something much more significant than the terms of our personal relationship. There was a subtext to this conversation that I couldn't quite grasp, layers of meaning that remained just out of reach.

The waitress appeared at our table, breaking the tension. "You folks ready to order some food?"

I realized I hadn't even looked at the menu, hadn't thought about eating since Elsa had walked through the door. "Give us a few more minutes," I said.

When we were alone again, Elsa seemed to have made some kind of decision. She leaned forward, her voice dropping to barely above a whisper.

"Can I tell you something in confidence?"

I nodded, though every instinct I had was screaming that I was about to hear something I didn't want to know.

"I think you're in danger."

The words hit me. After everything that had transpired recently, the warning took on new significance. "What kind of danger?"

"The kind that comes from asking the wrong questions about the wrong people." She glanced around the restaurant, as if checking to make sure we weren't being overheard. "Someone knows you've been investigating certain activities, and they're not happy about it."

"What activities? What investigation?"

"You know what investigation." Her eyes met mine, and I saw fear there, genuine fear that sent ice through my veins. "The question is, what are you going to do about it?"

I stared at her, my mind racing. Either she was telling the truth and I was in more trouble than I'd realized, or she was lying and trying to manipulate me for reasons I couldn't fathom. Either way, the game had just changed in a fundamental way.

"Who told you this?" I asked.

"Someone who cares about your wellbeing."

"Elsa, who?"

She didn't answer, but the slight tightening around her eyes was confirmation enough.

"What do you want from me?" I pressed.

"Be smart. Please understand that some stones are better left unturned, some questions are better left unasked." Elsa finished her margarita and signaled for another. "It's not too late to walk away."

"And if I don't?"

"Then you might not get another chance to make that choice."

We sat in silence for a moment, the weight of her words settling between us like a physical presence. The mariachi music continued in the background, cheerful and incongruous given the turn our conversation had taken. Other customers laughed and talked around us, oblivious to the drama playing out in our little corner of the restaurant.

"Is that why you're here?" I asked finally. "To deliver a message?"

"I'm here because I care about you," she said, and for the first time since she'd walked in, her voice sounded completely genuine. "I'm here because I think you're a good man who's gotten in over his head, and I don't want to see you get hurt."

"And if I choose to keep digging? Keep asking questions?"

She looked at me for a long moment, and I saw something that might have been sadness in her eyes. "Then I hope you're as good at this job as you think you are."

The waitress brought Elsa's second margarita and stood waiting for our food order. I ordered enchiladas I didn't want, and Elsa asked for a quesadilla she probably wouldn't eat. We were both going through the motions now, playing out the scene for the sake of appearances.

When we were alone again, I made a decision that I knew I'd probably regret.

"Let's say, hypothetically, that I wanted to walk away from whatever investigation has people so concerned," I said. "What would that look like?"

"Simple. You stop surveillance, you stop asking questions, you stop trying to connect dots that other people would prefer remain unconnected." She leaned forward again, her voice urgent. "You focus on other cases, other problems. There's no shortage of people in need of your type of assistance in Los Angeles—find something else to occupy your time."

"And in return?"

"In return, you get to keep living your life. You get to keep your job, your freedom, your health." She paused. "You get to keep seeing me, if that's something you want."

There it was—the carrot to go with the stick. Stop investigating, and I could have a relationship with this beautiful, intelligent woman who claimed to care about my wellbeing. Keep digging, and face consequences that were still vague but increasingly ominous.

"I need to think about it," I said.

"Don't think too long." She reached across the table and took my hand again. "Some offers have expiration dates."

Our food arrived, and we made small talk while we ate, carefully avoiding the subjects that had dominated our conversation. She told me about her childhood in San Francisco, her years at Berkeley, her decision to become a journalist. I found myself wanting to believe her stories, wanting to trust the woman sitting across from me despite every red flag my professional instincts were throwing up.

When the check came, I insisted on paying, and she didn't argue. We walked out into the warm evening air together, and for a moment it felt almost normal—like a real first date between two people who were genuinely interested in getting to know each other.

"This was nice," she said as we reached the sidewalk. "I hope we can do it again soon."

"Where's your car?"

"I took a rideshare. I didn't want to worry about driving after drinking." She smiled. "Plus, I was hoping you might offer to give me a ride home."

The request was reasonable, innocent even. But I remembered her earlier invitation to her apartment, remembered the way she'd turned every conversation back to personal territory, remembered the warning she'd delivered wrapped in concern for my safety.

"I'd be happy to call you another ride," I said. "My car's a bit of a mess right now."

She studied my face for a moment, then nodded. "That's fine. I understand."

While we waited for her ride, she moved closer to me, close enough that I could smell her perfume—something subtle and expensive that made me think of garden parties and summer evenings. When the car arrived, she turned to face me.

"Think about what I said, Bolt. Think about what's really important to you."

Before I could respond, she rose up on her toes and kissed me, soft and brief but with just enough heat to leave me wanting more. Then she was in the back seat of the car, waving goodbye through the window as they pulled away into traffic.

I stood on the sidewalk for a few minutes after she left, trying to process everything that had happened. The kiss had been unexpected, adding another layer of complexity to an already complicated situation. But it was the warning that dominated my thoughts—the implication that someone knew about my surveillance of Elena, that my investigation had attracted attention from people who were willing to take action to stop it.

The connection between Elsa's warning and my conversation with Russo wasn't lost on me. Both interactions had been about backing down, about walking away from investigations or contracts that other people wanted to see ended. The timing couldn't be coincidental.

I walked back to my car, my mind churning with questions and possibilities. Either Elsa was exactly what she appeared to be—a former thief and now journalist and money launderer who was genuinely concerned about my safety—or she was something else entirely, someone whose agenda remained hidden beneath layers of charm and apparent sincerity.

Just before I got back into the Porsche, Vicky texted: Tam O'Shanter at 8 p.m. It was 6 p.m. then. Two hours to kill. I sniffed my pits to make sure I was clean. A little funky, but not unreasonably so. I could drive back to Playa Del Rey, but the traffic might bite me in the ass. I decided to head to the dojo in Pasadena. I'd go buy a new shirt on Colorado and then take a shower there. It would be good to see Master again.

The drive to Pasadena gave me time to think about my conversation with Russo. The hitman had been professional, calculating, but not unreasonable. He was a businessman first, someone who understood that the best contracts were the ones that didn't end with complications. My offer had given him something to consider—the possibility of a long-term relationship with Elena's organization versus a one-time payday that came with significant risks.

But I also knew that men like Russo didn't abandon lucrative contracts easily. Seven figures was serious money, the kind of payday that could set someone up for years. And there was always the possibility that whoever had hired him wouldn't take kindly to him backing out of the deal. Contract killers who developed reputations for unreliability didn't stay in business long.

I found myself thinking about Elena and the position she was in. Her father was dying, she was preparing to take over a criminal empire, and she had enemies who wanted her family eliminated before the transition could take place. No wonder she'd seemed so tense during our meetings, so careful about who she trusted and what information she revealed.

The more I learned about the Chesnokov situation, the more complicated it became. Elena wasn't just inheriting legitimate businesses—she was stepping into a world where violence was a standard business practice and where showing weakness could be fatal. If she was going to survive the transition, she'd need allies, people she could trust to protect her interests.

Maybe that's where I fit into her plans. Not just as someone who could investigate threats, but as someone who could neutralize them when necessary. The thought made me uncomfortable, but I couldn't deny that it made sense from her perspective.

As I drove through the familiar streets of Pasadena, I found myself checking my rearview mirror more often than usual, looking for cars that might be following me, for signs that the danger Elsa had warned me about was more immediate than I'd realized.

By the time I reached Pasadena, I'd made a decision. I was going to keep digging, keep asking questions, keep following the trail wherever it led. But I was also going to be more careful, more systematic, more aware of the risks I was taking because whatever game I'd stumbled into, the stakes had just gotten a lot higher, and the rules had just gotten a lot more dangerous.

I parked on Green Street and walked one block to Colorado and Banana Republic. I found a new button-down in my size, paid and walked back to Green.

There was a class in session when I arrived at the school. I looked toward Master Parker's office, but it was empty. Another black belt was teaching a class of mixed level students: brown, green, blue, and purple belts were working through techniques and forms. I bowed before stepping on the mat and walked back to the men's locker room and showers. I grabbed a clean towel and proceeded to the last shower in the row.

The hot water felt good against my skin, washing away the tension from my encounters with both Russo and Elsa. But as I stood under the spray, I couldn't shake the feeling that I was being pulled in multiple directions by forces I didn't fully understand. Elena wanted protection for her family. Elsa wanted me to back off from my investigation. Russo wanted seven figures for killing Elena's father. And somewhere in the middle of it all, I was trying to figure out what the right thing to do was.

When I was almost finished, I heard a voice from outside the shower curtain say, "don't you say 'hello' anymore?" It was Master. "You were AWOL. Not in your office and not teaching."

"Even masters need to evacuate their bowels at times."

I turned off the water and drew the curtains back as I toweled off. "I have a date, and I was a little funky. I hope you don't mind, Master."

He smiled and walked away. "Come see me after you get dressed."

I dried off, put on deodorant, combed my hair, and dressed in my new shirt. I gathered my things and proceeded to see Master Parker in his office. The classes had been dismissed, but I bowed on and off the mat as protocol required. Respect is most important in the martial arts.

Master Parker was seated behind his great desk looking over some paperwork. As I entered the doorway, he motioned me to sit. I took the chair closest to the desk and sat down.

"A date, huh? It's been a while, no?"

"True. I've been busy." Master Parker looked up at me and shook his head. "Don't be too busy for love, Grasshopper," he said. He called me Grasshopper whenever I was being a nitwit in his estimation. The term was drawn from the '70s television series "Kung Fu." Grasshopper was the lead character Caine's nickname.

When Caine was a boy, he asked blind Master Po how he could function without seeing. Po asked Caine to close his eyes and describe what he could hear. Caine explained that he could hear the water flowing in a nearby fountain and birds in a nearby cage. Po then asked if Caine could hear his own heartbeat or the grasshopper at his feet. Caine hadn't noticed the insect. Caine then asked Po, "Old man—how is it that you hear these things?" Po's reply was, "Young man, how is it that you do not?" From that point on, Po affectionately called Caine "Grasshopper." Master Parker always used "Grasshopper" as an affectionate way to correct my ignorance.

"True, my Master. That is why I am going."

"Who is the lucky girl?"

"Victoria." Tatum Parker's face lit up. "Good. I like her."

"Jenny and you. Maybe you both should join us?"

"Get out," Tatum Parker said with a laugh. "See you soon."

But as I stood to leave, Master Parker's expression grew more serious. "Bolt," he said, his voice taking on the tone he used when he was about to impart wisdom. "You seem troubled. More than usual."

I paused in the doorway, considering whether to share my concerns. Master Parker had always been more than just a martial arts instructor to me—he was a mentor, someone whose judgment I trusted implicitly. But this situation was complicated in ways that were difficult to explain.

"I'm working a case that's gotten more complex than I expected," I said finally.

"Complex how?"

"The kind where it's hard to tell who the good guys are."

Master Parker nodded slowly. "In my experience, the most dangerous situations are the ones where everyone believes they're the good guy. When righteousness meets righteousness, violence often follows."

"What do you do when you're caught in the middle?"

"You remember that your first obligation is to yourself and those you care about. You can't save everyone, Grasshopper. Sometimes the best you can do is choose the lesser evil and live with the consequences."

The advice was practical, unsentimental, and probably exactly what I needed to hear. But it also reminded me of how alone I was in this situation. Elena, Elsa, Russo—they all had their own agendas, their own reasons for wanting me to act in particular ways. The only person I could truly trust was myself.

"Thank you, Master."

"Be careful, Bolt. And remember—sometimes the greatest victory is knowing when to retreat."

I exited the school, got into the Carrera, and headed toward Los Feliz, Master Parker's words echoing in my mind. The greatest victory is knowing when to retreat. But retreat to where? And at what cost.

CHAPTER 19

EARLY BIRD

I arrived at the Tam O'Shanter fourteen minutes later. The time was seven fifty. The heavy wooden door groaned open, releasing a cloud of aromatic smoke that wrapped around me like an old friend's embrace. Stepping inside felt like crossing a threshold into another world—one where time moved slower and dreams took shape over plates of prime rib and pints of ale.

The dining room stretched before me in warm, amber light, all dark wood paneling and burgundy leather banquettes that had absorbed decades of whispered conversations and boisterous laughter. Wrought iron chandeliers cast dancing shadows across the Scottish tartans that adorned the walls, while the massive stone fireplace crackled with a fire that seemed to have been burning since the restaurant's founding in 1922.

This was where Walt Disney held court with his imagineers, I'd heard, sketching characters on napkins and spinning tales that would soon flicker to life on silver screens across America. The very walls seemed to pulse with creative energy, as if they had absorbed every brilliant idea, every "what if," every eureka moment that had echoed through this space.

I slid into a corner booth, the leather creaking beneath me with the comfortable sag of countless previous occupants. The table bore the subtle scars of years—ring stains from glasses, tiny scratches from animated gestures during heated discussions about story arcs and character development. The servers moved between tables like actors in a well-rehearsed play, their crisp white shirts and dark vests giving them an Old-World dignity.

Vicky wasn't here yet. I checked my watch—nine minutes until she was officially late. I signaled the waitress and ordered a club soda, keeping my head clear for whatever the evening might bring.

Nine minutes came and went. I was halfway through my drink when the door swung open, and there she was. Vicky stood in the doorway for a beat, letting the light from outside create a halo around her auburn hair. She was wearing a black dress that hugged her curves like it was painted on, the hem just high enough to turn heads but low enough to keep it classy.

When her eyes found me, a smile broke across her face—slow, deliberate, the kind of smile that could stop traffic or start a fight. She made her way over, her heels clicking against the floor in a rhythm that matched my pulse.

"Hey, stranger," she said, her voice low and smoky, as she slid into the booth across from me. She leaned in and kissed me, quick but soft, her lips brushing mine just long enough to make my pulse kick up a notch. I caught the scent on her breath—whiskey, sharp and warm. She'd had a drink before arriving. Liquid courage, maybe.

"I don't remember you being tardy, ever," I said, keeping it light.

She laughed, a sound like ice clinking in a glass. "You know me, Jon. I move on my own time."

The waitress came to take our order—a cute girl about twenty-one with short brunette hair and a few tasteful tattoos on her arms. Her name was Emma, and she had that LA service industry polish that came from dealing with all types. We ordered drinks first—two margaritas, hers on the rocks, mine with a salt rim—and asked Emma to give us time with the menu.

"To old friends," Vicky said when the drinks arrived, raising her glass with that dangerous smile playing at the edges of her lips.

"To old friends," I echoed, clinking my glass against hers.

We settled into conversation over our drinks. Vicky told me she'd become a criminal defense attorney after we'd lost touch. Started in the public defender's office in Arlington, but after ten years of office politics she'd gone solo.

"Being a solo gives me all the money I want with all the flexibility I need," she said, swirling her margarita. "I can take the cases I want, turn down the ones I don't. No partners breathing down my neck, no office politics. Just me and the law."

"What kind of cases are you handling these days?" I asked, genuinely curious.

Her eyes lit up the way they always did when she got into her work. "Mostly white-collar stuff—embezzlement, fraud, some drug cases. I had this one client last month, a CFO who got caught skimming from the pension fund. Thought he was being clever, moving money through offshore accounts, creating shell companies. The problem with these executive types is they always think they're the smartest guy in the room."

"Let me guess—he wasn't."

"Not even close. The FBI had been watching him for months. They had bank records, email chains, even recorded phone calls. My job wasn't to prove his innocence—it was to keep him out of federal prison for the next twenty years."

"How'd that work out?"

"Plea deal. Three years minimum security, full restitution. Could've been a lot worse." She took a long sip of her drink. "Then there's the other side of my practice—the real criminals. Had a gang member last week, kid barely nineteen, caught with enough fentanyl to kill half of Arlington. The thing is, he's not the guy they really want. He's just the mule, bottom of the food chain."

I leaned forward, interested. "So what's your play?"

"Cooperation. The kid gives up his supplier, maybe the guy above that, and he gets a reduced sentence instead of life without parole. But here's where it gets interesting—" She lowered her voice, leaning closer. "The supplier he'd have to flip on? Word is he's connected to some serious people. Mexican cartel money laundering through construction companies in Northern Virginia. The kind of operation where people who talk too much end up in the Potomac wearing concrete shoes."

"Sounds like you've got your hands full."

"That's putting it mildly. The kid's scared—rightfully so. His family's scared. Even I'm getting nervous, and I've been doing this for fifteen years. But that's the job, right? Sometimes you have to dance with the devil to get your client a fair shake."

Emma returned to take our food order. We both went with the prime rib—medium rare, loaded baked potato, Caesar salad. Classic choices for a classic place. As Emma walked away, I told Vicky about my work, keeping it general.

"Still in the retrieval business," I said. "Anything someone needs to retrieve, but either can't or won't involve the police, I'm the man for the job."

"Sounds sketchy. Anything?"

"Not really 'anything'. I do retain some standards, but it can be 'sketchy' as you say. I'm working on a case right now that's got me scratching my head. Big money involved, we're talking eight figures stolen from a political campaign. Should be straightforward: follow the money, find the guy, find the money, and bring the money back, minus my commission. But it's turning into something else entirely."

Vicky raised an eyebrow. "How so?"

I took a sip of my drink, choosing my words carefully. "Started simple enough. Campaign aide skims from her candidate's campaign fund, is fired, but the cash cannot be located. Standard stuff. But the deeper I dig, the more it looks like organized crime involvement. Money laundering, shell companies, offshore accounts—the whole nine yards. What should've been a quick grab-and-go turned into something that could get me or others killed if I'm not careful."

"Jesus, Jon. Can you back out?"

"Not really. I'm in too deep now, and I've got obligations. But it's got me concerned. Used to be you could count on crooks being stupid. These days, they're getting smarter, more connected. The gal I'm chasing isn't just some desperate thief who got in over her head. I think she's part of something bigger, and that something bigger doesn't like people asking questions."

Our food arrived, and we shifted to lighter topics as we ate. The prime rib was perfect—tender, juicy, with just the right amount of char on the outside. The kind of meal that reminded you why some places become institutions.

"Remember that steakhouse in Georgetown we went to?" Vicky asked, cutting into her meat. "That place with the terrible service but amazing food?"

"Martin's Tavern. You sent back your steak three times because it wasn't cooked right."

"It wasn't! I ordered medium, they brought me shoe leather." She laughed. "You were so embarrassed, trying to tip the waiter extra to make up for my attitude."

"You were being unreasonable."

"I was being particular. There's a difference."

We talked through dinner, the conversation flowing easily despite the years between us. The restaurant had filled up around us—couples on dates, business dinners, groups of friends celebrating something or nothing at all. The fire crackled in the hearth, and the servers moved with practiced efficiency, keeping glasses filled and plates cleared.

By the time we finished dessert—bread pudding with whiskey sauce that was worth the calories—it was nearly nine o'clock, and the restaurant was winding down for the night. Emma brought the check, and I covered it despite Vicky's half-hearted protest.

"Where to now?" she asked as we stepped outside into the cool Los Feliz evening.

I looked across the street at The High Low, a dive bar that was the perfect contrast to the Tam O'Shanter's old-world elegance. Where the restaurant was all warm wood and leather, The High Low was neon and vinyl, the kind of place where the drinks were strong and the conversation was honest.

"How about we continue this over there?" I suggested, nodding toward the bar.

"Perfect. I wasn't ready to call it a night anyway."

The High Low was exactly what you'd expect from its exterior—a no-frills neighborhood bar with a long wooden counter, red vinyl stools that had seen better days, and a jukebox that played everything from Patsy Cline to The Replacements. The lighting was dim enough to hide imperfections and encourage confessions.

We found two stools at the end of the bar, away from the handful of other patrons scattered throughout the room. The bartender was a weathered guy in his fifties with graying hair and forearms covered in faded tattoos. He looked like he'd heard every story twice and believed none of them.

"What'll it be?" he asked, wiping down the bar in front of us.

"Jameson, neat," I said.

"Make it two," Vicky added.

The whiskey was smooth, with just enough bite to remind you it was working. Vicky held her glass up to the light, watching the amber liquid catch the neon glow from the beer signs behind the bar.

"So, tell me more about this case that's got you worried," she said, settling into her stool.

I took a sip of whiskey, feeling it warm my throat. "Remember I mentioned the organized crime angle? Turns out the money my gal stole is being laundered by some Russian mobsters. They've got an entire enterprise set up around the laundering operation. And I think they are on to me because the warehouse where most of the cash started was basically wiped clean when I got there."

"Ah. The Russian mob are not the nicest guys in the world."

"Exactly. So now I'm not just looking for the money—I'm potentially walking into some serious muscle who won't take kindly to me 'retrieving' millions of laundered money."

Vicky studied me over her glass. "You could walk away."

"Could. But I won't. I've got a reputation to maintain, and backing down from this would hurt that reputation. Plus, there's something about this case that doesn't add up. The gal I'm chasing—she's too smart to have just randomly decided to steal from a powerful politician and think she would get away with it. Either she's incredibly stupid, which the evidence suggests she's not, or there's more to this story."

"Like what?"

"Like maybe she didn't steal the money at all. Maybe she's being set up, used as a scapegoat for something bigger. Or maybe she's working with someone, and that someone is using her as a front. Either way, I need to find out what the truth is."

The bartender refilled our glasses without being asked. The bar was settling into its late-night rhythm—quieter conversations, more thoughtful drinking, the kind of atmosphere where people told the truth because lies took too much energy.

"What about you?" I asked. "Any of your cases keeping you up at night?"

Vicky swirled her whiskey, considering. "The gang member I mentioned—the one with the fentanyl? I think I'm going to have to withdraw from his case."

"Why?"

"Because representing him has become hazardous to my health. I got a call yesterday, an anonymous voice telling me it would be 'unfortunate' if my client decided to cooperate with federal investigators. The caller suggested I might want to advise my client to take whatever sentence the prosecutor offers and keep his mouth shut."

"Jesus. You report it to the police?"

"What am I going to tell them? Someone called and made vague threats? They'd take a report and file it away. Meanwhile, I've got to decide if defending this kid is worth potentially ending up as a cautionary tale."

I studied her face in the bar's dim light. "You're scared."

"Damn right I'm scared. I've handled drug cases before, but this feels different. Bigger. The money involved, the level of organization—it's like they have people everywhere. Prosecutors, judges, cops. How do you fight a system that's compromised from the inside?"

"Carefully," I said. "Very carefully."

We drank in silence for a moment, both lost in our own thoughts. The jukebox was playing something slow and melancholy—Johnny Cash, maybe, or Willie Nelson. One of those voices that sounded like it had lived through everything and survived to tell about it.

"You ever think about getting out?" Vicky asked suddenly, echoing a conversation we'd had hours earlier at the restaurant, but with more weight now. "Not just the cabin in the woods fantasy but really getting out. Different careers, different lives, somewhere the past can't find us?"

I looked at her, seeing something vulnerable in her expression that she usually kept hidden. "Every day. But then I wake up the next morning and go back to work, because it's what I know how to do. It's who I am."

"Maybe that's the problem. Maybe we are what we do, and what we do is dangerous."

"Maybe. But it's also necessary. Someone has to do the work we do, even if it's messy and dangerous and keeps us up at night. Someone has to stand between the predators and their prey, even if we get torn up in the process."

She smiled, but it was sad around the edges. "Look at us, Jon. A couple of middle-aged warriors, sitting in a dive bar, talking about cases that could get us killed. When did we become these people?"

"Gradually," I said. "Then all at once."

The bartender was starting to clean glasses and wipe down surfaces, the universal signal that last call was approaching. I checked my watch—nearly midnight. Time had slipped away from us the way it always did when the conversation was good and the whiskey was smooth.

"I should probably head out," I said reluctantly. "I've got an early meeting tomorrow."

"With who?"

"Not who, where. I'm driving out to Desert Center. I have a lead on where the new money laundering facilities are located. If I'm lucky, I can find the stolen campaign funds, 'retrieve' them, and be on my way back to L.A. before the sun rises. And by early, I mean four AM."

Vicky made a face. "Four in the morning? That's not early, that's obscene."

"Early bird gets the worm."

"The early bird can have it. I prefer to let someone else catch the worm and then steal it from them around ten AM with a cup of coffee."

I laughed, finishing the last of my whiskey. "That's always been your approach."

"It's served me well so far."

I stood up, pulling out my wallet to settle the tab. Vicky caught my wrist gently.

"This was good, Jon. Really good. I'd forgotten how easy it was to talk to you."

"Yeah," I said, and meant it. "It was."

I left money on the bar, enough to cover our drinks and a generous tip for the bartender who'd kept our glasses full and our conversation private. Vicky stood too, smoothing down her dress, suddenly looking like she was trying to decide whether to say something else.

"Call me tomorrow?" she asked. "After you get back from Desert Center?"

"Count on it."

I walked her to her car, a sleek BMW parked half a block down from the bar. The streets were quiet now, just the occasional car passing and the distant hum of the city that never quite goes to sleep. She unlocked her car and turned to face me.

"Be careful tomorrow, Jon. With this case, with everything. I know you think you're invincible, but you're not."

"I know."

She stood on her toes and kissed me, longer this time, her hand resting on my chest. When she pulled away, her eyes were serious.

"I mean it. Be careful."

"I will."

I watched her drive away, her taillights disappearing into the Los Angeles night. Then I walked to my own car, parked in a lot that smelled like oil and regret. The city was still humming around me—distant sirens, the low rumble of late-night traffic, the faint pulse of music leaking from other bars still serving the night shift.

The drive back to Dockweiler took me through neighborhoods that were settling into their late-night rhythm. Past convenience stores with bulletproof glass and security cameras, past apartment buildings where people were just getting home from second jobs or just heading out to third ones, past the invisible boundaries that divided the city into territories of hope and despair.

I pulled into the lot where I kept Coach, my thirty-seven-foot home on wheels. The rain had started again, a soft patter against the windshield that would probably continue until dawn. I cut the engine and sat for a moment, letting the quiet settle over me.

The evening with Vicky had been good—better than I'd expected. The conversation, the food, the easy rhythm of two people who'd known each other well once upon a time. But underneath it all was the current of danger that ran through both our lives now, the sense that we were both dancing on the edge of something that could go very wrong very quickly.

Her case with the gang member and the cartel connections. My recovery case that was turning into something much more complicated and dangerous. We were both in over our heads, probably, but too stubborn or too proud or too committed to back down.

I climbed out of the car, the rain cold against my skin, and headed inside Coach. The space was compact but efficient—a small kitchen, a dinette that converted to a bed, a tiny bathroom, everything I needed and nothing I didn't. A stack of case files sat on the table, reminders that the work never stopped.

I kicked off my shoes and made a cup of tea, something to take the edge off the whiskey and help me wind down. Through the small window, I could see the lights of LAX in the distance, planes taking off and landing in an endless cycle of arrivals and departures. People coming and going, starting new chapters, escaping old ones.

My phone buzzed with a text from Vicky: *Thanks for tonight. Sweet dreams, stranger.*

I typed back: *Sleep tight. Talk tomorrow.*

The rain continued its gentle assault on Coach's roof, a steady rhythm that was almost hypnotic. I finished my tea and got ready for bed, setting my alarm for five AM to give myself time to review my notes once more before the meeting.

As I lay in the narrow bed, listening to the rain and the distant sounds of the city, I thought about Vicky's question: *You ever think about getting out?* The honest answer was yes, more often than I cared to admit. There was something appealing about the idea of walking away from it all—the danger, the uncertainty, the constant knowledge that the next case could be the one that got you killed.

But even as I entertained the fantasy, I knew it was just that—a fantasy. This work, dangerous as it was, was what gave my life meaning. The missing woman I was trying to find, the money I was trying to recover, the people who needed someone to stand between them and the predators—that mattered. That was worth the risk.

I closed eyes, letting the sound of the rain carry me toward sleep. Tomorrow would come early, and Detective Valenzuela would either have something useful or he wouldn't. Either way, I'd be ready. In this business, you had to be.

Early bird gets the worm, I'd told Vicky. But as I drifted off to sleep, I couldn't shake the feeling that in this particular case, the worm might have teeth.

CHAPTER 20

UPPER HAND

The drive to Desert Center took me through some of the most desolate country in Southern California. Highway 10 stretched endlessly ahead, cutting through Joshua Tree National Park and into the Mojave Desert, where the only signs of civilization were the occasional gas station and the skeletal remains of abandoned buildings that had been left to bake under the merciless sun.

My Porsche 911 wasn't exactly built for desert surveillance work. The sleek black sports car stood out like a neon sign against the beige landscape, but it was the only vehicle I had available on short notice. The information from Detective Valenzuela had led me here—to coordinates that corresponded to a mobile home and warehouse complex about ten miles outside the tiny desert community of Desert Center, population 167 on a good day.

According to the financial records I had, this location was listed as a "storage facility" owned by one of Chesnokov's shell companies. But the satellite images I'd pulled up showed something more interesting—a cluster of buildings surrounded by a high fence, with what looked like a small airstrip nearby. This wasn't just storage; this was a distribution center.

I'd been driving back and forth along the access road for the past hour, trying to get a sense of the security situation without being too obvious about it. The property was set back about half a mile from the main highway, connected by a dirt road that kicked up clouds of dust visible for miles. Not exactly ideal for covert reconnaissance.

On my third pass, I counted four vehicles parked near the main warehouse: two black SUVs, a white panel van, and a red pickup truck that had seen better days. I didn't recognize any of them from my previous surveillance of Chesnokov's operations, which could mean either that these were different people or that Chesnokov was being extra careful about operational security.

What I didn't see was Ivan's distinctive Mercedes sedan. Ivan Volkov was one of Chesnokov's lieutenants, a thin, nervous man with the kind of eyes that suggested he'd done things that kept him awake at night. If Chesnokov was here personally, Ivan would be here too. The fact that his car was missing suggested either that this was a lower-level operation or that Chesnokov himself wasn't on site.

I pulled alongside one of several dumpsters that provided a modicum of concealment out here in the middle of nowhere and called Karl.

"What's up, boss?" he answered on the second ring.

"I need you to run a license plate check for me. Also, I need to know if you've had any reports of unusual activity in the Desert Center area in the past few weeks."

"Desert Center? What the hell are you doing out there?"

"Following up on the Chesnokov investigation. I think I've found one of his distribution points and new money laundering enterprise."

There was a pause, and I could hear Karl talking to someone else in the background. When he came back on the line, his voice was more serious.

"Bolt, if you've found something connected to Chesnokov, you need to call it in to the feds. This isn't something you should be handling alone."

"I'm just doing reconnaissance. But I need to know what I'm walking into."

"Give me the plates."

I read off the license numbers I'd memorized from the vehicles at the warehouse. Karl put me on hold while he ran them through the system.

"Interesting," he said when he came back. "Two of those vehicles were reported stolen in Los Angeles within the past month. The panel van is registered to a company that doesn't exist, and the pickup belongs to a guy who's been dead for three years."

"What about activity reports?"

"Nothing official. But I've got a friend in the Riverside County Sheriff's Department who works that area. He says there's been an uptick in small aircraft traffic at some of the private airstrips out there. Planes coming and going at odd hours, usually without filing proper flight plans."

That confirmed my suspicions. Chesnokov was using the Desert Center location as a waystation for smuggling operations—drugs coming up from Mexico, money going out to offshore accounts, all of it moving through the desert where law enforcement presence was minimal and witnesses were rare.

"How far out are you from backup if things go wrong?" Karl asked.

"Riverside County Sheriff is probably forty-five minutes away, Highway Patrol maybe thirty if they're already on the road."

"That's not good enough. You should wait for federal agents."

"By the time federal agents get organized and get out here, whatever's happening at that warehouse will be long gone. This might be my only chance to get hard evidence against Chesnokov."

"Bolt—"

"I'll be careful. But the only chance we have to recover the campaign funds is to locate where the laundering is happening. Money is fungible after all. I don't care which twelve million I retrieve as long as I can retrieve it."

I hung up before Karl could argue with me further. He was right, of course—going in alone was dangerous and probably stupid. But I'd been doing this long enough to know that sometimes you had to take risks to get results. The safe play didn't always lead to justice or a good result.

I pulled away from the dumpster toward the warehouse complex, but this time I continued past the access road for another mile before pulling off onto a barely visible dirt track that led into the desert scrub. The Porsche wasn't built for off-road driving, but it managed to navigate the rough terrain well enough to get me out of sight of the main highway.

I parked behind a cluster of Joshua trees and grabbed my Glock from the glove box and made sure I had my slide-rule periscope. I also took a pry bar I kept in the frunk as backup. The pistol was probably overkill for a reconnaissance mission, but given who and what I was dealing with, I wasn't taking any chances. Better to have a gun and not need it than to need it and not have it.

The walk to the warehouse complex took about twenty minutes across desert terrain that was equal parts sand, rock, and thorny vegetation that seemed designed specifically to tear holes in clothing and skin. The afternoon sun was brutal, and I was sweating heavily by the time I reached the perimeter fence.

The fence was eight feet high and topped with razor wire, but it wasn't electrified or monitored by cameras that I could see. This was security designed to keep out casual trespassers and curious locals, not trained investigators or serious criminals. Chesnokov was either overconfident or understaffed out here in the boonies.

I made my way around to the back of the property, staying low and using the natural terrain for cover. The warehouse was a large, prefab metal building that looked like it had been assembled from a kit. Next to it was a smaller structure that appeared to be living quarters—probably the mobile home mentioned in the financial records.

From my position behind a pile of concrete drainage pipes, I could see two men standing near the front of the warehouse, smoking cigarettes and talking in what sounded like Spanish. They were both armed—I could see the outlines of pistols under their shirts—but they seemed relaxed, more like guards on routine duty than sentries expecting trouble.

The back of the warehouse was less well defended. There was a service door about fifty feet from where I crouched, and I couldn't see any guards in that area. The challenge would be getting from the fence to the building without being spotted by the men out front.

I waited until both guards went inside, then made my move. The fence was difficult to climb because of the razor wire, but I managed to get over it without doing too much damage to myself or my clothes. The service door was secured with a Master padlock that looked substantial but wasn't particularly sophisticated.

The pry bar made short work of the lock. I'd learned a few things about breaking and entering during my agency career, mostly from observing the techniques used by criminals. It wasn't a skill I was proud of, but it was occasionally useful.

The interior of the warehouse was dark and stifling hot. Rows of wooden crates were stacked from floor to ceiling, creating narrow aisles that disappeared into the shadows. Each crate was stenciled with Chinese characters and shipping information that suggested they'd come through the Port of Long Beach.

I used the flashlight on my iPhone to examine the nearest crate more closely. The wood was new, and the shipping labels indicated the contents were listed as "decorative pottery" with a declared value of fifty dollars per crate. Given that there were probably two hundred crates in the warehouse, that suggested a legitimate cargo value of about ten thousand dollars.

But ten thousand dollars' worth of pottery didn't require this level of security or this remote location. Whatever was in these crates was worth considerably more than the shipping manifests indicated.

I used the pry bar to carefully open one of the crates near the back of the warehouse, working slowly to minimize the noise. The top came off with a soft creak, revealing a layer of straw packing material. Underneath the straw was what appeared to be decorative ceramic bowls, exactly as advertised.

But something felt wrong. The crate was lighter than it should have been for the amount of pottery it supposedly contained, and the bowls themselves felt hollow and fragile. I lifted one out carefully and examined it more closely.

The bottom of the bowl had a small hole that had been plugged with wax. I scraped away the wax with my thumbnail and found that the bowl was indeed hollow—and filled with white crystalline powder that I was fairly certain wasn't flour.

Methamphetamine. Chesnokov's people were smuggling drugs inside fake pottery, probably manufactured specifically for this purpose somewhere in China or Mexico. It was an elegant system—the crates looked legitimate enough to pass casual inspection, and even if customs agents opened a few boxes, they'd see exactly what the shipping manifests claimed.

I was photographing the contents of the crate when I heard footsteps approaching from the front of the warehouse. I quickly replaced the bowl and the straw packing, but there wasn't time to properly secure the crate lid.

The footsteps were getting closer. I could hear voices—at least two men, speaking in a mixture of Spanish, Russian and English. They were moving through the warehouse, apparently conducting some kind of inventory or inspection.

I moved deeper into the maze of crates, trying to find a hiding place or an alternate exit. The warehouse was larger than it had appeared from outside, with several smaller rooms branching off from the main storage area. I slipped into what looked like an office or break room, but there was no window and only one door.

I was trapped.

The voices were getting closer. I could make out individual words now—they were discussing shipping schedule and delivery routes. One of them mentioned "Viktor" and something about a problem with "the bitch," which I assumed was a reference to Elsa.

I pressed myself against the wall next to the door, hoping they would pass by without checking the room I was hiding in. But my luck ran out when one of them noticed the damaged crate I'd been examining.

"¿Qué es esto?" one voice said. "This box is open."

"Maybe it came loose during shipping," another voice replied, this one with a thick Russian accent.

"No, look. Someone pried it open. The lock on the back door—it's broken too."

There was a moment of silence, then the sound of weapons being drawn and safeties being clicked off.

"Search the building," the Russian voice commanded. "Someone is here."

I had maybe thirty seconds before they found me. The room I was hiding in had no windows and no other exits, but there was a ventilation grate near the ceiling that might lead to the roof. I climbed onto a desk and tried to remove the grate, but it was secured with screws that I couldn't loosen quietly.

Footsteps approached the door. I drew my Glock and took position behind the desk, knowing that if shooting started in this confined space, my chances weren't good.

The door burst open and a figure appeared in the doorway, backlit by the warehouse lighting. I started to raise my weapon, but something hard and heavy struck the back of my head with tremendous force. The world exploded into stars and pain, and then everything went black.

I have no idea how long I was unconscious. When awareness began to return, it came in fragments—the taste of blood in my mouth, the smell of motor oil and desert dust, the sound of voices speaking in languages I didn't understand.

The first thing I realized was that I was hanging from something, my arms stretched above my head and my feet dangling several inches off the ground. The second thing I realized was that there was something metallic and sharp pressed against my throat and the base of my neck.

"He's waking up," someone said in accented English.

Cold water hit my face with shocking force, causing me to gasp and sputter. My vision cleared enough to see that I was suspended from the warehouse rafters by a rope tied around my wrists. Around my neck was a device I recognized from medieval torture museums—a heretic's fork, a two-pronged metal instrument that would pierce the flesh under my chin and at the base of my throat if I allowed my head to drop.

Several men stood around me in a rough circle. I counted five, all armed, all watching me with the kind of casual interest that suggested they'd done this before. They were a diverse group—two looked Hispanic, two appeared to be Eastern European, and one had the lean build and weathered skin of someone who'd spent serious time in prison.

"Good afternoon, Mr. Bolt," one of the Eastern Europeans said. He was tall and thick through the shoulders, with graying hair and the kind of scars on his knuckles that came from hitting people with his bare hands. "I apologize for the dramatic awakening, but we need to have a conversation."

"Let me guess," I said, trying to keep my voice steady despite the pain in my head and the metal points pressing against my throat. "You're Kiril Chesnokov."

"Nyet. Chesnokov is coming. You disappoint me. Your reputation for deductive reasoning precedes you but clearly is undeserved."

"Maybe getting my noggin smashed in has something to do with that."

The warehouse door opened with a metallic screech, and sunlight streamed in, creating a silhouette in the doorway. The figure that entered was large and imposing, moving with the confident stride of someone accustomed to being in charge. As he approached, I could see his features clearly broad Slavic face, silver hair, expensive clothes that looked out of place in the desert setting. This was definitely Kiril Chesnokov. I had a slight recognition from my previous observation of him on Melrose, but my brain was still trying to overcome a likely concussion.

"Mr. Bolt," Chesnokov said, his accent much lighter than his subordinates'. "You have been a wery persistent thorn in my side."

"I get that a lot."

"I'm sure you do. The question is, why have you been following me? What do you hope to accomplish?" The time for being coy was long gone. This was do or die time.

"I'm investigating the theft of campaign funds from Senator Goldstein. She hired me to track down Elsa Kieger and the money."

"Ah, yes. Elsa can be a challenge. A very unfortunate situation."

"Unfortunate for her, maybe. Taking money from a powerful senator is just dumb."

Chesnokov smiled, but there was no warmth in it. "I will tell the senator to let it go. Her money no longer exists."

It was clear Chesnokov was planning to end me so I needed to consider my options. Telling Chesnokov everything else I knew about Elsa and Elsa's relationship with Elena would probably get her killed, assuming she wasn't dead already. But refusing to answer would definitely get me killed, probably sooner rather than later. Also, knowing Chesnokov was dying could give me the leverage I'd need to escape.

"I'm a retriever, Chesnokov. I retrieve things. Elsa took a lot of money that didn't belong to her. I believe you laundered or are laundering the money for her, however, she's also involved in your other businesses now and she has no idea how much extra trouble she's gotten into."

"An interesting theory. Do you have any evidence to support these accusations?"

"Enough to cause you problems if it gets to the right people."

"I see. And where is this evidence now?"

"Safe. If something happens to me, it goes to the FBI and the DEA simultaneously. Along with detailed information about your operations, including this warehouse."

It was a bluff, but a reasonable one. Chesnokov had no way of knowing whether I'd taken precautions or not, and in his position, he couldn't afford to assume I was lying.

Chesnokov studied me for a long moment, then nodded to one of his men. "We'll discuss this further after you've had some time to consider your situation."

They left me hanging there as the sun set and the warehouse grew dark. The heretic's fork made it impossible to rest—every time I started to nod off from exhaustion or pain, the metal points would dig into my flesh, sending jolts of agony through my neck and shoulders. It was a fiendishly effective torture device, designed to cause maximum suffering while leaving the victim technically alive and conscious.

Hours passed. Occasionally, one of Chesnokov's men would come by to check on me, sometimes offering water or asking if I was ready to talk. I refused both. The water was probably drugged, and talking would only confirm what they suspected about the evidence I claimed to have.

By the second day, I was beginning to hallucinate from sleep deprivation and dehydration. The warehouse seemed to shift and move around me, and I started hearing voices that weren't there. The pain from the heretic's fork had become a constant background sensation, no longer sharp but instead a dull, persistent agony that made it difficult to think clearly.

Chesnokov returned on the afternoon of the third day, accompanied by different men than before. These looked more professional—better dressed, better armed, more disciplined. Reinforcements, probably brought in from Los Angeles.

"Have you reconsidered your position, Mr. Bolt?"

"Go to hell," I managed to croak. My throat was raw from thirst and the constant pressure of the metal points.

"I was hoping you would be more cooperative. But I understand that some people require more persuasion than others."

He nodded to his men, who began untying the rope that held me suspended from the rafters. I collapsed to the concrete floor, unable to support my own weight after three days of hanging. They removed the heretic's fork, and I felt blood trickling down my neck from the wounds it had left.

"Unfortunately," Chesnokov continued, "the traditional methods don't seem to be effective in your case. So, we're going to try something more modern."

Two of his men dragged me to a metal chair that had been clamped to a four feet by eight feet sheet of half inch thick plywood which was resting on the concrete warehouse floor. They strapped me down with leather restraints that looked like they'd been designed specifically for this purpose. One of them began assembling what looked like a car battery connected to a transformer and some steel wool.

I'd heard about this kind of torture during my FIDA career—electric shock applied through steel wool that would burn and conduct electricity simultaneously. It was extraordinarily painful and left marks that could be explained as accidental burns. The kind of technique that left victims alive but permanently damaged.

"This is your last chance to cooperate voluntarily," Chesnokov said. "Tell me where you've hidden the evidence, and this ends quickly. Continue to resist, and I promise you that the next few hours will be the longest of your life."

The man with the electrical equipment approached the chair, steel wool in one hand and electrodes in the other. I could smell the ozone in the air as he powered up the transformer.

"I understand you used to be a federal agent of some sort," Chesnokov said conversationally. "Twenty-three years, several commendations for bravery. I respect that kind of dedication to duty. But this isn't about duty anymore, Mr. Bolt. This is about survival."

The first shock hit me like a sledgehammer to the chest. Every muscle in my body contracted simultaneously, and I bit my tongue hard enough to taste blood. The steel wool burned against my skin, sending waves of agony through my nervous system.

"Where is the evidence?" Chesnokov asked calmly.

I tried to answer but only managed a strangled gasp. The electrical burns on my chest felt like brands, and I could smell my own singed flesh.

The second shock was worse. This time they held it longer, and I felt my consciousness starting to slip away as my body convulsed against the restraints. When it ended, I was gasping like a fish out of water, unable to form coherent thoughts.

"Mr. Bolt? Can you hear me?"

I nodded weakly, not trusting my voice.

"I want you to understand something. I take no pleasure in this. You seem like a decent man who was simply doing his job. But you've become a threat to my organization, and I cannot allow threats to persist."

The third shock was the worst yet. I felt something fundamental give way inside my chest, and my vision began to tunnel toward blackness. This was it—either I talked now, or I was going to die in this chair in a warehouse in the middle of the desert. But before I could say anything, the darkness closed in completely, and I lost consciousness.

When I woke up, I was lying on the concrete floor, still strapped to the chair but no longer connected to the electrical equipment. Chesnokov was standing over me, checking his watch with apparent impatience.

"How long was I out?" I asked.

"About twenty minutes. Long enough for me to realize that you're either remarkably stubborn or remarkably stupid."

"Probably both."

"Indeed. But I'm beginning to suspect that you may have been telling the truth about the evidence. If you were bluffing, you would have broken by now."

I didn't respond. My chest felt like someone had taken a blowtorch to it, and I wasn't sure I could survive another session with the electrical equipment.

"Here's what's going to happen," Chesnokov said. "I'm going to give you some time to recover. Then we're going to continue this conversation in a more comfortable setting. Perhaps a change of scenery will help you remember where you put those files."

His men lifted the chair and carried me toward the front of the warehouse. Through the open door, I could see the sun setting over the desert, painting the sky in shades of orange and red that would have been beautiful under different circumstances.

A black SUV was waiting outside, engine running. They loaded me, still strapped to the chair, into the back of the vehicle. Chesnokov climbed into the passenger seat and nodded to the driver.

"Where are we going?" I asked.

"Somewhere more private," Chesnokov replied. "Somewhere we can take our time and explore more creative approaches to our problem."

As the SUV pulled away from the warehouse, I caught a glimpse of my Porsche in the distance, still hidden behind the cluster of Joshua trees where I'd left it. It seemed like a lifetime ago that I'd parked there, full of confidence about conducting a simple reconnaissance mission.

Now I was a prisoner of one of the most dangerous criminals on the West Coast, and the evidence that could bring him down was sitting in a safe deposit box that no one else knew about. If Chesnokov killed me—and he probably would, eventually—his operation would continue, more people would die, maybe even Elsa Krieger.

I closed my eyes and tried to conserve what strength I had left. If an opportunity for escape presented itself, I would need to be ready to take it. But as the SUV carried me deeper into the desert, away from any hope of rescue or discovery, I began to accept the possibility that I might not survive to see another sunrise.

The investigation that had started with a theft of campaign funds was about to end with a missing private investigator. Unless I could find a way to turn the tables on Kiril Chesnokov, this warehouse in Desert Center would be the last recon I ever worked.

The SUV's headlights cut through the growing darkness as we drove toward whatever fate Chesnokov had planned for me. Behind us, the warehouse grew smaller and smaller until it disappeared entirely, swallowed by the vast emptiness of the Mojave Desert.

But something had changed in the dynamic between Chesnokov and me. His admission that he believed I was telling the truth about the evidence meant I had leverage—not much, but enough to keep me alive a little longer. And in my experience, a little longer was sometimes the upper hand you needed to find a way out of an impossible situation.

CHAPTER 21

QUIET RIOT

The cold shock hit me like a sledgehammer to the skull. Water cascaded down my face, streaming over my swollen eyes and split lips, pooling at my feet in the concrete dust below. My body jerked involuntarily against the ropes, every nerve ending screaming as consciousness crashed back into me like a freight train.

"Good morning, sunshine," came the gravelly voice from somewhere in front of me. I forced my eyes open, squinting through the haze of pain and water droplets clinging to my lashes. This warehouse looked different in what I assumed was daylight—though it was hard to tell with the boarded windows and dim industrial lighting. Shafts of pale-yellow light sliced through gaps in the corrugated metal walls, casting long shadows across the concrete floor.

My shoulders were on fire. How long had I been hanging here? Hours? A day? Time had become meaningless, measured only in waves of agony that rolled through my body with each labored breath. The rope around my wrists had cut deep grooves into my skin, and I could feel dried blood caked around the bindings. My ribs screamed with every expansion of my lungs, and I was pretty sure at least two were cracked, maybe broken entirely.

I counted the figures moving in my peripheral vision. Two. Only two of Chesnokov's men remained. Where were the others? Had they given up on me? Had they assumed I was already dead, or close enough that it didn't matter? The thought should have been comforting, but instead it filled me with a cold dread. Two men were still two too many if I couldn't get myself out of this mess.

The one who'd thrown the water—a stocky man with arms like tree trunks and a face that looked like it had been carved from granite with a dull chisel—set down the empty bucket with a metallic clang that echoed through the warehouse. His partner, tall and lean with nervous energy that radiated off him like heat from an engine, was pacing near the far wall, occasionally glancing toward the loading dock where pale light leaked around the edges of the massive doors.

"Boss ain't coming back," the nervous one said, his voice carrying easily in the cavernous space. He had a slight accent—Eastern European, but not Russian. Czech, maybe, or Polish. "Been six hours. Something went wrong."

The stocky one—let's call him Granite Face—shrugged his massive shoulders. "Don't matter. We got our orders. Keep him alive until Chesnokov says otherwise." He looked at me with dead eyes, the kind of look a butcher gives a side of beef. "Though he didn't say nothing about keeping him comfortable."

Nervous Energy stopped pacing and pulled out a pack of cigarettes, tapping one free with shaking fingers. "I need some air. This place stinks like piss and blood." He shot a glance in my direction. "Mostly blood."

"Go," Granite Face said without looking away from me. "I'll keep our friend here company."

I watched through half-closed eyes as Nervous Energy headed for a side door I hadn't noticed before, probably leading to an alley or back lot. The heavy door squealed on its hinges as he pushed it open, letting in a brief gust of fresher air that smelled of rain and exhaust fumes. Then it slammed shut, leaving just me and Granite Face in the echoing silence.

For a moment, neither of us moved. I let my head hang forward, feigning unconsciousness while I tried to assess my situation. The rope around my wrists was rough hemp, tied with sailor's knots that had only gotten tighter as I'd struggled. My feet barely touched the ground, just enough to take some of the pressure off my shoulders but not enough to give me any real leverage. The beam I was hanging from looked solid—probably steel, part of the warehouse's original construction.

Granite Face walked over to a folding table I hadn't noticed before, positioned just outside my field of vision. I heard the scrape of metal on metal, then the ominous hum of electrical equipment powering up. My stomach dropped. I knew that sound.

"You know," he said conversationally, as if we were discussing the weather, "I was getting bored just watching you hang there like a piñata. Though maybe we could have some fun while my partner smokes his cancer sticks."

The humming grew louder, more insistent. I could smell ozone in the air, that sharp metallic scent that comes before a thunderstorm. Or before someone gets electrocuted.

Granite Face came back into view, and my blood turned to ice water. In his hands was a device that looked like it had been cobbled together from spare parts—a car battery connected to jumper cables, with what looked like a modified stun gun attached to the business end. The whole contraption was held together with electrical tape and the kind of creative engineering that suggested its maker had learned electronics from the wrong side of the law.

"Now, I ain't no electrician," he said, hefting the device with obvious satisfaction, "but I got a knack for making things hurt just right. Enough juice to light you up like a Christmas tree, but not enough to stop your heart. Usually."

He set the battery down at his feet and began unwrapping the cable, the metal clamps at the end catching the weak light like predatory teeth. The makeshift stun gun sparked once, twice, sending blue arcs of electricity dancing between the prongs.

"The thing about electricity," he continued, advancing toward me with the deliberate pace of a man who had all the time in the world, "is that it finds the path of least resistance. Through your nervous system, across your skin, sometimes right through your heart if you're unlucky. Makes you dance real pretty."

I could feel my heart hammering against my ribs, adding a new dimension to the symphony of pain that was my existence. This was it. This was how I was going to die—tortured to death in an abandoned warehouse by a psychopath with a homemade electric chair. The irony wasn't lost on me. After all the bullets I'd dodged, all the fights I'd survived, I was going to be killed by some reject from a high school shop class.

But as Granite Face raised the stun gun toward my chest, something inside me shifted. Maybe it was desperation, maybe it was rage, or maybe it was just the stubborn refusal to die that had kept me alive this long. Whatever it was, I felt a strange calm settle over me like a blanket.

"Enough," I said.

The word came out as barely more than a whisper, but in the silence of the warehouse it might as well have been a gunshot. Granite Face stopped mid-stride, the stun gun crackling in his hand.

"What's that?" he asked, leaning closer. "You got something to say?"

I lifted my head slowly, meeting his dead eyes with my own. "I said enough. I'll talk."

For a moment, he just stared at me, as if he couldn't quite process what he'd heard. Then a slow smile spread across his face, revealing teeth that had seen better decades.

"Well, well," he said, lowering the stun gun slightly. "Look who finally found his voice. Here I was thinking you were some kind of tough guy." He laughed, a sound like gravel in a cement mixer. "All it took was a little more juice to loosen your tongue."

"Not here," I said, my voice still barely audible. "Too exposed. Someone might hear."

He glanced toward the door where his partner had exited, then back at me. "Ain't nobody gonna hear nothing. We're in the middle of the fucking desert."

"The FBI," I whispered. "They're looking for me. If they find this place..."

Granite Face's smile faltered slightly. He was stupid, but not completely without survival instincts. The last thing he wanted was to explain to the authorities why he was in possession of a homemade torture device and a half-dead former federal agent.

"FBI?" he demanded, stepping closer. "You're lying."

I let my head fall forward again, as if the effort of speaking had exhausted me. "My partners," I gasped. "They know... know where I went. When I don't check in..."

"Bullshit." But there was uncertainty in his voice now. Fear. Good.

"Cut me down," I said. "I'll tell you everything. About the evidence I've collected, about people trying to infiltrate Chesnokov's organization, and why the vultures are circling. All of it."

He stood there for a long moment, the stun gun still crackling softly in his hand. I could practically see the gears turning in his head, weighing the possibility of information against the pleasure of causing pain. Finally, greed won out, as I'd known it would.

"You try anything funny," he said, moving closer, "and I'll fry you like bacon. You understand me?"

I nodded weakly, playing up the defeated prisoner act. He leaned in closer, close enough that I could smell the vodka on his breath and see the scars crisscrossing his knuckles. Close enough.

My legs shot up like coiled springs, wrapping around his neck in a scissor hold that cut off his air supply before he could even register what was happening. The stun gun flew from his hand, clattering across the concrete floor as his body went rigid with surprise.

He clawed at my legs with his meaty hands, trying to break the hold, but I had leverage now and twenty-years of close-quarters combat training. I squeezed tighter, feeling his pulse hammering against the inside of my thighs as his face turned red, then purple.

"Shh," I whispered, as if comforting a child. "Just go to sleep."

He thrashed for another few seconds, his body's autonomic systems fighting the inevitable, then went limp. I held the position for another ten count, making sure he was truly unconscious, then released him. He crumpled to the floor like a sack of cement, out cold but still breathing.

Now came the hard part. With Granite Face unconscious at my feet, I had to get myself free from the ropes before Nervous Energy finished his smoke break and came back to find his partner taking an unscheduled nap.

I looked up at the beam I was hanging from, following it back to where it connected to the warehouse's support structure. The rope was looped over the beam and tied off to a cleat on the far wall—standard rigging, probably left over from when this place had been a working warehouse. If I could somehow swing myself over there...

I began to rock back and forth, building momentum like a kid on a playground swing. Each movement sent fresh waves of agony through my shoulders and ribs, but I gritted my teeth and kept going. Back and forth, back and forth, the rope creaking ominously with each swing.

On the fifth swing, I managed to hook my foot around a vertical support beam. Using it as leverage, I pulled myself up just enough to take the pressure off the rope around my wrists. My shoulders screamed in protest, but I could feel the circulation returning to my hands.

The knots were tight, swollen with my blood and pulled taut by hours of my body weight, but they were still just knots. I worked my fingers on the hemp, feeling for the weak points, the places where the rope had stretched or frayed. There—a small gap where the binding had loosened slightly.

I worked at it with my fingernails, ignoring the pain as the rough hemp tore at my skin. One strand, then another, then a whole section gave way. The rope slackened, and suddenly I could move my hands.

It took another precious minute to fully free myself, unwinding the remaining coils of rope from my raw wrists. When I finally dropped to the floor, my legs nearly buckled. I'd been hanging for so long that my body had forgotten how to support its own weight.

I flexed my fingers, trying to get feeling back into them, then looked around for a weapon. The stun gun lay where Granite Face had dropped it, still connected to the car battery by the jumper cables. I picked it up, testing its weight. It would have to do.

That's when I heard the side door squeal open. I also recognized the telltale signs there was a dust storm brewing outside. The wind was whistling and a small cloud of dirt blasted through the doorway.

"Hey, Yuri," came Nervous Energy's voice from the entrance. "A storm is coming. You better finish up with our—"

He stopped mid-sentence as he took in the scene: me standing over his unconscious partner, the rope hanging empty from the beam above, blood dripping from my wrists onto the concrete floor.

For a heartbeat, neither of us moved. Then his hand darted inside his jacket.

I was moving before his gun cleared the holster, diving to the side as the first shot echoed through the warehouse like thunder. The bullet sparked off the concrete where I'd been standing, sending chips of stone flying.

He fired again, and again, the muzzle flashes strobing in the dim light. I rolled behind a stack of empty pallets as wood splinters exploded around me. The acrid smell of gunpowder filled the air.

"You're dead!" he screamed, his voice cracking with adrenaline and fear. "You hear me? You're fucking dead!"

I counted the shots. Three, four, five. Most handguns held anywhere from six to fifteen rounds, depending on the make and model. Without being able to see what he was carrying, I had to assume he had at least one more shot, possibly many more.

The warehouse fell silent except for the sound of his labored breathing and my own heartbeat thundering in my ears. I could hear him moving, his footsteps echoing off the concrete as he tried to get a better angle on my position.

I looked around my makeshift cover, searching for anything I could use as a weapon. The stun gun was still in my hand, but its reach was limited and it would only work if I could get close enough to touch him. The pallets themselves were too heavy to throw, but...

There. A piece of rebar, probably left over from some long-ago construction project, lay half-hidden under a pile of construction debris. It was about three feet long, rust-covered but solid. Not much, but better than nothing.

I grabbed the rebar and crept toward the end of the pallet stack, trying to get a sense of where Nervous Energy had positioned himself. His breathing was loud and ragged—he was scared, running on pure adrenaline. That made him dangerous and unpredictable, but also prone to mistakes.

"I know you're behind there," he called out, trying to sound confident but failing miserably. "Ain't nowhere to run, tough guy. This warehouse is locked up tight."

He was lying, of course. The side door he'd used was still open—I could feel the draft from here. But he was also partially right. The loading dock doors were chained shut, and the main entrance was blocked by debris. The side door was the only way out, and he was positioned between me and it.

I heard the distinctive sound of a magazine being ejected and reloaded. So, he had more ammunition. That changed things.

Moving as quietly as I could, I began to circle around the warehouse, using the scattered debris and machinery as cover. My bare feet made almost no sound on the cold concrete, but every step sent shards of pain up through my body. I was running on pure adrenaline now, the same chemical cocktail that was keeping my opponent jumpy and dangerous.

I could see him now, crouched behind an overturned table about thirty feet away, his gun trained on the pallet stack where he thought I was hiding. His hands were shaking, and sweat had soaked through his shirt despite the chill in the air.

The smart move would have been to try to reach the side door, to escape while I had the chance. But something primal in me, something that had been building since the moment I'd been strung up like a piece of meat, demanded satisfaction. These men had tortured me, humiliated me, left me to die in this godforsaken place. Running away felt like letting them win.

No. This ended here.

I crept closer, the rebar clutched tightly in my right hand, the stun gun in my left. Twenty feet. Fifteen. Ten. He must have heard something—the scrape of my foot against debris, or maybe just the instinctive awareness that comes when death is stalking you in the dark. He spun around, the gun swinging toward me in a smooth arc.

I threw the rebar like a spear, putting every ounce of strength I had left into the throw. It caught him in the shoulder, spinning him around and sending his shot wild. The bullet ricocheted off a steel beam somewhere above us.

Then I was on him, crossing the remaining distance in three long strides. He tried to bring the gun around again, but I grabbed his wrist with my free hand, forcing the barrel away from my body. The stun gun in my other hand found his ribcage, and I pulled the trigger.

Blue electricity arced between the prongs, and his body went rigid as fifty thousand volts coursed through his nervous system. He screamed, a high, keening sound that echoed off the warehouse walls, then collapsed as his muscles seized up.

But he wasn't done. Even as he writhed on the ground, his hand still clutched the pistol. I could see him fighting the electrical shock, trying to regain enough control to pull the trigger.

I hit him with the stun gun again, this time holding it against his neck. The second jolt did what the first had failed to accomplish—his eyes rolled back in his head and his body went completely limp. The gun slipped from his nerveless fingers, clattering across the concrete.

I stood over him for a moment, breathing hard, the stun gun still crackling in my hand. He was alive—I could see his chest rising and falling—but he'd be out for a while. Long enough for me to get out of here.

I picked up his pistol, checking the magazine. Eleven rounds left, plus one in the chamber. A Glock 19, just like mine, reliable and familiar. I tucked it into the waistband of my pants, then looked around the warehouse one more time. My phone was lying on the floor near my former gallows. I picked up and tried to check messages. It was dead. Damn! I put it in my pocket and moved toward the exit.

Granite Face was still unconscious where I'd left him, though he was starting to stir slightly. In a few minutes, he'd be awake and angry. I needed to be long gone by then.

The side door was still open, spilling pale afternoon light and dust into the warehouse. I could hear traffic in the distance, the normal sounds of the interstate highway system going about its business, oblivious to the life-and-death struggle that had just played out in this forgotten corner of the desert.

I walked toward the door, my bare feet picking up dust and debris with each step. Every movement was agony—my ribs protested with each breath, my shoulders were on fire, and I was pretty sure I had a concussion from all the times I'd been knocked unconscious over the past however many hours.

But I was alive. Against all odds, against Chesnokov's best efforts, I was still breathing.

The alley behind the warehouse was narrow and cluttered with dumpsters and abandoned shopping carts. The air smelled of rotting garbage and stagnant water, but after the close, blood-scented atmosphere of the warehouse, it was like breathing pure mountain air. Until the dust storm picked up its pace.

I looked both ways, trying to get my bearings in the haze. The sun was high overhead, filtered through a layer of gray clouds and the haze kicked up by the haboob that made everything look washed out and surreal. Based on the angle of the light, I guessed it was early afternoon, maybe one or two o'clock. I'd been hanging in that warehouse for at least twelve hours, possibly longer.

To my left, the alley opened onto what looked like a main street surfaced with decomposed granite. I-10 was in the distance. I could hear but couldn't see the cars passing by; there was the distant hum of traffic. To my right, the alley seemed to dead-end against another building. The choice was obvious.

I started walking toward the street, trying to look as normal as possible despite the fact that I was shirtless, bleeding, and armed with a stolen pistol; the dust provided the right amount of concealment. Just another day in the life of a private investigator.

As I reached the mouth of the alley, I got my first good look at my surroundings. We were still in Desert Center, I thought, but I needed to get an idea of where my 911 was parked. When Chesnokov and his men moved me from the first warehouse, I couldn't be sure if we went one mile or ten. I spun around and squinting under the sunshine I tried to focus on which way I needed to move.

And there, parked about a block away like a beacon of hope, was my Porsche. They must have driven us back after I was unconscious or I was so disoriented that my geographic orientation was way off.

It sat exactly where I'd left it before this whole nightmare began, the black paint dulled by a coating of desert dirt but otherwise intact. No broken windows, no flat tires, no obvious signs of tampering. Either Chesnokov's men had been too busy torturing me to bother with my car, or they'd been saving it for later.

I half-walked, half-jogged toward it, trying to ignore the stares from the few migrant workers I passed. A shirtless, bloody man stumbling down the dirt road wasn't exactly inconspicuous, but this wasn't the kind of neighborhood where people asked too many questions.

The car's doors were locked, of course, and my keys were God knows where—probably still in the pocket of whatever shirt they'd stripped off me back in the warehouse. But locks had never been much of an obstacle for someone in my line of work.

I looked around to make sure no one was watching too closely, then used the butt of the Glock to smash the passenger-side window. The safety glass held together as it shattered, creating a spider web of cracks that I was able to push through with minimal noise.

I reached through the broken window and unlocked the door, then slid into the familiar embrace of the Porsche's leather seats. The interior smelled of expensive car care products. For a moment, I just sat there, letting the familiarity wash over me like a warm bath.

Then reality reasserted itself. I was still in hostile territory, still bleeding, still very much in danger. Granite Face and Nervous Energy would wake up eventually, and when they did, they'd come looking for me. I needed to get out of here, and fast.

Hot-wiring a modern car isn't like it is in the movies. You can't just yank some wires out from under the dashboard and touch them together. Modern vehicles have sophisticated anti-theft systems, computer-controlled ignitions, and all sorts of electronic safeguards designed to prevent exactly what I was trying to do.

Fortunately, this particular Porsche was my Porsche, and I'd made some... modifications over the years. Nothing illegal, of course, just some practical adjustments that might come in handy in my line of work. Like the hidden bypass switch tucked under the dashboard, or the spare ignition module hidden in the glove compartment.

I found the bypass switch and flipped it, then retrieved the spare module from its hiding place. It took me about thirty seconds to swap it with the factory unit, and another ten seconds to activate the emergency start sequence I'd programmed years ago and hoped I'd never need to use.

The engine turned over on the first try, purring to life with the distinctive rumble that only a well-tuned German sports car can produce. I'd never been so happy to hear that sound.

I put the car in gear and pulled away, trying to resist the urge to floor it and tear out of there like a bat out of hell. The last thing I needed was to attract attention from the police, not when I looked like I'd been through a meat grinder and had a stolen gun tucked in my waistband.

As I drove through the small desert outpost, heading for the highway that would take me back to the civilized part of Southern California, I tried to process what had just happened. I'd been captured, tortured, and left for dead, but somehow, I'd managed to turn the tables on my captors and escape. It should have felt like a victory. Instead, it felt like the beginning of something much worse.

The highway stretched out ahead of me, four lanes of asphalt leading back toward the heart of the city. In the rearview mirror, Desert Center was already fading into the distance, just another collection of anonymous buildings in an anonymous part of Riverside County.

But I knew I'd be back. Whatever Chesnokov was planning, whatever operation had been worth torturing me to protect, it wasn't over. Men like him didn't just disappear when their plans hit a snag. They adapted, they evolved, they found new ways to achieve their goals. And when they did, I'd be waiting for them.

The Porsche ate up the miles, carrying me away from the warehouse where I'd nearly died and toward an uncertain future. My ribs ached with every breath, my shoulders burned like fire, and I could taste blood in my mouth, but I was alive. More importantly, I was free.

And as long as I drew breath, I would make sure that the men who had done this to me would pay for every moment of agony they'd inflicted. Not because I was vindictive or cruel, but because it was my job. Because somewhere in this city, other innocent people were depending on me to stop men like Chesnokov from carrying out their plans.

The warehouse grew smaller in my rearview mirror until it disappeared entirely, swallowed by the urban sprawl. But the memory of what had happened there, the feeling of helplessness as I hung from those ropes, the sound of electricity crackling in the air—those would stay with me forever.

They would remind me why I did this job, and what the stakes really were.

I pressed down on the accelerator, and the Porsche responded eagerly, surging forward into the afternoon traffic. Behind me, the past was already becoming history. Ahead of me, the future waited, uncertain and dangerous and full of possibilities.

I reached for the radio, Sirius XM 80's on 8. The song playing was "Cum on Feel the Noize" by Quiet Riot. Indeed, I thought. Feel the noise, Chesnokov. I don't give a shit that you are dying of stage four cancer. You're gonna die sooner rather than later. Count on it.

CHAPTER 22

GAME ON

The coach's door felt heavier than usual as I pushed it open, my shoulder screaming in protest. Every muscle in my body had something to say about the past three days, and none of it was complimentary. I dropped the stolen Glock on the small dinette table and stood there for a moment, listening to the familiar hum of the refrigerator and the distant rumble of highway traffic. Home sweet aluminum home—if you could call a recreational vehicle home.

I plugged in my phone so that it would be somewhat charged in the next half hour or so. Then I proceeded to the bathroom and shower.

The mirror in the tiny bathroom showed me exactly what I expected, and somehow worse. Three days of running, hiding, and fighting had left their mark. The cut above my left eyebrow had scabbed over, creating a ridge that made me look like I'd gone a few rounds with a meat tenderizer. My lip was split in two places, one side swollen enough to give me a permanent sneer. Blood had scabbed on my throat where the Heretic Fork sliced the skin there. Dark purple bruises bloomed across my ribs like abstract art, and when I lifted my shirt, I could see the full canvas of damage. Yellow was already creeping around the edges of the purple—my body's way of keeping track of time.

But it was my hands that told the real story. Knuckles raw and split, fingernails broken, and a long scrape across my palm where I'd grabbed the chain-link fence during my entry into Chesnokov's compound. These hands had done what they needed to do, and they'd paid the price.

I turned the shower handle, waiting for the ancient water heater to remember its job. The first blast was ice-cold, then gradually warmed to something approaching human temperature. The coach's shower was barely big enough for someone my size, but it was private, and right now that was worth more than a five-star hotel suite.

The hot water hit my shoulders like a blessing and a curse rolled into one. It felt incredible and agonizing at the same time, washing away three days of desert dust, blood, and the kind of sweat that comes from genuine fear. I closed my eyes and let my mind drift back to Desert Center, trying to piece together exactly how I'd managed to walk away from that mess.

Chesnokov had been ready for me—that much was clear from the moment I'd approached the warehouse. The whole thing smelled like a setup from the beginning, but sometimes you walk into the trap anyway because it's the only door available. His men had been positioned perfectly, exits covered, escape routes blocked. They'd done their homework. What they hadn't counted on was the storm.

Mother Nature had provided the cover I needed, turning the desert into a sandblaster's workshop. Visibility dropped to maybe ten feet, and I'd used the distraction to slip out of their perimeter, but not before collecting some intel that made the whole ordeal worthwhile.

The water pressure was starting to fade—another charm of coach living—so I quickly shampooed my hair, wincing as my fingers found a tender spot where someone's boot had connected with my skull. The shampoo ran pink down the drain, carrying away the last physical evidence of Desert Center. The memories would stick around longer.

I learned three important things during my extended visit to Chesnokov's hospitality suite. First, he was definitely moving something big through the area, something that required military-grade security and enough firepower to invade a small country. Second, whatever he was moving was time-sensitive, the kind of job where delays cost more than money. And third, he was expecting someone else, someone important enough to make Chesnokov nervous.

That last part was what had saved my skin. When his men had cornered me in the warehouse, Chesnokov was gone, and that changed everything. Suddenly, I went from priority target to minor inconvenience. They'd tied me up instead of putting a bullet in my head, which gave me the opening I needed when the storm hit.

I turned off the water and reached for the threadbare towel hanging on the back of the door. Every movement was a reminder of the past seventy-two hours, but I was alive to feel the pain. That counted for something.

The coach felt different now, smaller somehow, like the walls had moved closer together while I was gone. Maybe it was just the knowledge that Chesnokov knew where I lived. This place had been sanctuary for months, but sanctuary was a luxury I could no longer afford.

I pulled on clean clothes—jeans and a black t-shirt that didn't require any complicated arm movements—and tried to inventory my next moves. First priority was medical attention. I'd done enough field medicine over the years to know when I was outside my skill set, and the throbbing in my ribs suggested at least one crack, maybe two.

The second priority was Maggie. She'd been expecting updates, and three days of radio silence would have her climbing the walls. Being tied up and tortured left little opportunity to "reach out and touch someone."

The third priority was figuring out what the hell Chesnokov was really up to and why my investigation into Elsa's theft had wandered into his crosshairs. I understood the laundering operation, but there must be something more, otherwise why were Elena and Trisha involved? The connection was there; I just couldn't see it yet.

I picked up my phone from the kitchen counter, booted it up, and saw it was thirty percent charged. There were seventeen missed calls from Maggie, forty-three text messages, and one voicemail from Dr. Roth confirming an appointment I'd missed two days ago. The digital clock on the microwave read 6:47 AM. I'd been gone longer than I thought.

And there was a text from Elsa. It read, "Jon, we need to talk. Can we meet? Soon?" I immediately thought Chesnokov contacted Elsa after my improbable escape from his lair in the desert and wanted to get another stab at me. I had to think through this, and in my current physical state I was not able to focus very well. I needed medical attention first.

Dr. Roth's private number was programmed into my speed dial for good reason. Steven Roth had been patching up people like me for thirty years, first as an Army medic in Vietnam, then as an ER doctor in Detroit, and finally as a discreet private physician who asked the right questions and forgot the right answers. He'd saved my life at least twice and my freedom more times than I could count.

The phone rang four times before switching to voicemail. Roth's gravelly voice came through the speaker, professional but warm. "You've reached Dr. Steven Roth. Leave a detailed message, and I'll get back to you as soon as possible. If this is a medical emergency, hang up and call 911."

"Doc, it's Bolt," I said after the beep. "I need to see you today if possible. Nothing life-threatening, but I've had a rough couple of days and could use your professional opinion on some injuries. Call me back when you get this."

I hung up and stared at Maggie's contact information for a long moment. She was going to be furious, and she had every right to be. Partners don't disappear for three days without warning, especially when they're working a case that's already turned deadly.

Her phone rang twice before she picked up.

"BOLT!" The volume nearly blew out my eardrum. "Where the HELL have you been?"

"Good morning to you too, sunshine," I said, trying to inject some lightness into my voice. "Miss me?"

"Miss you? MISS YOU?" Her voice climbed another octave. "I thought you were DEAD! Your car hadn't moved in three days, you didn't answer your phone, and the last text I got from you was 'heading out to follow a lead.' Do you have any idea what I've been going through?"

The raw emotion in her voice hit me harder than any of Chesnokov's punches. Maggie was tough as nails, had been through hell and back in her own right, but the fear bleeding through her anger was genuine. I'd put her through that, and there was no excuse good enough to make it right.

"Maggie, I'm sorry," I said, dropping the attempt at humor. "I'm okay. I'm alive. I'm back at the coach, and I'll explain everything, but I need you to know that I'm safe."

"Safe?" She was crying now, the anger mixing with relief in a way that made my chest tight. "You disappear for three days working a case where people are already trying to kill us, and you think 'I'm safe' covers it?"

"You're right," I said. "You're absolutely right, and I'm sorry. The situation went sideways faster than I expected, and I couldn't risk contacting you until I was clear."

"What situation? Where did you go? And don't you dare give me some vague bullshit about following leads."

I could hear her pacing, the way she did when she was trying to burn off adrenaline. Three days of worry could generate a lot of adrenaline.

"I went to Desert Center," I said. "Following up on the Elsa connection we discussed. It turned into more than I bargained for."

"Desert Center? That's two hundred miles from here. What's in Desert Center?"

"Apparently, some very unfriendly people with very serious hardware," I said. "Look, I know I screwed up by not checking in. I should have found a way to let you know I was okay, but communications were... complicated."

"Complicated how?"

I looked at my reflection in the coach's small window, seeing the cuts and bruises that told the story better than words could. "Let's just say I spent some unplanned time as a guest of people who don't believe in the hospitality industry."

There was silence on the other end for a moment, then a sharp intake of breath.

"Jesus, Bolt. Are you hurt?"

"Not too bad," I said, automatically minimizing the damage. "But you should see the other guys."

It was a weak joke, but I heard her snort out a laugh despite herself.

"That's not funny."

"It's a little funny."

"It's not." But her voice was calmer now, the initial panic settled into the kind of worry that could be managed. "Are you really okay?"

"I'm vertical and breathing under my own power," I said. "Everything else is just details."

"Details like what? How badly are you hurt?"

Before I could answer, my phone buzzed with an incoming call. Dr. Roth's name appeared on the screen.

"Maggie, I need to take this call. It's my doctor calling back."

"Your doctor? How badly—"

"I'll call you right back, I promise. Give me five minutes."

I clicked over to Roth's call before she could protest further.

"Doc, thanks for calling back."

"Bolt." His voice carried the weight of three decades patching up broken people. "Your message sounded like you tangled with a wood chipper. How bad is it?"

"Probably not as bad as it looks, but bad enough that I figured I should have a professional take a look."

"Can you get to a hospital?"

"Doc, you know I can't."

There was a pause, and I could practically hear him weighing his options. Steven Roth understood the kind of life I lived, the gray areas where official medical records could become legal complications. He'd built his private practice around people who existed in those gray areas.

"Can you see me today?" I asked.

"What kind of injuries are we talking about?"

"Contusions, lacerations, possible rib fracture. Nothing arterial, nothing that's getting worse, but enough that I'd feel better having someone who knows what they're doing take a look."

Another pause, longer this time.

"Can you be here at ten?"

I checked the clock. It was just after seven, which gave me enough time to finish with Maggie and maybe grab some breakfast that didn't come from a vending machine.

"Yeah, I can make ten. Should I come to the office or your home office?"

"Home," he said without hesitation. "And Bolt? I hope to Christ you don't require surgery."

"You and me both, Doc."

He hung up without further pleasantries. Steven Roth was a man who believed in efficiency, especially when it came to patching up people who couldn't afford to be patched up in public.

I called Maggie back immediately. She picked up on the first ring.

"Five minutes, my ass. What did the doctor say?"

"He's going to see me at ten. It's nothing serious, just want to make sure I didn't miss anything important."

"What kind of injuries?"

"The kind you get when you spend three days playing hide and seek with people who take the game very seriously."

"Bolt..."

"I'm okay, Maggie. Banged up, but okay. And I learned some things that are going to help us with Elsa's case."

"What kind of things?"

I settled into the coach's small dinette, trying to find a position that didn't make my ribs scream. "The kind of things that suggest we're on the right track, but we're dealing with people who have a lot more resources than we initially thought."

"Meaning?"

"Meaning we need to be very careful moving forward. These aren't street-level players. They have serious money, serious connections, and serious firepower."

"Are you talking about Chesnokov?"

The name hung in the air between us like a loaded gun. I hadn't mentioned Chesnokov by name a lot in my previous conversations, but Maggie was smart enough to connect the dots.

"Among others," I said carefully. "Look, I know you want details, and you deserve them, but I'm not thinking clearly enough right now to give you the full picture. Can we meet after I see the doc? Maybe around noon?"

"Where?"

I thought about that. The coach was compromised, and Maggie's apartment might not be safe either if Chesnokov decided to expand his interest in my personal life.

"How about the diner on Fletcher? The one with the terrible coffee and the amazing pie?"

"Mabel's?"

"That's the one. Noon?"

"I'll be there." She paused. "Bolt?"

"Yeah?"

"Don't disappear on me again. I mean it. If something happens to you and I don't know about it, I'll track you down in the afterlife just to kill you myself."

"Understood."

"Good. And Bolt?"

"Yeah?"

"I'm glad you're okay."

The line went dead, leaving me alone with the familiar sounds of the coach and the weight of everything that had happened over the past three days. I looked around the small space that had been home for the better part of a year, seeing it with new eyes. The dinette that served as my office, the tiny kitchen where I'd made thousands of cups of coffee, the narrow aisle that connected the front cab to the living area. It wasn't much, but it had been mine. Now it felt like a target.

I opened the small refrigerator and pulled out a bottle of water, downing half of it in one go. Dehydration was probably contributing to the pounding in my head, along with whatever cocktail of chemicals Chesnokov's people had used to keep me compliant during the early stages of my captivity.

The memory of those first few hours was still fuzzy around the edges. I remembered walking into the warehouse, the feeling that something was wrong, and then a sharp pain in my neck followed by darkness. When I'd come to, I was zip-tied to a chair in what looked like a converted office space, facing a man who introduced himself as Kiril Chesnokov as if we were meeting at a cocktail party.

Chesnokov was not what I'd expected. The intelligence reports had described him as a mid-level player in the Eastern European crime scene, someone who specialized in moving contraband across international borders. What they hadn't mentioned was his intelligence, his education, or his complete lack of the theatrical brutality that characterized most of his peers.

He'd questioned me with the patience of a college professor, asking about my investigation into Elsa's theft with genuine curiosity. When I'd refused to answer, he hadn't threatened me with violence. Instead, he'd simply waited, as if my cooperation was inevitable and he had all the time in the world. It was that patience that had scared me more than any threat could have.

The phone rang, startling me out of the memory. I checked the caller ID, expecting to see Maggie's number, but it was a number I didn't recognize.

"Hello?"

"Mr. Bolt?" The voice was male, middle-aged, with a slight accent I couldn't place.

"Who's asking?"

"A friend. I believe you recently visited some mutual acquaintances in the desert."

My blood went cold. "I think you have the wrong number."

"I don't think so. You spent three interesting days with Mr. Chesnokov, and you left quite an impression."

I was already moving, grabbing my keys and the small go-bag I kept packed for emergencies. If they had my phone number, they probably had my location.

"What do you want?"

"To talk. Nothing more. Mr. Chesnokov was... disappointed that your conversation was cut short by circumstances beyond his control."

"Tell Mr. Chesnokov that I'm a busy man."

"I'm sure you are. But perhaps you might find time for a brief conversation. There are aspects of your current investigation that might benefit from additional perspective."

I was at the coach's door, scanning the parking area for anything that looked out of place. Everything seemed normal—too normal, maybe.

"I'll pass, thanks."

"Mr. Bolt, I think you misunderstand. This is not a threat or coercion. Mr. Chesnokov genuinely believes you are pursuing the wrong people for the wrong reasons, and he would like the opportunity to provide some clarity."

"Clarity?"

"About Elena Pavlov. About who she really wants, and why."

That stopped me cold. "Go on."

"Not over the phone. Are you familiar with the Observatory Café on Mount Wilson?"

"Yeah."

"Tomorrow, 2 PM. Come alone, and come prepared to listen. If you're not satisfied with what you hear, you're free to leave. You have my word."

"Your word doesn't mean much to me."

"Perhaps not. But the truth might."

The line went dead.

I stood in the doorway of the coach, keys in hand, trying to process what had just happened. Chesnokov wanted to meet, and he was claiming to have information about Elena's motivations. Was it about her desire to 'inherit' her father's business after his demise or something else? It could be a trap—probably was a trap—but it was also the first break in the case I'd had in weeks.

The Observatory Café was public, which made it harder to stage an ambush, but not impossible. Mount Wilson was isolated enough that help would be a long time coming if things went wrong. On the other hand, if Chesnokov really did have information about Elena, I couldn't afford to ignore it.

I looked at the clock. It was 8:30, which gave me an hour and a half before my appointment with Dr. Roth. Time enough to grab some breakfast and think through my options.

The diner down the road from Dockweiler was the kind of place that served coffee strong enough to wake the dead and breakfast that came with a side of arterial blockage. The waitress knew me by name and always had my usual ready before I sat down: black coffee, wheat toast, and whatever looked freshest on the grill.

"Honey, you look like hell," she said as I slid into my usual booth. "What happened to your face?"

"Walked into a door."

"Must have been some door."

"You should see the door."

She poured coffee without being asked, the dark liquid steaming in the chipped ceramic mug. "You want your usual?"

"Just coffee today. My stomach's not quite ready for solid food."

She gave me a look that suggested she'd heard that excuse before from men who'd had rough nights, but she didn't push it. That was another thing I liked about this place—they minded their own business.

I sat in the booth, sipping coffee that could strip paint and watching the morning traffic build on the street outside. Normal people heading to normal jobs, dealing with normal problems. Part of me envied them their mundane concerns, their predictable schedules, their reasonable expectation that they'd make it home alive at the end of the day.

But only part of me. The truth was, I'd tried the normal life, and it hadn't taken. There was something in my wiring that required a certain level of chaos, a certain amount of uncertainty. Maybe it was all my years with FIDA: never stopping until I got what I wanted from a suspect. Maybe it was just who I was. Either way, I'd learned to accept it.

The coffee was working its magic, clearing some of the fog from my head and bringing the world into sharper focus. I pulled out a small notebook—one of several I carried—and started making notes about everything I could remember from Desert Center.

Chesnokov's operation was bigger than I'd initially thought. The warehouse complex had been substantial, with multiple buildings and enough security to suggest they were protecting something valuable. I'd counted at least eight guards during my brief tour, all armed with military-grade weapons and wearing tactical gear that wasn't available at the local Army surplus store.

The timing was important too. Chesnokov had been expecting someone—someone important enough to make him nervous. The phone call that had interrupted my interrogation had changed his entire demeanor, shifting his focus from me to whatever was coming down the pipeline.

And then there was the question of how Elena, Elsa, and Trisha were connected to all of this. Chesnokov claimed to have information about Elena's real motives, which suggested either he wasn't responsible for her or he was playing a much deeper game than I'd given him credit for.

My phone buzzed with a text message from Maggie: "Ran Elsa's financials again. Found something interesting. Can't wait until noon."

I finished my coffee and left a ten on the table. The waitress waved goodbye as I headed for the door, calling out, "Take care of yourself, honey."

If only it were that simple.

The drive to Dr. Roth's house took me through some of the nicer parts of town, where the houses had yards and the streets had trees. Steven lived in a modest ranch-style home that had been converted to accommodate his private practice. The home office was accessed through a separate entrance on the side of the house, allowing his patients to come and go without disturbing his family life.

I pulled into the driveway at exactly 10 AM and walked around to the side entrance. Before I could knock, the door opened to reveal Dr. Roth himself—all six feet and change of him, with steel-gray hair and the kind of hands that had seen everything the human body could endure.

"Christ, Bolt," he said, looking me up and down. "You look like you went ten rounds with Mike Tyson."

"Feels like it too," I said, following him into the examination room.

The space was equipped like a small emergency room, with everything needed to handle trauma cases that couldn't or wouldn't go to a hospital. Roth had saved more than one life in this room, patching up people who existed in the margins of society.

"Sit on the table," he said, washing his hands at a small sink. "Start from the top and tell me everything that hurts."

"Everything hurts, Doc."

"Then we'll start with everything and work our way down." He put on latex gloves and approached the examination table. "What happened to your face?"

"Someone didn't like my sense of humor."

"Their loss." He tilted my head to examine the cut above my eyebrow. "This is going to need a few stitches. When did it happen?"

"Two days ago, maybe three. Time kind of warped."

"It's already started healing, but not cleanly. I'm going to have to open it back up and do it right." He moved to my split lip. "This one's not as bad. Just keep it clean and try not to smile too much."

"Shouldn't be a problem."

He continued his examination, making notes on a clipboard as he went. "Contusion on the left cheek, minor swelling around the left eye, abrasions on both hands consistent with defensive wounds or climbing. What else?"

"Ribs," I said. "Left side, about three or four inches below the armpit."

He had me remove my shirt, and I heard him whistle low when he saw the full extent of the bruising.

"Someone worked you over pretty good," he said, gently probing the discolored area. "Take a deep breath."

I did, wincing as the movement sent a sharp pain through my side.

"Again."

The second breath was easier, but the pain was still there.

"I don't think anything's broken," he said, "but you've got some serious soft tissue damage. Are you having any trouble breathing?"

"Only when I laugh."

"Then you should be fine." He continued his examination, checking my range of motion and looking for signs of internal bleeding. "Any dizziness? Nausea? Blurred vision?"

"Headache, but I think that's mostly dehydration and lack of sleep."

"When's the last time you had a full meal?"

I had to think about that. "Maybe four days ago."

"Jesus, Bolt. You can't run on empty and expect your body to heal itself." He moved to a cabinet and started pulling out supplies. "I'm going to clean and stitch that cut, give you some antibiotics to prevent infection, and prescribe some pain medication for the ribs. But you need to eat, you need to sleep, and you need to take it easy for at least a week."

"Can't do it, Doc."

"Can't or won't?"

"Both."

He was preparing a local anesthetic, drawing the clear liquid into a syringe. "This is going to sting a little."

The injection felt like a bee sting, but within a few minutes the area around the cut was numb. Roth worked with the practiced efficiency of someone who'd done this thousands of times, cleaning the wound and closing it with small, precise stitches.

"You know," he said as he worked, "I've been patching up people like you for thirty years, and I've noticed something."

"What's that?"

"The ones who think they're bulletproof are usually the first ones to prove they're not."

"I don't think I'm bulletproof, Doc. I just don't have a choice."

"There's always a choice." He tied off the last stitch and applied a small bandage. "The question is whether you're going to make it before or after it's made for you."

He moved to another cabinet and pulled out a bottle of antibiotics and a smaller bottle of pain pills. "Take one antibiotic twice a day with food—and I mean real food, not coffee and whisky. The pain medication is for when the ribs get unbearable, but don't drive or operate machinery while you're taking them."

"Thanks, Doc."

"Don't thank me yet." He sat down across from me, his expression serious. "Bolt, I don't know what kind of trouble you're in, and I don't want to know. But whatever it is, it's escalating. This is the worst I've seen you, and that's saying something."

"I'll be careful."

"Careful isn't enough anymore. You need to be smart. The human body can only take so much abuse before something gives way permanently."

I put my shirt back on, every movement a reminder of the past three days. "I hear you, Doc."

"Do you? Because I've had this conversation with too many people who thought they were listening, and some of them aren't around to have follow-up appointments."

"I'll try to be more careful."

"Try harder." He stood up and walked me to the door. "And Bolt? Next time you disappear for three days and come back looking like this, consider the possibility that whatever you're chasing isn't worth dying for."

"I'll keep that in mind."

"See that you do."

The door closed behind me with a soft click, leaving me alone in the morning sunlight with a bottle of pills and the uncomfortable knowledge that Dr. Roth was probably right. Whatever I was chasing was dangerous enough to have already cost me three days and nearly cost me a lot more.

But Elena Pavlov, Elsa Krieger, and Trisha Goldstein were all taking up residence in my head, rent free, and if Chesnokov really did have information about Elsa, I had to pursue it. Even if it meant walking into another trap. Even if it meant proving that I wasn't nearly as bulletproof as I sometimes pretended to be.

I sat in my car for a moment, looking at the bottle of pain medication. The smart thing would be to take one now, go back to the coach, and sleep for twelve hours. Let my body start the healing process while my mind processed everything that had happened. Instead, I started the engine and headed toward Fletcher Avenue. Maggie was expecting me at noon, and she'd found something in Elsa's financials that couldn't wait. Whatever it was, it might be the key to understanding how everything was connected to Chesnokov's operation. Or it might be the key to getting us both killed. At this point, those seemed like equally likely possibilities.

The clock on the dashboard read 11:15. Just enough time to grab some real food before meeting Maggie, if I could keep it down. My body needed fuel if it was going to heal, and Dr. Roth was right about running on empty.

I pulled into a small grocery store and bought a turkey sandwich, a banana and a pint of whole milk. Not exactly a balanced meal, but it was protein and vitamins, easy to digest, and more than I'd had in days.

I ate in the parking lot, watching people come and go with their shopping carts and their everyday concerns. A woman loading groceries into a minivan while her kids argued in the back seat. An elderly man struggling with a bag of dog food. A teenager on his phone, gesturing animatedly as he talked.

Normal life continued all around me, completely unaware of the undercurrents of violence and corruption that flowed just beneath the surface. Sometimes I wondered what it would be like to be that oblivious, to live in a world where the biggest worry was whether the milk was past its expiration date.

But then I thought about Elsa, and the choice between ignorance and justice seemed pretty clear.

I finished the sandwich and headed for Mabel's Diner, ready to hear what Maggie had discovered and to start planning our next move. Whatever Chesnokov wanted to tell me tomorrow, I needed to be prepared for the possibility that he was lying, that he was telling the truth, or that the truth was more complicated than either of us realized. In my experience, it was usually the latter. The game was definitely on, and the stakes kept getting higher. But I'd been playing high-stakes games for a long time, and I wasn't ready to fold just yet. Even if I was starting to wonder if I had enough chips left to see it through to the end.

CHAPTER 23

FLOOD WATERS

Mabel's Diner looked exactly like it had since 1962—red vinyl booths cracked with age, checkered linoleum that had seen better decades, and the kind of fluorescent lighting that made everyone look like they were recovering from the flu. The coffee was terrible, the pie was legendary, and the clientele consisted mostly of people who'd given up on impressing anyone with their choice of restaurants. In other words, it was perfect for the kind of conversation Maggie and I needed to have.

Through the glass entry door I spotted her in the back corner booth before she saw me, her laptop open and papers spread across the table like she was conducting a board meeting. Her auburn hair was pulled back in a ponytail, and she was wearing the kind of focused expression that usually meant she'd found something that would complicate my life in interesting ways.

The bell above the door announced my arrival with a cheerful jingle that seemed wildly inappropriate given the circumstances. Maggie looked up, and I saw her take in my appearance—the fresh stitches above my eyebrow, the way I was moving carefully to protect my ribs, the general aura of someone who'd recently been used as a punching bag.

"Jesus Christ, Bolt," she said as I slid into the booth across from her. "When you said you were banged up, I thought you meant maybe a black eye and some bruises."

"This is just the visible damage," I said, trying for lightness and not quite achieving it. "You should see my ego."

She wasn't buying the humor. "What the hell happened out there?"

Before I could answer, our waitress appeared—a woman in her sixties with bottle-blonde hair and the kind of no-nonsense attitude that suggested she'd seen everything at least twice. Her name tag read "Dolores," and she looked at me like I was a stray dog that had wandered in from the rain.

"Coffee?" she asked.

"Please. And maybe some pie if you've got anything that won't require too much chewing."

"Apple pie's soft enough for a baby," Dolores said. "You want ice cream with that?"

"Why not. Life's short."

"Ain't that the truth, honey." She poured coffee into a thick ceramic mug and headed back toward the kitchen, leaving Maggie and me alone with the weight of everything that had happened over the past three days.

"Start talking," Maggie said, closing her laptop and giving me her full attention. "And don't you dare give me any of that 'need to know' bullshit. I'm your partner, which means I need to know everything."

I took a sip of coffee that tasted like it had been filtered through a dirty gym sock and tried to figure out where to begin. "You know how sometimes you get a feeling that you're walking into something bigger than you initially thought?"

"Yeah."

"Well, I was wrong. This isn't bigger than I thought. It's bigger than I could have imagined in my worst nightmare."

I told her everything, starting with my decision to follow up on the Chesnokov lead and ending with my escape from the Desert Center compound during the sandstorm. I didn't spare any details—the interrogation, the casual professionalism of Chesnokov's operation, the phone call that had changed everything, and the growing certainty that Elsa's theft was connected to something much larger than simple embezzlement. I added the little tidbit about Elsa's text less than twenty-four hours after I was nearly killed by Chesnokov's henchmen.

Maggie listened without interruption, her expression growing more concerned with each detail. When I finished, she was quiet for a long moment, processing everything I'd told her.

"So let me get this straight," she said finally. "You walked into what you thought was a small-time money laundering operation and discovered what might be a major criminal enterprise with international connections."

"That's about the size of it."

"And now Elsa wants to meet with you to discuss or do what?"

"I assume to either get additional information from me or take another swipe, so to speak."

"You know it's a trap, right?"

"Almost certainly."

"But you're going to see her anyway."

"Haven't decided yet."

Dolores appeared with a slice of apple pie that looked like it had been cut by someone who believed in generous portions. The ice cream was already starting to melt, creating a small lake of vanilla around the crust.

"Anything else?" she asked.

"We're good for now," I said.

She nodded and moved on to terrorize other customers, leaving us alone again.

"What did you find in Elsa's financials?" I asked, taking a bite of pie that was sweet enough to make my teeth ache.

Maggie reopened her laptop and pulled up a spreadsheet that looked like it had been designed by someone with a serious addiction to color coding. "This is where it gets interesting. You know how we traced her theft back to the Goldstein campaign funds?"

"Yeah."

"Well, I decided to dig deeper into her personal accounts, see if there were any other patterns we'd missed." She turned the laptop so I could see the screen. "Look at this."

The spreadsheet showed a series of transactions going back six months. Most were routine—rent, groceries, credit card payments, the usual financial flotsam of modern life. But highlighted in yellow were a series of deposits that didn't fit the pattern.

"Five thousand here, seven thousand there," Maggie said, pointing to the highlighted entries. "Always in cash, always deposited at different branches, always just under the federal reporting requirements."

"Classic money laundering technique. Stay under the radar, spread it around, make it look like legitimate income."

"Exactly. But here's the interesting part." She clicked to another tab, revealing a different view of the same data. "The timing of these deposits correlates almost perfectly with a series of withdrawals from accounts connected to the Goldstein campaign."

I studied the screen, seeing the pattern she'd identified. "She wasn't just stealing from the campaign. She was laundering money through it."

"It gets better. Or worse, depending on your perspective." Another click, another spreadsheet. "I cross-referenced the deposit dates with some other databases I may or may not have legitimate access to."

"Maggie—"

"Don't ask, don't tell. The point is, these dates correspond with some interesting activities in the world of international finance. Specifically, large cash transactions in Eastern European markets."

The pieces were starting to come together, forming a picture that was both clearer and more disturbing than anything I'd imagined. "You're saying Elsa was part of an international money laundering operation."

"I'm saying Elsa was a small cog in a very large machine. The question is whether she knew it."

I thought about my conversations with Elsa, trying to remember any signs that she'd been aware of the larger implications of her actions. Her nervousness when discussing the details of the theft, her evasiveness about her motivations, the way she'd seemed genuinely surprised by the violent reaction her actions had provoked.

"I don't think she knew," I said finally. "I think she thought she was just stealing campaign funds. She had no idea she was stepping into the middle of an international criminal conspiracy."

"Which would explain why everyone's been trying to kill you," Maggie said. "You're not just investigating a simple theft. You're investigating their entire operation."

"And now Elsa wants to meet."

Maggie closed the laptop and leaned back into the booth. "What do you think she really wants?"

"That's the million-dollar question." I finished my pie and pushed the plate away. "Could be she wants to recruit me. Could be she wants to eliminate me. Could be she genuinely believes I'm chasing the wrong people and wants to set me straight."

"Or it could be all three."

"Or it could be all three," I agreed.

We sat in comfortable silence for a moment, the weight of our discoveries settling between us like a third person at the table. Outside, the afternoon traffic was building, normal people heading home from normal jobs to normal lives that didn't involve international criminal conspiracies or meetings with dangerous men in isolated locations.

"There's something else," Maggie said, her voice careful in a way that suggested she was about to drop another bombshell.

"Of course there is."

"I ran some background checks on our three women—Elena, Elsa, and Trisha." She pulled out a manila folder and opened it on the table. "Turns out they have more in common than we initially thought."

The folder contained printouts of what looked like official documents—birth certificates, passport records, university transcripts. I picked up the first page and started reading.

"Elena Pavlov, born in Kiev, Ukraine, 1985. Immigrated to the United States in 2003. Studied business and finance at UCLA." I looked up at Maggie. "This doesn't seem unusual."

"Keep reading."

I picked up the next document. "Elsa Krieger, born in Prague, Czech Republic, 1986. Immigrated to the United States in 2004. Studied business and finance at USC."

The pattern was starting to emerge. I grabbed the third document.

"Trisha Goldstein, born in San Francisco, USA, 1987. Studied business and finance at USC."

I looked up at Maggie, who was watching me with the expression of someone who'd just solved a particularly complex puzzle.

"Two of the three women," she said, "are from Eastern European countries that were former Soviet satellites. They immigrated to the United States within a two-year period. All three studied business and finance at local universities with Trisha and Elsa at USC. Trisha most likely recommended Elsa to her mom the senator, but I'm still tracking down their class schedules to confirm they were classmates and friends."

"Good work, Mags. They're connected."

"I think they're more than connected. I think they're part of the same operation."

The implications hit me like a physical blow. If Maggie was right, then Elsa's embezzlement wasn't an isolated incident. It was part of a coordinated effort to infiltrate financial institutions and political organizations throughout Southern California.

"How many others do you think there are?" I asked.

"Could be dozens. Could be hundreds. This kind of operation takes years to set up, requires careful planning and significant resources."

"The kind of resources that someone like Chesnokov might have access to."

"Exactly."

I pulled out my phone and stared at it for a moment, thinking about the call I'd received that morning. Elsa claimed she wanted to provide clarity about Elena's motivations. Now I was beginning to wonder if what she really wanted was to find out how much I'd discovered about the larger operation.

"I have to take this meeting," I said.

"No, you don't. We can turn everything we've found over to the FBI and let them handle it."

"And spend the next six months in protective custody while they try to unravel a conspiracy that probably involves people in their own organization?"

Maggie was quiet for a moment, considering the implications. We both knew that an operation of this scope would require corruption at multiple levels of government and law enforcement. Trusting the wrong people could get us killed quickly.

"So, what's the plan?" she asked.

"I meet with Elsa tomorrow. Try to find out what she really knows and what she really wants."

"And I do what?"

"You stay safe. This is already bigger than anything we've handled before, and if something happens to me—"

"Nothing's going to happen to you."

"Maggie—"

"Nothing's going to happen to you because you're not going alone." She closed the folder and fixed me with a look that I'd learned to recognize over our years working together. It was the look that said she'd made up her mind and no amount of arguing was going to change it.

"The meet is at the beach, at Coach. I suggested the Observatory Café on Mount Wilson. Public place, but isolated. She demurred saying 'I love the beach. It relaxes me.'" Maggie's look could have slaughtered a rhino.

"Are you out of your fucking mind, Bolt. You can't be alone with her in your place. What is wrong with you?"

"I learned my lesson. Trust me, Mags."

"You're a man. Trust's got nothing to do with it."

Maggie avoided looking directly at me for a few moments. She was obviously preparing her next thoughts.

"Ok. If you're too stupid or horny to not do this, then I'm going to be nearby on stakeout."

"Maggie, no. She might be setting me up. You could get pulled into the maelstrom. If this goes bad, I need someone who can get word to the authorities."

"Which is exactly why I'm going to be there."

"No."

"Yes."

"Maggie, this isn't a debate. These people have already demonstrated that they're willing to kill to protect their operation. I'm not putting you in that kind of danger."

"Bolt, with all due respect, fuck that noise." She leaned forward, her voice dropping to the kind of whisper that somehow carried more weight than shouting. "We're partners. We've been partners for three years, through cases that have involved the cartels, fucking terrorists, and drug dealers. I didn't sign up for this job to stay safe, and I sure as hell didn't sign up to abandon my partner when things get dangerous."

I opened my mouth to argue, but she held up a hand to stop me.

"Besides," she continued, "you're injured, you're probably still concussed despite what Dr. Roth says, and you're about to walk into a meeting with someone connected to people who've already proven they can capture and torture you. You need backup, whether you want to admit it or not."

She was right, and we both knew it. My ribs ached with every breath, my head was still pounding despite the pain medication, and the stitches above my eyebrow were a constant reminder of how close I'd come to not walking away from Desert Center.

"Fine," I said. "But we do this smart. You park on the other side of the parking lot. Stay back, out of sight, with a clear line of communication. At the first sign of trouble, you call for backup and get the hell out of there."

"Agreed."

"And if something does happen to me, you take everything we've discovered and get it to someone who can use it. Someone outside the local law enforcement community."

"Nothing's going to happen to you."

"Promise me, Maggie."

She was quiet for a moment, then nodded. "I promise."

Dolores appeared at our table with the check, her expression suggesting she'd seen enough intense conversations in her time to recognize one when it was happening.

"You folks okay?" she asked.

"Just fine," I said, pulling out my wallet. "Thanks for the pie."

"Anytime, honey. And take care of yourself, okay? You look like you could use some looking after."

After she left, Maggie and I sat for a moment longer, both of us processing the weight of what we'd discovered and what we were planning to do about it.

"There's one more thing," I said finally.

"When is the meeting supposed to happen?" Maggie said.

"She's coming to the coach this afternoon."

Maggie stared at me like I'd just announced my intention to juggle live grenades. "Please tell me you're not serious."

"Dead serious."

"Bolt, how are we to plan for any contingencies? We have..." Maggie looked at her phone. "A few hours. What the ever lovin' fuck!"

"It'll be okay, Mags. Really. She just wants to talk."

"Really? We just established that she's part of an international money laundering operation. She could be coming to kill you."

"Or she could be coming to warn me. Or to ask for help. We don't know what her real role in all this is."

"We know enough to know that meeting with her is a terrible idea."

"Maybe. But it's also an opportunity to get some answers."

Maggie closed her eyes and took a deep breath, the kind that people take when they're trying to summon patience from sources they're not sure exist.

"Chesnokov's people already know you live at the beach, correct?"

"Which is why I'm not staying there much longer regardless."

"And you think it's safe to meet her there?"

"I would have preferred somewhere public, but I think it's safer than meeting her somewhere isolated where she might have backup waiting."

Maggie opened her eyes and looked at me with the expression of someone who was rapidly running out of patience with my decision-making process.

"Fine," she said. "I'll be ready. I need to put some things together for the stakeout. Let's get out of here."

We left Mabel's together, walking out into the late morning sunshine that seemed too bright and cheerful for the kind of day we were having. In the parking lot, Maggie paused beside her car.

"What time is she coming?"

"She didn't say exactly. Just this afternoon."

"I'll be in position by three. Try not to get yourself killed before then."

"I'll do my best."

She got in her car and drove away, leaving me alone with my thoughts and the growing certainty that I was about to make another in a long series of questionable decisions. But that was the nature of this job—sometimes you had to walk toward the danger in order to find the truth. The trick was knowing when you were walking toward answers and when you were walking toward a bullet.

I drove back to Dockweiler Beach slowly, taking a circuitous route and checking my mirrors frequently. If Chesnokov's people were watching me, I didn't spot them, but that didn't mean they weren't there. Professional surveillance was like professional magic—if it was done right, you never saw the trick.

The beach parking area was nearly empty when I arrived, just a few dedicated surfers and the occasional jogger taking advantage of the perfect weather. I parked the Porsche in its usual spot and spent a few minutes walking the perimeter of the coach, looking for anything that seemed out of place. Everything appeared normal, but normal was a relative concept when your life had been threatened by international criminals.

Inside the coach, I made fresh coffee and tried to think through my approach to the conversation with Elsa. If she really was part of Chesnokov's operation, then she might be coming to pump me for information about what I'd discovered. If she was innocent, she might be coming to warn me about dangers she'd become aware of. If she was somewhere in between—a small player who'd gotten in over her head—then she might be coming to ask for help.

The problem was that all three scenarios required different strategies, and I wouldn't know which one I was dealing with until she arrived. That was assuming she was coming alone, which was far from guaranteed. For all I knew, this was an elaborate setup designed to eliminate a problem that had become too dangerous to ignore.

I checked Nervous Energy's Glock, making sure it was loaded and easily accessible. I'd lost track of my gun back at the warehouse in the desert, but this would substitute nicely with a few changes.

Since Nervous Energy was part of a huge criminal conspiracy, it was more than likely there are one or more unsolved murders committed with his weapon. I didn't want to become part of any murder investigations simply because a slug from my new Glock matched those collected at a crime scene.

I kept several extra Model 19 barrels at any one time. You just never know when something goes awry, and you need to dispose of a barrel so your slugs cannot be matched.

I disassembled the Glock, replaced the barrel with a new blued one, and reassembled the weapon. I racked the slide several times to test fit and finish.

I took Nervous Energy's old barrel and went on a short walk to the shoreline. There were only a few people walking, biking, or jogging along the bike path on the beach, but the path was over a hundred yards away from the shoreline.

I picked up several larger stones and seashells and began tossing them into the ocean. I found a large oblong stone on the moist sand, picked it up, and threw it as far as I could into the drink. Immediately after, I threw the barrel too. I finished up my diversion throwing an additional four seashells and stones into the mighty Pacific. Then I walked back to the coach.

I positioned myself where I could see both the beach approach and the parking area, settled in to wait, and tried not to think too hard about all the ways this could go wrong.

The afternoon stretched on with the kind of languid pace that made every minute feel like an hour. I found myself watching the waves with the kind of obsessive attention usually reserved for surveillance operations, noting the rhythm of the sets, the way the wind was affecting the surf, the patterns of foam that marked where the water met the sand.

It was almost four o'clock when I saw her Buick SUV approaching down the beach access road, kicking up sand as it navigated the uneven surface. She parked about twenty-five yards away—close enough for conversation, far enough away to make a quick escape if necessary—and sat in the car for a moment before getting out.

She was wearing jeans and a white blouse that managed to look both casual and expensive, her blond hair pulled back in a way that emphasized the sharp lines of her face. Even knowing what I now knew about her potential connections to international criminal organizations, I felt that familiar tug of attraction that had gotten me into this mess in the first place.

She walked toward the coach with the kind of predatory grace that suggested either exceptional physical fitness or professional training in movement and observation. When she was close enough to speak without shouting, she stopped and looked around the beachfront setup with an expression I couldn't quite read.

"Well," she said, "this is certainly isolated."

"I prefer 'private,'" I replied, standing up from my chair but keeping my distance. "Coffee's fresh if you want some."

"I'd like that."

I went inside to pour two cups, my ears tuned to any sounds that might suggest she wasn't alone. But all I heard was the steady rhythm of the waves and the distant cry of seagulls hunting for their afternoon meal.

When I came back outside, she was standing by the water's edge, looking out at the horizon with the kind of thoughtful expression that people wear when they're trying to decide how much truth they can afford to tell.

"Beautiful view," she said, accepting the coffee cup.

"It has its moments."

"Mind if I sit?"

I gestured to the camp chair I'd set up for guests, then settled back into my own chair, close enough for conversation but far enough away to react if things went in an unexpected direction.

"So," I said, "to what do I owe the pleasure?"

She was quiet for a moment, staring into her coffee cup like it might contain answers to questions she hadn't figured out how to ask yet.

"I heard you had some trouble out in the desert," she said finally.

The casual way she said it sent a chill down my spine. "Word travels fast."

"Word travels at the speed of money and violence. You managed to step into the middle of something that involves both."

"Care to elaborate?"

She took a sip of coffee and looked at me over the rim of the cup, her blue eyes unreadable. "How much do you know about the case you're working on?"

"I know it started as a simple embezzlement investigation and turned into something considerably more complex."

"Complex. That's one way to put it."

"What would you call it?"

"Dangerous. For everyone involved."

We sat in silence for a moment, the weight of unspoken implications hanging between us like smoke from a discharged weapon. I had the distinct feeling that we were both circling around the same central truth, each waiting for the other to make the first move toward honesty.

"Elsa," I said finally, "I'm going to ask you a direct question, and I'd appreciate a direct answer."

"Okay."

"Are you part of whatever Chesnokov is running out of Desert Center?"

Her reaction was immediate and genuine—surprise, followed quickly by something that looked like fear.

"Really, Jon? What kind of question is that?"

"The kind that might keep us both alive."

"You think I'm working for Chesnokov?"

"I think you're connected to this mess in ways you haven't told me about. I think Elena's using you to help her take over her father's business, and this whole mess has become something bigger than either of us initially realized. And I think you know more about what that something is than you've been willing to admit."

She was quiet for a long moment, and I could see her weighing her options, trying to decide how much truth the situation required.

"You're right," she said finally. "I do know more than I've told you. But not because I'm working with anyone. Because I've been trying to stay alive long enough to figure out how to get out of this mess."

"What kind of mess?"

"The kind where you discover that people you trusted have been using you as part of an operation you never agreed to participate in."

The pieces were starting to come together, forming a picture that was both clearer and more disturbing than anything I'd imagined.

"Tell me about Elena," I said.

"Elena Pavlov is not who she claims to be."

"I'm listening."

Elsa stood up and walked toward where the sand began, her posture tense in a way that suggested she was fighting an internal battle between self-preservation and the need to unburden herself of secrets that had been eating at her.

"Elena, Trisha, and I were recruited in college," she said without turning around. "Not recruited exactly—more like identified and cultivated. We were all students, all studying business and finance, all in need of money to pay for our education."

"Recruited by who?"

"People who said they represented legitimate business interests. People who offered us part-time work that paid well and didn't seem to require anything more than basic bookkeeping and financial processing."

"Money laundering."

"We didn't know that's what it was. At least, I didn't. They made it sound like we were helping legitimate businesses navigate complex international banking regulations."

She turned around to face me, and I could see the genuine distress in her expression.

"By the time I figured out what was really happening, I was in too deep to get out safely. They had financial records that implicated me in illegal activities, personal information that could be used to destroy my life, and a network of people who were very good at making problems disappear."

"So, you stayed."

"I stayed. For five years, I processed money, moved funds between accounts, and told myself that I was just following orders from people who knew better than I did. I told myself that I wasn't hurting anyone, that I was just a small cog in a machine I didn't really understand."

"And Elena?"

"Elena was different. She was smarter than the rest of us, more ambitious, and a lot more ruthless. She figured out what we were really doing long before I did, and instead of being horrified, she was excited. She saw it as an opportunity."

"To do what?"

"To climb the ladder. To become more than just a processor. To become someone important in an organization that spanned multiple countries and controlled millions of dollars. She is her father's daughter."

The picture was getting clearer, but it was also getting more frightening. If Elsa was telling the truth, then Elena wasn't just trying to take over her father's organization after his demise. She was an active participant in an international criminal conspiracy.

"What about Trisha?"

"Trisha tried to get out. About six months ago, she told Elena she was done, that she wanted to disappear and start over somewhere safe."

"And?"

"And Elena told her that wasn't an option. That she knew too much to just walk away."

"So, what happened?"

Elsa was quiet for a moment, and when she spoke again, her voice was barely above a whisper.

"I'm not sure how, but Elena convinced Trisha to stay on for a few more months."

It was beginning to make sense. Elena was trying to leverage everyone, including me, to help her in her "palace coup." If Trisha left, Chesnokov or his lieutenants would be tipped off that something was askew. If this was all true, then Elsa was taking an enormous risk by talking to me. More than that, she was taking an enormous risk by continuing to exist.

"Why are you telling me this?" I asked.

"Because Elena's planning something. Something big. Something that's going to bring a lot of attention to the organization, and when that happens, people like me are going to become liabilities."

"What kind of something?"

"I don't know exactly. But she's been making moves, transferring large amounts of money, establishing new accounts, setting up what looks like an exit strategy."

"You think she's planning to disappear with a significant amount of the organization's money."

"I think she's planning to disappear with all of it."

That changed everything. If Elena was planning to steal from her father instead of taking over his enterprise, then the violence that had been directed at me wasn't about protecting a money laundering operation. It was about preventing a much larger theft that could destroy the entire organization.

"How much money are we talking about?"

"I don't know exactly. Hundreds of millions, maybe more. Elena has access to accounts all over the world, and she's been consolidating assets for months."

"And you think her father knows about this."

"I think he might be the one trying to stop her."

We sat in silence for a moment, the weight of Elsa's revelations settling between us like a third person at the beach. The waves continued their endless assault on the shore, and I found myself wondering if I was looking at the ocean or looking at a metaphor for the forces that were slowly eroding everything I thought I knew about this case.

"There's something else," Elsa said.

"Of course there is."

"Elena knows you're investigating her. She knows about your trip to Desert Center."

"How could she know that?"

"Because she has people inside the organization. People who report to her instead of to her father."

The implications were staggering. If Elena had turned members of Chesnokov's organization against him, then Vinny might have an opening to execute the contract on Chesnokov.

"You need to get out of here," Elsa said. "Tonight."

"I can't do that."

"Why not?"

"Because if I run now, Elena gets away with hundreds of millions of dollars, and people like you remain trapped in an organization that will eventually kill them to protect its secrets."

"And if you don't run, Elena gets away with hundreds of millions of dollars and you end up dead."

She had a point. But running wasn't an option, not when I was this close to understanding the full scope of what Elena had been planning.

"There has to be another way," I said.

"Like what?"

"Like stopping her before she can disappear."

Elsa stared at me like I'd just suggested we solve our problems by flapping our arms and flying to the moon.

"Jon, you don't understand. Elena isn't just smart and ruthless. She's paranoid and prepared. She's been planning this for months, maybe years. She has contingencies for her contingencies."

"Then we'll have to be smarter."

"We?"

"You want out of this organization, right? You want Elena stopped before she can eliminate the people who know too much about her plans?"

"Of course, but—"

"Then help me stop her."

Elsa was quiet for a long moment, and I could see her weighing the risks and benefits of what I was proposing. On one hand, helping me would put her in direct opposition to a woman who had already demonstrated her willingness to eliminate problems permanently. On the other hand, doing nothing would leave her at the mercy of someone who viewed her as a liability to be managed.

"What did you have in mind?" she asked finally.

"I don't know yet. But I've got until tomorrow afternoon to figure it out."

"That's not much time."

"It's the time we have."

She finished her coffee and set the cup down on the sand beside her chair. "If I help you, if we somehow manage to stop Elena, what happens to me? I'm still guilty of money laundering, still connected to an international criminal organization."

"We'll figure that out when we get there. Right now, the priority is staying alive long enough to see tomorrow night."

"You make it sound simple."

"It's not simple. But it's possible. With your knowledge of the organization and my experience with this kind of investigation, we might actually have a chance."

"And if we fail?"

"If we fail, then Elena disappears with hundreds of millions of dollars, Chesnokov probably kills us both, and the organization continues operating with new management and new procedures."

"Well," Elsa said with a smile that didn't reach her eyes, "when you put it that way, how can I refuse?"

The sun was starting to set, painting the Pacific in shades of orange and gold that would have been beautiful under other circumstances. Right now, they just reminded me that I was running out of time to figure out how to stop a criminal conspiracy that spanned multiple countries and involved more money than most people saw in several lifetimes. But I was also feeling closer to Elsa than before this conversation. Was she working me or was she being honest. Fear can cause people to react in very illogical ways. Maybe this was one of those times.

"Do you want to stay the night," I said before I even knew I was going to ask.

"Yes," Elsa replied coyly.

I led her into the coach following closely behind. She still smelled great. Perfume and stress do that. I closed and locked the door behind us. Elsa looked around the interior of my home on wheels. "Where?" she said. I grabbed her hand and led her back to the bedroom. I closed the bedroom door behind us per my habit, and we got busy.

The flood waters were definitely rising, and I was starting to wonder if I had enough sandbags to keep from drowning, but for the next few hours it was going to be a lot of fun. Like the old limerick: she offered her honor, he honored her offer. All night long, it was offer and honor.

CHAPTER 24

EARNEST MONEY

The first thing that penetrated my consciousness wasn't the gentle rocking of the RV or the distant sound of waves lapping against the shore. It was the smell—rich, savory bacon sizzling in a pan, the distinct aroma of fresh coffee brewing, and underneath it all, the comforting scent of eggs cooking in butter. For a moment, I lay there with my eyes closed, letting the domestic symphony wash over me like a warm blanket.

Sunlight filtered through the RV's small windows, casting golden rectangles across the rumpled sheets. I could hear Elsa moving around in the galley, the soft pad of bare feet on the vinyl flooring, the gentle clink of dishes and utensils. She was humming something under her breath—a melody I didn't recognize but found oddly soothing.

I checked my phone. Karl texted to confirm our meeting at noon. I replied with a thumbs-up emoji. I still use the default yellow skin color emojis because I'm not letting myself get caught up with any "cultural appropriation" debates.

Last night came flooding back in vivid detail. The way she'd looked in the moonlight streaming through the windows, her skin was luminescent and warm beneath my hands. The taste of coffee on her lips, the soft sounds she made when I kissed that sensitive spot just below her ear. The way she'd moved against me, all curves and heat and desperate need.

I'd let my guard down. Completely, utterly, dangerously. For the third time in a month. What was it about this woman that made me a complete imbecile? It's because I'd allowed myself to just be a man instead of a retriever. No ulterior motives, no hidden agendas, no carefully constructed covers or personas. Just me, raw and honest and vulnerable in a way that should have terrified me. And it was incredible.

But now, in the harsh light of morning, reality was seeping back in like cold water through cracks in a dam. I was still an investigator working on a case. Elsa was still a woman I'd met under less than honest circumstances, and who was the keystone of the investigation. And no matter how genuine last night had felt, no matter how much I wanted it to be real, I couldn't shake the ingrained paranoia that came with my profession.

Trust no one. Question everything. Assume everyone has an angle.

The motto had kept me alive for over a decade, but right now it felt like a lead weight in my chest.

I rolled out of bed, my bare feet hitting the cool floor of the RV's sleeping compartment. My reflection caught my eye in the small mirror mounted on the wall—disheveled hair, stubble shadowing my jaw, and the fading yellow-green bruises from my encounter with Chesnokov's men still visible along my ribs. I looked like what I was: a man who'd been through hell and was trying to pretend he was healing.

I pulled on a pair of board shorts from the small dresser, the fabric soft from multiple washings and bleached by salt water and sun. The RV's air conditioning hummed quietly, but I could already feel the heat building outside. It was going to be another scorcher.

"Good morning, sleeping beauty," Elsa called from the galley as I emerged from the sleeping area. She stood at the small stove, spatula in hand, wearing nothing but one of my button-down shirts. The white cotton hung loose on her frame, falling to mid-thigh and leaving her long legs bare. Her hair was tousled from sleep, and she had that soft, satisfied glow that comes after a night of good loving.

She looked absolutely devastating, and for a moment I forgot how to breathe.

"Morning," I managed, my voice still rough with sleep. "Smells incredible in here."

"I hope you're hungry," she said, flashing me that smile that had gotten me into trouble in the first place. "I may have gone a little overboard."

She wasn't kidding. The small galley counter was covered with food—a plate piled high with crispy bacon, scrambled eggs that looked perfectly fluffy, hash browns golden brown and steaming, fresh fruit cut into neat sections, and what appeared to be homemade biscuits. The coffee maker was gurgling contentedly, filling the air with the rich aroma of freshly brewed caffeine.

"Where did all this come from?" I asked, genuinely impressed. "I'm pretty sure my refrigerator wasn't this well-stocked yesterday."

She laughed, a sound like wind chimes in a gentle breeze. "I may have made a quick run to the store while you were still unconscious. You sleep like the dead, by the way. I was gone for over an hour and you didn't even stir."

Something cold twisted in my stomach at those words, but I pushed it down. So, she'd left while I was sleeping. Big deal. People did that all the time. It didn't mean anything sinister. Did it?

"Hope you don't mind," she continued, turning back to the stove to flip the hash browns. "I used your credit card. The one from your wallet. I'll pay you back, of course."

The cold feeling in my stomach intensified. She'd gone through my wallet? While I was sleeping? Every instinct I'd developed over years of undercover work was screaming warnings at me, but I forced myself to keep my expression neutral.

"No problem," I said, though my voice sounded strained even to my own ears. "Thanks for thinking of breakfast."

If she noticed my discomfort, she didn't show it. Instead, she began plating the food with the efficiency of someone who clearly knew her way around a kitchen.

"Coffee?" she asked, already reaching for two mugs from the small cabinet above the sink.

"Please."

She poured two cups of the dark, fragrant liquid, adding cream to hers and leaving mine black, just the way I liked it. How did she know that? Had I mentioned it last night, or was she just guessing?

Stop it, I told myself firmly. *You're being paranoid. She made breakfast, not a bomb.*

We sat across from each other at the small dinette table, the morning sun streaming through the windows and casting everything in a warm, golden glow. The food was exceptional—the eggs were perfectly seasoned, the bacon was crispy without being overdone, and the biscuits practically melted in my mouth.

"This is amazing," I said, and I meant it. "Where did you learn to cook like this?"

"My grandmother," she replied, cutting a piece of biscuit and using it to soak up some egg yolk. "She was from the old country—Ukraine—and she believed that the way to anyone's heart was through their stomach. She taught me that cooking for someone was an act of love."

The way she said it, the soft smile that played at the corners of her mouth, the warmth in her eyes—it all felt genuine. Real. But then again, I'd learned long ago that the best lies were the ones wrapped in truth.

"Tell me about her," I said, taking a sip of coffee and studying her face over the rim of my mug.

Her expression grew wistful. "She was incredible. Came to America with nothing but the clothes on her back and a head full of recipes. Built a life from scratch, raised five children, outlived two husbands, and never lost her accent or her sense of humor." She paused, lost in the memory. "She used to say that as long as you could make someone smile with your cooking, you'd never truly be alone in the world."

"Sounds like a wise woman."

"She was. I miss her every day."

We ate in comfortable silence for a while, the only sounds the gentle clink of silverware against plates and the distant cry of seagulls outside. It was peaceful, domestic, normal in a way that my life rarely was. Part of me wanted to freeze this moment, to bottle it up and save it for the dark times when the job got too heavy and the world seemed too cruel.

But another part of me—the part that had kept me alive through countless dangerous assignments—was cataloging every detail, looking for inconsistencies, searching for tells that might indicate this was all an elaborate performance.

"So, what's the plan for today?" Elsa asked, breaking the comfortable silence. "More lounging on the beach? Maybe some snorkeling? I noticed you have quite the collection of gear stowed away."

"Actually, I have some errands to run," I said, watching her reaction carefully. "Business stuff, unfortunately. Pretty boring."

"Oh." Was that disappointment in her voice, or relief? "Anything I can help with?"

"Thanks, but no. Just some financial stuff I need to take care of. Probably take most of the day."

She nodded, spearing a piece of fruit with her fork. "No worries. I should probably head back to my place anyway." I sensed she was projecting insecurity that her welcome was waning.

"You're welcome to stay here if you want," I heard myself saying before I could stop the words. "I mean, if you want to hang out on the beach or whatever. Just lock up if you leave."

The smile she gave me was radiant. "Really? You trust me alone in your space?"

Trust. There was that word again. "Sure," I said, hoping I sounded more confident than I felt. "What's the worst that could happen?" Famous last words, as it turned out.

After breakfast, Elsa announced she was going to take a shower. I watched her disappear into the small bathroom, heard the water start running, and tried not to think about what she looked like under the spray. Instead, I forced myself to focus on the tasks ahead.

I retrieved my laptop from its secure compartment—a hidden space I'd built into the RV's cabinetry that wasn't visible unless you knew exactly where to look. The laptop was a high-end machine, encrypted and secured with military-grade software, but still small enough to be portable. I set it up on the dinette table and booted it up.

The financial transfers I needed to make were routine but necessary. Moving money between various accounts, maintaining the complex web of identities and assets that kept my resources intact. It was tedious work, requiring multiple passwords and authentication steps, but it was also crucial to my operation and my life.

I logged into the first account—a legitimate checking account. The balance was healthy, reflecting the salary of a successful businessman with diverse investments. From there, I transferred funds to a secondary account in the Cayman Islands, then from there to a third account in Switzerland. The money would eventually find its way back to various U.S. based financial institutions, but the path it took would be so convoluted that even the best forensic accountants would have trouble following the trail. Asset protection at its best. My spendthrift trust assets were protected by Tatum Parker, but my personal money required additional safeguards to dissuade potential litigants.

It was while I was executing the third transfer that I heard the shower shut off. Elsa's voice drifted through the bathroom door, humming that same melody from earlier. The sound was muffled by the thin walls, but somehow intimate in the close confines of the RV.

I finished the transfer and moved on to the next account. This one required biometric authentication—a fingerprint scanner built into the laptop's frame. The technology was cutting-edge, virtually impossible to fool, and one of the reasons I'd chosen this particular machine.

The bathroom door opened just as I was logging out of the final account. Steam billowed out, carrying with it the scent of shampoo and soap and something distinctly feminine. Elsa emerged wrapped in a towel, her hair darker and wet against her shoulders, droplets of water still clinging to her skin.

"Feel better?" I asked, closing the laptop and sliding it back into its hiding place.

"Much," she said, moving toward where she'd left her clothes draped over a chair. "Nothing like a hot shower to wake you up properly."

She dropped the towel with casual confidence, apparently unconcerned about her nudity. I tried to look away, to give her privacy, but found my eyes drawn to the graceful curve of her spine, the way the morning light played across her skin. She caught me looking and smiled. "Like what you see?"

Heat flooded my cheeks. "Sorry, I—"

"Don't apologize," she said, pulling on her underwear with deliberate slowness. "I like that you're looking. Makes me feel... appreciated."

She finished dressing with the same unhurried grace, each movement designed to catch and hold my attention. By the time she was fully clothed, my mouth was dry and my pulse had quickened significantly.

"So," she said, settling onto the small couch and patting the cushion beside her. "You sure you have to run those errands? Because I was thinking we could have a little 'round two' before you go."

The invitation was clear, her meaning unmistakable. And God help me, I was tempted. The rational part of my brain was screaming warnings, reminding me of all the reasons this was a bad idea, but the man in me—the part that had been lonely for too long—wanted nothing more than to pull her into my arms and lose myself in her warmth again.

But I couldn't. Not now, not with so much riding on the work I had to do today.

"Rain check?" I said, getting to my feet. "I really do need to take care of this stuff, and if I don't leave soon I'll be late for my first appointment."

She pouted playfully. "Fine, abandon me for your boring business meetings. But you owe me, Mr. Successful Businessman."

"I'll make it up to you," I promised, grabbing my keys from the counter. "Stay as long as you want. There's plenty of food, the beach is right outside, and the entertainment system has every streaming service known to man. Just lock up if you decide to leave."

She stretched languidly on the couch, like a cat in a patch of sunlight. "I might just take a nap, actually. It was a long day yesterday, plus... other activities... have me more tired than I expected."

I kissed her goodbye—a soft, lingering kiss that tasted of coffee and possibility—and then I was out the door, walking across the blacktop toward where I'd parked the Carrera the night before.

The meeting with Karl was set for noon at a small café in El Segundo, far enough from the tourist areas to avoid casual observation but public enough to discourage any unpleasant surprises. The clock in the 911 showed 10:05. I had time to visit a few banks to clean up some financial issues.

My first stop was the Citizens Business Bank on Rosecrans. I parked in front of the building and went inside, approaching the teller window. There was a short line with two other people waiting: a guy about thirty or thirty-five wearing an ill-fitting t-shirt and two-inch plugs in each earlobe.

I get that I'm an old man, but really? What's the point of disfiguring your ears like that? I'd love to see this guy when he's eighty or ninety, if he lives that long. He'll either have earlobes hanging below his neck or he'll have the skin removed and be sans earlobes.

Behind Mr. Clean was an older lady about sixty years old. She was holding that vestige of the twentieth century, a checkbook, in her hands.

I gave up writing checks years ago. Paying with Zelle, Venmo, or Apple Pay was so much simpler. And all my bills are auto-paid online.

Mr. Clean visited the teller when he was called forward. His visit lasted less than five minutes. I thought, 'have fun playing video games' as he left the bank.

Grandma's visit to the teller window took substantially longer. I really hate waiting in lines, and the angry young man inside hates it even more.

Grandma wrote a check for some unknown amount as she talked incessantly with the teller. She tore the check out of the checkbook, but her angle of attack sucked. The check tore down the middle instead of along the perforations.

She put the torn piece of check to the side and then carefully removed the other piece that was remaining in the checkbook. And when I say "carefully," she popped each perforation individually and slowly. Truly, the whole process felt like it took hours. It was actually only a few minutes, but you know how time expands when you're waiting.

Grandma finally finished her visit to the teller ten minutes later. By then the line behind me was six people. I saw the bank manager, or who I assumed was, speaking with the lone teller. From their conversation I inferred there were no additional tellers available to assist the growing line of customers. I guess I needed to find a different bank.

When I finally got up to the teller window I said, "Busy morning, huh?"

"Yeah," the teller said. "Two people called in sick today. I don't get it."

"What are you gonna do? People are lazy, am I right?"

"So right. How can I help you?"

I asked her to check my account balance. She told me to put my ATM card into the reader and enter my PIN. I did as I was told.

"Do you want verbal or should I print out the balance?"

"Print out please."

She printed the balance statement and slid it under the window. Fifty-five thousand was in the account. Good. That would work for a while.

I thanked the teller and said, "I hope you get some backup soon." And I walked away.

I visited two other banks in the South Bay in the next hour and a half. All told, I had ready access to two hundred fifty thousand dollars in cash if needed. Enough for most emergencies.

I headed back to Main Street in El Segundo and found a parking space in front of the Original Rinaldi's. Rinaldi's is a local El Segundo café that has been serving up sandwiches, salads, and other American casual food since 1973. The submarine sandwiches are second to none. You can almost feel the love when eating one.

I walked in the place, and I found Karl already seated at a corner table, nursing a cup of coffee and pretending to read a newspaper. He was an unremarkable man in his fifties, the kind of person who could disappear into a crowd without effort. One of his superpowers was an almost supernatural ability to find patterns in financial data that others missed.

"You look like hell," he said without preamble as I slid into the seat across from him.

"Charming as always, Karl. How's Gina?"

"Expensive," he replied dryly. "Her nesting instinct has her buying stuff on Amazon all day long. We get three or more deliveries a day, literally. But you're not here to discuss my financial woes."

He slid a manila folder across the table. Inside there were dozens of pages of financial records, bank statements, wire transfer receipts, and other documents that represented weeks of painstaking investigation.

"I've been able to trace approximately seven million of the embezzled funds," Karl said, his voice low and professional. "Most of it went through the Cayman Islands initially, then got bounced through a series of shell companies in Panama. Classic money laundering operation—sophisticated but not particularly original."

I flipped through the documents, noting the dates and amounts. The trail was complex but followable, assuming you had the right resources and expertise.

"What about the other five million?" I asked.

Karl's expression darkened. "That's where things get interesting. And by interesting, I mean frustrating as hell. The trail went cold about six months ago. One day the money's moving through the usual channels, the next day it just... vanishes."

"Vanishes how?"

"Cash withdrawals, mostly. Small amounts, spread across dozens of different accounts and locations. Someone was very careful to stay under the reporting thresholds, but when you add it all up..." He shrugged. "Five million dollars, converted to cash and scattered to the winds."

I leaned back in my chair, processing the information. "Any theories?"

"A few," Karl said, pulling out a second, thinner folder. "Based on the timing and the methods used, I'd say whoever's behind this is planning to use the cash for operations that need to stay off the books. Drugs, maybe. Or weapons. Possibly both."

"Prostitution, protection rackets, gambling," I added, thinking of Chesnokov's various enterprises. "All cash businesses that are hard to track."

Karl nodded. "Exactly. It's the perfect setup for someone who wants to expand their operations without leaving a paper trail. They've got seven million laundered and legitimized for the above-board stuff, and five million in cash for everything else."

It made perfect sense. Chesnokov wasn't just stealing money—he was building a war chest. The question was, what was he preparing to fight?

"There's something else," Karl said, his voice dropping even lower. "I've been monitoring some of the accounts we've identified, watching for any new activity. There was a transaction this morning that caught my attention."

He pulled out a single sheet of paper, a bank statement with several lines highlighted in yellow.

"Someone accessed one of the secondary accounts—one we thought was dormant—and moved twenty-five thousand dollars to an untraceable cryptocurrency wallet. The transaction happened about two hours ago."

A chill ran down my spine. Two hours ago, I'd been having breakfast with Elsa. Two hours ago, she'd been telling me about her grandmother's cooking and looking absolutely innocent.

"You're sure about the timing?" I asked, though I already knew the answer.

"Positive. The transaction was authorized at 10:17 AM local time, using legitimate login credentials. Whoever did this had access to the account passwords and security information."

My blood turned into ice water. The only person who could have accessed those passwords was someone who'd been watching me type them. Someone who'd been in my RV while I was conducting my financial transfers. Someone like Elsa.

I thanked Karl, paid for our coffee, and left the café in a daze. The drive back to the RV passed in a blur of anxiety, growing dread, and anger. Part of me was hoping—praying—that I was wrong, that there was some other explanation for the timing of the theft. But as I pulled into the parking area near my RV, I could see that Elsa's car was gone. The space where it had been parked was empty, marked only by a small oil stain on the asphalt.

I unlocked the coach's door and stepped inside, immediately noticing the changes. The space felt different somehow—too clean, too organized. The dishes from breakfast had been washed and put away.

The bed had been made with military precision. Even the towels in the bathroom had been folded and hung neatly on their racks.

It was the kind of thorough cleanup someone did when they were trying to eliminate evidence of their presence.

I went straight to the hidden compartment where I kept my surveillance equipment. The coach had multiple cameras and recording devices—a precaution that had seemed paranoid when I'd installed them but now looked like the smartest decision I'd ever made. The recordings from the morning told a story that made my stomach turn.

After I'd left, Elsa had indeed taken a nap—for about twenty minutes. Then she'd gotten up, put on a bikini, and gone for a swim in the ocean. Normal enough behavior for someone spending a lazy morning at the beach. But then she'd come back inside, dried off, and gone straight to the hidden compartment where I kept my laptop.

I watched in horrified fascination as she found the concealed space with the efficiency of someone who knew exactly what they were looking for. She'd had some kind of device with her—a small electronic tool that she used to bypass the compartment's lock.

The laptop came next. She'd booted it up and begun working, her fingers flying over the keyboard with practiced ease. From the camera angle, I couldn't see exactly what she was doing, but it was clear she knew her way around the system. She connected a thumb drive into one of the laptop USB ports.

Then came the part that made my hands shake with rage. She'd danced. Actually danced, naked and uninhibited, right there in my living space while she waited for some kind of software to install. It was a performance of pure contempt—a celebration of how thoroughly she'd fooled me.

The final insult came when she'd accessed my laptop a second time, this time to execute the financial transfer Karl had told me about. Twenty-five thousand dollars, stolen with the same casual ease as someone picking up loose change from a dresser.

By the time I'd finished watching the recordings, I was shaking with a combination of fury and self-recrimination that threatened to overwhelm me. I'd been played. Completely, utterly, professionally played by a woman who'd made seducing marks look as easy as breathing.

I logged into my financial accounts to confirm what I already knew. The money was gone, transferred to an encrypted cryptocurrency wallet that would be virtually impossible to trace. Twenty-five thousand dollars—not enough to bankrupt me, but enough to hurt. More importantly, it was proof that I'd been compromised.

But it wasn't just about the money. It was about what Elsa now knew about me. She'd had access to my laptop, my financial records, and my communications. She knew I wasn't who I claimed to be. She knew I was conducting surveillance on Elena and her. And if she knew, then Chesnokov knew.

I slumped into the dinette booth where we'd shared breakfast just hours earlier, the taste of coffee and betrayal bitter in my mouth. How had I been so stupid? How had I let my guard down so completely? The answer was simple and humiliating: I'd been lonely. Tired of living in shadows, tired of pretending to be someone else, tired of going to bed alone night after night while I chased criminals through an underworld of violence and corruption.

Then my thoughts went off in a different direction: one of recrimination and revulsion. Vicky was available and we clearly connect, and we have connected for many years. She would never betray me, or at least I thought not. So, why then did I fall completely for Elsa's bullshit? Little head thinking.

When Elsa had smiled at me across the table at El Mariachi, when she'd laughed at my jokes and looked at me like I was interesting and attractive and worth her time, I'd wanted it to be real so badly that I'd ignored every warning sign. And ignore the fact that she was a brazen woman who stole millions from a powerful United States Senator.

The accent that came and went depending on her mood. The way she'd deflected personal questions with humor and charm. The fact that she'd approached me after knowing I was investigating her, I should have been more discerning. All red flags that I'd chosen to ignore because I'd wanted to believe in the fantasy she was selling.

My phone buzzed with an incoming text message. For a wild moment, I hoped it might be from Elsa—an explanation, an apology, something to make sense of what had happened. Instead, it was from an unknown number: "Thanks for the earnest money. Consider it a down payment on future services.—E."

Earnest money. A real estate term for the deposit a buyer makes to show they're serious about a purchase. She was telling me that the twenty-five thousand was just the beginning, that she expected more payments in the future.

I stared at the message until the words blurred together, rage and shame and something that might have been heartbreak churning in my chest like a toxic cocktail. She'd played me perfectly, right down to the morning-after breakfast and the casual intimacy that had made me feel special. Every smile, every touch, every breathless moment in the darkness had been calculated and performed with the skill of a master manipulator. And the worst part was, even knowing what she was, even seeing the evidence of her betrayal with my own eyes, part of me still wanted to believe it had been real.

I deleted the text message and powered off my phone, then sat in the silence of my violated sanctuary and tried to figure out what the hell I was going to do next. Outside, the ocean continued its eternal rhythm, waves rolling onto the shore with mindless consistency. Seagulls cried in the distance, and somewhere a radio was playing classic rock at low volume. The world continued on its axis as if nothing had changed, as if I hadn't just discovered that the woman I'd made love to was using me for financial gain. A tale as old as time.

But everything had changed. My trust was betrayed, my security was compromised, and somewhere in this city, Chesnokov was probably laughing at how easily his honey trap had worked. I'd let my guard down for one night, allowed myself to feel human for a few precious hours, and it had cost me everything.

The irony wasn't lost on me. I'd spent days trying to infiltrate Chesnokov's organization, looking for weaknesses and vulnerabilities I could exploit. Meanwhile, he'd found mine in a matter of hours and exploited it with surgical precision.

I looked around the coach that had been my home for the past several years, noting all the small ways Elsa's presence had contaminated the space. The coffee mug she'd used still sat in the sink, lipstick traces still visible on the rim. The pillow she'd slept on still bore the impression of her head. The air still carried the faint scent of her perfume.

It all had to go. Every trace of her, every reminder of my colossal failure in judgment. I needed to sanitize this place like a crime scene, then figure out how to salvage what was left of my operation.

But first, I needed to follow up with Karl and Maggie. The breach in security was too serious to handle alone, and there was always the possibility that Elsa had planted surveillance devices of her own while she'd been here.

I retrieved a secure satellite phone from another hidden compartment and dialed Karl's number. The phone rang twice before he answered.

"Using the satellite phone, boss. It's bad then?"

"You were right. Elsa stole twenty-five grand and made the crypto transfer," I said. "I need the coach swept."

There was a pause, then Karl's voice came back sharp and professional. "I'll be there in an hour with the team."

I closed my eyes, the shame burning in my chest like acid. "Karl. I'm fully compromised. She got me with a honey pot."

"Jesus Christ, Bolt. Please tell me you didn't—"

"I did everything she needed me to do," I said, cutting him off. "Financial access, operational intelligence, probably location data. They've got enough to burn me and half the operation. And Chesnokov probably knows too."

Another pause, longer this time. When Karl spoke again, his voice was carefully controlled. "Understood. It's not great, but it happens."

"Not to me it doesn't. I'm pissed!"

"Ten-four. See you in sixty."

The line went dead, leaving me alone with the consequences of my actions.

I had an hour to see what I could uncover before Karl's team of cyber-nerds showed up. They were a bunch of young, whip-smart young women and men who could not only detect if Elsa left any surveillance equipment or software, but could trace where any information extracted was being sent and plant a trojan horse, a worm, or any other number of hacker infiltrations in the receiving site. They were really that good.

I started with the laptop, removing the hard drive and preparing it for testing and potential destruction. The RV's microwave would serve as a crude but effective electromagnet, scrambling the data beyond any hope of recovery. Then I began gathering the other sensitive materials—documents, photographs, surveillance equipment, weapons—anything that could link me to the investigation or endanger others.

As I worked, my mind kept returning to the morning's events, looking for clues I'd missed, moments where I should have known something was wrong. The way she'd known how I liked my coffee. The efficiency with which she'd found my hidden compartment. The casual mention of having gone through my wallet while I slept.

All signs that she was far more than she appeared to be. But what haunted me most was the memory of how she'd felt in my arms, warm and real and responsive to my touch. Had any of it been genuine, or was she such a consummate professional that she could fake even that? I suppose it didn't matter now. Real or fake, she was over.

I placed all the electronics on the dining table for easy access to the team. I then began my search for listening or other data collection devices. That's when I found it—a small electronic device, no bigger than a coin, stuck to the underside of the dinette table with industrial adhesive. A listening device, sophisticated and expensive, the kind of equipment that only serious professionals had access to.

I stared at the bug for a long moment, marveling at the thoroughness of Elsa's operation. She hadn't just stolen from me—she'd been monitoring me, probably transmitting everything I said and did back to Chesnokov in real time.

How long had it been there? Had she planted it this morning, or had she somehow gotten into the coach before? The thought that she might have been watching me for days made my skin crawl.

I added the device to my collection of evidence, then finished my sweep. Three more bugs in various locations around the coach, each one professionally placed and nearly invisible unless you knew what to look for. They'd been thorough. I had to give them that.

Nearly an hour passed when I heard several vehicles pulling up outside; at least two were motorcycles. I opened the door and saw Karl pulling up in his classic Mercedes followed by an early 1970s Datsun 510, a 1987 Buick Grand National, a mid-2000s Kawasaki Ninja 600, and a fairly new Harley-Davidson Sportster. Each driver or rider either exited or dismounted, and the bike riders removed helmets.

This was Karl's rag-tag team: Billy O'Lahey, Michelle "Mickey" Sanders, Donovan Platt, and Sandra "Don't Call Me Sandy" Miller. They each waved as they gathered "cleaning" equipment from the trunks of the cars and headed towards the coach.

"Howdy, Bolt," Billy said.

"How's it hangin', Billy?"

"To the left today."

Mickey and Sandra each gave me a big hug. "You ladies are looking fine today." It was a lie. Mickey was dressed in a black skin-tight bodysuit with several strategically cut and cauterized holes in it. Her hair, though pulled back in a bun on top, looked like it had not been washed in a week. Sandra was wearing dirty blue jeans and a nearly thread-bare t-shirt emblazoned with the saying, "Pull my finger." Her cat-eye glasses taped together on the bridge with duct tape.

"When are you going to get new glasses, Sandra?" I said.

"Never!"

Donovan gave me a high-five as he walked by saying, "please don't fuck up again, Bolt." I gave Karl a "thanks for nothing, pal" look.

This team was efficient. They swept, scanned, and visually analyzed all the evidence I'd laid out and the entire interior of the coach in fifteen minutes, each team member calling out what had been discovered as Sandra logged everything in her laptop.

Billy said, "It looks like all the data was being sent to the same IPv4 address 101.1.1.1. I'm going to try a SQL Injection to see what we can shake loose." Billy typed furiously on his keyboard for a few minutes, and then said, "That should do it. I'll collect the data and analyze it. I'll send you the report in a few hours."

Ten minutes later, the team was done. They gathered their equipment and left. Once again, Sandra and Mickey gave goodbye hugs and a kiss on the cheek. Donovan threw a finger gun my way and made a fart sound with his lips. Billy shook my hand and said, "adios, amigo. I'll get you that report soon."

Karl stood beside me as his troops left the Dockweiler parking lot. He put his hand on my shoulder. "It'll be okay, boss. Just be more careful." No shit, Sherlock.

I took a look around the coach. It had been my sanctuary, but now it had been tainted, and it was my fault. I trusted Karl's team had cleaned or deactivated any threats, and Billy would get some level of retribution for me. Now I had to extract payback from the bitch, my new nickname for Elsa.

I locked the coach and walked towards the Carrera. I took the Glock in the Safe Carry holster from the glove box. As I stood inside the open driver's door, I undid my belt and pants, slid them down to my knees, and strapped the Safe Carry around my waist. I pulled up and re-buttoned my pants and tightened my belt. I was ready if things went south. I was no longer going to be the prey. Now I was the hunter. Permanently.

I got in and started the flat six, and I pulled out of the parking area without looking back. I called Maggie as I left the parking lot and hung a left on Vista Del Mar. She answered immediately.

"I hope that orgasm was worth it."

"They were," I said. Maggie let out a huge guffaw. "Multi-orgasmic are we? Tell it to the tourists. What's up?"

"What're you doing now?"

"Just chillin'." That meant she was high, but I didn't care.

"I'm on my way over. You talked to Karl?"

"Of course I did. Karl tells me everything. I'm spending a few days in the Marina at my mom's old place." Maggie inherited a small, ocean view unit when her mother died several years ago. She doesn't rent it out for income because her parents left her plenty of cash as well, but she's also superstitious her mom's "spirit" will leave if someone else lives there.

"I need to plan my revenge, and you're my revenging angel, right?" I said.

"Fuckin'-A I am. When will you be here?"

"About twenty. See you then." I ended the call and sped onto the 105 east. Hopefully, traffic was light.

As I drove I kept thinking about what a schmuck I had been. Never get involved with a suspect in an investigation. This rule is hard and fast. Just like Fight Club. And I broke the fuck out of it. Dumb Ass!

The drive to Maggie's also gave me time to think, to process what had happened and plan my next moves. The operation wasn't necessarily over. Depending on how much Elsa had learned and how much she'd shared with Chesnokov, there might still be ways to salvage the investigation. But it would require revising the plan.

I had gathered a lot of intelligence already, much of it still useful. But Chesnokov, Elsa, and probably Elena would all adjust how they would handle me from now on. I'd need to find new ways to get close to them. All the work of the past weeks, all the relationships I'd built and the intelligence I'd gathered, would have to be considered tainted.

And somewhere in the back of my mind, a small voice kept whispering the most dangerous question of all: What if it had been real? What if, despite everything, Elsa had felt something genuine for the man she'd been sent to betray?

I pushed the thought away, focusing on the road ahead and the uncertain future that waited at the end of it. There would be time for what-ifs and might-have-beens later, when the immediate crisis was resolved and I could afford the luxury of doubt.

Right now, I had a job to do and a cover to maintain, at least until I reached the extraction point. After that, Bolt the businessman would cease to exist, and I'd become someone else entirely.

The cycle would begin again, as it always did in this business. New name, new history, new lies to tell and maintain. Another chance to get close to the criminals and gather the evidence needed to bring them down.

But as I drove toward my rendezvous with Maggie, I couldn't shake the feeling that something fundamental had changed. The professional detachment that had served me so well for so many years felt cracked and fragile, damaged by a few hours of intimacy with a woman who'd seen me as nothing more than a mark to be exploited.

Maybe that was the real cost of Elsa's betrayal—not the money she'd stolen or the security she'd compromised, but the piece of my humanity she'd taken with her when she walked away.

The marina appeared ahead of me, a cluster of white boats bobbing in the afternoon sun. Maggie's mom's condo in the Marina City Club had a wonderful view of the Pacific. That would help calm me down as I planned my next move against Elsa and Chesnokov.

I parked the Porsche and exited the parking structure, took the elevator to the seventh floor and walked to Maggie's apartment number seven-fourteen. I rang the doorbell and waited. A few seconds later the door swung open and there was Maggie, dressed in a ratty bathrobe, smiling. Then she blew a big cloud of dope smoke directly in my face. "Welcome to my world, whore," she cackled. I walked into her unit and closed the door behind me, coughing lightly.

And somewhere else, Elsa was probably counting my money and laughing at how easy it had been to seduce the lonely private investigator who'd thought he was so much smarter than everyone else.

The joke was on me, as it turned out. In a business built on deception and betrayal, I'd been the one foolish enough to believe in the possibility of something real.

It was a mistake I wouldn't make again.

CHAPTER 25

LOW TIDE

The view from Maggie's condo was stunning. Her living room window overlooked the entire Basin E of Marina Del Rey with its mega-yachts, sailing sloops, and other pleasure craft. I was staring out the window watching a mid-sized sailboat heading out for a morning run when Maggie said, "here," and gave me a piping hot cup of black coffee. I took a small sip testing the temperature, and I was glad because had I gulped it, I'm certain I would now have second degree burns in my throat.

"Geez, Mags, could you have gotten this any hotter?"

"Pussy," she said.

Maggie sat down on the love seat across the room from where I was standing. She gestured with her eyes for me to sit on the sofa. I was still processing my great fuck-up with Elsa so I did sit down. I was staring at the floor with my hands clasped together for a minute or so. I've noticed that time seems to expand in silence. That one minute seemed an eternity until Maggie spoke.

"Tell me how it happened."

I looked up at her, this woman who'd been my anchor through countless operations, my voice of reason when the world got too dark. Her ratty bathrobe was tied loosely around her waist, and her hair looked like she'd stuck her finger in an electrical socket, but her eyes were sharp and focused despite the lingering haze of marijuana smoke in the room.

"I broke the cardinal rule," I said simply. "Got involved with a suspect."

"No shit, Sherlock. I got that much from Karl. What I want to know is how a veteran agent with your experience let some honey trap bitch turn him inside out." She took a long drag from the joint she'd been nursing and studied me through the smoke. "You've been doing this for what, over twenty years? You've seen every con, every angle, every way criminals try to manipulate law enforcement. So, what made this one different?"

I leaned back against the sofa cushions, trying to find words for something I didn't fully understand myself. "She was good, Maggie. Really good. It wasn't just the physical attraction, though that was part of it. She made me feel... normal. Like I could just be a guy instead of a P.I. for a few hours."

"Bullshit," Maggie said, but not unkindly. "You've had plenty of opportunities to feel normal over the years. Hell, you've got Vicky, who's been carrying a torch for you since forever. This wasn't about wanting normal. This was about something else."

She was right, and we both knew it. I'd been telling myself that loneliness had made me vulnerable, that I'd just needed human connection after months of living in shadows and lies. But the truth was more complicated and more embarrassing.

"I wanted to be the kind of man she seemed to think I was," I admitted. "Successful, confident, worth seducing. When she looked at me across that table at El Mariachi, when she laughed at my jokes and touched my hand, I felt like I mattered. Not as an investigator with a gun who might get her out of a mess she made, but as a person."

Maggie nodded slowly. "There it is. The ego trap. Oldest trick in the book, and you walked right into it with your eyes wide open."

"I know that now. Doesn't make me feel any less stupid."

"Good. Feeling stupid might keep you alive next time." She stubbed out the joint and leaned forward, her expression serious. "But we're not here to beat you up about your poor judgment. We're here to figure out how to turn this clusterfuck into an advantage."

"What do you mean?"

"Think about it, Bolt. Elsa seduced you, stole your money, and planted surveillance devices in your RV. But she also showed her hand. Chesnokov's organization now knows you're not who you claim to be, which means they'll adjust their behavior accordingly. They'll either try to eliminate you or try to use you. Either way, it gives us information about how they operate."

I hadn't thought about it that way. In my anger and embarrassment, I'd been focused on what I'd lost rather than what I might have gained.

"Plus," Maggie continued, "Karl's going to trace where all that surveillance data was being sent. We might get a look inside their operational structure; maybe identify new players or safe houses we didn't know about before."

"Assuming they don't just disappear now that they know I'm compromised."

"Maybe. But criminals are predictable in their unpredictability. They'll think they've won, think they've neutralized you as a threat. That overconfidence might make them sloppy."

I stood up and walked back to the window, watching the boats rock gently in their slips. A group of pelicans was diving for fish near the jetty, their movements precise and efficient. I envied their single-minded purpose.

"There's something else," I said without turning around. "The way Chesnokov treated Elsa at the smoke shop on Melrose. He hit her, humiliated her in front of everyone. She's not his partner in this—she's his asset, just like I was supposed to be her..." I stopped mid-sentence. Thinking about that incident made me angry all over again, but now not because Kiril hit Elsa, but because now I was thinking she deserved what she got.

"Bolt!" Maggie yelled. "What the fuck?" I looked over at Maggie then down at my hands. In my anger-fugue state I had unconsciously crushed one of Maggie's multiple bongs she had on display. "Damn, sorry Mags. I'll get you another," I said.

"I don't care about the fucking bong. Where did you go?"

"It's everything about Elsa. It's making me a little mental, but she's in deeper than I thought. Chesnokov owns her, probably has for a while. And there's more—Elena Pavlov is looking to take over Chesnokov's organization. He's dying."

This got Maggie's full attention; she sat up straighter. "How do you know?"

"Elena told me. She's actually Chesnokov's daughter."

Maggie jumped up. "Holy shit. You're kidding me. She's trying to take over the organized crime family of one of the biggest Russian mobsters on the west coast, who happens to be her father, and who also is dying?"

"Stage four pancreatic cancer."

Maggie stopped, stared at me with her mouth hung open, and did a pantomime of "mind blown" with her left hand. Then she said, "That changes everything. We thought we were dealing with a simple embezzlement scheme, but now..."

"She's stealing because she's a klepto, and not just from Senator Goldstein and me, but probably from Chesnokov too. Which makes her vulnerable in ways we didn't know about before."

"And desperate. Desperate people make mistakes; take risks they wouldn't normally take." Maggie reached for her laptop, her fingers already moving across the keyboard. "We need to revise our entire approach. If Elena's planning a takeover she could be working with Elsa.

They were together at the Kabbalah Center. That may or may not be relevant. I need to dig into see how close they are."

I sat back down, feeling some of the weight lifting from my shoulders. This was what I'd needed—Maggie's analytical mind cutting through the emotional chaos and finding the tactical opportunities hidden beneath the surface.

"There's something else to consider," I said. "Elsa's text message about 'earnest money' and 'future services.' She's expecting more payments from me, which means she thinks the relationship is ongoing."

"Or she's just fucking with your head."

"Maybe. But what if she's not? What if there's a way to turn this around, make her think she's still playing me while I'm actually playing her?"

Maggie looked up from her laptop, her expression skeptical. "That's dangerous territory, Bolt. You already proved you can't maintain objectivity where she's concerned."

"That was before I knew what she was. Before I understood what makes her tick. I'm not going to fall for the same trick twice."

"Famous last words from every man who's ever gotten in over his head." She closed the laptop and fixed me with a hard stare. "But I can see the wheels turning in that devious little brain of yours. What are you thinking?"

I stood up and began pacing, the plan forming even as I spoke. "Elsa thinks she's won. She's got my money, she's compromised my security, and she's probably expecting me to either disappear or come crawling back begging for mercy. What she's not expecting is for me to approach her as an equal."

"An equal how?"

"As someone who might be willing to work with Chesnokov's organization. Think about it—I'm a businessman with access to significant financial resources and international connections. From their perspective, I could be useful for money laundering, offshore banking, maybe even legitimate business fronts."

Maggie was shaking her head before I finished speaking. "Too risky. They'll see right through it."

"Not if I sell it right. Elsa proved I'm not as clean as I pretended to be—I've got multiple bank accounts, encrypted communications, sophisticated security measures. That doesn't scream 'innocent businessman' to people in their line of work. It screams 'fellow criminal who got caught.' And considering my past, which I'm certain they are aware of, they probably consider me a compadre."

"And you think they'll just welcome you into the family?"

"I think they'll be curious enough to keep me alive while they figure out how to use me. And that gives us time to gather intelligence from the inside."

Maggie was quiet for a long moment, her analytical mind working through the possibilities and pitfalls. Finally, she sighed and reached for another joint.

"It's insane," she said, lighting up and taking a deep drag. "Completely fucking insane. Which probably means it might actually work."

"You think so?"

"I think you're going to do it regardless of what I say, so I might as well help you do it right." She exhaled a cloud of smoke and looked at me seriously. "But we're going to need backup plans. Multiple extraction scenarios, dead drops for intelligence, code words for emergency situations. And you're going to wear a wire every single time you meet with any of them."

"Agreed."

"And if I say abort, you abort. No arguments, no heroics, no trying to salvage the mission. You get out immediately."

"Understood."

She nodded and turned back to her laptop. "Give me everything you know about Elsa's patterns, her habits, where she likes to go. I'll start building a psychological profile we can use to manipulate her right back."

For the next three hours, we worked through every detail of my interactions with Elsa, analyzing her behavior for weaknesses and inconsistencies. Maggie's questions were sharp and clinical, forcing me to examine moments I'd rather forget and admit to observations I'd been too embarrassed to voice.

"She's a chameleon," Maggie concluded as we reviewed her notes. "Changes her accent, her mannerisms, even her vocabulary depending on who she's with and what she wants from them. That's a survival mechanism, usually developed in childhood. She's probably been manipulating people since she was a kid."

"So how do we get through her defenses?"

"We don't. We make her think she's getting through ours." Maggie pulled up a new document on her laptop. "The key is to give her exactly what she expects to see—a wounded, angry man who's been outsmarted but is too proud to admit it. Let her think she's still in control while we gather everything we need to destroy Chesnokov's entire operation."

By late afternoon, we had the framework of a plan. It was risky, complicated, and dependent on my ability to maintain emotional control in situations designed to test it. But it was also our best chance to salvage something from the wreckage of my blown cover.

"One more thing," Maggie said as I prepared to leave. "Vicky called while you were in the bathroom. She knows something happened, and she's worried about you."

I felt a stab of guilt. In all the chaos of the past few days, I'd barely thought about Vicky and how my actions might affect her. She'd been nothing but loyal and supportive, and I'd repaid that by sleeping with a criminal and getting myself compromised.

"What did you tell her?"

"That you were dealing with some operational difficulties but that you were okay. She didn't buy it, of course. That woman has better instincts than half the operatives I know."

"I'll call her later."

"You'll call her now," Maggie said firmly. "Before you do anything else. She deserves better than radio silence while you chase after some criminal bitch who played you for a fool."

She was right, as usual. I pulled out my phone and dialed Vicky's number, stepping out onto Maggie's balcony for privacy. The call went to voicemail, which was probably for the best. I wasn't sure I could have maintained my composure if I'd had to lie to her voice.

"Hey, it's me," I said after the beep. "I know Maggie probably told you something's going on, and she's right. I can't give you details, but I'm okay. Just dealing with some complications in the case. I'll call you tomorrow when things are clearer. Take care of yourself."

I hung up and stood on the balcony for a moment, watching the sun begin its descent toward the horizon. The marina was beautiful in the golden light, all the boats gleaming white against the blue water. It was the kind of scene that should have been peaceful, but I felt anything but calm.

Somewhere out there, Elsa was probably planning her next move, confident that she'd neutralized me as a threat. Chesnokov was probably congratulating himself on the successful honey trap operation. And Elena was probably hovering around her ailing father preparing to strike when the opportunity arose.

In twelve hours, I'd begin the most dangerous phase of the case—voluntarily walking back into the web of criminals who'd already proven they could manipulate me. Everything would depend on my ability to stay one step ahead of people who made their living by staying one step ahead of everyone else.

But for the first time since I'd watched those surveillance recordings of Elsa dancing naked in my RV, I felt like I had a chance. Not just to salvage the operation, but to turn the tables on the people who'd played me.

The game was far from over. In fact, it was just beginning.

I went back inside to find Maggie cleaning her laptop screen with obsessive precision. "Second thoughts?" she asked without looking up.

"None. When do we start?"

"Tonight. I've been monitoring the social media accounts we identified for Chesnokov's organization. There's going to be a party at one of his clubs—invitation only, very exclusive. The kind of event where a wealthy businessman might go to network with other wealthy businessmen who don't ask too many questions about each other's tax returns."

"Club Mirage?"

"No, this one's classier. Club Azure, downtown. More upscale clientele, better security, and probably where Chesnokov conducts his real business." She handed me a printed invitation. "Karl worked his magic. You're now on the guest list as Marcus Kellerman, pharmaceutical sales executive with interests in international distribution."

I studied the invitation. It was elegant, expensive-looking, the kind of thing that would appeal to people with more money than sense. "And if Elsa's there?"

"Then you'll have your chance to start the next phase of the game." Maggie's smile was sharp and predatory. "Just remember—this time, you're not the mark. You're the hunter."

The plan was set. In a few hours, I'd walk into another of Chesnokov's establishments, but this time I'd be armed with knowledge and purpose instead of naive hope. This time, I wouldn't be seduced by a beautiful woman with a hidden agenda.

This time, I'd be the one doing the seducing.

As I left Maggie's apartment and headed toward my car, I felt the familiar surge of adrenaline that came before a dangerous operation. The fear was still there, the uncertainty and the very real possibility of failure. But underneath it all was something I hadn't felt in days: the cold, professional confidence that had kept me alive through the years. Elsa thought she'd broken me. Chesnokov thought he'd neutralized a threat. They were about to learn how wrong they were. It was low tide in the marina and for the organization.

The Porsche's engine roared to life as I pulled out of the marina parking garage, and for the first time since this whole mess began, I was smiling. It wasn't a pleasant smile—it was the kind of expression predators wore when they caught sight of prey.

The real game was about to begin, and this time I intended to win.

CHAPTER 26

CLOUD NINE

Club Azure lived up to its name—everything was bathed in shades of blue, from the LED lighting that pulsed along the walls to the azure-tinted glass that separated the VIP areas from the main floor. The invitation Maggie had procured got me past the velvet rope and the mountain of muscle who served as the bouncer, but once inside, I was on my own.

The club was exactly what I'd expected from one of Chesnokov's upscale establishments: expensive, exclusive, and crawling with the kind of people who did their real business after midnight in soundproof rooms. The main floor throbbed with electronic music while beautiful women in designer dresses moved between tables occupied by men in thousand-dollar suits who looked like they'd never done an honest day's work in their lives.

I made my way to the bar, ordered a scotch neat, and began the delicate process of appearing interested but not desperate. I'd played similar roles before, but never with so much personal baggage weighing on my performance.

The bartender was a study in calculated indifference—attractive enough to earn good tips, professional enough to ignore whatever illegal activities might be happening around her. She served my drink without conversation, which suited me fine. I wasn't here to make friends with the staff.

I'd been nursing my scotch for about twenty minutes, watching the crowd and trying to identify the players, when I saw them. Elsa and Elena, moving together through the crowd like predators who'd temporarily joined forces. They were dressed to kill—literally, in Elena's case, given what I now knew about her plans for her father's organization.

Elsa wore a black cocktail dress that hugged every curve, her platinum hair styled in an elegant updo that exposed the graceful line of her neck. She looked every inch the sophisticated socialite, nothing like the woman who'd danced naked in my RV while surveillance equipment recorded every moment. Elena was in midnight blue, her dark hair flowing loose around her shoulders, projecting an aura of dangerous beauty that made men turn to stare as she passed.

They moved to the dance floor, and I watched with professional detachment as they began to move together. It wasn't sexual—it was business. They were clearly working together, their movements coordinated, their attention split between each other and the crowd around them. This wasn't two women out for a night of fun; this was a strategic meeting disguised as socializing.

I shifted position to get a better view, noting the way other patrons gave them space. Some of that was simple attraction—both women were stunning enough to command attention anywhere they went. But some of it was fear. People in this crowd recognized power when they saw it, and both Elsa and Elena radiated the kind of dangerous charisma that came with connections to serious money and serious violence.

They danced for three songs, their heads close together during the slower moments, conducting a conversation that no lip reader could follow from my distance. I caught fragments of body language—Elena's sharp gestures, Elsa's more defensive posture—that suggested they were negotiating something. The terms of their partnership, perhaps, or the details of whatever scheme they were planning.

During a particularly intense exchange, Elena grabbed Elsa's wrist, her grip tight enough that I could see Elsa flinch. Even from across the crowded dance floor, the power dynamic was clear. Elena was the one in control, and Elsa was trying to maintain her value as an asset. It made sense now—if Elena was planning to take over her father's organization, she'd need allies. Elsa's skills as a manipulator and her apparent debt to Chesnokov would make her a valuable recruit.

Maybe Elsa was hoping that when—if—Elena took over, Elena would forgive Elsa's debt to the old man. It would explain the partnership, the coordination, the way they moved through the club like they owned it. Elsa wasn't just stealing from marks like me and Senator Goldstein; she was positioning herself for survival in a changing criminal landscape.

The music shifted to something darker, more intense, and their dance became more aggressive. Elena spun Elsa around, pulling her close from behind, whispering something in her ear that made Elsa's face go pale. Whatever Elena was telling her, it wasn't good news.

I finished my scotch and ordered another, maintaining my cover as a bored businessman with time to kill. The bartender served me without comment, but I caught her glancing toward the dance floor where Elsa and Elena continued their deadly ballet. Even the staff here knew to be careful around these two.

After another song, they separated. Elena headed toward the VIP section, moving with the confidence of someone who belonged there. Elsa remained on the dance floor for a moment, her composure cracking just enough for me to see the fear underneath. Then she composed herself, smoothed her dress, and headed in the opposite direction—toward the bar where I was sitting.

This was the moment Maggie and I had planned for. Elsa would see me, and I'd have to sell the performance of my life as if I didn't know about surveillance equipment or stolen money or blown covers. I'd just be a man who'd been played by a beautiful woman and was too proud to admit how badly it had hurt.

She approached slowly, as if she hadn't noticed me until she was almost at the bar. Her acting was flawless—surprise, then uncertainty, then a carefully calculated mixture of guilt and defiance.

"Jon?" she said, her accent shifting subtly toward something more refined, more European. "What are you doing here?"

"Elsa." I kept my voice level, neither welcoming nor hostile. "Small world."

She ordered a martini, extra dry, and turned to face me. Up close, I could see the strain around her eyes, the tension in her shoulders. Whatever Elena had told her on the dance floor had shaken her more than she wanted to admit.

"I suppose you're angry with me," she said.

"Should I be?"

It was a good response—not denying anger but not confirming it either. Let her wonder exactly how much I knew, how much I'd figured out. The key to this performance was to appear wounded but not broken, suspicious but not certain.

"I never meant for things to go as far as they did," she said, and for a moment I almost believed her. The regret in her voice sounded genuine, but then I remembered the surveillance footage, the stolen money, the careful way she'd planned every moment of our time together.

"Which things?" I asked. "The sex, or the theft?"

She flinched, a micro-expression that confirmed I'd hit the mark. "It wasn't supposed to be theft. It was... complicated."

"Twenty-five thousand dollars complicated?"

"You don't understand the situation I'm in." Her voice dropped to a whisper, and she moved closer, her perfume mixing with the alcohol on her breath. "There are people I owe, Jon. You know who. I needed that money to stay alive."

It was a good sob story, and she delivered it with just the right mixture of vulnerability and desperation. If I hadn't known about her connection to Chesnokov, about Elena's plans, about the web of lies she'd constructed around our entire relationship, I might have believed her.

"And the surveillance equipment?"

This time she couldn't hide her surprise. Her martini glass paused halfway to her lips, and I saw her calculate rapidly behind those beautiful blue eyes.

"I don't know what you're talking about," she said finally.

"The listening devices; the keystroke logging software. The way you recorded everything we did together." I leaned closer, matching her whisper. "Did you enjoy listening to the playback?"

She set down her glass and turned to face me fully. The mask of vulnerability slipped, replaced by something colder and more calculating.

"You're smarter than I gave you credit for," she said.

"Not smart enough, apparently. But I'm learning."

We stared at each other for a long moment, two predators sizing each other up. Around us, the club continued its nightly ritual of excess and indulgence, but our little corner of the bar had become an island of tension in the sea of artificial pleasure.

"What do you want, Jon?" she asked finally.

It was the opening I'd been waiting for. Time to flip the script, to become the hunter instead of the prey.

"To make a deal," I said.

She laughed, but there was no humor in it. "With me? After what I did?"

"With your employer."

That got her attention. She straightened slightly, her eyes sharpening with interest and wariness.

"I don't have an employer. I work for myself."

"Bullshit." I finished my scotch and signaled for another. "Nobody plants surveillance equipment that sophisticated without backing. You moved twenty-five thousand dollars onto the blockchain. Why? You need to hide it from someone. And nobody gets invited to dance with Elena Pavlov without serious connections."

The mention of Elena's name hit her like a physical blow. She glanced quickly toward the VIP section, then back to me.

"You don't know what you're talking about," she said, but her voice lacked conviction.

"I know enough. I know you're not the independent operator you pretended to be. I know you're working for someone with reach and resources. And I know that Elena might be interested in doing business with me. We've had some discussions previously."

"Why would you want to do business with people who robbed you?"

"Because they proved they're good at what they do." I met her stare directly. "And because I might have use for those skills."

She studied my face, looking for tells, for signs of deception or desperation. I gave her nothing but calm confidence, the expression of a man who'd been backed into a corner and decided to come out fighting.

"Even if what you're suggesting were possible," she said carefully, "what makes you think you have anything she wants?"

"Elena confided in me about her father's illness. She wants my help gaining control. She already offered me a shitload of money to do that. I could probably agree to help her provided she jettisons you."

Her eyes widened slightly. I was describing Elsa's nightmare scenario where she was standing alone, just like the cheese. I believed her childhood trauma made this scenario almost unbearable.

"Please, Jon, please don't," she said.

"You deserve whatever you have coming. But maybe I'll be merciful. Just maybe."

She was silent for a long moment, her mind working through the implications. If I was to throw her under the proverbial bus, it could be the end of Elsa Krieger. If I decided to be a 'good guy' she would live to fight another day. I could see the wheels turning and the concern on her face.

"I'd need to make some calls," she said finally.

"I'd expect nothing less."

She stood, smoothing her dress and checking her appearance in the mirror behind the bar. The professional mask was back in place, hiding whatever emotions might be churning underneath.

"How do I reach you?" she asked. She obviously knew I would change my phone after the shenanigans in the coach. I pulled out a business card of one of many aliases I use during casework and wrote a number on the back. "This phone stays on. Twenty-four hours."

She took the card, studying it briefly before slipping it into her purse. "If this is some kind of setup—"

"If this is a setup? You kill me. Be glad I'm giving you a chance to make amends." She nodded and started to leave, then turned back. "For what it's worth, Jon, I really didn't want to hurt you."

"But you did anyway."

"Yes. I did."

She walked away, her heels clicking against the polished floor as she headed toward the VIP section where Elena was holding court. I watched her go, noting the way other patrons moved aside for her, the deference that suggested she was more than just another beautiful woman in an expensive dress.

I finished my third scotch and left a generous tip, playing the role of disconnected businessman to the end. As I walked toward the exit, I felt the weight of eyes on me—security cameras, human surveillance, the invisible watchers who made places like Club Azure possible. By tomorrow, every detail of my appearance and behavior would be analyzed by people who made their living by spotting deception.

But as I stepped out into the cool night air, I felt another surge of adrenaline that came with high-stakes operations. This was what I was good at—walking the knife's edge between success and disaster, using my enemies' greed and ambition against them. The real test would come when they called.

My phone rang at 7:30 AM the next morning, jolting me awake from the first decent sleep I'd had in days. I'd returned to my coach after leaving Club Azure, spent an hour debugging the surveillance equipment Maggie's techs had missed, and finally collapsed into bed around 3 AM. The phone's shrill tone cut through my dreams like a knife through silk.

"Hello, Senator," I answered, recognizing Nancy Goldstein's number. "Thanks for waking me up."

"Not funny, Mr. Bolt. It's my daughter." The voice was scared and cracking. I was suddenly alert. Trisha was in trouble. I saw her just the other day at the Red Bull Lounge in Redondo. And Senator Nancy Goldstein, the woman whose political career had survived three decades in Washington through a combination of shrewd intelligence and careful image management, was in full freak-out mode. It was off-putting but understandable.

"How can I help you, Senator?"

"It's about my daughter, Trisha. I'm getting worried. Trisha hasn't called or texted for almost a week now, which isn't like her."

I could hear the strain in her voice, the careful control of a woman who was used to managing crises but was struggling with this one. "When did you last speak with her?"

"Last Tuesday. She called to tell me she was fine, that she was staying with friends in West Hollywood. But since then, nothing. Her voice cracked slightly. "I think something's happened to her."

The desperation in her voice was real, maternal fear cutting through political polish. But something about the timing bothered me. I'd just confronted Elsa at Club Azure and now Trisha was missing? Maybe it was a coincidence, but I didn't believe in coincidence.

"Senator, I have to tell you that I did see Trisha a few days ago in Redondo Beach so she's probably okay."

She paused, and I could hear her breathing carefully, trying to maintain control. "Will you go find her to make sure? Please? I need to know she's safe."

I was already reaching for my clothes. "Do you have an address for where she's staying?"

"I do. It's an apartment in West Hollywood. I'll text you the details."

The address came through thirty seconds after we hung up: 1247 Fountain Avenue, Apartment 4B. It was the kind of neighborhood where aspiring actors and musicians went to struggle artistically while trust fund kids went to slum convincingly. Either way, it was the perfect place for a senator's daughter to disappear into the urban background.

I showered quickly, dressed in khaki chinos and a black t-shirt, and headed out to find Trisha Goldstein. The drive from Playa Del Rey to West Hollywood took forty-five minutes in morning traffic, giving me time to think about the complications this new development might create.

If Trisha was really in trouble—kidnapped, hurt, or worse—then I had a moral obligation to help regardless of the politics involved. But if this was just another episode in her ongoing rebellion against her mother's expectations, then I might be walking into a family drama that would compromise my already precarious position with the Chesnokov investigation.

The apartment building was a converted 1920s Spanish colonial that had seen better decades. The kind of place that charged premium rent for vintage charm while providing minimal maintenance and maximum attitude from the management. I found a parking spot on the street and studied the building's layout from my car.

Four stories, fire escapes on the east and west sides, a security door that looked like it had been bypassed so many times that residents probably didn't bother with keys anymore. The kind of place where people minded their own business and expected others to do the same.

Apartment 4B was on the top floor, accessible by a stairway that creaked with every step. The hallway smelled like old cigarettes and new marijuana, with undertones of cooking spices and industrial disinfectant. I could hear music, television, and muffled conversations coming from behind the various doors, the soundtrack of urban anonymity.

I knocked on 4B and waited. No answer. I knocked again, harder this time, and called out: "Trisha? It's Bolt. Open up."

Still nothing. But I could smell something from inside the apartment, something chemical and acrid that made my sinuses burn. I'd encountered that smell before, in crack houses and meth labs and the apartments of users who'd stopped caring about ventilation or basic safety.

The lock was a joke—three minutes with my picks and I was inside, hit immediately by the full force of the chemical stench that had been seeping under the door. The apartment was a disaster zone: empty pizza boxes, scattered clothes, drug paraphernalia covering every available surface. And there, in the center of it all, hunched over a glass pipe like a worshipper at a toxic altar, was Senator Nancy Goldstein's daughter.

Trisha Goldstein had been beautiful once. I'd seen the family photos in her mother's office in Malibu, the carefully staged campaign events where she stood beside her parents with a practiced smile. That girl was gone. The woman on the couch was a shadow, her once-lustrous hair now stringy and unwashed, her designer clothes replaced by stained sweatpants and a tank top that hung loose on her diminished frame.

She hadn't noticed me yet. The meth had her complete attention, her movements slow and deliberate as she prepared another hit. Her hands shook—not from nerves, but from the chemical dependency that had taken over her life. The drug didn't discriminate between senators' daughters and street kids. It devoured them all with equal hunger.

"Trisha," I said, my voice cutting through the oppressive silence.

She jerked up, the pipe clattering to the floor. Her eyes were wide and unfocused, pupils dilated despite the dim lighting. For a moment she just stared at me, her brain struggling to process my presence through the chemical haze.

"Who... who are you?" she stammered, her voice hoarse and cracked. "How did you get in here?"

I stepped into the apartment, closing the door behind me. The locks were pathetic—a motivated twelve-year-old could have picked them. "It's Bolt, Jon Bolt. I saw you a few days ago in Redondo Beach. Your mother hired me."

Recognition flickered across her features, followed immediately by anger. "My mother," she spat, struggling to her feet. She swayed slightly, catching herself against the arm of the couch. "Of course she did. Can't have her precious image tarnished by her junkie daughter, can she?"

"She's worried about you."

"Bullshit." The word came out as a hiss. "She's worried about her polls. About what the press will say when they find out Senator Family Values has a daughter who smokes meth in back alleys."

I took another step closer, my eyes scanning the room for weapons, exits, anything that might become relevant in the next few minutes. Years of agency work had taught me that desperate people were unpredictable people, and Trisha Goldstein looked desperate enough to do something we'd both regret.

"When's the last time you ate?" I asked.

The question seemed to catch her off guard. "What?"

"Food. When did you last have a real meal?"

She blinked, her drug-addled mind struggling with the concept. "I don't... yesterday? Maybe the day before. Time's kind of... fuzzy."

It was worse than I'd thought. Senator Goldstein had mentioned she'd been missing for a while, but looking at her now, I suspected she'd been on this particular bender much longer. The weight loss, the pallor, the way she moved like her bones were made of glass—this wasn't a recent development.

"Your mother wants you to come home," I said.

"My mother wants me to disappear." She laughed, but there was no humor in it. "Do you know what it's like being the daughter of someone who's supposed to be perfect? Every mistake, every stumble, every human moment gets turned into a campaign liability. I was in rehab by sixteen because God forbid anyone find out I smoked pot at a party."

I'd heard variations of this story before. Rich kids, poor kids—addiction was an equal opportunity destroyer, but the wealthy ones usually had more elaborate justifications for their self-destruction.

"So, you decided to show them what a real scandal looks like?"

Her eyes flashed with anger. "You don't know anything about me."

"I know you're killing yourself to hurt them. I know you're smart enough to realize how stupid that is."

She moved faster than I expected, her hand swinging toward my face in a wild, drug-fueled arc. But speed and coordination were two different things, and meth had stolen most of the latter. I deflected the blow easily, catching her wrist and holding it steady.

"Let me go!" she screamed, struggling against my grip. "Leave me alone! You don't care about me! Nobody cares about me!"

I released her wrist and stepped back. She stumbled, catching herself against the wall, her chest heaving with exertion and emotion.

"You're right," I said. "I don't know you. But I know your mother does care, whether you believe it or not. And I know you're worth more than this."

She stared at me for a long moment, her eyes searching my face for something—sincerity, maybe, or just another lie to add to the collection she'd been fed over the years. Whatever she found there must not have satisfied her, because she suddenly bolted for the door.

I could have stopped her easily, but something told me not to. Instead, I followed at a distance as she stumbled down the stairs of the apartment building and out to the street, where a beat-up Honda Civic sat parked at the curb. She fumbled with the keys, dropping them twice before managing to get the door open.

The engine turned over on the third try, belching black smoke into the afternoon air. I jogged back to my Carrera, parked a block away, and followed as she pulled into traffic with the erratic driving patterns of someone whose reflexes were compromised by narcotics.

She headed south, weaving between lanes with reckless abandon. Other drivers honked and swerved to avoid her, their faces twisted with anger and fear. I stayed three cars back, my heart hammering as I watched her nearly clip a city bus at the corner of Sunset and Highland. Somehow she got onto the 101 freeway heading toward downtown Los Angeles. Trisha cut across four lanes of traffic at the 101-110 interchange, and miraculously didn't hit another car or cause an accident. The Honda continued southbound on the 110.

The chase continued for thirty minutes, winding through Hollywood, University Park, South Los Angeles, Harbor Gateway and into San Pedro. I had a sinking feeling about where she was heading even before she turned onto the approach to the Vincent Thomas Bridge. The massive green suspension bridge stretched across the harbor like a steel and concrete gateway to oblivion, and too many desperate people had seen it as exactly that over the years.

Trisha's Honda lurched to a stop in the emergency lane halfway across the span. I pulled over behind her, leaving my hazard lights flashing as I got out. The wind whipped across the bridge with enough force to sting my eyes, carrying the salt smell of the ocean four hundred feet below.

She was already out of her car, moving toward the railing with the determined gait of someone who'd made a decision. The barrier was higher than most bridges—nearly six feet of concrete and steel designed specifically to prevent what she was planning—but it wouldn't stop someone who was truly committed.

"Trisha!" I called out, but my voice was lost in the wind and traffic noise.

She had her hands on the rail now, testing its height. Cars rushed past in both directions, their drivers oblivious to the drama unfolding in their peripheral vision. This was Los Angeles—everyone was too busy to notice one more person having a breakdown on a bridge.

I broke into a run, my feet pounding against the concrete sidewalk. She heard me coming and turned, her face streaked with tears I hadn't noticed before. The wind whipped her hair across her features, making her look even younger and more fragile than she already was.

"Stay back!" she screamed. "Don't come any closer!"

"Trisha, you don't want to do this."

"How do you know what I want?" She grabbed the top of the barrier, pulling herself up with the desperate strength of someone running on pure adrenaline. "How does anyone know what I want? Nobody's ever asked!"

I was fifteen feet away now, close enough to see the way her whole body was shaking. Not from the drugs this time—from fear and desperation and the terrible weight of whatever had brought her to this moment.

"I'm asking now," I said, slowing my approach. "What do you want, Trisha?"

"I want it to stop," she sobbed. "I want the pain to stop. I want to stop disappointing everyone. I want to stop being a burden."

"And you think this will accomplish that?"

She had one leg over the barrier now, her balance precarious in the gusting wind. One strong gust, one moment of wavering, and she'd be gone. I could see the harbor spread out below us, dotted with ships that looked like toys from this height.

"It'll accomplish something," she said. "It'll make a statement."

"What statement? That your parents' enemies were right about them? That they couldn't even keep their own daughter safe?"

Her face crumpled. "They don't care about keeping me safe. They care about keeping me quiet."

I took another step closer. Ten feet now. "Then prove them wrong. Come down from there and tell your story. Tell it your way, not their way."

"Nobody will listen."

"I'm listening."

She looked at me then, really looked at me for the first time since I'd found her in that apartment. I saw something shift in her expression—not hope, exactly, but maybe the faintest possibility of it.

"My whole life," she said, her voice barely audible over the wind, "I've been a prop in their show. The perfect daughter. The campaign asset. Even my problems had to be the right kind of problems, handled the right way, with the right kind of discretion."

"So, stop being their prop."

"I don't know how to be anything else."

That's when I saw my chance. She was wavering, both literally and figuratively, her second leg still on the bridge side of the barrier. I launched myself forward in a tackle that would have made my high school football coach proud, wrapping my arms around her waist and pulling her backward with all my strength.

We hit the concrete hard, her body underneath mine as we tumbled away from the railing. She fought like a wildcat, scratching and punching and screaming, but the meth had sapped most of her strength. I held on tight, absorbing the blows as she struggled to break free.

"Let me go!" she shrieked. "Let me go! You don't understand!"

"I understand enough," I grunted, wincing as her elbow connected with my ribs. "I understand you're not thinking clearly right now."

She kept fighting for another minute before exhaustion began to set in. Her movements became less coordinated, more desperate than effective. Finally, she stopped struggling altogether, her body going limp beneath mine.

"I hate you," she whispered, but there was no real venom in it.

"That's okay," I said, still not letting go. "Would it make you feel better if you could hit me?"

She looked up at me with surprise. "What?"

"You want to hit someone, hit me. I can take it. Might make you feel better."

"You're serious?"

"Dead serious. But no weapons, and when you're done, you're done. Deal?"

She nodded, and I slowly released my hold on her. We both got to our feet, her movements unsteady on the wind-swept bridge. I spread my arms wide, making myself an open target.

"Go ahead," I said. "Get it out of your system."

The beating lasted five minutes and felt like fifty. She hit me with everything she had—fists, elbows, knees, whatever she could manage. I stood there and took it, letting her work through whatever demons were driving her. She pummeled me with the desperate fury of someone who'd been holding everything inside for too long.

When she finally collapsed from exhaustion, I knelt beside her and waited for her tears to subside. Then I helped her to her feet and led her to the Porsche, calling for a tow truck for her Honda while she slumped in the passenger seat like a deflated balloon.

The ride back to Dockweiler was silent except for the hum of the engine and the occasional sniffle from my passenger. My coach was parked in its usual spot, close enough to the ocean that you could hear the waves if the traffic wasn't too heavy.

Trisha followed me inside without comment, her movements automatic and disconnected. I pointed her toward the bedroom and told her there were clean sheets in the closet. Within minutes, I could hear the steady breathing of someone who'd finally found the exhaustion that comes after a complete emotional and physical breakdown.

She slept for fourteen hours. When she finally emerged, showered and wearing clean clothes from my emergency stash, she looked better.

Not good—the hollowed cheeks and dark circles under her eyes would take weeks to heal—but better.

I had breakfast ready: scrambled eggs, whole wheat toast, and coffee strong enough to wake the dead. She picked at the food, eating slowly, mechanically.

"How do you feel?" I asked.

She set down her fork and looked at me. "Empty," she said finally. "Like someone scooped out everything inside me and forgot to put it back."

"That's the meth talking. Your brain chemistry is all screwed up right now. It'll take time to balance out. At least you got some good sleep. You were on cloud nine."

We talked for the next hour. About her life, her parents, the pressure of growing up in the political spotlight. About the drugs, the rebellion, the desperate need to be something other than a campaign asset. Slowly, carefully, she began to open up about the pain that had driven her to that bridge.

"Why didn't you just take me home?" she asked eventually.

"Would you have stayed?"

"No."

"Then what would have been the point?"

By the time she finished her second cup of coffee, color had returned to her cheeks and some clarity to her movements. It was a start—just a start, but more progress than I'd expected.

My phone buzzed with a text message from an unknown number: "Interested in your proposal. Meeting tonight. Will send details."

Elsa. The game was moving to the next level, and I had a senator's daughter sleeping in my RV while I prepared to walk back into the world of criminals who'd already proven they could manipulate me.

But as I looked at Trisha, saw the first signs of hope returning to her eyes, I realized that sometimes the most important cases weren't the ones that paid the bills. Sometimes they were the ones that reminded you why you'd chosen this life in the first place.

The real game was just beginning, on multiple fronts. And for the first time in days, I felt ready to play.

CHAPTER 27

BORN AGAIN

I've always believed that truth has a way of clawing its way out, no matter how deep you bury it. It's like a splinter under your skin—small, nagging, festering until you dig it out with a knife. That's what I was doing now, standing in Elsa's office, the late afternoon sun slicing through the blinds and painting her face in stripes of light and shadow. She sat behind her desk, all polished elegance, her manicured nails tapping a rhythm on the mahogany. But her eyes—those sharp, calculating eyes—betrayed her. They flickered with something I'd learned to recognize over the years: guilt.

"Elsa," I said, my voice low, deliberate. "We need to talk."

She tilted her head, a practiced smile curling her lips. "Bolt, darling, you sound so serious. What's this about?"

I didn't answer right away. Instead, I pulled my phone from my pocket, opened the video, and set it on her desk. The screen glowed to life, showing grainy security footage from camera in my coach. There she was, clear as day, her fingers dancing across a keyboard, siphoning funds from my account. The timestamp didn't lie. Neither did the numbers flashing across the screen.

Her smile froze, then melted into something brittle. "I told you I needed the money. I will make it up to you," she said, her voice tight.

"How? Sex? You're overestimating your worth in that department, sweetheart." I could see my ploy was getting to her. She was a sexual manipulator, and questioning her sensuality hit her to the core.

"Don't get me wrong. It was good. Just not twenty-five K good."

Her gaze darted to the door, then back to me. She was calculating her escape, but I wasn't about to let her slip away. Not this time. "You have a problem, Elsa. I think you have a problem. You took twelve million dollars, Elsa. Where is it? It's gone. You want to explain that?"

She leaned back in her chair, crossing her arms, trying to regain control. "You're blowing this out of proportion. Maybe there's a mistake. A glitch in the system. You know how these things happen."

"A glitch?" I raised an eyebrow, letting the word hang in the air like a bad joke. "A glitch that funnels millions into offshore accounts linked to your name? Try again."

Her composure cracked, just for a second, but it was enough. She stood, pacing to the window, her heels clicking against the hardwood. "Alright, fine," she said, her voice dropping to a whisper. "I... I have a problem, okay? I've had it since I was a kid. Kleptomania. I take things. I don't even mean to sometimes—it's just... an impulse."

I stared at her, letting the silence stretch. Kleptomania? That was her play? I'd recently been observing Elsa—her sharp mind, her ruthless ambition, the way she could charm a room full of donors or bury an opponent of the senator with a single well-timed leak. She wasn't some compulsive shoplifter swiping candy bars. This was calculated. Deliberate. But I'd play along, see how deep she'd dig her own grave.

"Kleptomania," I repeated, my tone flat. "You're telling me you stole twelve million dollars because you couldn't help yourself?"

She turned to face me, her eyes wide, pleading. "It's not like that. It started small—little things, you know? But then... it got out of hand. The money, it was just... there. And I needed it."

"Needed it for what?" I pressed, stepping closer. "What could you possibly need twelve million dollars for?"

She hesitated, her fingers twisting together. "I... I have other problems, Bolt. Drugs. Shopping. Partying. It adds up. You don't know what it's like, living under this kind of pressure. The campaign, the senator, you—everyone expects me to be perfect. I just... I needed an escape."

I almost laughed. Drugs? Shopping? Partying? Elsa was good, I'd give her that. She could spin a story better than most, but I wasn't buying it. Not for a second. "Twelve million dollars," I said, my voice hard. "That's not an escape, Elsa. That's a heist. And you didn't spend it all on coke and designer handbags. So, where's the rest of it?" Her face paled, and for the first time, I saw real fear in her eyes. "I don't know what you're talking about," she said, but her voice wavered.

I straightened, my decision made. "Get your coat," I said. "We're going for a drive."

She blinked, caught off guard. "A drive? Where?"

"You'll see."

The road stretched out before us, a ribbon of asphalt cutting through the sprawl of Los Angeles. The sun was dipping low, painting the sky in shades of orange and purple, but I barely noticed. My hands gripped the steering wheel of the old 911, the engine's rumble a steady counterpoint to the storm brewing in my chest. Elsa sat in the passenger seat, her arms crossed, her body tense. She hadn't said a word since we left her office, but I could feel her eyes on me, searching for a way out.

I didn't give her one.

We pulled into the Public Storage on Oxnard Street in Van Nuys, the lot quiet except for the hum of distant traffic. The place was a maze of low, beige buildings, each one lined with identical roll-up doors. I parked near unit 47, popped the frunk, and pulled out a black duffle bag. It was heavier than it looked, loaded with tools and other necessary things I hoped I wouldn't need. I also picked up two similar empty duffles.

"Get out," I said, my voice calm but unyielding.

Elsa hesitated, then complied, her heels clicking against the pavement. "Bolt, what are we doing here?" she asked, her tone laced with unease.

I didn't answer. Instead, I walked to the unit, the filled duffle slung over my shoulder. The roll-up door was secured with a heavy padlock, glinting dully in the fading light. I set the bag down and turned to her. "Open it." She stared at me, her brow furrowing. "What?" "The lock," I said, nodding at the door. "Open it." She laughed, but it was forced, brittle. "I don't know what you're talking about. I've never been here before."

I didn't have time for her games. I reached into the duffle, pulled out a pair of bolt cutters, and snapped the lock in one clean motion. The metal clattered to the ground, and I kicked it aside. Elsa's eyes widened, but she didn't move.

I rolled up the door, revealing a cramped 5' x 5' storage space packed with boxes. The air inside was stale, tinged with the faint smell of mildew. I stepped in, shoving aside a stack of cardboard boxes to reveal a larger one tucked in the back. It was heavy, reinforced with tape, and unmarked. I dragged it into the open and used my knife to slice through the tape.

Inside, neatly stacked, were bundles of cash. At least twenty million, maybe more, wrapped in plastic and organized like bricks in a wall. The sight of it hit me like a punch to the gut—not because of the money, but because of what it meant. Elsa hadn't just betrayed me. She'd betrayed everyone who'd trusted her, everyone who'd believed in the campaign. She must have scammed Chesnokov too, or Elena.

I turned to her, my jaw tight. "Twenty million dollars," I said, gesturing at the box. "Give or take. Not bad for a kleptomaniac."

Elsa's face crumpled, and she took a step back, her hands raised as if to ward me off. "Bolt, I can explain," she stammered. "I was going to return it, I swear. I just... I needed to hold onto it for a while. Please, you have to believe me."

"Believe you?" I said, my voice low, dangerous. "After everything? You think I'm that stupid?"

Tears welled in her eyes, but I wasn't moved. I'd seen her cry on cue before, charming donors or dodging questions from the press. "Please," she whispered. "I'll give it all back. Every cent. Just... don't hurt me."

I stepped closer, towering over her. "Payback's a bitch, Elsa," I said, my voice cold as steel. "You should've thought of that before you decided to screw me over."

Her eyes darted to the open door, and I saw the moment she made her decision. She bolted, her heels slipping on the concrete as she lunged for the exit. But I was faster. I grabbed her arm, yanking her back, and before she could scream, I wrapped my arm around her neck in a sleeper hold. She struggled, clawing at my arm, but I tightened my grip, cutting off her carotids just enough to make her go limp. She slumped against me, unconscious, her body a dead weight.

I lowered her to the ground, my heart pounding. I wasn't a killer—not yet, anyway—but I was done playing nice. I started sorting through the cash, pulling out the senator's eight million and my four million.

I placed Senator Goldstein's share in one empty duffle and my share in another. Combined, both filled bags must have weighed over two hundred pounds. I carried each duffle separately to the car, placing the senator's bag in the shotgun seat and mine in the frunk. The rest of the cash could stay in Public Storage, for all I cared. Let someone else find it. Let it be someone else's problem.

From the equipment duffle, I pulled out two gallon jugs—one of bleach, one of white vinegar. I set them on the floor and grabbed a plastic basin from the corner of the unit. I poured the liquids in, the sharp, chemical smell hitting me as they mixed, releasing a faint haze of chlorine gas. It wasn't enough to kill her—not immediately—but it would make sure she didn't wake up feeling refreshed.

I slung the duffle over my shoulder, picked up the cut lock, and left the open one on the ground. I rolled the door down, the metal groaning as it sealed the unit shut. Then I walked back to my car, the weight of the remaining tools heavy against my back, the weight of what I'd done heavier still.

As I drove away, the storage facility shrinking in my rearview mirror, I felt something shift inside me. Not guilt, not regret, but a strange, hollow clarity. I'd been reborn in that moment, not as a hero or a villain, but as something else entirely. Someone who'd finally stopped trusting, stopped hoping, and started doing what needed to be done.

The road stretched out before me, endless and uncertain, and for the first time in a long time, I felt free.

CHAPTER 28

LAST CALL

The phone felt heavy in my hand, heavier than it should've for something so small. Maybe it was the weight of what I was about to do, or maybe it was just the lingering ache in my knuckles from the day before. Either way, I punched in Senator Nancy Goldstein's number, the digits burned into my memory from all the back-and-forth about the campaign funds and Tricia's chicanery over the last many days. The line rang twice before her voice came through, crisp and commanding, like she was addressing a committee instead of answering a call from me.

"Mr. Bolt," she said, not a question, just a statement. "What's this about?"

"I've got something for you," I said, keeping my tone even. "Something you'll want to see."

A pause, the kind that told me she was weighing her options, measuring me like a chess piece. "Come to the Malibu house," she said finally. "Seven o'clock. Don't be late."

The line went dead before I could respond. Typical Nancy. Always calling the shots, even when she didn't know the game. I glanced at my watch—4:15 p.m. Plenty of time to kill before I needed to be in Malibu. I grabbed the duffle bag from the corner of my apartment, the one stuffed with the senator's money, and headed for my Carrera. The engine roared to life, a familiar growl that steadied my nerves as I pointed the car west toward the coast.

Malibu was a different world from the grit of Van Nuys, all sun-bleached cliffs and ocean breeze that smelled like salt and money. I pulled into the parking lot of the Marmalade Cafe just off the Pacific Coast Highway, the kind of place where the salads cost more than a decent steak downtown. My stomach was rumbling, and I figured a quick dinner would keep me sharp for whatever was coming. The hostess, a blonde with a smile too bright for minimum wage, led me to a table by the window. I ordered a burger—medium rare, no frills—and a black coffee, then leaned back to watch the parade of Malibu's elite through the glass.

The place was packed with the usual crowd: tech bros in designer sneakers, yoga moms clutching reusable water bottles, and a few aging surfers who looked like they'd washed up from the '70s. I chewed slowly, savoring the burger's char, but my mind was elsewhere. Elsa's face kept flashing in my head—her panicked eyes, her desperate pleas, the way her body went limp in my arms. I pushed the thought down, focusing on the coffee's bitter bite instead. Regret was a luxury I couldn't afford.

After dinner, I wandered through the Malibu Country Market, a glossy outdoor plaza where the rich came to play at being ordinary. The stores were a fever dream of excess—$12 cupcakes dusted with edible gold, artisanal cheeses that cost more per pound than my car payment, and boutiques selling cashmere scarves nobody needed in 70-degree weather. A woman in a linen jumpsuit brushed past me, her arms loaded with shopping bags, her perfume sharp enough to cut glass. I caught her glance, a quick flicker of disdain, like I was some drifter who'd wandered into her kingdom. I smirked and kept walking. Let her think what she wanted. I wasn't here for her approval.

The sun was dipping low, painting the sky in shades of pink and gold, so I headed toward Malibu Lagoon to clear my head. The trail around the lagoon was quiet, just the rustle of reeds and the distant crash of waves. I walked slowly, my boots crunching on the gravel path, my eyes on the water where egrets stood like statues, their reflections shimmering in the still surface. Out here, away from the city's noise, I could almost pretend I was someone else—someone who didn't carry the weight of what I'd done, what I was about to do. But the duffle bag in my frunk was a reminder I couldn't shake. Twelve million dollars, give or take, minus my cut. Blood money, maybe, but it was mine all the same.

At a quarter to seven, I climbed back into the Carrera and drove the short distance to Senator Goldstein's estate. The house was a sprawling Mediterranean-style mansion perched on a bluff, all white stucco and red tile, the kind of place that screamed power without trying too hard. I parked in the circular driveway, grabbed the duffle from the frunk, and walked to the front door. The weight of the bag pulled at my shoulder, but I barely noticed. My focus was razor-sharp now, every sense dialed to eleven.

I rang the doorbell, the chime echoing like a church bell. The door swung open, and there was Hobbs, the senator's right-hand man, all six-foot-four of him, built like a linebacker with a face that never smiled. "Mr. Bolt," he said, his voice a low rumble. He reached for the duffle, but I pulled it back, keeping my grip firm.

"I've got it," I said, my tone polite but unyielding. "Personal delivery."

Hobbs raised an eyebrow but didn't argue. He stepped aside, gesturing for me to follow. Instead of the main living room, he led me to a smaller antechamber down a hallway lined with abstract art that probably cost more than a Wilshire apartment. The room was sparse but elegant—a mahogany desk, a leather armchair, and a flat-screen TV mounted on the wall, muted, showing the local news. I set the duffle on the floor beside my feet and leaned against the desk, waiting. The air smelled faintly of lavender, probably from some overpriced diffuser in the corner.

Less than a minute later, Senator Nancy Goldstein swept into the room. She was every inch the politician—tailored blazer, silver hair pulled back in a sleek bun, eyes that could cut through steel. But there was a weariness to her I hadn't noticed before, a faint sag in her shoulders, like the weight of her office was finally catching up. She extended a hand, and I shook it, her grip firm but not aggressive.

"Mr. Bolt," she said, her voice smooth, practiced. "You've been busy."

"You could say that," I replied, nudging the duffle with my boot. I unzipped it, revealing the stacks of cash inside, neatly bundled and smelling faintly of ink and plastic. "Eight million. Twelve million, minus my one-third. Count it if you want."

Her eyes flicked to the money, then back to me. "I trust you," she said, but there was an edge to her voice, like she was testing me. "You've always been reliable."

I nodded, keeping my expression neutral. "Elsa Krieger wasn't. She took your money, funneled it through offshore accounts and the Russian mob, stashed most of it in a storage unit in Van Nuys. I got it back—most of it, anyway. Your daughter's safe, too. Tricia's at home, probably cursing my name, but she's alive."

Nancy's face softened at the mention of Tricia, but only for a moment. "Elsa," she said, her voice tightening. "What happened to her?"

Before I could answer, movement on the TV caught my eye. The muted news broadcast had shifted to a breaking story, the screen showing aerial footage of the Public Storage on Oxnard Street. Yellow police tape fluttered in the wind, and a reporter stood in front of the facility, her mouth moving silently. The ticker at the bottom read: *Woman Found Dead in Van Nuys Storage Unit, Cause of Death Asphyxiation by Chlorine Gas.*

I nodded at the TV. "Turn it up."

Nancy grabbed a remote from the desk and unmuted the sound. The reporter's voice filled the room, clipped and urgent. "Authorities are investigating the death of a woman found in a storage unit on Oxnard Street in Van Nuys earlier today. The victim, identified as 38-year-old Elsa Krieger, appears to have died from asphyxiation caused by exposure to chlorine gas. Police are treating the case as suspicious and are asking for anyone with information to come forward."

Nancy's eyes locked onto mine, sharp and searching. "What happened to Ms. Krieger?" she asked, her voice low, dangerous. I held her gaze, unflinching. "You have your money and your daughter, Senator. Be content in that."

For a moment, neither of us moved. The air in the room felt thick, charged, like the moment before a storm breaks. Then I zipped the duffle closed and turned for the door. "We're done here," I said, not looking back.

Hobbs followed me out, silent as a shadow, but I could feel his eyes boring into my back. I climbed into the Carrera, the engine's roar cutting through the quiet of the Malibu night. As I pulled onto the Pacific Coast Highway, the ocean stretching dark and endless to my right, I felt that same hollow clarity from the day before. No guilt, no regret—just the road ahead and the weight of choices I'd made.

Elsa was gone. The money was delivered. Tricia was safe. And me? I was still Bolt, still walking the line between right and wrong, knowing full well I'd crossed it more times than I could count. But that's the thing about last calls—they don't always mean the end. Sometimes, they're just the beginning of something new.

I pressed the gas, the Carrera surging forward, and let the night swallow me whole. In my rearview mirror, the lights of Malibu faded to pinpricks, and ahead lay only darkness and possibility. I'd been reborn in that storage unit, shed my old skin like a snake, and emerged as something harder, colder, more pragmatic. The world was full of people like

Elsa—predators dressed up as allies, thieves masquerading as friends. I'd learned to speak their language, to play by their rules.

The phone buzzed on the passenger seat. A text from an unknown number: *Need your help. Big case. Big money. Are you interested?*

I glanced at the message, then back at the road stretching endlessly before me. The city lights blurred past in streams of white and red, and somewhere in the distance, sirens wailed—the sound of other people's problems, other people's pain. I'd built a reputation on cleaning up messes, on finding truth in a world that preferred comfortable lies. The work wasn't glamorous, but it was honest in its own twisted way.

I typed back a single word: *Yes.*

Whatever came next, I'd be ready for it. I'd learned the hard way that loyalty was a currency that could be counterfeited, that trust was a luxury the wealthy couldn't afford to give and the desperate couldn't afford to expect. But information—cold, hard facts—that was something I could count on. That was something I could use.

The Carrera's engine hummed beneath me, a mechanical heartbeat that matched my own. I was Jon Bolt, private retriever, problem solver, and as of today, a man who'd finally stopped pretending the world was fair. There was work to be done, money to be made, and justice—my own particular brand of it—to be served.

The night stretched ahead, full of possibilities and shadows, and I drove toward whatever waited in the darkness, ready for anything.

THE END?